Rokubei, seeing Yoshi's concern for Hiromi, drew his sword, stepped forward, and with one quick slash parted Hiromi's robes in an explosion of blood and entrails. Hiromi's eyes bulged, his arms clutched his belly, trying vainly to hold himself together. He fell to his knees, staring in horror at the gouts of blood that coursed over his hands, his face twitched, once, and died...

The life of the sword demanded payment once more...

Charter Books by David Charney

SENSEI
SENSEI II: SWORD MASTER

SENSEI II
SWORD MASTER

DAVID CHARNEY

ℂ

CHARTER BOOKS, NEW YORK

SENSEI II: SWORD MASTER

A Charter Book/published by arrangement with
the author

PRINTING HISTORY
Charter Original/June 1984

ISBN: 0-441-79264-2

Charter Books are published by The Berkley Publishing Group,
200 Madison Avenue, New York, New York 10016.
PRINTED IN THE UNITED STATES OF AMERICA

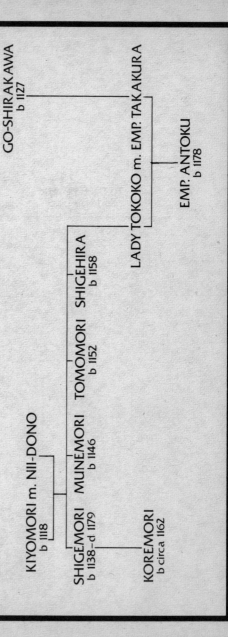

THE TAIRA

GO-SHIRAKAWA
b 1127

LADY TOKOKO m. EMP. TAKAKURA

EMP. ANTOKU
b 1178

KIYOMORI m. NII-DONO
b 1118

SHIGEMORI
b 1138 – d 1179

MUNEMORI
b 1146

TOMOMORI
b 1152

SHIGEHIRA
b 1158

KOREMORI
b circa 1162

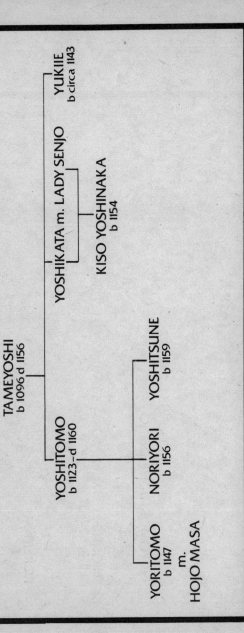

THE MINAMOTO

TAMEYOSHI
b 1096 d 1156

YOSHITOMO
b 1123–d 1160

YORITOMO
b 1147
m.
HOJO MASA

NORIYORI
b 1156

YOSHITSUNE
b 1159

YOSHIKATA m. LADY SENJO

KISO YOSHINAKA
b 1154

YUKIIE
b circa 1143

BOOK I

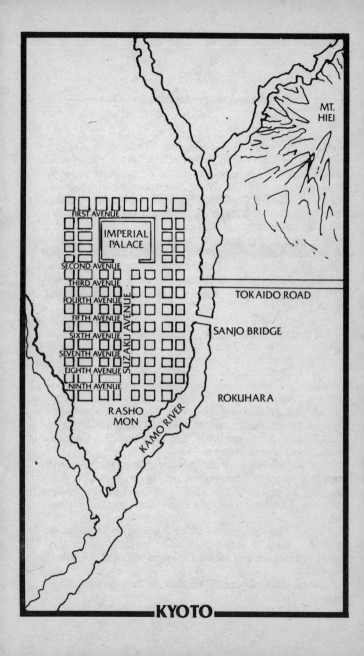

one

———◆———

Northeast of Kyoto, Mount Hiei was covered with a silvery quilt. The air was cold and silent except for the hiss of wind and the crack of an occasional tree limb breaking under its crown of snow. The first rays of Amaterasu, the sun goddess, reflected from the ice fields, defining the edges of low-hanging clouds in amber and gold. Wind feathered snow from every projecting surface. It was the second month of 1181.

A white fox, almost invisible against the snow, scrabbled for shelter, burrowing away from a strange monster that lurched down the rocky road from the ancient cemetery on the mountainside. As the figure loomed closer, the cowering fox saw two heads, four arms, two legs dangling, and two legs slipping on the treacherous ice.

Two men. One carrying the other.

The younger man, face strained, gasped a plume of vapor from his open mouth. The older man's hood was open and an ice film covered his hawk-nosed face. His eyes were closed; his head lolled spinelessly from side to side. No vapor came from his nose or from his bloodless lips. His lined face was peaceful in death.

The younger man was *Sensei* Tadamori-no-Yoshi. A few hours earlier, in the cemetery field, he had faced the older man, Lord Chikara, in a sword battle. The duel resulted in Chikara's death . . . and almost his own.

A shout echoed from the mountainside, and the warrior staggered to a halt, swaying on widespread legs. The wind tugged at his robe, lifting a torn edge to reveal a crude bandage at his hip. Blood oozed out to soak his under-robe and *hakama*, pants-skirt.

He stared through snow-encrusted lids at the source of the shout, too spent to move. A hundred yards below, a gray-haired man waved and shouted from an oxcart at the side of the road.

"Yoshi, what happened?" shouted the man through cupped hands.

3

Yoshi stared blankly. He shook his head, releasing a faint cloud of dislodged snow, then slowly sank to the ground.

Yoshi became aware of the erratic movement of the oxcart. He heard the ice compacting under the iron-bound wheels. Steam formed with every breath in the frigid air and was quickly dispersed by the wind that pierced the oxcart walls. Yoshi lay still. Every time the wheels revolved, the cart lurched and a sword of fire stabbed his hip. He had not been aware of pain on the way down from the cemetery; his mind had closed out the agony that came with each step. Now, immobile on a straw-filled pallet, he slipped back into the trance that had taken him after the duel as he had knelt for hours before Chikara's corpse and the ghosts of the past battled for his soul.

Yoshi moaned and felt someone's hand press on his fore-head. He tried to open his eyes but failed; his head fell back as his mind spiraled down into a roiling sea of memories.

Since birth, his life had been intertwined with Chikara's. It was Chikara, lord of an adjacent estate, who married Yoshi's childhood love, Nami, the daughter of one of Lord Fumio's many sisters. Nami had spent her summers as a guest at Lord Fumio's *shoen*, estate, in far-off Okitsu. It was there that Yoshi was left in her company for an entire season. He was sixteen years old that year, and he had fallen deeply in love.

Yoshi was fresh from three years at the Confucian Academy in Kyoto, a model of sophistication to his fourteen-year-old cousin. His white face powder, blackened teeth, soft-colored silk robes, and scented fan had impressed her. Her delicacy, fine-boned beauty, and sensitivity to poetry had enchanted him.

They had spent an idyllic summer exchanging confidences and thrilling to each other's touch. His feelings were unspoken, but Yoshi assumed that one day he would return to claim his cousin's hand in marriage.

Three years later, a foppish Yoshi, the perfect product of court society, returned to Okitsu to attend Nami's wedding to Chikara. The wedding brought bitterness and jealousy to Yoshi's heart, and led to tragedy and Yoshi's exile.

Despite his androgynous appearance, his lack of muscula-ture, and his limpid manner, Yoshi was brave. He was also jealous, hot-tempered, and ready to take any position that put him in opposition to Nami's future husband.

Yoshi insulted the older man and was challenged to a duel. He was no match for Lord Chikara; in the end, Yoshi fled the estate, lucky to be alive. From then on, Chikara loomed as an evil influence over Yoshi's life, causing pain and loss at every turn.

Yoshi took refuge with a sword smith. In four years of labor at the forge, he changed from an effete courtier to a taciturn young man of great physical strength. Later he became apprenticed to a famous sword master. Dedication to learning the way of the sword and unswerving loyalty to his master eventually earned him the title *sensei*, teacher and sword master. When Yoshi's master died in an ambush by a former student, Yoshi, wrongly, blamed Chikara.

After Yoshi inherited his master's school, he immersed himself in teaching the martial arts and achieved a measure of contentment if not happiness.

Meanwhile, the political situation of Japan was in ferment. Two families fought for political control and the wealth it represented. The Taira clan, under the leadership of Taira Kiyomori, ruled the country from behind the throne. Their rivals, the Minamoto, were banished to the northern provinces. In an attempt to neutralize the Taira's evergrowing strength, the wily old cloistered Emperor, Go-Shirakawa, ordered Kiyomori, the Taira Prime Minister, to accept Minamoto on the Imperial Council. Kiyomori agreed, thinking he could control the enemy if he brought their leaders to Kyoto. He invited them to send representatives.

Chikara saw to it that the Minamoto representatives died in duels with Taira swordsmen.

Because of Chikara's campaign against them, the Minamoto asked Yoshi to join the Council in their name. Against his will, he accepted. Thus, if it had not been for Chikara, Yoshi would never have returned to Kyoto and would never have seen Nami again.

Once in Kyoto, he was repeatedly challenged by the Taira, who made the mistake of thinking him an easy target. Their mistake was fatal. The Minamoto councillors were overjoyed as Yoshi defeated their enemies in a series of duels. The losses were a major blow to the Tairas' pride, but killing Taira courtiers was not Yoshi's goal; his quarrel was with their leader, Lord Chikara. And Lord Chikara ignored him.

Despite the danger, Yoshi visited Nami and proclaimed his love in a night of passion and mutual discovery. The next day, Yoshi publicly challenged Lord Chikara, and the Taira lord accepted. If Yoshi won, he would achieve an important victory for the Minamoto and the opportunity to win Nami.

But it had not been that simple.

Yoshi winced as he remembered the scene... was it only last night? His mother, Lady Masaka, and Nami had come to his quarters to beg him not to face Chikara. When their pleas had failed, Lady Masaka told him the secret she had carried since Yoshi's birth.

In her youth, she had known Chikara at the court. They had been lovers for one night. The next morning, when no love poem came, she knew she had been compromised. She fled the court determined to become a nun. Before she could take her vows, she discovered she was pregnant and left the monastery in shame. She traveled far from Kyoto to seek out her cousin, Lord Fumio, and ask for sanctuary on his *shoen*. Fumio accepted her without question and she gave birth to Yoshi on a tempestuous night filled with thunder and lightning.

Until last night, only Lady Masaka had known the truth: Lord Chikara was Yoshi's father.

And Yoshi had killed him.

Yoshi had spent a long night at his dead father's side, the supernatural worlds of good and evil battling for Yoshi's soul. Was the life of a sword master good if it caused the death of friends, relatives... his own father? Long ago he had learned that an evil blade meant an evil soul. How could he avoid evil and escape the wrath of the gods?

A sob racked his body, his shoulders convulsed, and a tear stained his cheek.

"Yoshi?" The voice belonged to his uncle, Lord Fumio, the gray-haired gentle old warrior who had taken the place of his father during his childhood.

Yoshi turned away and pressed his cheek against the pallet, feeling the rough weave, a thousand pinpricks on his icy flesh. The dry, cold straw filled his nostrils with an odor that seemed to be composed of rot, decay, and death. Chikara? Where was Chikara? He was instantly filled with revulsion and struggled to raise himself.

"Please, do not move," said Fumio gently.

Yoshi closed his eyes. He felt consciousness slip away again. He sighed and sank into darkness.

Fumio studied him through tear-filled eyes. How the boy had changed since growing to manhood. The once soft, undefined features were now hewn in smooth granite: broad cheekbones etched by years of hard physical effort, a small nose delicately formed for a face so strong, a sensitive mouth set in a powerful jaw, and pale skin, clean-shaven and set off by shiny black hair pulled back into a tight top-knot.

Fumio lifted Yoshi's head tenderly and pulled his hood up to protect him from the cold. Fumio's rough-skinned, craggy features were solemn; in the harsh winter light he looked every one of his sixty years.

Yoshi was either asleep or unconscious; there was nothing more to do until he was under the care of priests and healers.

"This morning, Lady Masaka confessed her secret to me," Fumio whispered. He leaned closer to see if Yoshi heard. There was no response.

"There are many things to consider." Fumio spoke to himself in a soft voice, half whisper, half chant. "That Chikara was your father is a matter between you and the ghost world, but in this world you have done irreparable damage. By killing Lord Chikara, you upset the equilibrium of the court. The Prime Minister depended on Chikara for his ability to lead the ministers, for his leadership of the Imperial army, and for the extra support his wealth provided. Yoshi, you may have signed your death warrant. Kiyomori will never forgive you for the chaos you've caused." His brow furrowed; he knew that Yoshi had had no choice. Honor prevented any other course.

Lord Fumio was torn. "I am a staunch ally of the court," he said to the unconscious Yoshi. "Everything I am I owe to the Taira clan. The shade of Lord Chikara will deal with you in the next world, but I must deal with my Taira allies here."

Yoshi did not stir. A crust of ice formed on his upper lip as vapor from his breath condensed. Fumio carefully brushed it clear. "No doubt," he continued, "your mother will be overjoyed that you are alive. I cannot imagine that she will mourn the death of your father; she has hated him since he deserted her so many years ago."

It was easy for Fumio to predict Lady Masaka's reaction. Nami, on the other hand, was now Chikara's widow and free to choose her own life. She had never suffered the strictures of convention, so there was no way to guess what she would do.

"Nami says she wants to leave Kyoto with you and flee to the north. If she does, she will be giving up Chikara's wealth and her position in the court. She says these are not important, but I say she must think of more than the moment. She has a responsibility to Chikara's name. To leave so precipitously would be an unforgivable insult to her husband's memory. The scandal would destroy you both." Fumio wrung his hands, and since Yoshi could not see, he brushed a tear with his sleeve. He murmured, "Dear boy, what *can* I do to save you from the pain I see ahead?"

Yoshi lay unmoving. Only the cloud of vapor from his breathing showed him to be alive. Fumio twisted around to stare through the front latticework. Amaterasu had risen farther, and her rays bathed the capital in an orange-red glow. The cart was on the lower reaches of Mount Hiei, approaching the city. Giant Cryptomeria trees bowed their snow-laden branches, supplicating the travelers as they passed.

Fumio saw a large group of warrior-monks, wrapped in heavy winter robes, marching up the road from the northern gate. He had to squint against the glare to see them clearly; the white and light-tan robes blended with the snow. The monks used their wooden *geta*, clogs, to stamp their way through the snow and ice. The bulk and shape of their robes indicated that they wore battle armor underneath. Many carried *naginata*, four-foot blades of steel set on wooden shafts. Some two dozen supported a *mikoshi*, a portable shrine, suspended from two sturdy poles. The shrine was intricately carved, the corners of the lacquered roof turned up in the Chinese style. Heavy brass fittings reinforced the support poles. Fumio knew these *sohei*, warrior-monks, often descended from their mountain temples when they disagreed with an Imperial edict. When they did not get their way, the monks deposited the shrine at the Imperial Palace, striking superstitious fear in the hearts of the courtiers until the court retracted the ill-favored edict.

As the monks' party passed the oxcart, some of the monks tried to peer inside. One, more brazen than the others, called to the driver, demanding to know whose carriage dared pass the monks of Enryaku-ji. He seemed surprised at the answer.

Behind the monks, beggars and criminals skulked around the gate. A year of famine and unrest in the home provinces had created a society of homeless vagabonds who lurked on the outskirts of the capital, beggars hoping for charity and thieves looking for victims. These outcasts had melted into the surrounding countryside with the arrival of the armed monks and were warily returning to the gate as the last of the monks passed through.

As the cart entered the city gate, a flock of wild geese rose from the ice-filled Imperial pond and fluttered overhead, breaking the silence with a cacophony of horn-blast calls.

Fumio's home was in the second ward, a prestigious address close to the Imperial enclosure. The grounds covered a full *cho*, nearly four acres, and were surrounded by a high wall of white-painted stone. At the covered area for carriages, the oxcart ground to a halt. One of Fumio's retainers opened the gate and the cart lurched over the crossbeam that ran from gatepost to gatepost.

"We are home," said Fumio, adjusting his robe and gently shaking Yoshi awake.

The oxcart crunched its way along the path to the southern entrance of the main hall. There it stopped with a shudder. The driver dropped back from the oxteam and pounded a callused palm on the door. "We have arrived, my lords," he announced, and bent to unhitch the team from the front of the cart so Fumio and Yoshi could descend with proper dignity.

Fumio grasped Yoshi's arm to help him, but Yoshi shrugged off the helping hand. "Am I a weakling to need help for a battle wound?" he asked. "Stand aside, Uncle, so I may alight on my own two feet."

Fumio felt a stir of pride. Misguided though he might be, Yoshi was a true samurai.

Yoshi walked to the entrance without faltering, but he left a trail of red on the snowy path.

Fumio hurried ahead to open the way. A servant peered from under the eaves, mouth agape at the sight of Yoshi, deathly pale, weaving slightly but standing by himself. Then, as Fumio and the servant watched, and before either could move in his direction, Yoshi collapsed into the ever-widening red pool at his feet.

two

"Yoshi must die," said Chomyo, the priest, his thin, pale face as cold as the wind that whined through the latticework walls. Outside, the morning sun was breaking the horizon; inside, the monastery hall was dark as night. Charcoal braziers gave off a dull red glow and very little heat. The thick smell of incense and burning oil filled the air. Guttering oil lamps on triangular pedestals cast dim light to separate the four figures that knelt in the middle of the floor.

They wore heavy outer robes, cowls thrown back, exposing shaved heads. Three were bearded; only the priest who had spoken was clean shaven. The waxing and waning flames alternately lit and shadowed his sharp features as he leaned toward his audience, pressed his fist to the hardwood floor, and repeated his statement: "Yoshi must die."

"If the *kami*, divine spirits, will allow," said a monk who was so large that even sitting cross-legged he was almost as tall as a man standing. "Earlier, I told you of this morning's events; let me repeat." He paused and studied his companions. They were silent, impassive. Only the faint crackle of an ember and the soughing wind broke the silence. The speaker cleared his throat. "Very well. I shall proceed," he said. "This morning, an oxcart carrying Tadamori-no-Yoshi, a Minamoto councillor, was seen returning from Mount Hiei. He has no right to be alive. I suspect something supernatural in his ability to escape death. More than once Taira swordsmen have tried to kill him and failed. Last night, he fought Lord Chikara, Minister of the Right. They met at the hour of the rat, midnight, almost eight hours ago. Lord Chikara was the most skilled swordsman in Japan, yet he fell to Yoshi's attack. There is no longer doubt in my mind—we are facing a man who is in league with the *kami* and only divine intervention can stop him."

"I heard and understood your report, Gyogi," said Chomyo dryly. "You are correct that Yoshi is no ordinary man, but remember that except for Chikara, the Taira were amateurs, fools who had no right to bare a sword in anger. I am a *gakusho*,

10

a warrior-priest, yet even I understand the awesome powers of a sword master. Yoshi is a *sensei,* a professional teacher of the sword. Last night he met our champion and should have fallen. It was decreed otherwise."

Chomyo's mouth pursed, his nostrils pinched. He continued, "I do not believe Yoshi's strength is a result of supernatural interference. He does not represent the spirit world. We do. We will recite sutras and make offerings. We will pray for help. Nevertheless, we will not depend on prayer alone. We will plan for Yoshi's downfall, and when we succeed, we will offer a ceremony of thanksgiving."

Another monk broke in, his voice thick with the accent of a peasant farmer. He was one of those who had fled their farms during the famine of 1180, the year when the floods had washed out the country's crops. Nominally priests, these men were called *sohei* and served the monastery as warrior-monks. "I hold no brief for this Yoshi," he grunted. "If you say he must die, so be it. As far as I can see, he is only a man. You say he may be in league with the spirit world, but I see no difference between him and the other courtiers with their fancy robes and superior airs. He will bleed and die like any of us and I will help kill him . . . yet I do not understand why his death is so important."

"Muku," said Chomyo caustically. "You do not have to understand to do your work, but I want you to realize the gravity of our situation. Our temple, Enryaku-ji, has been rival to the temples of Todai-ji and Kofuku-ji for two hundred years. Since the great monk Saicho founded our first chapel during the reign of Emperor Kammu, we have controlled the northern approach to Kyoto. Saicho's wisdom in choosing Mount Hiei put us in a position of power. We retain this power because of the support of Taira Kiyomori, the Prime Minister. He shaved his head and became one of us years ago. Today, Kiyomori instructed me to kill Yoshi. He made this a condition of his continued support.

"Know you, Muku, there are three forces engaged in a struggle for control of Japan: the Taira clan, the Minamoto clan, and our Tendai monks. Kiyomori and his Taira family rule over Kyoto and the home provinces. His rivals in the north, the clan of the Minamoto, are supported by the monks of Todai-ji, our mortal enemies. If the Minamoto gain strength or, Buddha forbid it, if they should prevail over the Taira, our temple will be weakened and perhaps even destroyed. Do you understand? Anyone who helps the Minamoto contributes to our downfall. Since Yoshi came to the Imperial Council, he has threatened our very existence. Some say his actions brought on the Prime Minister's ill health. Some say Yoshi put a curse on the Prime Minister and only Yoshi's death can save us. Kiyomori believes that to be true. So . . . Yoshi must die."

Kangen, the last monk, was a soft-featured, handsome man, his face decorated by a moustache and beard, in the Chinese style. "I know this Yoshi," Kangen said in a cultured accent edged with jealousy. He paused until Chomyo lifted his brows and nodded as if to say go on.

"Yes," continued Kangen. "When we were young, we were fellow students at the Confucian Academy. Muku is right. Yoshi is no different than other courtiers. In school, he was known for his prowess at perfume smelling and poetry reading. He was an indifferent swordsman and a physical weakling, a country bumpkin acting the courtier. Hardly an opponent to worry about. Yet, somehow he bested Chikara. Gyogi has suggested supernatural interference . . . perhaps the explanation is simpler. Perhaps a dishonorable trick of some kind. I cannot imagine him winning fairly even with the aid of a *kami*."

Chomyo fingered his beads. "Do not underestimate your childhood acquaintance," he advised. "Yoshi was once the courtier you describe, but I doubt that you would recognize him today. Recently, his story became known to the court and, through my spies, to me. Fifteen years ago, he left the easy life of the capital, a fugitive from the Imperial guards. He has suffered much and learned much. Now his life is steeped in the practice of the martial arts.

"So forget your memories of the young courtier; he no longer exists. Even if we disregard the spirit world, tonight Chikara faced a man of iron, a fighting machine that has survived a dozen attempts on his life."

"We cannot disregard the spirit world," rumbled the giant, Gyogi. "He would be dead if they had not interfered."

Chomyo stared at him coldly. "But he still lives," he said. "Shall we lay down our arms then and let him destroy us? No! I cannot accept that. We will enlist the spirit world on our side."

Chomyo spoke firmly. "We will not act hastily. We will take every precaution in case he is truly allied with the spirits of the underworld. We need a plan, a foolproof plan that uses his own strength against him."

"And where will we find such a plan?" asked Kangen.

"I have one ready. A plan that cannot fail, knowing Yoshi's character. However, before we discuss the plan we must purify ourselves at the washbasin, then offer prayers asking Buddha for help. We will look for a sign..."

As Chomyo spoke, bells from the thousand temples of Mount Hiei rang and pealed, sounding eight in the morning, the hour of the dragon.

"Listen," said Chomyo. "Buddha smiles on our enterprise. He has hastened to send an auspicious sign. Now we need not fear the spirit world; it is on our side. We cannot fail if we are patient and await the proper moment."

three

On the thirteenth day of the third month, a taboo on travel was decreed by the Imperial astrologers. There were no objections from the court since the day offered little to encourage travel. Unseasonably warm weather had melted most of February's snow, leaving a residue of slush in the muddy streets. Purple-gray clouds, whipped by high winds, rushed across the sky, and streamers of low-lying mist gave the city an air of gloom and foreboding. Rain started after dawn and continued through the day, drumming on tile, bark shingles, and thatch roofs.

No courtiers were abroad. Even Suzaki-Ōji, the main street, was deserted except for occasional commercial workers, dressed in straw rain capes and wide hats, hurrying to the seventh ward. A trio of half-starved dogs splashed through puddles and bared their fangs at the strange shapes formed by the rain-whipped mist. The city seemed to be under an enchantment; a visitor would be hard pressed to recognize the "City of Purple Hills and Crystal Streams," with low clouds covering the surrounding hills and the rain turning streams into torrents of muddy water.

At Rokuhara, his opulent estate, Taira Kiyomori, the *Daijo-Daijin*, Prime Minister, was alone in the open south hall of his mansion. Kiyomori was short and stocky. He had taken his vows and shaved his head twelve years ago, at fifty-one. The bare skull, thick neck, generous nose, and sensuous lips gave him a look of physical strength despite his years. He wore a heavy yellow *naoshi*, court cloak, with a green undercloak that showed through the wide sleeves. His loose court trousers matched his undercloak. Though he had spent the morning alone, he wore a formal black silk *koburi* on his head. A fan lay in his lap.

Kiyomori had all the dividing screens removed, and he sat cross-legged in lonely splendor on a raised dais. His only concession to comfort: a woven mat and a yellow silk uphol-stered elbow rest. Except for two unlit charcoal braziers and a ceramic vase full of yellow spring flowers, the dark, polished wood floors extended unbroken to the outer wall. Around him, the huge room was empty. He had insisted that the bamboo shades of the south wall be rolled up, leaving him exposed to the elements.

"I feel my days are near an end and I wish to be at one with nature," Kiyomori had said. "The wind warms my bones and the sight and sound of rain fills me with peace."

Heiroku, his ancient majordomo, had exchanged glances with the Yin-Yang healer; they were upset, but Kiyomori sounded so rational they remained silent.

Kiyomori had been acting strangely for months. No one could judge what his next mood would be; one moment he was lost in a dream, the next moment, raving at anyone within reach. These had been difficult months for his family and the staff. However, today the *Daijo-Daijin* was calm and preoccupied; the servants were careful to be quiet. No one dared to disturb him.

He had been sitting silently for several hours, watching the rain dimple the water of his pond, when his wife's lady-in-waiting arrived with a message scroll. The servants expected an outburst when the young lady interrupted the *Daijo-Daijin*'s meditation; they were pleasantly surprised and a trifle jealous when he accepted the message silently. He took the scroll with one thick-fingered hand and touched the girl's cheek with the other.

"Your name, child?" he asked.

"Shimeko," she responded.

"Wait, little Shimeko," he said as he removed the crimson ribbon from the heavy mulberry paper. He glanced at the calligraphy. "My wife, Hachijo-no-Nii-Dono, requests an interview," he said aloud. "How strange. She has not left her northern wing for weeks and now she claims she must tell me something of importance. What can the foolish woman want?"

He nodded to Shimeko, who knelt before his dais; his eyes shone with amusement and a hint of lechery. Shimeko was beautiful. Her skin was smooth and her eyes luminous under carefully painted brows. She stared down and trembled under his gaze.

Kiyomori sighed. The young ones no longer found him attractive. Once it would have been different . . .

Taira-no-Ason Kiyomori of Rokuhara! Even in the Imperial Palace they spoke his name with respect. His sons were of the second and third rank; sixteen of his immediate relatives were fifth rank or above. No one in the court commanded more power than Kiyomori. It was not mere chance of birth that had given him this position. No. Foresight and planning . . . years ago, he had shrewdly formed a special guard of young men, fourteen to sixteen years old, who patrolled the streets of Kyoto investigating rumors of disloyalty. There were nearly three hundred of them, distinctive with their short hair and cherry-red robes. They pried into every corner of the city: inns, houses of pleasure, commercial establishments, even private homes. They reported only to Kiyomori. Power! He had held it firmly in his grasp, and he had used it well. Many of the less fortunate envied him, but they kept their peace under the threat of the red-robed youths.

Then had come his sickness. And fear of the next world. Kiyomori had never been a religious man. He had defeated the monks at the Gion shrine in 1146. He had fought against the monks again, ten years later, during the Hōgen incident. Then sickness and the threat of death had changed his views. At age fifty-one, he developed terrible abdominal cramps. His face turned red as he burned with a high fever. Some said it was retribution for his actions against the temple. Shaken by thoughts of the afterworld, Kiyomori embraced religion. He took his monkish vows at Enryaku-ji and became known as the lay-priest of Rokuhara.

The sutras, the prayers, the offerings, and the purifications did their work. He healed; the fever abated, the cramps disappeared, and Kiyomori, not caring what the "good people" thought, was back to his old life, eating too much, drinking too much, and ignoring the sensibilities of the court by frequenting the houses of pleasure.

Kiyomori frowned at Shimeko; it was not her fault that she reminded him of his age and mortality. He felt one of his uncontrollable rages building. With an effort, he smiled at Shimeko with what he meant to be endearing charm. She was terrified.

"Tell the Nii-Dono I will receive her immediately," he said, feeling the anger mount when she did not respond. "Immediately!"

Shimeko scuttled backward on her knees, forehead pressed to the floor.

Kiyomori sighed again. He was doomed. He felt it in the tremors that attacked his hands, in the stabbing pain that hit his belly, and in the hot flush that made his face burn and covered him with a film of perspiration.

The tranquil mood of the morning was shattered. The sound of the rain made his head ache and the soft pearl-gray light in the garden made his eyes sting.

An inauspicious day.

Kiyomori gave up attempts at meditation. His mind wandered freely. He wondered if he was right in using political pressure to force the monks to act against Yoshi. Of course he was right, he told himself. That was the purpose of political power. Let Chomyo and the monks earn his support. Yoshi was Yoritomo's agent; the monks belonged to Kiyomori. He stirred restlessly. How much of his present illness was due to Yoshi's interference? The loss of Lord Chikara had been a major blow. Kiyomori had depended on Chikara to control the council. Without Chikara, the Taira family was immeasurably weakened. And Chikara's death was a personal blow . . . a loss of face for the entire family. How had Yoshi defeated Lord Chikara, the Taira's greatest champion? If Yoshi had the spirit world supporting him, Kiyomori would answer with the religious power of the monks. They would prevail. They had to!

Kiyomori's attention came back to the present. He scowled. Where was the damn woman? First she sent a foolish young girl to bother him, then she kept him waiting. He waved his fan desultorily, trying to cool the heat that radiated from his shaved skull. It was no use; the heat rose from some central point in his abdomen, a *kami* burrowing in his vitals to torture him.

"I come to inquire about your health, my lord."

It was the Nii-Dono. She had slipped in silently and taken a place on her knees in front of the dais. She was a small woman, fine-boned, short and thin. Her hair was combed into two thick wings of gray-tinged black that almost reached the floor. Her face was wide across the middle, with deep hollows under the cheekbones. Her long slim eyes were sunken in shadows. When she spoke, she showed teeth that had been carefully blackened with a mixture of iron and tannic acid. White powder made her hard face masklike.

The Nii-Dono had grown accustomed to power and had learned to use it with ruthless subtlety to achieve her ends. Still, she acknowledged that Kiyomori was not to be trifled with and that as a woman, her power was only a reflection of his.

Life had not always been easy or pleasant for Hachijo-no-Nii-Dono. Even her name was only a reflection of her position: Hachijo-no-Nii-Dono meant "person of the second rank from Eighth Street." Rank was hers because of her marriage. Yes, what she was she owed to Kiyomori, and her loyalty to him was complete if occasionally grudging.

Kiyomori tightened his jaw and hissed through clenched teeth, "You are straining my patience, woman. You asked to see me on a matter of importance. Speak before I grow angry."

"Forgive me, my lord. I would not intrude if I did not have your best interests at heart. I am worried about your health and felt it important."

"An important interruption." Kiyomori's voice dripped sarcasm.

"I think so. My lord, at the risk of offending you, I wanted to report a dream that brought me awake in tears." The Nii-Dono hesitated. She knew that the *Daijo-Daijin* believed in the significance of dreams, but she waited for a sign to continue.

Kiyomori's head hurt. He would have liked to send her away, yet . . . his curiosity was too strong. He nodded.

"I had a vision," continued the Nii-Dono, "of the next world, and in it, the dread king Emma-Ō sent a flaming chariot to bring you to his throne. I tried to wake, but the underworld held me in thrall. The chariot was fearsome; yellow flames lit the sky, and its wheels thundered as it rolled through the gates of Rokuhara. It was surrounded front and back by two monsters, one with the head of a horse, the other with the head of an ox."

Kiyomori's eyes opened wide. He was repulsed by the dream, but found himself listening avidly to find out how it ended.

"Yes, yes," he hissed. "Then what happened?"

"I asked who the chariot was for; I cried out when they told me. They had come for you, my lord. I begged them. I pleaded. 'Why?' I cried. 'He is a good man.' They were not to be dissuaded. They said you had gained evil karma. Because you burned the hundred-sixty-foot-high statue of Vairochana in the Kofuku-ji temple, King Emma-Ō sentenced you to the hottest of the underworld hells: the Avichi hell, where rebirth and pain are unceasing."

Kiyomori moaned. The dream confirmed his worst fears. There was no escaping the significance of what the Nii-Dono had told him. Even Baku, the dream-eater, would reject such a dream.

The monks of Kofuku-ji hated him. Because of what had happened at their temple, he was doomed. If it hadn't been for pressure from the Minamoto, the burning of the temple would never have happened.

It was the Minamoto. They were at fault. Not he!

Kiyomori glared at his wife, not seeing her, only half hearing her words.

"When I awoke," she was saying, "I immediately ordered gifts sent to all the temples. The monks of Mount Hiei are offering sutras at every shrine. Everything is being done to save your soul."

"Get out!" shouted Kiyomori. His neck bulged and drops of perspiration ran down his face. His skin had turned bright red again. He swelled up, and his face congested with rage.

The Nii-Dono's eyes widened; she hastily backed away. She had told Kiyomori her dream, torn between genuine solicitude and a touch of malice. Her feelings about him had always been mixed; she loved him for the tenderness he had shown her in the past and for the social position he gave her in the present. Few women achieved the second rank, and she had reached that exalted position only because of her relationship to Kiyomori.

As she retreated across the broad expanse of floor, she saw him collapse inward. Within moments, he turned into a shriveled old man. The Nii-Dono raised a hand in consternation and started back to help him.

"No!" His voice grated, his brows furrowed, and he resembled the dread king of her dream. He muttered, his voice like the rasp of raw silk, "Minamoto Yoritomo," and then, "Tadamori Yoshi."

She fled to her northern wing, the two names echoing in her head. She understood what ate at his vitals. Oh yes, she understood. Twenty years ago . . . it had been called the Heiji insurrection. The Minamoto clan had attacked and set fire to the Sanjo Palace in an attempt to kidnap the Emperor. They had failed due to Kiyomori's determined defense and brilliant counterattack. He had defeated and killed the Minamoto leader and had had the opportunity to destroy the entire clan. He had methodically captured and beheaded virtually every important clan member until Tokiwa Gozen, the leader's widow, appealed to him to spare her young sons.

The Nii-Dono smiled grimly. She had warned him to stand firm, but Tokiwa's radiant beauty had swayed Kiyomori into what was to prove the biggest mistake of his life. Against his principal wife's advice, he had acted like a stallion in heat and had taken Tokiwa to be his concubine.

The old fool exiled Yoritomo, the oldest son, and spared the others. Now his act of generosity had returned to haunt him. No wonder he cried the name Yoritomo in anger. The same Yoritomo was sending hired assassins, like the councillor Tadamori Yoshi, to destroy what Kiyomori had built.

The Nii-Dono felt tears streak the white powder on her cheeks. Her poor lord! To suffer for a good deed done in the past. Her face hardened into a mask of resolve. She would help him. She knew what to do. Yoshi would be destroyed first, then she would see to Yoritomo.

She clapped her hands for her lady-in-waiting. Shimeko responded at once.

"Summon Kiyomori's sons," she ordered. "I want them here tonight by ten, the hour of the boar. I will need them to order the red-robes on a special mission."

four

Yoshi regained consciousness in a spacious room of his uncle's Kyoto estate. His head was resting on a wooden pillow box. A tray with a pot of tea and a bowl of fresh flowers were at his side. He pushed aside the *futon* and realized that Nami was kneeling near him, her back to a painted *shoji* screen. Her eyes were closed, and her lips moved in silent prayer. He studied her appreciatively, realizing he had not seen her in bright light for almost a year.

Nami's hair fell in two ebony waterfalls, parted and tied by a crisp silk bow halfway down her back. She was dressed in mourning: her over-robe was black glossed silk to match her hair. Under it, a series of thin robes of varying dark shades of gray. The gray silk fanned out from her wide sleeves and contrasted elegantly with the black over-robe. Her face was ivory smooth, her nose delicate and symmetrical. Yoshi felt a rush of desire. Here she was at last.

Nami opened her eyes. Her lips stopped their prayer and turned into a tentative smile. "Dear Yoshi, I find myself again acting as nurse and healer. Would you like some tea?"

"Time for tea later. How long have I been here?"

"You arrived on our doorstep yesterday morning, more dead than alive and showing no more sense than I would expect from you. Walking unaided with so grievous a wound!"

"Not really serious. I've had worse wounds in the past. We'll say no more about it. I want to know what happened to Lord Chikara's body."

"Uncle arranged everything. His retainers left for Mount Hiei the moment you were comfortably in bed. Do not concern yourself. My lord will be given a full ceremonial funeral, as befits his station."

"I am desolate that our duel turned out so tragically. Lord Chikara died bravely. Whatever acts he committed before our duel, I cannot forget that he was your husband and my father. It seems that whenever I draw my sword, evil is the result. In the past, I had little choice. I fought in response to challenges or to protect myself against attack. This time, I was the challenger. I forced Chikara to fight me. I told myself it was for the Minamoto cause, for the Emperor, and for revenge, but I fear that part of my true motive was selfish: to win you."

Nami reached for Yoshi's hand. "It is done," she said softly. "Blaming yourself will serve no purpose."

"Not just blame. I must reevaluate my life. Nami, I am wearied of killing. My swords are a symbol of death. What kind of life can we look forward to if at every turn I must draw my blade and commit murder? I am a *sensei*, a teacher. I want to teach. I am not guilty of false pride when I say I am one of the finest swordsmen in the Empire. I have proved my ability again and again."

"No one doubts that, Yoshi."

"Then why must I kill to stay alive? I want you and I want peace to live my life as a *sensei*. I am ready to leave this unhappy place at a moment's notice—today, if you will join me. Yoritomo will need me to teach his warriors in the days ahead."

Nami edged closer to Yoshi's *futon*. She placed a tender hand on his forehead. "No, my beloved, I cannot leave Kyoto so soon."

"But we love each other. There are no more obstacles in our path. The sooner we leave Kyoto, the sooner we can start our life together."

"I have certain responsibilities first. How can you be so uncaring? I have duties to my late husband until the *Shijuku-Nichi*, forty-ninth-day services, are over. I cannot consign him to Emma-Ō's judgment without interceding on his behalf."

Nami believed that each person died seven deaths before being consigned to his fate in either the *Gokuraku*, paradise, or the *Jigoku*, hell. The seven deaths took place over forty-nine days, with the departed's soul hovering in limbo while ten celestial judges decided his eventual fate. This neutral period was called *Chuin*, and Nami believed that sincere prayers could influence the judges in making their decision. The size of the formal ceremonies, the number of mourners, and the sincerity of the family were all important in that final reckoning.

Lord Chikara's first death had come when Yoshi severed his spinal cord. Seven days later would be his second death, and an important mourning ceremony. Friends and associates would come to pray for Chikara's salvation. They would make offerings, recite sutras, and burn candles and incense.

Chikara's fate for ten thousand years might depend on the proper observation of the *Shonanuka,* the first seven-day service. Nami was constrained by custom and belief to see to it that daily food offerings were placed on the home altar, since Chikara's spirit would reside there until it was released at his final death on the forty-ninth day.

Nami, as Chikara's widow, was responsible for arranging the death services. She was officially in mourning, and to ensure Chikara's passage to the Western Paradise, she would have to avoid colored clothing, wearing either white, gray, or black, abstain from meat and fish, and avoid carnal pleasures.

Only after the great ceremony of the seventh death would she be free of constraints. Then, Chikara's belongings would be distributed to friends and family and his soul would be free to leave the earth.

Yoshi was contrite. "Forgive me for being so thoughtless. Your duty to Lord Chikara is as important as any duty of my own. I understand. Yet I will find it difficult to wait the forty-nine days without the solace of your touch."

"We can see each other daily without touching."

"I may find that impossible." Yoshi made an impromptu poem.

> *"New-formed plum blossoms*
> *Bring promise of early spring*
> *Yet if one flower*
> *Should hide its face from the sun*
> *The promise stays unfulfilled."*

Nami was touched. She responded, "The blossoms will open, my dear. We have waited so many years, another seven times seven days will pass." And she returned an impromptu poem of her own.

> *"As the mayfly darts*
> *And flies in the warmth of spring*
> *And then disappears*
> *So will swiftly go the days*
> *Until we at last are joined."*

"The days may pass swiftly to the world outside, but will seem an eternity to me if I am denied your touch," said Yoshi.

"When you are well enough to walk, you will return to your own quarters and I will see you only at the seven-day ceremonies."

"How can I leave you?"

"Think of duty and of your relationship to my dead lord. We owe him every chance to reside in the Western Paradise."

"You are right. I will return to my court duties tomorrow. My wound is of no consequence. I will miss you, but there is nothing to be done about it."

"When the mourning period is over and I can shed my black robe, we will plan our future. My life will be in your hands. If you wish to leave Kyoto for the north, so be it. I hold no brief for Yoritomo and his Minamoto brigands, but where you go I will go . . . happily and willingly."

"I love you, Nami."

"And I love you, Yoshi."

five

On the fifteenth day, the weather was unseasonably warm. All signs of winter snow were gone and plum blossoms opened their white faces to the rays of the sun. A special council meeting was held in the Great Hall of the Palace of Administration.

The councillors marched in single file, a solemn procession. They separated as they passed through the massive red-lacquered columns and glided to their places under the sweeping expanses of the high roof. The councillors of Divination and Wardrobe and the councillors of Ceremonial Rituals and Education turned to the left. The others, the Ministers of War, Medicine, Housekeeping, Carpentry, and representatives of the provinces, turned to the right. Each took his place at his kneeling mat. The highest ranking members were near the empty center dais, where Kiyomori normally presided. The others, in descending rank, knelt on two platforms that diverged from the higher center dais. The cloistered Emperor, Go-Shirakawa, sat opposite the councillors, listening and watching from a private vantage point behind a great painted screen.

Inside the Great Council Hall, the normal dignity of the Council was disturbed by a constant undercurrent of whispering. News had spread through the council, news that brought fear to some, elation to others. The day before, Taira Kiyomori, *Daijo-Daijin*, was taken to his bed with a terrible illness.

One councillor of the Left whispered to the next that he had heard directly from Kiyomori's household that the Prime Minister was burning with fever and the healers were bathing him with cold water to reduce his temperature.

The recipient of this news repeated it to his neighbor. "Taira Kiyomori is burning with fever. Even cold water fails to cool him." The story passed through another transition and became, "Kiyomori has a rare sickness. His fever burns so that cold water boils when it touches his body."

In three more transitions it became known that, "The *Daijo-Daijin*'s skin is so hot that even the healers cannot approach him, and furthermore, when cold water is poured on him, it immediately boils off in clouds of smoke and shooting flames. His room has become like the hottest hells of the dread king Emma-Ō. Woe to our leader. His evil karma has at last overtaken him."

The Taira Ministers of the Left were shaken. They knew of Kiyomori's killing of the monk Saiko and of his burning of the one hundred-sixty-foot-high Buddha. They concluded that no matter how one rose in the ranks of man, one could not escape his karma.

Yoshi knelt among a group of fifth-rank Minamoto councillors. He wore full court dress. He had a *koburi* on his head, its black silk reflecting dull light from the oil lamps. His dark blue over-robe was patterned with a lighter blue Minamoto crest; it spread around him, framing his silk *hakama*. Bright sky-blue under-robes showed through his wide sleeves. He wore padded formal shoes, and his wand of office lay at his side. The agitated whispers of rumor were, so far, confined to the Taira councillors; Yoshi and those beside him knelt patiently waiting for the official opening of the meeting.

Presently, the deep boom of a gong announced the arrival of Kiyomori's son Munemori, who took his place on the center dais and solemnly opened the council meeting with a prayer to Amida Buddha. Of Kiyomori's sons, Munemori was the oldest and the most ineffectual. His lack of ability and confidence made him vacillate between indecisiveness and bullying stubbornness—which he saw as a sign of strength. After the opening ritual, Munemori hesitated. His round, soft face bore little resemblance to his father's. Munemori had a small, mean mouth and spoke in a voice more reminiscent of a lady-in-waiting than a warrior. Everyone, including his father, despised him.

Munemori stared at the councillors, pursing his lips and nodding to himself. His full court dress in the *sakura* combination, red and white, made him look even less masculine than usual. Yoshi, who had once admired and emulated this androgynous look, was mildly repulsed.

Having drawn his thoughts together, Munemori plunged into the reason for the special council meeting. "Minamoto Yoritomo has been building his strength in the northern mountains. His army is a collection of rough mountain men, farmers, laborers, professional samurai, and other uncultured brutes.

Yoritomo wants control of our court and our Emperor. If we do not stop him before he grows more powerful, he will destroy us. Spies tell me that these brigands are preparing for an armed assault against our beloved Emperor. This is a situation we cannot tolerate, and I have been chosen by my father, the *Daijo-Daijin*, to lead an expedition to chastise these rebels."

Munemori's shifting eyes and limpid manner took some of the bellicosity from his words, but the Taira ministers and councillors unanimously applauded and declared themselves ready to follow Munemori's leadership. Most of them had no personal experience of battle; their idea of following bravely in Munemori's footsteps consisted of sending their retainers and samurai.

The five Minamoto representatives, including Yoshi, were at a loss. The Taira majority ignored them as they discussed plans to punish the Minamoto leaders.

Yoshi whispered to Hiromi, a Minamoto councillor, who sat at his left, "These fools are creating a situation they may well regret."

Hiromi was Yoshi's only friend in the council. It was Hiromi who had journeyed to Sarashina to plead with Yoshi to accept the council seat. Yoshi had liked him on sight. Hiromi was not a prepossessing figure. He was slight, almost birdlike, with small bones and a narrow face. But his eyes shone with intelligence, and despite his serious, pedantic manner—self-deprecating but kind—he had a keen sense of humor. A good and gentle man, worried and solicitous of Yoshi's well-being. Hiromi felt responsible for bringing Yoshi to the court and for placing his life in jeopardy.

With all his gentleness and lack of warlike qualities, Hiromi was a confirmed believer in the justice of the Minamoto cause and was willing to fight to the death for it.

Hiromi's prominent teeth shone in a nervous smile. "We may all regret their rashness," he said. "If it were not for the Taira's respect for your sword, they would turn on us now."

"In this atmosphere, no Minamoto is safe. I suggest that immediately after this meeting you take the others and leave for the north."

"And you?"

"I have personal reasons to stay. Do not worry about me. I have already proved that I can survive against their best."

"Yoshi, Munemori is dangerous because he is a fool and a

coward. He will set his father's red-robed guards against you. Be careful."

"Hiromi, I have endured much because I had a goal in mind Now that goal is at hand. I will not give it up through fear."

"May Amida protect you."

The Taira councillors left their places and clustered around the dais congratulating Munemori for his warlike words. Yoshi grasped Hiromi's sleeve. "Now is the time to leave," he said, "before false courage makes them do something foolish. Hurry!"

Hiromi rose to his feet and bowed. *"Hai,* yes," he said. "I will see to it that the others are outside the city gates before nightfall."

"And you?" asked Yoshi.

"I will remain in the city as long as you are here. I have no fear of these courtiers as long as you are here to protect me."

Hiromi and the others swept from the hall looking to neither left nor right as they passed into the darkness away from the lamps. Yoshi was the only councillor still kneeling in place. It was as though he were surrounded by an invisible wall. The Taira assembled in groups, pumping up their courage. Groups formed, broke up and reformed, all speaking in breathless tones, urging each other on to feats of bravery.

Even the cloistered Emperor, Go-Shirakawa, came from behind his screen. Go-Shirakawa loathed Munemori, yet he felt the current of enthusiasm that resulted from Munemori's words was too strong to deny. For political reasons, he joined the Taira councillors to show his support.

Yoshi felt this was a bad sign for the future. He knelt impassively as the groups swirled around his position, pointedly ignoring him.

After twenty minutes of brave display, Munemori called the meeting back to order. The Taira reluctantly returned to their mats.

"Some of our councillors seem to lack the sense of loyalty we expect," he said, pointedly staring at Yoshi and the empty spaces around him. "Yet they are members of our council. Well . . . any member who cannot support the goals of our beloved Emperor by supporting my father, the Prime Minister, should resign. If the Minamoto representatives continue to obstruct our path, they will be removed . . . by force, if necessary."

Munemori hesitated. His threat seemed to have depleted his last energy. His mouth pursed again. "In the next two days you will be informed as to the formation of my new army. This council meeting is now adjourned.

"Namu Amida Butsu."

six

Kiyomori was almost unrecognizable: a white stubble of hair grew around his pate, his eyes were sunken in dark sockets, the skin on his neck hung in loose folds.

The healers had treated him with *moe-kusa*, the traditional powdered leaf cone. The burning of the *moe-kusa* on Kiyomori's skin should have adjusted the yin-yang balance that flowed through the twelve channels of *chi*. Once that balance was returned, his fever should have abated. The treatment, however, succeeded only in adding twelve painful burns to his other symptoms.

He thrashed about, unable to find a comfortable position. "*Ata, ata,* hot, hot," he gasped. The healers brought holy water from Mount Hiei. They filled a stone tank and lowered him into it. The pain of the cold water touching his burns made him twist uncontrollably, and he had to be taken out.

Most of the time he was unaware of his surroundings and moaned unintelligibly.

The Nii-Dono was constantly present. Her heavy jasmine perfume and the crisp rustle of her silk over-robe contrasted with the smell of Kiyomori's sickness and the soggy sounds of his body flailing about on the wet sheets.

On the morning of the twenty-first day of the third month of 1181, Kiyomori's eyes focused and he lay still. He watched the healers fussing with the overhead bamboo pipe that dripped water to cool his fevered body. Heiroku, Kiyomori's major-domo, saw the change and hurried to his master's side.

Kiyomori whispered, "Send them away. They are useless."

Heiroku's bald head bobbed up and down. "Yes, my lord, yes," he said, tears streaming from his eyes. "What else can I do?" He had served Kiyomori for over forty years and felt genuine grief at his imminent loss.

Kiyomori struggled to raise himself on his elbows. His naked body sagged wetly against the sheets. His skin had taken on the pale shine of a fish's underbelly. Heiroku had to turn his face away.

"Bring me Go-Shirakawa, the cloistered Emperor. I have orders for him."

"And the priests?"

"When I have done with the cloistered Emperor and my sons, there will still be time for priests. Now, act at once. The healers out. Go-Shirakawa here..." Kiyomori sank back on the sheets.

"Healers out. Out!" ordered Heiroku. "You heard my master."

"We cannot leave him. He is in our care. You have no authority to order us away," said one of the healers, the one who had burned the *moe-kusa*.

"Guards!" shouted Heiroku.

"No need, no need. We are leaving," said a second healer hastily. He grasped his protesting colleague's arm and drew him away.

A red-robed guard who was stationed in the hall opened the *shoji* screen and entered at Heiroku's cry.

"See these men out," said Heiroku. "Then return with a messenger. Kiyomori is calling for the cloistered Emperor."

An hour later, a ruffled and angry Go-Shirakawa knelt at Kiyomori's bedside. His large nose wrinkled in distaste at the sour odor in the room. He carefully adjusted his purple brocaded robe to avoid stains from the dampness around the *Daijo-Daijin*.

Go-Shirakawa had long nursed a hatred of the *Daijo-Daijin*. Go-Shirakawa needed Kiyomori's strength to support the throne, but resented his policy of placing relatives in positions of power. They often clashed, and Kiyomori usually came out the victor.

For weeks, Go-Shirakawa had been under virtual house arrest. In the guise of protecting him, Kiyomori's samurai surrounded his palace. The infernal red-robes were in every corner of the grounds. Go-Shirakawa could hardly enjoy his gardens without a silent red-robed youth standing guard beside him.

No wonder that as Go-Shirakawa knelt near the dying Kiyomori he felt no sorrow. His mind, rather than being filled with grief, raced ahead with plans and plots to remove Kiyomori's family and his influence from the court. He listened to Kiyomori's "orders" with a curled lip, his eyes narrowed.

"You will see to it," murmured the *Daijo-Daijin*, "that my son Munemori is given the same support you have given me. I have instructed him to mount an offensive against the Minamoto. See that he has full command of the Imperial troops."

"I will see that everything runs smoothly," said the cloistered Emperor, resenting the authority in Kiyomori's tone. *It is I who gives the orders, not this coarse warrior. How dare he speak to me this way?* he thought. Go-Shirakawa nodded. *Today he can speak to me as he will; tomorrow he will be on his way to the court of Emma-Ō, king of the next world. Amida Nyorai Butsu.*

"Help Munemori control the monks. They, as much as the Minamoto, cause our problems." Kiyomori twisted in a spasm of pain, splashing water on Go-Shirakawa's robe.

The cloistered Emperor drew back in distaste. *This situation is insufferable,* he told himself.

"And I want you to remove the Minamoto spy Yoshi from the council. I have arranged to repay him for the trouble he has caused me."

Go-Shirakawa's beady eyes grew smaller. Everyone in the capital knew of Yoshi's actions. The cloistered Emperor had heard Yoshi's inflammatory speech when he was first introduced to the council. Yoshi had antagonized the entire Taira contingent, but at the same time, he had sworn fealty to the throne. An idea planted itself in Go-Shirakawa's crafty mind. Rather than take revenge upon Yoshi, he would use him . . . to Go-Shirakawa's advantage.

"Enough. You will follow my wishes."

As you have followed mine, thought Go-Shirakawa ironically. He smiled thinly and said, "Of course."

After the cloistered Emperor had been seen to his palanquin, the Nii-Dono came to Kiyomori's chamber with their three sons, Munemori, Tomomori, and Shigehira.

They shuffled in uncomfortably. Their father was a difficult man and gave each of them cause to be nervous in his presence. Kiyomori had loved his oldest son, Shigemori, without reservation, but Shigemori had died five years ago, leaving the ineffectual Munemori next in line for Kiyomori's position.

They took positions around their father's bed. The Nii-Dono knelt in the background behind a light screen. She had already decided what she would do for her lord and had informed their sons. Yoshi's time would come soon, and afterward, the rebel Minamoto Yoritomo's.

Kiyomori spoke in a hoarse whisper. Each word took a great effort. "We have always supported the Imperial line," he said. "Before any of you were born, my life was devoted to our

Emperor and our court. I have been well rewarded for my loyalty. My family enjoys great wealth and position and will continue to enjoy the fruits of my labor. I ask of you one small favor in return.

"You have undoubtedly prepared an ornate funeral. That is of no interest to me. I would prefer to be burned and buried without great ceremony, but..." Kiyomori turned a baleful glare on each son in turn. "I want the heads of Yoshi and Lord Yoritomo mounted on stakes before my tomb.

"That is all I ask of you."

The Nii-Dono could not contain herself. She scuttled from behind her screen and threw herself at her husband's side. "It shall be done," she cried. "I have already planned for the first head to be presented to you. Your red-robed guards will collect Yoshi's head before the week is out."

"Then I am content," said Kiyomori. His lids lowered, and for a moment his family held their breaths as he hovered in the space between this world and the next. Then, as his sons and his principal wife wiped tears with their sleeves, Kiyomori murmured, "Send for the priests."

seven

The next few hours were marked by the priests' desperate attempt to reverse the course of Kiyomori's *mono-no-ke;* they guessed this evil influence had gained entry to his body when he was exposed to the noxious spring winds.

The abbot of Enryaku-ji, Jichin, came from Mount Hiei and denounced the efforts of the healers. Jichin lit incense in the four corners of the room, sending up clouds of smoke and sweet scent, then he declared, "Due to an error in judgment, the healers have treated Lord Kiyomori for an excess of yin. They have worsened his condition. He suffers from too strong a flow of yang. To bring his *chi* into balance, we must treat him with acupuncture needles."

Unfortunately, the earlier treatment had left painful burns on each of the twelve channels of *chi,* and when the abbot attempted to insert the needles, Kiyomori screamed and thrashed wildly, pulling away from the source of pain.

The abbot reconsidered. "It is an evil *kami* of great strength, possibly the ghost of the monk Saiko whom Kiyomori killed. Medicine alone cannot help. We will have to attack the *kami* directly through the intervention of a *yorimashi.*"

This news registered through Kiyomori's cloak of pain and he howled like a lost soul. His back arched up in a bow, his teeth clenched, and his lips drew back as he struggled to throw off the wet sheets.

"Amida Buddha Nyorai," he cried, seeking forgiveness. Because he had once tortured and beheaded the monk Saiko, he knew he would find no mercy from the court of Emma-Ō.

The abbot asked an assistant to prepare for an exorcism ceremony. Monks brought rice and salt, which they scattered in the four corners of the room. A priest was sent for the *yorimashi.* The medium would accept the evil spirit in her own body after the abbot's spells and incantations drove it out of Kiyomori.

Then the abbot called on the ferocious Shinto god Fudo, who had vowed to give his believers a six-month extension of their lives. "Preserve our beloved chancellor for the time you have promised. He is a true believer and we beseech you to allow him his full period of grace."

Kiyomori had appealed to Amida Buddha. The healers had applied *moe-kusa*. Jichin himself had attempted to insert the acupuncture needles, and then had called for Fudo's promised extension. Now, Jichin could only pace the floor, recite sutras, and wait for the *yorimashi*.

She came too late.

At the end, Kiyomori slipped silently into the limbo of *chuin;* his fate was in the hands of the ten celestial judges.

The word spread quickly through the Rokuhara; servants wailed and tore at their breasts. Where would they go now? Samurai stared at each other with stony faces. Cast from Rokuhara as wandering *ronin,* their lives would be as petals floating on the stormy Kamo River. Only the special guard of red-robed youths felt unselfish sorrow; they were a fanatic core of believers in Kiyomori's greatness. They, too, would be cast rootless into the world, but they thought first of their master. Tears welled up unbidden, and they asked each other how could they repay those who had caused their master ill.

The Nii-Dono was brought from her northern wing. Lady Shimeko followed in attendance, impassively listening to her mistress's orders to priests, samurai, and servants. The Nii-Dono seemed in complete control of herself. No one could guess that under the facade of white face powder she felt a terrible emotional loss. Whatever Kiyomori had done, she had never ceased to love him.

Jichin, the abbot, accepted her instruction with head bowed. He had failed to save the most powerful man in Japan. Jichin announced loudly, "This lay priest Jōkai, also known as Taira Kiyomori, shall be given as great a funeral as befits his station."

"He requested a modest cremation and burial of his bones," said the Nii-Dono. "However, it would be unseemly if we did not honor his contributions to this world and if we did not raise the people to influence the ten judges of Emma-Ō. So I charge you to make preparations for a funeral that will assure my lord passage to the Western Paradise."

"So it shall be," intoned Jichin.

Accordingly, that night, the body of Kiyomori was taken to the temple, where it was bathed in hot water and wrapped in clean white cotton. The body was then carried to the main hall, where it was dressed in full court robes. The Nii-Dono had chosen his clothing: a deep red over-robe, a full set of white and peach *hitatares,* ceremonial swords in his *obi,* and an *eboshi* tied on his head with white ribbons.

Attendants seated the body in the square golden coffin. Kiyomori's head was placed between his knees in a reverent position. Bags of vermilion were packed around him to support him in place. At his feet was silver to pay his passage to the Western Paradise. The priests sprayed him with aromatic ointments and spread a white linen cloth over him. The lid was lowered and sealed while the priests burned incense.

The Nii-Dono and Kiyomori's three sons gathered around the coffin to spend the night praying for divine intervention.

Go-Shirakawa arrived with an entourage of courtiers. With Kiyomori's death, he had been released from restraints. There were no red-robes in his party. He mounted the temple steps alone. "I bring gifts of silver in honor of my dear friend and compatriot," he said with a malicious twinkle in his half-closed eyes.

"We accept the gift in the spirit in which it is offered," countered the Nii-Dono.

Shigehira, the most aggressive of the sons, said, "Rather than bring gifts, you could show respect for my father by bringing Yoritomo and his lacky Yoshi to justice."

"In time, young man, in time," answered the cloistered Emperor. "For every man there is a time and place for justice. The Imperial Council will see that proper rewards and penalties are given to those that deserve them."

Munemori lisped, "But I am the head of the council. My father said . . ."

Go-Shirakawa interrupted with a contemptuous wave of his hand. "Your father is dead. We have many decisions to make. The future may hold change and surprise for all of us."

"The samurai lords will follow me . . ."

"Perhaps." Go-Shirakawa turned his back insultingly.

Munemori was stunned. His nose reddened and his eyes became damp and unfocused. Shigehira, seeing his distress, stepped in front of his brother. "We have the samurai of Rokuhara and the special guards," he said. "They will support my father even in death. Can it be that there are surprises even one as august as yourself cannot foresee?"

Shigehira was rewarded by a glare of ill-concealed hatred from the cloistered Emperor. "After the funeral, young man, we will see who is most surprised."

• • •

Nami attended Kiyomori's funeral service with the old Empress, Ken-shun-mon-in. Nami sensed tension in the atmosphere the moment she arrived. The ladies-in-waiting were nervous and constrained.

Outside the temple, the ladies-in-waiting were surrounded by warrior-monks and shepherded to a small room at one side of the temple, while the Empress paid her respects alone. Young red-robed guards were stationed at every door. The ladies milled about, unsure how to react. They felt like prisoners of the temple.

Earlier, Nami had been consulted on the Empress's clothing. She had suggested the proper dull mourning colors, but Ken-shun-mon-in decided on clothing that was at the borderline of good taste. She wore an outer robe of deep purple with a pattern of fuchsia brocade. Under the purple were eight under-robes in colors ranging from coral to deep red. The bright red showed at her sleeves and hem. When she walked, her silken linings rustled like the breeze through the Cryptomeria forest.

The subtle insult was not lost on the Nii-Dono, and although the Empress presented her with flowers and sweets, the Nii-Dono's face remained a rigid white mask as she accepted the gifts.

Nami wore the black over-robe and the gray under-robes she had affected since Lord Chikara's funeral, just over forty-nine days before. The tension within the Empress's party communicated itself to her. She was uncomfortable in the presence of priests, and the heavy incense made her queasy. She was relieved when the Empress returned and led the group of ladies to the carriages that waited at the temple gate.

With the Empress's departure, the councillors of third rank or above came, singly and in pairs, to offer gifts of silver, incense, flowers, and candy. Each recited a sutra and offered words of condolence.

Yoshi came with his friend Hiromi. Although they had opposed Kiyomori in the struggle for court power, Yoshi insisted upon coming to the temple to intercede for the Prime Minister's soul.

They arrived at the temple at the hour of the tiger, about four in the morning. Councillors of the fifth rank had been told they would be welcome when those of higher rank left. Yoshi and Hiromi tied their horses outside the wall, straightened their clothing, and entered the gate only to find their way barred by a squad of special guards.

The red-robes had appeared silently from the fog around the gate. There were about a dozen of them, led by a tall, slim youth who glared malevolently at the two councillors.

"You are not wanted here," he said.

Hiromi pulled back as though stung; this was an unheard-of insult from a lowly guard to a councillor of the fifth rank. He opened his mouth to retort.

Yoshi held his arm and shook his head admonishing caution. "We are members of the Imperial Council," said Yoshi quietly. "Surely you mistake us for others."

"No mistake," said the youth in a grating monotone. "We have our orders." His hand was on the pommel of his sword.

Yoshi bent close to Hiromi and whispered, "Be calm. Make no overt moves. These men are armed; we are not." As a sign of respect to Kiyomori, Yoshi had left his swords at home.

"Do you know who we are?" demanded Yoshi.

"Yoshi and Hiromi, the Minamoto traitors," answered the youth. "The Taira family does not want you here. You have safe conduct . . . tonight."

Yoshi noticed the hesitation and the implied threat. His face was stony. "We leave in peace. We have no wish to disturb the dead."

As Yoshi and Hiromi backed through the gate, moonlight revealed a group of warrior-monks watching them from the temple veranda. One was a giant who towered two heads above his companions, one had the coarse features of a peasant, and the third had a familiar face, soft and featureless. Yoshi could not recall why the third monk seemed familiar. Someone he had met in the past, perhaps. The monks did not interfere, but they seemed to be studying Yoshi intently. There was nothing friendly in their faces.

Yoshi heard slow music and the chanting of the priests. Even from the gate, he was aware of the heavy incense covering a faint smell of death.

The unseasonably warm weather had continued and the air was oppressively damp. The temple grounds were covered by mist. Yoshi and Hiromi mounted and turned their horses away. As they rode off, the three monks and the red-robed guards disappeared behind them, looking like a preview of the next world.

An inauspicious night.

eight

The next morning the fog had thickened; low-lying hollows were filled with gray billowing clouds. Hiromi's cart appeared out of the fog and stopped at Yoshi's gate just after dawn. Neither man had had more than three hours of sleep, but since they were accustomed to a court schedule that often started at four in the morning, they felt nothing unusual in the circumstance.

Hiromi wore a court cloak, as befitted his fifth rank. His thin, intelligent face was lugubrious as he greeted Yoshi.

"Does the coming funeral make you so sad?" asked Yoshi.

"Not at all," was the response. "It is the only ray of brightness in a day that may end in disaster."

"How so?" Yoshi was patient. He knew Hiromi would make his point in a roundabout and pedantic way.

"I found a message waiting when I arrived at my living quarters."

"Yes?"

Hiromi pulled a folded mulberry paper note from his cloak and handed it to Yoshi. His hand trembled.

Yoshi unfolded the stiff paper and glanced at the hastily brushed in characters. The calligraphy was nervous, jagged, angular; the message fit the spirit of the characters. *There is a plot to kill Yoshi and present his head to the Nii-Dono. The red-robes will act today. Be warned.* There was no signature.

"You see?" said Hiromi. "We must avoid public places. Especially the funeral celebration. Kiyomori's guard will be there in force."

"They won't attack me at the funeral, out of respect for their master. Anyway, I will not run nor hide in fear."

"Better to live in fear than to be cut down by a hundred fanatics. Our days in Kyoto are at an end; soon we will leave for Kamakura. Yoshi, if you hide for a few days, we can leave together. Your life will be a symbol of our success. If they take your head, we will have failed."

"Your arguments have merit, Hiromi, but the Taira will not

39

take my head if I do not threaten them. However, if they give me no choice, I will protect myself. Wait for me."

Yoshi left Hiromi waiting in the cart while he went back in his house to don his armor: a lightweight jacket of leather scales attached to each other with brightly colored cords. Yoshi fastened thick leather shoulder plates in place with a red ornamental bow. He completed his armor with breast plates at right and left. He covered the armor with a loose robe, then he placed two swords in his *obi*, sash, and a handful of *shuriken*, sharp-edged throwing stars, in his pockets.

He flexed his leg. The wound at his hip was stiff but not painful. He was well satisfied. He would try to avoid battle, but if it was forced on him, he was ready. He thought of the distress he had felt after his last duel. He did not want to use his sword for evil . . . but if he had to protect his life? . . . He had momentary qualms, thinking that if he had more strength of character he would go without weapons. No! That was asking too much of a mere human. He was part of his culture. A sword master!

The funeral procession left Kiyomizu temple at the hour of the dragon, about eight in the morning. The fog changed to a steady drizzle, turning the streets to mud wallows. Despite the inclement weather, the entire city appeared for the funeral.

The procession would cross the Sanjo, Fifth Street, Bridge, before noon. Every cross street on the route was jammed with horse, oxcart, and pedestrian traffic. Almost a thousand carriages and carts jostled and bumped, throwing up sprays of muddy water to despoil the courtiers' finery.

Imperial edicts specified the exact nature of carriage allotted for each rank and denied the use of the carriage to anyone below fifth rank. Like many other well-meaning but unenforceable laws, this one was ignored by all. Anyone who could afford a carriage rode. The carriages included huge Chinese-style vehicles, drawn by teams of oxen, ornately decorated with gabled roofs so large, they had to be mounted by ladders. These carriages were assigned to Kiyomori's family and other high officials. Twin oxen carriages with split-palm thatched roofs comprised the somewhat smaller carriages of ministers of the third and fourth rank. Single oxen pulled the board carriages of the fifth and sixth rank. Merchants, scribes, and others of no rank had their own equipages to jostle and mud-spray their neighbors.

Yoshi and Hiromi shared a one-ox carriage. Their driver was one of the most vociferous on the road and his shouts, curses, and threats accompanied the bumping and rattling of the carriage. Yoshi sat quietly on the plank seat while Hiromi, in the spirit of the day, leaned out and threatened anyone who came too close. His prominent eyes glistened with a mischievous light. He seemed completely unlike his usual professorial self.

Samurai dressed in full armor, with quivers of twenty-four arrows at their backs and two swords at their waists, rode between the carriages; they added to the confusion by cursing those who got in their way.

A few royal palanquins, each carried by a team of six bearers and preceded by armed soldiers, forced their way to the front followed by envious glares. Despite a cortege of twenty samurai, even the Imperial palanquin, borne on the shoulders of thirty-two men, had difficulty traveling from the Imperial Palace to the bridge.

Go-Shirakawa accompanied the three-year-old Emperor Antoku in this giant vehicle. The child Emperor was fascinated by the scene outside and clapped his hands whenever he saw a carriage collapsed by the roadside with a broken wheel or a bent axle.

Go-Shirakawa sat on a thickly padded seat and, ignoring the strictures of the mourning period, morosely ate sweet beancakes. He felt himself well rid of Kiyomori, but he knew that an incorrect decision or alliance at this point of political flux could cost him his throne and his head. He had played the game of power for many years and was determined to play and win again.

The gold phoenix on top of the royal palanquin bobbed steadily forward until it reached the banks of the Kamo River, the scene of the funeral procession.

Kiyomizu temple was on the east side of the Kamo, a short distance south of the Rokuhara estate. It had been chosen for the services because of its proximity to Kiyomori's mansion. The parade of mourners started at the temple, passed Rokuhara, and continued across the Sanjo Bridge.

Hiromi's driver, by dint of great effort and much shouting, manuevered the cart to a point in the front row, where Yoshi and Hiromi could watch the procession as it crossed the bridge. Imperial guards had cleared a wide, flat area at the bridge approach and Yoshi and Hiromi had an excellent view; they

were on the south side of the clearing opposite the Imperial
Phoenix Palanquin.

The funeral cortege was appropriate for the rank of *Daijo-
Daijin,* Prime Minister. The *hosho,* an attendant on foot, dressed
in a red-bordered black robe with a bearskin thrown over his
shoulders, led the cortege. He wore a grotesque wooden mask
with four gold coins for eyes. He shook a spear in his right
hand and a shield in his left to scare away the evil *kami.*

Next came a double row of one hundred white-robed monks,
carrying flowers arranged in ten-foot-high pyramids. Behind
them marched more monks, bearing flags inscribed with Kiyomori's virtues and selections from his favorite sutras.

The Imperial Bureau of Ceremonies specified the number
of funeral musicians permitted for each rank. As *Daijo-
Daijin,* Kiyomori was entitled to one hundred forty drums, two
hundred ten flutes and recorders, four gongs, and four cymbals.
The musicians played slow, doleful music in keeping with the
solemnity of the occasion.

The square coffin was set on an ox-drawn cart behind the
musicians. It lumbered to a stop every ten paces as the priests,
monks, attendants, and musicians halted to rest.

The *moshu,* chief mourner, wearing tattered homespun and
cloth-covered straw sandals, followed the coffin cart. He limped
and staggered to show his deep sorrow at the death of the
master.

Behind the chief mourner, another attendant carrying the
ihai, memorial tablets honoring the deceased, led the relatives
and friends, who trod slowly, ostentatiously wiping tears with
the sleeves of their white robes.

Usually, the parade would have been completed by the servants and staff of Rokuhara carrying cakes for the poor, but
this time there was one more group to be counted. Eyes straight
ahead, faces of stone, the special guard marched silently in the
rear. Their red robes were covered by white over-robes in
respect for their dead leader.

Slowly, stopping every few seconds, the half-mile-long
procession continued, accompanied by the measured beat of
the drums and the keening wail of the flutes and recorders.
Fine rain dampened the marchers and muted the sounds made
by the musicians.

Hiromi's ox shifted and snuffled nervously as Imperial soldiers forced the carriage back to make space for the funeral
cortege. The jam of carriages formed a nearly solid wall, and

soldiers pushed back the rear carriages to make room for those in the front.

There was a stir as a team of oxen, driven to distraction by fear, pulled against their traces, slipped in the mud, and over-turned their carriage, trapping themselves in their yokes. The soldiers, accompanied by the wails of the driver and the shouts of the passengers, killed the oxen and chopped them free of their traces. Unfortunately, the dead oxen did not respond to orders to move and the soldiers were left with a dilemma of their own making. They solved the problem by arresting the driver and leaving the dead oxen in the middle of the street.

By noon, the first part of the rain-soaked procession reached the main avenue and turned south to the Rasho-Mon gate. The cremation was to take place in the marshy fields south of the city where Kiyomori had requested that his bones be buried.

The attendants, bearing food gifts for the needy, passed Yoshi's vantage point. Then carriages in the rear ranks began to leave, again creating disorder as carriages crushed litters and litter-bearers slipped in the mud, dumping their passengers into the wet street.

As Yoshi and Hiromi ordered the driver to turn their cart, Yoshi saw a group leave the funeral cortege. There were ten of them, garbed in white over-robes that showed flashes of red at the collar and sleeves. Their bulky shapes indicated battle armor underneath.

The white-clad special guards had not looked at him, but Yoshi recognized the young man who had turned him from the temple gate the night before. Yoshi did not want to draw his sword again. His own life was of little importance; he was ready to face the consequences of a life with the sword. How-ever, Hiromi's life was another matter; he should not suffer for Yoshi's past mistakes. Yoshi had an overwhelming pre-monition of evil. Hiromi was an innocent, and innocents often seemed to pay for Yoshi's sins.

"Hiromi, leave the cart," Yoshi said urgently. "Take the driver and go on foot to Sixth Street. Wait for me there."

"I want to stay with you."

"Impossible! Kiyomori's red guards are surrounding us. They want me. If you stay, they will show you no mercy. Go!"

"All the more reason for me not to leave. You'll need my help."

"Hiromi, please. You are my only friend in Kyoto. I do not want to lose you. You cannot help me. If you stay, you will be a hindrance and may pay with your life. They do not want you. Leave me now!"

"I cannot. I am responsible for you. I must help."

"Do you have a weapon?"

"No."

"Then don't be a fool." Yoshi opened the cart door and pushed Hiromi out unceremoniously.

Hiromi staggered backward and fell into the mud. His robe caught in the stays and traces. He was furious. His expression was a mixture of rage, surprise, and hurt. His usually thoughtful, good-humored face betrayed his confusion as he sputtered incoherently.

"Take the driver and go!" ordered Yoshi.

The driver heard, and understanding Yoshi's tone, jumped from his seat and disappeared among the carriages.

Yoshi saw the red-robed leader coming toward him. The other nine had melted into the jam of carriages and were nowhere to be seen.

It was too late for Hiromi to run. He stood forlornly next to the traces, trying to clean the wet mud from his robes. The rain ran down his face, mixing with tears of anger and frustration.

"Tadamori-no-Yoshi," announced the youth, peeling off his white over-robe and exposing his red uniform. "I am Oguri-no-Rokubei, seventeen years of age. My father fought at the side of Lord Taira Kiyomori in the Hōgen rebellion, gaining glory for himself and our family. I owe absolute allegiance to my lord, alive or dead. I formally challenge you to face me so I may honor my vow to present your head at the tomb of my master."

Hiromi stood straddle-legged, bent over, wringing the hem of his robe with both hands; his *eboshi*, twisted by his fall, gave him a comical appearance. His prominent eyes bulged; his large teeth shone from his open mouth and a mixture of rain and tears made his face glisten. He was unarmed. Slowly, he rose to his full height and dropped the robe. He straightened his *eboshi* and composed his features.

"Young man, you are interfering with two members of the Imperial Council. You are impertinent and I will lodge a formal complaint with your superiors." Hiromi had assumed his most pedantic manner, and though his full height only brought him to the youth's shoulder, he sounded confident and secure: the teacher lecturing the recalcitrant student.

"Get out of my way," snarled Rokubei.

Hiromi involuntarily took a step backward, then pulled himself together and marched toward Rokubei.

"Hiromi. No!" shouted Yoshi, stepping out of the front of the cart onto the traces.

Rokubei, seeing Yoshi's concern for Hiromi, drew his sword, stepped forward, and with one quick slash parted Hiromi's robes in an explosion of blood and entrails. Hiromi's eyes bulged, his arms clutched his belly, trying vainly to hold himself together. He fell to his knees, staring in horror at the gouts of blood that coursed over his hands and mixed with the rain and mud in the street.

"I shall certainly report this . . ." he said as he collapsed onto his face, twitched once, and died.

Yoshi was desolated by *mono no aware*, the sense of the pathos of life. We are truly mayflies, he thought; we dance through life for brief moments and then we are gone, peasants or kings, no more important than the cicada, singing in the night forest, no more permanent than the spring frost that melts at Amaterasu's smile.

The life of the sword demanded payment once more. Yoshi had chosen a path years ago and he could not change the results. No matter how much he wanted to shun battle, the presence of his swords drew tragedy as a magnet drew iron dust. He had come to the funeral fully armed. Perhaps if he had left his swords and armor at home, the gods would have seen to it that he and Hiromi survived.

As it was, he knew his duty. There was no escape. Yoshi cleared his mind of extraneous thoughts. He drew his long sword, jumped to the ground, and moved toward Rokubei.

Rokubei shuffled backward, holding his blade in both hands in a defensive position. Simultaneously, he shouted a command. Nine red-robed youths, stripped of their white coverings, stepped out from among the solid phalanx of carriages, swords extended and ready. They quickly fanned out to surround Yoshi.

nine

The last of the funeral cortege disappeared down Fifth Street, escorted by the Imperial police. Carts, carriages, and litters were lined up side by side while their occupants avidly watched the drama being laid out before them. Hundreds of spectators stayed in place. A woman screamed and was immediately silenced. Yoshi saw the phoenix head atop the Imperial palanquin in the forefront of the spectators. Only the Emperor and his entourage were permitted to ride in this luxurious manner. The thirty-two bearers stood silently at their positions. There would be no help from them.

Yoshi lunged forward in a feint and struck at Rokubei, who retreated under the attack.

He sensed a movement on his right and turned, instinctively parrying a strike. He lunged after the attacker, who quickly withdrew. Yoshi spun in a circle, studying each of the red-robes as they closed in upon him. They were all young, some no more than children of fifteen. This was small comfort since Yoshi was certain that they were an elite group chosen for their ability with the sword. Indeed, he saw no area of weakness in the wall of red. They held their weapons like experienced warriors.

The red-robes were disciplined and well rehearsed. The wet ground was in their favor as it made Yoshi move carefully. Red-robes at varying points in the circle, in apparently random order, stepped forward with one attack and immediately retreated. The youths were restricted to their one-at-a-time pattern; otherwise they would obstruct each other's efforts. Yoshi spread his legs wide to maintain a firm base. The Emperor, the other spectators, the rain, the funeral, and Hiromi's pitiful body were forgotten, along with his desire to avoid using his sword in mortal battle.

Yoshi became a survival machine. His brow was clear, his eyes narrowed, his mouth firm but relaxed. He was aware of the faint odor of the field and the traces of incense and flowers left by the funeral cortege's passing. Rain continued to fall in a fine pattern, making his footing precarious. He felt the squish of grass under his bearskin boots and compensated automatically with every step. As each enemy made his attempt, Yoshi sensed the motion and took one lightning step to the side, parrying and countering smoothly.

Within seconds, Yoshi realized that the youths had arranged a preset order of attack; his mind narrowed the possibilities as his body reacted time after time. Nine attacks. No damage. The tenth man was due. He was directly behind Yoshi. As though he had eyes in the back of his head, Yoshi felt the air disturbance as the tenth swordsman moved. He twisted sideways, dropping to one knee and striking in a wide arc. The classic wagon-wheel technique.

First blood! Yoshi's blade slashed across the boy's thighs, cutting through meat, bone, and the major arteries. In a spray of blood, the boy gave a loud, keening shriek and fell. He dropped his sword and flopped back and forth like a beached fish as his blood spattered the men around him.

Yoshi did not hesitate. He sprang toward the opposite side of the circle, his sword flashing in the eight-sided pattern, then reversing into the butterfly and the windmill technique. His blade was a living thing that covered him on all sides. The red-robes gave way as Yoshi drove toward the wall of carriages.

"Stop him. Don't let him reach the carriages," shouted Rokubei, realizing that the advantage would be lost if Yoshi had the wall to protect his back.

One of the youths leaped ahead of the others with a shout of rage. "You've killed my brother," he cried, striking blindly at Yoshi. Yoshi was momentarily distressed by the undisciplined attack. Survive! He could not afford mercy or generosity. The wildly flailing boy died with his shout cut off at the throat, his head falling and rolling in the mud.

The next man lost his footing and skidded in an effort to dodge his companion's head. The skid was his undoing. Yoshi's sword slipped in under his shoulder plate, dismembering his left arm and sinking deep into his chest cavity.

In one more step, Yoshi was between the two teams of oxen. His sides were protected by double walls of nervous, stamping, and snuffling oxen.

"Pull back. Regroup," ordered Rokubei. There were now only seven against Yoshi.

Carriages and carts were frozen in place. People stared through bamboo blinds, fascinated or horrified—according to their nature—by the drama they observed.

In the Imperial palanquin, Go-Shirakawa had forgotten his sweet beancakes. His face was glued to the lattice, watching the field. He recognized Yoshi from the council, and as he watched, he formulated a plan. If the young man lived, Go-Shirakawa would have an important task for him. The fate of the Empire could be entrusted to such a brave and accomplished man.

Rokubei and his youths were huddled in a tight group opposite Yoshi. Rokubei organized them in twos and whispered three different sets of orders. At a clap of Rokubei's hands, the three pairs separated and slipped into the mass of vehicles.

Yoshi heard shouts and orders behind him and at both sides; he immediately understood Rokubei's strategy. The boys would strip away his protective wall of carts, one at a time, until Yoshi was exposed and trapped at the last cart.

There was a rending sound as a large carriage lost a wheel and crashed to the ground. Shouts of dismay filled the air. Under cover of the confusion, Yoshi climbed atop the roof of the carriage at his right. He sheathed his sword and, leaping six and eight feet at a time across the carriage tops, he reached the back of the jam. Two red-robes were abusing the occupants of the foundered carriage: six court ladies and an elderly lord. The ladies' cries and the lord's ineffectual orders added to the chaos. The youths' abuse served no purpose; the carriage could not move until it was repaired.

The old lord, his top-knot in disarray, his *eboshi* crushed on his head, his black over-robe torn, wrinkled, and wet, left the carriage to chastise the distraught young men. One of them raised his sword threateningly and the lord back-stepped quickly, putting his foot in a deep puddle and splashing himself with mud. He cried out in embarrassment and fear as the youth started to slice down.

The blow was never completed. Yoshi leaped to the street and, in a burst of swordplay, parried the strike, reversed his own blade, and slashed at the boy's arm just above the wrist-guard. Blade and hand fell into the puddle at the lord's feet. The lord gasped and turned fish-belly white, staring at the screaming youth, who held his forearm and pivoted in panic, spraying blood around him like a red ribbon.

Before the second youth could react, Yoshi had already cut through armor and flesh with one powerful stroke.

Yoshi shook his blade to clear it of blood and sheathed it

with a click. He estimated the height of the roof of another
great carriage and sprang up to catch an ornamental overhang.
He used his arms to pull himself up onto the roof. His strategy
was clear. For the first time since the red-robes had surrounded
him, he had them in separate groups; two more pairs and Rokubei. Yoshi raced along the tops of the carriages, jumping over
ox teams, and balancing precariously on the Chinese-style roofs.

Yoshi heard them before he saw them. These two had had
more luck in clearing the carriages than their compatriots. Two
carriages were already turned and a third was being extricated
from the jam. The youths had their swords in their sheaths.
The first was dead before his sword was out; the second died
as he blindly slashed at the ghost who had appeared from above.

Three left.

Yoshi crouched under the belly of a palm-thatched carriage
and checked in all directions; he hoped to gain the advantage
of surprise by locating the enemy first. He found himself among
a forest of iron-bound wheels and the legs of nervous oxen.
He was surrounded by the heavy smell of ox dung mixed with
the cloying scent of the fish oil that lubricated the axles. Yoshi
was sweating profusely under his armor. There was no breeze
under the wagons; he felt suffocated in a warm, dry pocket.
There might be safety in remaining hidden, but that was not
Yoshi's way. He had been trained never to turn his back on
an enemy, and whatever the odds, to fight to the death. When
possible, common sense said, divide your enemies and fight
them individually; when that is not possible, fight with every
survival trick at your command.

He heard a young-sounding voice nearby. Yoshi slipped out
from under the carriage, sword in hand. There they were, not
six carriages away, arguing with the occupants. Yoshi heard
an older woman's remonstrating voice and an angry rejoinder
from the red-robe. Then cries, complaints, and whimpers from
a group of young women who had been frightened by the
youths' rough manner. The women's cries turned to screams
as Yoshi emerged like an angry *kami* from behind the next
carriage. He held his sword with both hands, point up at a
forty-five-degree angle, poised for action.

The closest youth jumped away with a warning to his companion. Yoshi was on him, a hawk on a rabbit. His blade
whistled through the air, striking the boy's sword. The boy's
fingers opened involuntarily under the force of the blow and
the sword fell to the mud. The boy was helpless. In the

millisecond before the ringing sound made by the vibrating blade stopped, Yoshi was acutely aware of everything around him. It was as though the world stopped. He saw the young face, open-mouthed but staring defiantly. The rain had loosened the youth's top-knot, and hairs hung to his collar. He was handsome, despite the scars of a childhood pox. About sixteen, the age Yoshi had been when he left Kyoto so long ago. Yoshi hesitated, again beset by a wave of melancholy. These were children. How could he continue to kill them? He tightened his jaw. Do it, he told himself. Do it!

Yoshi's hesitation had given the boy's partner his chance. Yoshi felt a blow on his right shoulder. The wetness of the lacquered armor saved him. The red-robe's blade was partially deflected by the shoulder plate and the stroke that might have cut into Yoshi's arm only numbed it. He spun around, freeing his short second sword with his left hand.

Now Yoshi understood why he was still alive. This red-robe was merely a child. He seemed no more than fourteen years old. He didn't have the power to cut through armor. His expression, however, warned Yoshi not to take him lightly. The young face radiated cold intelligence and malice.

There was no time to think. Another sword strike was already on its way. Yoshi ducked, feeling his hair stir from the closeness of the blade.

Yoshi's short sword was only eleven inches long, hardly more than a dagger. The boy, though not physically strong, was quick and competent. Yoshi shifted to the side, keeping both boys in his line of sight. The older one had regained his sword and his composure; he was trying to slip behind Yoshi.

Yoshi placed his back to the wagon wheel and arced his short blade back and forth in a protective pattern. The boys were well trained; they separated and approached Yoshi from both sides. As soon as he turned to one, the other would lunge at him from behind. Yoshi's speed and sensitivity saved him again and again. He was in a state of *mizu no kokoro,* his mind as open and clear as a tranquil pond. He felt the movement of the air as ripples in the pond of his mind and parried on instinct alone.

Soon one of the boys would succeed in wounding him. Yoshi had to make a decision; he could not win a purely defensive battle. Though his blade was unsuited for attack, he would have to fight his way out of the carriage jam and onto the open ground. The disadvantage in the field would be the addition of

Rokubei; the advantage would be freedom to move in any direction to confuse his enemies.

The decision was made for him by the younger boy, who shouted for Rokubei's help. Without a long sword, three competent swordsmen would be beyond even Yoshi's abilities.

Yoshi parried, and instead of turning to defend his back, lunged at the older youth. One foot was inside the boy's line of attack. Now, the short blade gave Yoshi the advantage as the boy tried to shorten his grip to strike at the *kami* that was pressing against him, chest to chest, and pushing the point of the blade under his chest plates.

Yoshi's short sword sank to the hilt, sliding from hard armor into soft flesh. Blood rushed down Yoshi's blade, covering his hand and wrist and saturating his rain-wet sleeve. The younger boy struck at him from behind in a frantic effort to save his companion. Yoshi flung his head back and forth, avoiding the young boy's attack by sheer instinct. Yoshi's short blade touched bone and stuck. Too late to retrieve it, he grabbed at the dead boy's arm, prying his fingers from the long sword.

The younger boy was screaming incoherently as he struck again and again, missing Yoshi's head, his blade deflected by Yoshi's armor.

Now Yoshi had the sword. He felt sick at the thought of killing one so young, but he knew that this time he could have no mercy. Kill the child or die. He started a combination, a feint at the boy's head to be followed by a body strike. The boy should raise his sword to block the head blow, leaving his body exposed. Any competent swordsman would have protected his head, but the hysterical boy didn't even raise his blade, instead he launched a wide arcing strike at Yoshi's midsection. The blades hit simultaneously. The boy's head lifted from his shoulders in a graceful arc and, like the round leather ball in the popular game of *kemari*, rolled under the wagon, startling the oxen. The terrified oxen stamped and shuffled around the strange object; one hoofed foot landed on it, crushing the fine bones and grinding the broken sphere into the mud.

The boy's blade had cut into Yoshi's chest plate and rested against his exposed flesh. Yoshi pulled it loose and dropped it at his feet. He felt heartsick. A *sensei*, a teacher, a sword master, decapitating children. Though it was kill or be killed, he felt he had failed. The acrid smell of blood, ox dung, tallow, wet wood, and his own sweat made him sick.

Yoshi staggered into the clearing, castigating himself for what he had done. He was aware of people peering at him through the latticework walls of the carriages. What could they be thinking of him? He shuddered with revulsion. The evil spirits that led him to violence had betrayed him again. He was tired of death. Hiromi, the boys. Why? He felt a tear on his rain-washed cheeks. Poor Hiromi. It had not been his battle. The gentle, scholarly man had died because fate had put him in the wrong place.

Yoshi whispered, *"Namu Amida Butsu,"* to help Hiromi's soul on its trip to the ten judges. He told himself that the touch of death was lighter than a feather and that every man eventually had to leave this cycle of life. Cold comfort when it was his only friend who had left him to suffer the cycle of life alone.

Yoshi stepped out onto the open field. The wooden Sanjo Bridge was at his right; the Emperor's palanquin was surrounded by another mass of carriages ahead. The rain had lightened to a fine mist. Yoshi spread his legs and glared at the Emperor's palanquin and the thirty-two bearers who had not moved to help him. He lifted his sword in an ironic salute to the invisible occupants of the palanquin and threw it as hard as he could toward the rushing Kamo River. The blade twisted lazily through the air and landed, point first, to quiver in the railing at the bridge approach.

Suddenly, Yoshi was reeling forward, dropping to his knees, palms hitting the ground and sliding in the mud. His preoccupation with the palanquin had dulled his sensitivity. Rokubei had stealthily approached and, with hundreds of silent witnesses, struck at the back of Yoshi's throat. Only Rokubei's haste had saved Yoshi from instant death. The overanxious red-robed leader had miscalculated his distance, hitting Yoshi across the shoulders an inch below his throat line. The armor plates held, and Yoshi fell forward from the shock of the strike.

Rokubei was frenzied. He howled like a wild monkey and leaped at Yoshi's exposed back. The treacherous ground made him almost lose his footing. He slid, flailing his arms to maintain his balance.

Yoshi took the opportunity to roll away. At least he would die facing his killer.

Rokubei regained his balance; there was no reason to rush. Yoshi lay on his back in the mud. He had no sword. There was no cover for twenty yards in any direction. Rokubei's chest stopped heaving. The insane glare left his eyes, to be replaced by an expression of feral cunning. The corner of his upper lip quivered like that of a hunting dog scenting the kill. He raised his sword in preparation for the final stroke. Armor would not stop him this time. He sucked in a deep breath and planted his feet firmly.

Yoshi rolled onto his side. There seemed no way to escape. By the time he regained his footing it would be over. He shifted further, feeling a hard pressure at his hip.

The *shuriken!*

He had filled his jacket pockets with them before he left his house. Steel. Knife-sharp throwing stars, each about three inches in diameter. Each capable of killing an ox if properly placed.

Yoshi whipped his hand into his jacket. Rokubei's arms were already descending when Yoshi released a flight of three *shuriken*.

One split Rokubei's forehead, one removed an ear, the third whistled across the field to hit the framework of a cart with an audible whack.

Rokubei fell to his knees, his blade sinking into the muddy ground an inch from Yoshi's face. He slowly fell across Yoshi's legs, staring sightlessly at the soggy earth.

Yoshi lay in the wet field with tears in his eyes. He felt self-loathing, disgust. *Sensei* Tadamori-no-Yoshi, killer of children.

ten

On the twenty-third day of the third month, the sun shone brightly. Reed rainhats and capes were once more stored in their proper places. Pear blossoms opened, forsythia made a yellow border along the city wall, and the willows of Suzaku-Ōji filled their branches with delicate green streamers. Wild geese headed north, tiny black flags on the horizon. Amaterasu was apologizing for the abysmal weather during Kiyomori's funeral. Though the air was still crisp enough to pinch the skin and redden the cheeks, it did not discourage the good people from venturing out into the streets. Traffic had returned to normal.

At the hour of the snake, about ten in the morning, a group of high-ranking councillors and generals arrived at Yomei-Mon, the western gate to the Imperial enclosure. They came in three palm-leaf carriages, gold and silver roofs glinting in the morning sun, red and blue flags snapping in the brisk wind. The officials bounced over the ground beam and were halted by the watch station of the Imperial guards.

"I am Komatsu-no-Sammi Chujō Koremori," announced the leader, adjusting his *koburi*, headdress, "general and councillor of the third rank. I am here at the request of the cloistered Emperor."

The captain of the guard bowed repeatedly in welcome. "I am honored to be chosen to greet you. His Majesty is waiting. Please follow me." The captain waved his wand of office impatiently. The guards snapped to attention and formed a double line to accompany the general and his companions down narrow Saemon-Fu Street to the *Dairi*, Imperial Palace.

General Koremori wore a black cloak with gray and white under-robes. A white *hirao*, ribbon, was attached to his sword belt. His black *koburi* was tied under his chin with another white ribbon, and his baton of office was held firmly in his hand. He wore his colorless court costume, as he was in mourning for his grandfather, Kiyomori, the departed *Daijo-Daijin*.

General Koremori was only twenty years old, yet he felt

the responsibility for the future of the Taira rested on his shoulders. With both his grandfather and his father dead and with his ineffectual Uncle Munemori leading the clan, he was searching for an opportunity to gain power and prestige. He felt that if the fate of the Taira rested with Munemori, they would all be destroyed.

Koremori marched deliberately on thick-padded shoes, ignoring the shallow puddles left by yesterday's rain. He might have been a reincarnation of his grandfather, with his heavy shoulders and thick neck. He followed the old ways and wore a thin coat of white powder on his classically handsome features. Though he had had only one experience in battle, his walk was an imitation of the rolling gait of a samurai warrior. The other generals and councillors followed him without question. Despite his youth, Koremori was a natural leader.

The Imperial guards stopped at the palace entrance and faced each other in two formal lines, making a path for the distinguished guests. Koremori led the way up the stone steps. His party was shown to the reception hall, where Go-Shirakawa waited with Munemori kneeling at his side.

The reception hall was in the center of the palace. Its hardwood floors glowed with polish. Support beams crisscrossed overhead in dizzying patterns until they were lost in darkness. Even at the height of morning, the central hall received no light from the outside world. Oil lamps along the walls sputtered. The braziers were unlit, leaving the air cold and filled with the scent of dead ashes and burning oil.

Go-Shirakawa sat on a carved chair on a raised dais. It was the only chair in the room. Behind him were rare Chinese screens depicting scenes from the holy city of Ch'ang-An. A lacquered tray on his lap held a teacup and a bowl of sweetmeats. The kneeling Munemori pouted unhappily as the cloistered Emperor popped candies into his mouth and licked his stubby fingers.

"Ah, my councillors and generals," Go-Shirakawa said when he was ready.

Koremori said nothing. He bowed along with the others.

"Please kneel," said Go-Shirakawa. "I do not appreciate your hovering over me like black crows."

"Yes, Your Highness," muttered Koremori, his young face sullen. The officials sank to their knees, forming a semicircle to face the seated Emperor.

"Munemori asked me to summon you for this special meeting," said Go-Shirakawa. "You will note that all my war ministers are included but that we omitted invitations to those minor councillors who represent the Minamoto. I thought it best to let Munemori make his announcement without distractions."

Munemori squirmed uncomfortably as everyone waited for him to speak. After several painful seconds, he began. His voice cracked out too loudly in the silent hall. He immediately stopped and, in embarrassment, lowered his voice. His effort to sound commanding brought contemptuous sneers to the lips of some of the generals.

"I've called you here, in the presence of His Majesty, because you are responsible for the safety of the Imperial family and the security of our city. His Majesty is not pleased with the results of our struggle against the warrior-monks and the Minamoto barbarians.

"My illustrious father, Kiyomori, is dead. We must not let his death create dissension in our ranks. We must cooperate, putting our own special interests aside in the greater interest of prevailing over our enemies..."

"*Hai, hai,* yes, yes," grunted Koremori, his youthful features twisted in a subtle expression of distaste. "We want to cooperate; we want to conquer Yoritomo's evil band. Our point of contention is how to do it and who shall lead. I control three thousand samurai, plus another three hundred red-robed special guards. If I am placed in command, I swear to bring you Yoritomo's head on a pike. I volunteer to lead our armies against Yoritomo."

Go-Shirakawa leaned forward, his a bald head glistening in the light of the oil lamps. "Well spoken, my young general," he said softly. "However, I would remind you that as recently as four months ago you led our troops in a disastrous retreat at Fujikawa."

Koremori turned red with embarrassment. It was tasteless of the Emperor to mention the retreat in front of his Uncle Munemori and the other officials. A pulse vibrated in his jaw. The "battle" of Fujikawa had been his only military experience, and it had ended in complete disaster.

Koremori's army had camped on the western bank of the Fujikawa River. Spies informed him that a large force of Minamoto had crossed over the Hakone mountains and were on their way to the Fujikawa. General Saito Sanemori, one of Koremori's uncles, and an experienced veteran sixty-six years old, recommended they cross the river immediately and face the Minamoto at the foot of Mount Fuji.

The army had—for political reasons—been put under Koremori's command. He resented the authority of his more experienced uncle. To impress Sanemori with his ability to command, Koremori ordered the camp set on the plain facing the wide shallow river. November winds fluttered the red Taira pennants and ruffled the waters of the river and the reeds that clung to its banks. Ducks and geese beat their wings among the reeds looking for quiet pools to settle in.

Night fell suddenly in the shadow of the mountains and a flutist, playing a sad melody, cast a spell on soldiers and generals alike.

Sanemori, angry at Koremori's intransigence, stalked off, leaving the young general alone.

Koremori had forgotten to post sentries, an unforgivable oversight attributable to his lack of field experience and his agitated state of mind. General Sanemori, angry with his young nephew, said nothing. Those officers who realized that orders had not been issued kept their silence, fearing the general's anger. The main body of inexperienced troops slept soundly.

Only Koremori was awake. The wind of the eleventh month snapped tent flaps and whistled through the shore reeds. Suddenly, the birds, resting near the bank, lifted by the thousands at some unexpected noise. Their wings whirred and beat furiously as they flapped up in dark clouds. To Koremori, alone in his tent, the noise was like the roar of a mighty army. "Guards," he shouted bravely. "To arms. To arms. We are under attack."

The results were catastrophic. Instead of jumping to their posts and facing the unseen enemy, the green troops abandoned their positions, their weapons, and even their horses. Three thousand samurai and retainers, many only half clad, ran in a panic.

Koremori had no choice but to join them. He leaped on his horse and raced away at the head of his retreating army.

Was it the Minamoto? Was it only a sound in the night? No one could be sure where the truth lay.

By the time the bedraggled soldiers reached Kyoto, twelve days later, Koremori was being ridiculed at the Imperial court.

How cruel of Go-Shirakawa to mention it. Munemori saw Koremori's discomfort and hastened to say, "Our troops were overextended in far-off Suruga. We can not blame our fine young general for an honorable retreat. Blame rather the evil *kami* that eats away at the home provinces. Blame the famine that keeps our armies underfed. Blame Yoritomo and his rebels."

Go-Shirakawa studied the generals, who knelt in a group among the other officials. "Good men all," he murmured. "I place no blame, but none of you has met with success against the Minamoto. Last year Chikara and Oba Kagechika won over Yoritomo at Ishibashiyama. Small cause for rejoicing now that Chikara is dead and Kagechika unavailable. There is only one other general who has shown the ability to win. He is not here today. He is in the field with his troops, where a general belongs. I speak of Taira Shigehira, Munemori's youngest brother, the man who led his troops against the monks of Nara, the man who brought back the heads of one thousand *sohei*.

"So . . . where Chikara is dead, Koremori and Sanemori failed, one man can boast a record of success against our enemies. Taira Shigehira, young as he is, will lead the Imperial armies against Yoritomo's uncle, Minamoto Yukiie. Shigehira will command thirteen thousand men. When Yukiie is destroyed, we will turn our wrath against Yoritomo himself."

Munemori added, "As I said, we shall appoint Shigehira to go forth and bring us the head of Yoritomo."

General Sanemori applauded. Koremori glared. Though his Uncle Shigehira was only a few years older than he, Shigehira seemed destined for ever greater glory while Koremori was left behind. The other generals gradually joined Sanemori in ragged applause. Munemori was a weak fool, but he had summarized the Emperor's wishes neatly. They would all cooperate.

After Munemori and the last of the officials had departed, Go-Shirakawa clapped for his majordomo. "Bring me paper and a brush," he ordered.

He munched more sweets while he waited. His small eyes were thoughtful. He was walking a very narrow path on a very high cliff. It would be necessary to build a strong net to catch him if he slipped. The fate of Japan rested on his shoulders. Selfish as he was, he was dedicated to the country's best interests. He could survive under the Taira, but the Taira had grown corrupt and greedy. Without Kiyomori and Chikara, they lacked the strength to hold Japan together. Yoritomo was strong . . . perhaps the Empire would be better served if he held the reins of power. Go-Shirakawa had a long-range plan that might change the course of history and save the Empire . . . or destroy it!

The paper came. He brushed in the message, neatly folded the paper, and sealed it.

"Take this to the Minamoto councillor, Yoshi," the Emperor ordered. "Use discretion. No one must see you. Give it to Yoshi personally. Wait for an answer."

eleven

Yoshi's expression was serious. He had been silent during most of the meal. Lord Fumio strained to make polite conversation, but gave up in the face of monosyllabic answers and grunts. The servants finally cleared the trays and left.

The shutters were raised, leaving the south wall open to the gardens. It was midafternoon and sunny, but a stiff wind rustled the fresh foliage around the artificial pond. Bush warblers hopped and flew among the new leaves of the red maples, calling to each other in clear bell-like voices.

Nami came in after the servants finished. She wore a pale mauve over-robe lined with deep purple. Beneath it she wore a series of lightweight silk under-robes in various shades of orange. A crimson skirt flashed from the hem of the robe when she sat down to join the men.

Fumio tightened his lips as if to say something, then sighed and relaxed. Whatever he had intended to say remained unspoken.

Nami abruptly broke the silence. "Yoshi, forgive me for joining you uninvited," she said. "I must talk to you. You owe both your uncle and me an explanation for the terrible occurrence at the funeral. The court speaks of nothing else. You are called a monster. I know that is not true. You must have had good reason to kill those children."

"I am heartsick to think of it." Yoshi slumped wearily, as though under great pressure. "Yes, I had good reason. Those children—as you call them—were a well-trained cadre of assassins. I hate what I have done. I wish I had never learned to kill with my sword. I wish I would never again have to draw it in anger. I did not want to kill children, but when Hiromi was murdered and they raised their swords against me, I had no choice."

Fumio broke in. "Yet it was a terrible thing! Why is your life fraught with these situations? It must come from living by the sword." He nodded, satisfied with his analysis. "I wish you had chosen a different course."

"Like you, dear Uncle? I often think that I would, indeed, prefer a more peaceful life. I envy you your new position and the prestige and rank that comes with it. Lord Fumio, president of the court's department of archives. It has a nice ring."

Yoshi referred to the Imperial appointment that had promoted Fumio from a senior fourth rank to a junior third.

"My duties are light. The position is mostly ceremonial."

"And peaceful."

"Yes, nephew. Peaceful. I remember when I was your age. I had already led a full life of action. I felt it was time to marry and bear the responsibilities of my family."

Fumio had been awarded estates and a title for supporting the Emperor in battle. He had brought his bride to the *shoen* and prepared for a life of peace and happiness. His happiness was fated not to last. In less than a year, his wife had died in childbirth. Six months later an earthquake destroyed his castle. He was torn between taking his vows and retiring from the material world or using his lands and recently acquired wealth for the benefit of his three sisters and four brothers. The life of a monk did not appeal to him; he was a simple, direct man with no taste for the religious life. He decided to devote himself to playing the supportive uncle for the myriad children of his brothers and sisters.

Yoshi said, "I would like to build a family, too. However, that road is closed to me in Kyoto. And there you have the reason why I must take Nami and leave for Kamakura. With Yoritomo, we will be able to pursue our own happiness."

"Yoshi, please think beyond today. You are right to leave Kyoto, but Nami does not belong in Kamakura. She is accustomed to the life of the court. For her sake, go alone."

"There is no reason for Nami to stay behind. We go together." Yoshi reached out, took Nami's hand, and repeated, "We go together."

"Yes, I want to go, Uncle," said Nami eagerly. "I have done everything that duty required of Chikara's widow. It is now a week since the *Shijuku-Nichi*, the forty-ninth-day ceremony. My mourning period is over. There is no further reason for me to remain. Chikara's possessions have been distributed. My duty is done."

"Not so. The traditionalists will insist you wait, at least till after the hundredth-day service."

"The traditionalists?" Nami sneered in a most unladylike manner. "What do I care for the traditionalists? They will never be satisfied. They will expect me to cut my hair and remain a *mibojin*, widow, for the rest of my life. First the hundredth day, then the two hundredth day. No. I am still young enough to bear children. I choose to leave Kyoto with Yoshi to raise my own family."

"You were always headstrong," said Fumio. "I am not surprised at your decision. Yet, for my sake, stay a while longer. I need you here. My new position requires a woman in the north wing to manage my household."

Yoshi raised his brows. "My mother has satisfactorily managed your affairs for years. She still controls the staff."

"Not so. Yoshi, you have rarely visited me since your recovery. Your mother has been suffering from melancholia since your return to the court. I suppose it is the way of the world for sons to avoid old parents."

"How can you say that?" interjected Yoshi. "I've asked to see her several times. She always claims to be indisposed."

"Yes, yes. Of course she would. I thought when Chikara died she would rejoice in your safety. Somehow that has not happened. She sees no one. Even you, her son. She can no longer take care of the social needs of my household. Indeed, we take care of her."

"I will insist on seeing her before we leave, but leave we will."

Nami wavered in her determination. She owed so much to her uncle. How could she ignore his request for her own selfish reasons? "Perhaps," she said, "we should reconsider. We have many years before us. Yoshi, if your uncle and your mother need us . . ."

She was interrupted by a tentative knock on the *shoji*, screen.

"Yes? What is it?" asked Fumio with a trace of impatience.

"A message, my lord."

"Bring it to me later."

"The messenger claims it is urgent, sire."

"Oh, very well." Fumio shrugged. "Forgive me," he said to his guests. "The message is probably from my new bureau and is of small importance, but I must accept it."

Fumio's retainer handed him a scroll of heavy white paper. It was tied and sealed with the Taira insignia. The messenger withdrew as Fumio undid the red silk ribbon.

He read the brush strokes. "I have been summoned to Rokuhara, the Taira headquarters, at ten tonight. They ask me to be available for a mission of great importance." Fumio smiled.

"This may be an opportunity to use my military experience."

"Oh no," cried Nami. "You are beyond the days of military service. You are president of the Imperial archives. The Emperor will never release you from your official duties."

"The message is not from the Emperor but from the Nii-Dono, writing for her son Munemori. The mission is not specified, but . . ." Fumio smiled again, his thoughts going back to military triumphs of his youth. "Perhaps they need my mature advice in the coming campaign. The older generals remember and respect my military record."

Fumio's craggy face lit up with almost youthful enthusiasm. "Yes. I'm sure that's it. They want me to advise the young generals."

"What of the merits of the life of peace?" said Yoshi. "I find it strange that you are so gleeful at the opportunity to leave it."

"My advice to you does not change, but I have had peace for some thirty years. I welcome this last chance to serve the Taira."

"Yes, Uncle. You have lived a full life and I understand your desire to serve. For myself, I want to follow your advice and seek a life of peace. I have lived by the sword too long and am tired of fighting and killing. I love Nami. I would stay in Kyoto if I could, but here I am forced to fight every hand. Kiyomori's followers will not let me rest till I have killed them all or am dead myself."

"And when you reach Lord Yoritomo in Kamakura? What then? Will he let you live a life of peace?"

"Dear Uncle, I shall volunteer to train his soldiers. I am more valuable as a teacher of one hundred men than as a single swordsman. I love the art of the sword and will be content serving Yoritomo as best I can."

"I am relieved, Yoshi. I feared that as a soldier in the Minamoto army you would someday face me in battle. You are a son to me. I would find that situation an abomination. However, we each must do our duty as we see it. The world is large. I doubt that our paths will cross in war." Fumio rolled up the scroll and retied the ribbon. "The Taira have over thirteen thousand samurai warriors at their command. They will drive Yoritomo and his cousin Kiso back to the northern wilderness."

The long afternoon had been pleasant. Yoshi exchanged poems with Nami. He visited his mother and, despite warnings of her depressive condition, found her well and in good spirits.

She congratulated him on his plan to leave Kyoto with Nami. "There are those who would discourage you," she said. "I am not among them. You deserve a chance to build a family, and I will welcome the coming of your children. My life will be fuller knowing that you and Nami have the happiness you deserve."

Even Fumio, who originally was against Nami's departure, changed his mind. He wished Yoshi and Nami well for the future. His enthusiasm about actively serving the Taira made him forget his usual restraint, and after congratulating Yoshi and Nami, he spoke of his own future with joy. "They need me, these young generals. They need my knowledge and background. I feel young again. No more archives till the campaign is over. One last chance to prove I am of value."

At the end of this pleasant afternoon, when Yoshi left Fumio's estate, he noticed the giant monk who had been at the temple the night of Kiyomori's *otsuya* loitering near Fumio's mansion. The monk seemed to have business on the other side of Nijo Street, but it was the second time in a week Yoshi had seen him there.

Coincidence? Yoshi wondered.

Ever since the ambush at the funeral, he was extremely careful, alert to any possible threat. Now, as he guided his horse home, he saw his gate ajar.

Yoshi's small estate was on the western side of the main thoroughfare, in the northwest quarter, third ward—not too fashionable, but in keeping with his fifth rank. It was modest by the standards of his uncle's Shinden mansion or Chikara's small palace. The picket fence and tall hedges gave the three connected houses privacy, but the grounds were small. There was a flower garden, but no artificial pond, no bridges, no pavilions. A stone path led from the half-open gate to the main house: one large room divided by screens into several smaller rooms.

There were two smaller buildings in the rear, connected to the main house by covered walkways. Yoshi's retainer lived in one, the other was for guests.

Yoshi dismounted silently and tied his horse to a nearby orange tree. He stepped through the gate quickly.

The light was fading over Kyoto's western wall. Fireflies blinked in the dusk, making bright displays around the hedges.

The scent of orange blossoms filled the air. It was a setting that should have given Yoshi a sense of peace. Instead, he sensed danger.

The sun sank from sight. With infinite patience, Yoshi edged around to the covered corridor on the north side of the house. He climbed to the veranda, careful not to make a sound. He inched forward along the rail, avoiding the squeaky center of the flooring. He slid his long sword free and stepped quickly into the main room.

An old man knelt on the polished hardwood floor. He stared coolly at Yoshi. His heavily wrinkled features showed no fear, though he was unarmed. Yoshi recognized him as Yukitaka, an old and loyal retainer of the Emperor. Yoshi slipped his sword back into its sheath with relief. His determination not to use his blade to kill would not be tested this time.

Yukitaka held out a folded sealed square of mulberry paper. "The Emperor ordered me to give this to you personally," he said.

Yoshi watched him suspiciously; an ambush was still conceivable. Without looking away from the old man, he broke the seal and shook the paper open. A quick glance told him that the message, in the form of a poem, was indeed from the cloistered Emperor. The Emperor writing personally to Yoshi! How flattering!

Yoshi removed his hand from the pommel of his sword. "Forgive me for being suspicious. I was not expecting guests."

"I understand," said Yukitaka. "Your situation is common knowledge. Though I do not know the message my master sends, I believe it will be to your advantage to read it and obey it at once."

"Thank you, old man. You may go now."

"No. My master requests an immediate answer. I have waited several hours for your return. A few more minutes are of no importance." He bowed, his forehead scraping the floor.

Yoshi nodded. The calligraphy was splendid, a reflection of the quality of Go-Shirakawa's training in the court arts.

> *Fujiyama's crest*
> *The sliver moon greets the deer*
> *Silently nearing*
> *The safety of its white crown*
> *High above the red maples*

The brush strokes vibrated with controlled energy. Yoshi concentrated on the secondary meaning of the poem. It was unlikely that the Emperor would send a poem just to impress him with its aesthetic qualities. The poem contained a message, a message important enough for Go-Shirakawa to have written it personally and to have asked a messenger to wait for a reply.

Fujiyama, the sacred mountain whose name meant "never die," must represent Go-Shirakawa. The stealthy deer must then be Yoshi. There was an *engo*, echoing wordplay, involved in the "white crown high above the red maples." Obviously a symbol for the Minamoto and the Taira. White was the banner color of the Minamoto, red the color of the Taira. Was Go-Shirakawa suggesting sympathy with the Minamoto cause?

Yoshi raised his brows in surprise. The message, if he read it correctly, asked him secretly to approach Go-Shirakawa. The sliver moon was in the sky tonight. The end of the lunar month was at hand. In a few days the new moon that heralded the fourth month would appear.

Come secretly, the message said. Tonight.

The *shika*, deer, were safe from hunters in the mountains. It was when they descended to the plains and forests that they were hunted and killed. The Emperor's power would be the mountain that protected Yoshi from the Taira.

Yoshi asked Yukitaka to remain. He went to a low lacquered table in one corner of the main room, wet his inkstone, drew his brush through it, and in bold, sure strokes answered the cryptic poem.

> *A stealthy white deer*
> *Steals silently through the snow*
> *Of Fujiyama*
> *Leaving no track to be seen*
> *By Tsukiyomi's thin smile.*

He folded and sealed the thick paper. Even if Yukitaka were waylaid, the poem would be meaningless without its context. The Minamoto agent—white deer—would appear at Fujiyama—the Emperor's Palace, tonight under the thin crescent of Tsukiyomi, the moon god.

twelve

A thousand bells rang the hour of the rat, midnight, from the slopes of Mount Hiei. The night was warm and soft with the scent of a myriad of spring flowers. The air pulsed with the aromas of newly opened buds on cherry, plum, and pear trees. For most of the court it was a night for romance.

Yoshi arrived at the Suzaku-Mon, the main gate at the southern entrance to the Imperial enclosure. The Emperor may have asked him to "come silently," but the gate, with its connected guardhouse, was a hive of activity. Imperial troops marched the wall of the perimeter. Torches lit the gate approach almost as brightly as day.

Yoshi was dressed formally for his interview with the Emperor. He wore black silk headgear, a midnight-blue cloak, and wide-legged green trousers. He was unarmed—a test of his ability to survive without his swords. He tethered his horse at a flowering tree out of sight of the gate and moved to the edge of the lighted area, where he pressed against a tall hedge, trying to remain inconspicuous. He felt vulnerable to every passing stranger.

The traffic at the gate was not as heavy as during the day. Carts made routine deliveries to the Imperial kitchens; their interiors were inspected. Small carriages deposited courtiers who had been outside the enclosure on affairs of the heart; they were questioned regardless of rank. A few larger carriages brought delegations of officials to meetings; the Imperial government made no concession to the hour; many bureaus began working as early as the hour of the tiger, four in the morning, others worked from early evening until dawn.

The guards were well disciplined. Though individuals left the enclosure unquestioned, every incoming carriage was challenged and inspected before being allowed to bump over the crossbeam and onto the Palace grounds. Yoshi hoped to join one of the official delegations, but there was no way to do so without being noticed. The Emperor had been explicit. Clearly,

Yoshi was to come unseen and unannounced.

Tsukiyomi's thin crescent was well on its way to the horizon before Yoshi saw his opportunity. A cart full of fish was bouncing toward the gate when one of its wheels buckled. The cart tilted sideways, jamming itself in the middle of the road. The three fishermen and the driver crowded around it cursing freely.

Delivery of fish was at best a high-risk enterprise. At the spring tide, the sea off Saizaki was filled with *tai*, sea bream. They were easy to catch and were a favorite of the court. It was a race to bring the fresh fish from the coast to the Imperial kitchens; the cart that was delayed reached Kyoto with a cargo of rotten fish and the fishermen returned home without payment.

The fishermen were dressed in ragged cotton robes over loincloths. *Hachimaki*, head bands, held back their untidy hair. Their mouths opened in almost toothless grimaces as they shouted in shrill voices. They were representatives of the masses of population the court referred to as *esemono*, people of doubtful quality, semihumans. Yoshi's experiences in his years as a sword smith taught him that these men—outwardly coarse and unclean—were as honest and sensitive as any member of the court. There was much shouting and hand waving at the capsized cart. The driver gave orders while the three fishermen worked at cross purposes, accomplishing nothing.

Yoshi seized the moment. Hidden in the darkness across Nijo Street, Yoshi quickly peeled off his cloak and under-robes, folding them in an awkward bundle. He made a clumsy loincloth of his *obi*. He undid his hair, ruffled it, and tied a kerchief around his forehead as a *hachimaki*. With his muscular torso, he looked more like a worker than a courtier. The disguise, while not perfect, should pass.

The gate guards were laughing, calling out obscene remarks and giving mocking advice to the distraught fishermen. Yoshi stayed on the shadowed side of the cart. He joined the struggling men without a word. They started at him in surprise. Who would offer to help unfortunate laborers? This one looked like one of them, but there was something different about him. Perhaps it was that he was clean despite the bare torso.

Yoshi tossed his bundle into the cart. The odor of fish was overwhelming; this delivery was a race that might yet be lost. Some of the fish were already beginning to spoil.

Yoshi took a place under the cart. He positioned his shoulders

against a crossbrace and motioned the fishermen to hold the wheel.
Sweat poured from his body as he strained against the massive
weight. Saltwater and fish blood seeped through the floorboards
to pour onto his naked back. Veins bulged at his temples. Slowly,
with tremendous effort, he straightened his legs. An inch. And
the cart sank back to the cries of disappointment of the fishermen
and the jeers of the gate guards.

Again. Yoshi strained, teeth gritted, eyes closed to slits.
An inch. Another. One more. The cart was clear, the wheel
was snapped in place. Yoshi sank to his knees, spent with the
effort. The fishermen and the driver clustered around, thanking
him for saving them. Their breaths and the smell of their bodies
were even more unbearable than the stench of the fish.

Yoshi was breathing heavily. He needed air. He waved them
away.

"How can we repay you?" asked the driver. "We are poor
men."

"Ignore me. Go about your business. I will come along to
see that nothing else happens on the way to the kitchens."

So it was that shortly before three in the morning, Yoshi
was brought to Go-Shirakawa's presence by Yukitaka. His
clothing was rumpled and stained from the cart, but his hair
was combed and his *eboshi* in place.

"Everyone must know you are here," said the cloistered
Emperor.

"No, sire. I followed your instructions and arrived disguised
as a fisherman. No one saw me."

"I'm sure no one saw you. However...the smell!" Go-
Shirakawa held a perfumed handkerchief to his nose with one
hand and waved a painted fan with the other.

"Forgive me, sire," said Yoshi and recited an impromptu
poem:

> "Scents of red roses
> Waft through the great palace halls
> Sweet smells, but empty
> Of the nourishment in the
> White fish of Kamakura."

"Very good, very good indeed," chortled the Emperor, waving his fan faster. "I can see that you are the ideal choice for

my mission. A great warrior, and a fisherman that composes clever poems! Yes, yes. Your poem tells the truth; I receive little nourishment from the red roses since Munemori became their leader. Perhaps, my little white fish of Kamakura, we can arrange a more filling meal with your leader."

Go-Shirakawa studied Yoshi through narrowed eyes. "Are you ready to serve your Emperor and the people of Japan?" he asked.

Without hesitation, Yoshi answered, *"Hai,* yes!"

"Even if it places your life in danger?"

Yoshi said, "I consider my duty to my Emperor more important than my life." He hesitated.

Go-Shirakawa said quickly, "You have reservations. What are they?"

"I also have a duty and loyalty to the Minamoto," Yoshi answered. "I will not betray them."

"No need to. I want a loyal representative, one I can trust to serve our country's best interests. There will be dangers, but success will bring its own rewards."

"I am honored to serve regardless of reward." Yoshi bowed in acquiescence.

"This, then, is your mission. You will go to Kamakura and offer to serve Yoritomo. He will accept...he knows of your service to the Minamoto. You will act honorably on his behalf, but...you will always remember that the country and your Emperor are of prime importance. Your report on Yoritomo the man and Yoritomo the statesman will influence my decision as to whom I will support in the trying days ahead. Deliver my sealed message to Lord Yoritomo. Every minute lost lessens your chance of success. The Taira will try to stop you. Leave tonight. Immediately!" The Emperor hesitated, then added, "Perhaps you should take time for a hot bath and a change of clothing. At any rate, I want you to leave Kyoto before the sun rises."

"I must take my family, sire. We intended to leave shortly so there will be little delay."

"No delay!" Go-Shirakawa's eyes hardened to black stones. "I know your connection to Lord Chikara's widow. I give you my Imperial approval. Take her, but...you must leave tonight."

"I am here to obey, sire. I leave before daybreak."

"Start now."

"Hai."

Yoshi backed away, bowing deeply. Go-Shirakawa blew out through his lips in an expression of relief and sniffed at his perfumed handkerchief. The fate of the nation depended on a man who smelled of spoiled fish!

thirteen

Lord Fumio spent a quiet evening working on a project for the Imperial archives. Nami and Lady Masaka were busy in the north wing. He did not see them before his retainer brought around an oxcart and driver. At ten at night, he arrived at the two-storied gate of Rokuhara. He was dressed in a brocaded robe of thick cornflower-blue silk, official black *koburi* set squarely on his gray head, padded boots, wide-legged pants, and ceremonial swords at his side. He carried the official baton of the Imperial archives in his right hand and an iron fan in his left.

Fumio ignored the red-robed youths who patrolled the gate and grounds in great number. They were always stationed around Rokuhara, and if there were more of them than usual tonight, it seemed of no great consequence. The sentries passed his cart, and he found himself in front of the palace. He alit and dismissed his driver. He would enter the palace alone.

A few years ago, this area east of the Kamo River had been an unfashionable expanse of marshy fields. After the building of the Sanjo Bridge, Kiyomori changed it to the social and political center of Kyoto. The extensive grounds were covered with dozens of buildings, where Taira relatives made their homes. Tall walls enclosed mansions with roofs that extended in waves of tile until the main roofs disappeared in a maze of upturned corners and carved eaves. The beauty and luxury of Rokuhara rivaled the Imperial gardens of the Emperor. There were Chinese-style pleasure pavilions for moon viewing, dancing, perfume smelling, poetry reading, and wrestling matches. A racetrack paralleled the bank of the Kamo. Artificial ponds and streams were filled with frogs, croaking on their lotus blossoms. There were even special pavilions for fishing the streams and for waterfall watching.

To be invited to the Rokuhara by the Nii-Dono was an honor surpassed only by the Emperor's personal invitation to the Imperial Palace. Fumio's face maintained a disciplined formality; inside, he bubbled with an enthusiasm he had not felt in years. The Taira wanted him. At last, his experience and wisdom would be put to use.

Fumio had been flattered when the Imperial promotion lists were posted during the New Year's ceremonies. To be president of the archives was a high honor for a former warrior and country samurai. A high honor, but an empty one. How could he not be pleased that Rokuhara asked for his services in a more active capacity?

He mounted the broad steps at the entrance to the main hall. An honor guard of six soldiers met him. Mature soldiers, not the young red-robes who made Fumio feel uncomfortable. These were tough, hard-bitten veterans who marched with the unmistakable roll of the fighting man. Fumio nodded appreciatively. This was the way to be greeted.

The soldiers surrounded him. Two in front, two behind, one on each side. They brought Fumio into the main hall. The hall was almost a replica of the Imperial Great Hall—high ceilings crisscrossed with wood beams, and thick lacquered columns receding with mathematical precision into the darkness. The dais in the center had the only light, a series of oil lamps on high tripods. Fumio was surrounded by the smell of burning oil.

Hachijo-no-Nii-Dono watched him from a carved chair in the middle of the circle of light. She had forsaken the traditional screen of state and sat in the place reserved for the head of the Taira clan. Kneeling beside her were her three sons, Munemori, Tomomori, and young General Shigehira. The Nii-Dono wore a pale gray over-robe and varied shades from white to black under it: the mourning costume of a principal wife. Her face was lowered and the moving flames above her tiny figure cast harsh pools of darkness in her eye sockets and under her cheekbones. She solemnly followed Fumio's progress across the vast floor.

Fumio stopped before the dais and bowed to the Nii-Dono and her sons. For the first time, he felt uneasy. Why did that weakling Munemori and his brothers avoid his gaze?

"I am honored to be invited here. I hope to prove myself useful," said Fumio.

The Nii-Dono's voice was thin, almost shrill. "You *will* prove useful, Lord Fumio."

Munemori squirmed. Still avoiding Fumio's eyes, he said, "Mother, let us discuss our business."

The Nii-Dono ignored him. "We have questions for you, Fumio," she said.

"Ask, and I shall answer to the best of my humble ability."

"Are you loyal to our cause?"

"Of course."

"Would you give your life for us if necessary?"

"How can you ask me this? I have always been a staunch supporter of the Taira. My life is yours if you demand it."

"Yet you harbor one who has caused us great grief."

"Lady Hachijo, Yoshi has caused me even greater grief. I raised him and tried to instill in him a love of the Emperor and our clan. Yet circumstances conspired to turn him against us. If you knew the sad details, you would forgive him."

"Never! Fumio, my husband's dying words demanded Yoshi's head. I consider it a sacred trust that we carry out his wishes. Two heads will be placed before his tomb: Yoshi's and Lord Yoritomo's. Now tell me, will you help us?"

"No one has ever questioned my loyalty to the Taira. Madam, I respect you and the others of our family. Ask me to go into the field. Ask me to hunt down Lord Yoritomo. I will go without question. But Yoshi . . . I love the boy as if he were my own."

"We are aware of that. We also know he loves and trusts you. That is why we ask your help. Yoshi seems to have an almost supernatural ability to escape our wrath; every effort to capture or kill him has been frustrated." The Nii-Dono leaned forward, her face falling in deep shadow, her voice a hiss. "Pledge your loyalty. Pledge your every effort to help us against Yoshi," she demanded. "At this moment Yoshi is in a trap. He cannot escape. When the monks of Mount Hiei bring us his head, you will have nothing further to do. Your pledge will be fulfilled and you will have earned our complete support and loyalty. We will see to it that you are properly rewarded. Do you want to be a general of the armies? Granted! Do you want the return of your estates in Okitsu? Granted! Tell us your wishes, we will grant them."

"I am confused," said Fumio. "You want my pledge of loyalty. It is yours as it has ever been. Yes, I would like to be a general, but if I can serve you and the Emperor in a lesser capacity, that will suffice. I thought you brought me here to ask my advice for the young generals. If that was not your desire, then why am I here?" Brave words. Inside, Fumio felt a cold hand squeezing his heart. There was something he had never seen before in the Nii-Dono's face, something hardly sane.

"Platitudes," she snapped. "We need more than empty promises."

"My pledge is no empty promise," responded Fumio. A beading of sweat moistened his brow and covered his upper lip. His fingers holding the baton and the fan felt cold. Cold as death. The scene began to blur. It was as though he were living a ghastly dream. The Nii-Dono seemed to expand and contract as he watched. He became aware of his pulse pounding, of the six samurai who surrounded him, of the acrid smell of burning oil, of the unhappy expressions of the three men on the dais, and above all the mad glint in the eyes of Kiyomori's widow.

"If our trap fails, we call on you to give us Yoshi," the Nii-Dono suddenly screamed.

Fumio stepped back, startled. He felt the soldiers making a wall of armor behind him.

"That is impossible," said Fumio with simple dignity. "Yoshi is the same as my son."

"Take him!" snarled the Nii-Dono.

The unheard-of happened: Two samurai grasped Fumio's arms, holding him tightly in place. Common soldiers holding an officer of the third rank! Fumio struggled to reach his ceremonial sword—to no avail. He cursed, using words that had not passed his lips in the thirty-five years since his last military campaign. His hands were bound behind him and a sword prodded his back as he was led from the main hall.

"Mother, Fumio has always been our friend. How can you treat him so cruelly?" said Munemori.

The Nii-Dono curled a lip in contempt. "You are a weakling. But you must not also be a fool. If the monks succeed and bring us Yoshi's head, we can never trust old Fumio again. He must die along with every other member of his family. Remember what happened to your father because he spared Yoritomo. If the monks fail, we will use Fumio to draw Yoshi into a final trap—one from which he will not escape. So . . ." Her voice lowered and became even more deadly. "Even if Fumio agrees to help us, he will not leave Rokuhara alive."

Munemori looked to his brothers.

Tomomori turned away.

Shigehira shook his head in negation. "Munemori," he said, "you are wrong. Mother is right. There is no other possibility.

Fumio and his entire family must be destroyed. Our father's dying request is not to be taken lightly; we must put Yoshi's head before his tomb or lose face and power in the court."

"Spoken like a true Taira noble," said the Nii-Dono. "Though you are the youngest, I understand why the Emperor chose you to lead our armies." She turned to Munemori again. "Your weakness shames me. This is a time to harden our hearts. Though Fumio is an old friend, I will not hesitate to use him and discard him. That is the way of power. If you possess it, you must prove yourself strong enough to maintain it."

Fumio was chained to a post in absolute darkness. He was in a strong-walled room in a building that was used to accommodate prisoners of state.

After an hour of total silence, a group of red-robes entered with a pine torch; they put it in a holder mounted on the wall.

Lord Fumio held himself very straight. He would show no sign of weakness or fear. Nevertheless, he quivered inside. It had been many years since he was forced to submit to manhandling and threats. It took a major effort not to sink to his knees and beg for mercy. The hour he spent alone had given him time to reflect on his decision; he would never betray Yoshi. Whatever the cost to himself, he could bear the pain. He had no illusions as to his eventual fate. The Nii-Dono was far too committed to seeing Yoshi dead to allow Fumio to leave Rokuhara alive. Fumio was afraid but determined to die honorably.

A trio of youths were building a fire in an oven in the far corner of the room. With the light of the oven and the pine torch, Fumio could now make out his surroundings. He was chained to the center pole of a line of three. The room was large, with earthen walls on three sides. The fourth wall was constructed of heavy wood beams set at right angles to each other, making a grillwork. In front of this open wall was a raised dais with a thick wood block set upon it. Racks of tools and weapons were hung on the side wall next to the oven.

With a sinking heart, Fumio recognized his surroundings as the torture and execution room of Rokuhara. This large room had been authorized by the Emperor years ago, to confine prisoners of state and condemned criminals. Beyond the grillwork were seats from which spectators could watch an execution. Fumio remembered being outside that wall a year earlier to witness the beheading of a murderer.

His knees trembled and his fingers and toes turned to ice. Please, he wanted to shout, I am a man of peace, I have no quarrel here. Spare me! His resolve weakened; he asked himself what could it matter if he promised to deliver Yoshi. The Nii-Dono had said Yoshi was already dead. Were they merely trying to trick him? He could not live if he betrayed the one he considered his own son?

He watched as the red-robes heated a sword blade, joking among themselves as they held the white-hot steel toward him.

Fumio felt his knees tremble. He fixed his gaze on the open wall and chanted, *"Namu Amida Butsu."* The imminence of his death struck him with physical force. Death was so final. He had lived longer than most of his contemporaries, but he felt he had many years left. Could he give in? Would Yoshi understand? Yoshi was a good son; he would forgive.

No. No! Honor above all. Fumio bit down on his own tongue until blood poured from his mouth.

A red-robe came toward him with the white-hot blade extended. The damp air in the room sizzled from the heat.

"Submit and save yourself," said the youth.

"Call the Nii-Dono," said Fumio in an old man's voice.

"Give us your pledge; then we will call her."

The blade was three inches from his face. Fumio could feel his skin blister from the heat. He opened his mouth. Closed it. Gasped, *"Namu Amida Butsu-u-u-u."* An excruciating pain radiated from his chest down his left arm. His eyes bulged and sweat popped out on his livid face. He welcomed the pain. It atoned for the thought that he might have betrayed Yoshi.

"Never," he cried as his heart stopped.

fourteen

Leaving the ninefold enclosure proved easier than entering. Lovers from every part of the city who had spent the night behind the curtains of their paramours waited until cock crow before leaving to write their "next-morning" poems. But there were always those whose evenings ended early: the husband returned unexpectedly, the act of love ended too soon, the lady was indisposed. Yoshi blended into their ranks. Looking the perfect fifth-rank courtier and smelling like rotten fish, he left unchallenged. Though the guards rolled their eyes upward as he passed, they were disciplined enough to hold their tongues in his presence. Did he hear laughter as the gate closed behind him? No matter. There were more important things to attend. First, he would ride to the northwest quarter, wash and change; then call on Nami at Lord Fumio's estate and arrange to leave at once.

Yoshi left his house in the care of Goro, his old retainer. "I may be gone for some time," he warned. "Care for the house and grounds as though they were your own. I have left you enough silver for one year. If you need more, go to Lord Fumio. He will help you."

"It shall be done, sire. May Buddha smile on you."

In less than an hour it would be dawn. Lamps were being lit in houses all over Kyoto as officials and workers prepared for the coming day. Yoshi whipped his horse across the city. The streets were almost empty, and he arrived at Fumio's estate in minutes.

As he came close to Fumio's gate, he felt his scalp prickle. He guided his horse around the perimeter fence, dismounted, tied it to a fence paling, and walked to the back gate, which was used only by staff and tradespeople. Usually there were two sentries on duty. Tonight there were none.

Yoshi sniffed the predawn air. A breeze whipped across his face. His uncle's well-tended gardens were filled with flowering shrubs: Chinese pinks, moonflowers, and campion. Their scent filled the air, but under the sweet cover, Yoshi detected a sharp, acrid smell. Burning wood? Paper? All too familiar. He had encountered this odor when houses burned in the aftermath of earthquake. Yet there was no sign of flame, no touch of heat in the cool morning.

The moon gave little light. Yoshi felt his way carefully . . . carefully. He walked through the deserted north wing. There was no sign of his mother, no sign of the household staff. He felt surrounded by an invisible enemy. A palpable feeling of power lurked in the shadows.

Quickly, Yoshi passed through the covered corridor. He wanted to call Nami's name. His throat was dry, his forehead covered by a thin coat of sweat.

Someone was moving in the main hall! Yoshi silently made his way around the main hall to the armory. He wanted a sword to defend himself if necessary. He told himself that wearing swords did not mean using them. He chose two well-made blades. One went into his *obi*, the other stayed in his hand. He stole back to the main hall, stopped, listened. Whoever it was made very little noise. One man? Two? No more.

A rasping sound, a flare of light, and Yoshi stepped into the room alert for an ambush.

There was one man in the room. A monk dressed in white robes over battle armor. His shaved head shone in the faint light of a small brazier. His back was toward Yoshi, and he seemed unaware that he had company. Yoshi watched him strike a phosphor match and touch it to a mound of cloth and paper on the floor in front of him. The paper flared, but the cloth resisted the flame.

This was the odor Yoshi had detected. Apparently, the small fires had died out before catching the wood frame of the building.

In a society of paper, wood, and thatch homes, fire was a most dreaded enemy. Much of Kyoto had been burned in the flames that ran uncontrolled after the recent earthquakes. Anyone who would intentionally set fire to a house, knowing it might rage over half the city, was worse than a murderer. He threatened the fabric of the Empire.

The flame flared for a few seconds and died out again. The monk muttered under his breath.

Enough! Yoshi raised his sword and hesitated. A feeling of desolation swept over him. Did a curse follow wherever he went? Were those he loved doomed to suffer? If anything had happened to Nami or his mother, he would never forgive himself. Yoshi instinctively knew that the monk was his enemy, not Fumio's. He recognized him as one he had seen at the temple during Kiyomori's funeral ceremony. The monks knew that to harm Yoshi they had only to capture his family. That must be why they had watched Yoshi's movements for the past several days. Every man's hand was against him. Yoshi had expected the Taira to try to take their revenge, but this man was a monk. What quarrel did he have with the monks of Hiei?

Yoshi swallowed; his mouth was dry as summer earth. He remembered that last night, Uncle Fumio had gone to see the Nii-Dono. He was safe. But Nami; Mother! Amida help them. Don't let them suffer. He started to move forward, sword ready, and again he hesitated. He would not kill! He would protect himself but not harm the monk. Disarm him, capture him, let him live to tell what had happened to Nami, his mother, and the staff. Killing the monk would seal off his only source of information.

Yoshi stepped lightly through the piles of debris and ash. The monk realized he was not alone and dived forward, twisting to free his sword. He was quick. The sword was out before he stopped moving. Yoshi saw a glare of recognition and hatred. The monk's face was familiar. Soft and pale, with Chinese moustache and beard. There was no time for more hesitation.

Yoshi aimed a testing stroke at the man's head. As he expected, it was easily parried. The monk retaliated with a competent counter that made Yoshi retreat. Then the monk snarled Yoshi's name and pressed an attack combination that Yoshi easily blocked. "You don't remember me," the monk hissed as he withdrew. "Yoshi, the country bumpkin." Yoshi had not been called a country bumpkin since his youth at the Confucian Academy. The monk's face superimposed itself on an old memory. "Tsadamasa?" asked Yoshi tentatively.

The monk was breathing hard from the exertion of his few moves. His mouth was already open. Yoshi could hear gasps of air being sucked in and pushed out. "Once Tsadamasa," gasped the monk. "Now Kangen, warrior-monk of Enryaku-ji."

"So, Kangen. Now I remember you. You taunted me when I was a child. What do you want of me now? What have you done with my family?"

Kangen did not answer. He husbanded his strength and launched a vicious attack, driving Yoshi to the door. The smell of smoke clogged Yoshi's nostrils. His mind divided itself in two parts: one was aware of the monk's blade, the other sought the source of the fresh smoke. The fire, which had seemed dead, was nibbling at the pile of debris, throwing off smoke and flickers of flame. If Yoshi did not end this battle soon, the entire mansion would be ablaze.

"Enough, Kangen," said Yoshi coldly, and leaped toward the white figure, his blade a blur of continuous motion.

Kangen parried the first few strokes and retreated to the wall. Here, unable to go farther, he waved his sword in a windmill defense. Yoshi stayed just out of range for three passes of the blade, then with perfect timing, he stepped inside the circle and with a twist of his wrist disarmed the monk.

Kangen watched open-mouthed as his sword spun end over end, landing in a dark corner of the room. Before Kangen could react, Yoshi's short sword was pressed to his throat. Kangen shrank against the wall, cringing away from the point of the blade, which maintained just enough pressure to draw one drop of blood.

"Please," he said, fear drawn on his face. "Let me live. I know where your family was taken. Please." A tear rolled down his soft cheek, and his knees started to buckle.

fifteen

In the meditation hall of a small temple behind the great complex of Enryaku-ji, the *gakusho* and two warrior-monks were in close conversation.

"Can Kangen convince him?" asked the giant monk, Gyogi. "A man with his supernatural abilities..."

Chomyo interrupted brusquely. "Nonsense. He has no supernatural abilities. Stop playing the fool; Yoshi is human. No more, no less. A skilled warrior, subject to the same weaknesses as the rest of us. Let us hear no more about supernatural powers. We are the priests."

"You are right," muttered Gyogi. "It's just that he has been so fortunate..."

Chomyo broke in again. "His fortune is at an end. My plan will work, given his nature and what we know of his love for the woman."

Muku, the farmer, grumbled. "We should have waited at Lord Fumio's house and ambushed him. Your plan is too complicated. How do we know he will come here?"

"Muku, I respect you as a fighter. However, you must leave thinking and planning to me. I have studied Yoshi's character. I know him. He will not kill Kangen because his love for the woman is greater than his desire for revenge.

"I told Kangen to make every effort to kill Yoshi. He will fail, but he will be convincing. If he succeeds, by luck or trickery, our goal is achieved and we will release the hostages. If Kangen is bested, as I suspect he will be, our goal is still won. Yoshi will make him speak. Kangen will resist only until he feels genuinely threatened. He will tell Yoshi where we are. Once Yoshi knows that, he will come."

"When will that be?" asked Gyogi.

"My guess is that he will arrive within the hour."

"And if he waits till after daybreak?"

"Even better. We are not engaged in a formal samurai display of valor. When Yoshi clears the trees and is within sight

82

of the temple, I will ring the temple bell and ten archers will shoot without warning."

"Tell me again," said Muku. "Why are you so convinced he will fall to your archers?"

"There is only one way a man like Yoshi will approach. He will be angry and off balance. He will tell himself that monks are no match for him in combat. Since he is no fool, I think he will weigh the advantages and disadvantages of waiting for daylight. He will not wait, thinking there is an advantage in darkness against our superior numbers. Yoshi is a direct man . . . an honorable warrior. He will challenge us and face us with his sword."

"Supposing he enters the temple before the archers see him?"

"I am not a fool. There are sentries at every road from Kyoto. By the time he arrives at the clearing, they will be ready for him. As he approaches, the sentries will signal his progress with the hoot of an owl."

"We cannot fail?" Gyogi wrung his huge hands nervously. His belief in Yoshi's supernatural powers was written in broad strokes across his face.

Chomyo shook his head, a mixture of consolation and exasperation. "We cannot fail," he said confidently.

Chomyo, despite his air of confidence, was as nervous as Gyogi. He watched Muku's sullen bearded face and envied the farmer his direct, unimaginative nature. Of course nothing would go wrong. Yet . . . why did he feel a flutter in his belly? He reviewed his plan. It was perfect. He had studied Yoshi's character and his past history. He knew how he would react. Chomyo pictured him, at this moment, spurring his horse up the steep side of Mount Hiei, racing as fast as the treacherous ground would allow. Yoshi would arrive within the hour.

Chomyo fidgeted, clasping and unclasping his hand on the pommel of his sword. A *gakusho* was more a priest than a warrior, more a student of the sutras than a fighter. He was unaccustomed to taking an active part in an ambush. He shrugged away his unease. Let the *sohei* fight; he would supervise.

He detected the first streak of light on the far horizon. From the temple gate, he could see across the northeast plains and forests to the edge of Lake Biwa and beyond to the distant mountains.

The temple buildings overlooked a steep cliff. The road

from Kyoto led through a forest of Cryptomeria trees. Sentries were hidden among the trees along the road. When Yoshi drew closer, the owl hoot signal would be given by a chain of men, each signaling the next. The final approach to the temple was up a narrow set of stairs and onto a clearing surrounded by trees . . . trees that hid a score of archers.

Yoshi would have to leave his horse and walk up the stairs. When he came into the clearing, Chomyo would ring the bell signaling the archers to loose their arrows.

An owl hoot in the distance!

Chomyo felt his pulse race. He peered out to the edges of the clearing. The timing could not have been better. There was just enough light for him to make out vague white shapes, the archers hidden among the trees. They were ready.

Another hoot, this time closer. Yoshi was moving quickly.

"He comes," said Chomyo, forcing his voice to calm.

"Pray. Let us pray," said Gyogi tremulously.

Muku looked at the quivering giant with disgust. "Let him come," he growled. "I am not afraid. Let the archers fail, and I will show what I can do."

An owl hoot sounded at the edge of the clearing. In the distance a sheen of light reflected from a cloud to the surface of Lake Biwa. The forest below whispered in the breeze. The distant mountains were now visible as dark silhouettes. It would soon be daylight, and the smell of the air promised a perfect spring day.

A perfect morning to die, thought Chomyo as a figure separated itself from the trees, running awkwardly across the field toward the temple. Full armor . . . as though that would protect him from the power of the archers. His helmet was in place, his dark blue robe flew behind him as he ran. In the dim light, Chomyo fancied he could see the white Minamoto emblem on the midnight-blue robe.

Chomyo rang the bell.

The twang of bowstrings sounded before the echo, reverberating from the bell's vibration, stopped.

Twenty arrows converged on the single figure. Some were deflected by the armor, some penetrated with the unmistakable thud of arrows sinking into flesh. The archers renocked their bows and loosed twenty more arrows in a second flight. The blue robe seemed to deflate as the figure collapsed to the ground, arrows quivering like porcupine quills.

Muku grunted in disappointment and disgust.

"Praise be to Buddha," whispered Gyogi. "I never doubted that we would succeed."

"He is dead," said Chomyo soberly. "Our duty is done."

sixteen

Yoshi grabbed a handful of white robe and twisted it, holding Kangen in place. "Quickly," he said. His voice was all the more terrifying because it was so calm. "What have you done with my family?"

Kangen's reply was undecipherable. He choked and coughed. Disjointed words poured out. Yoshi applied pressure to the short sword. "You live only if you answer my questions. I have no time to waste. I will ask you one more time." Yoshi's powerful left arm lifted Kangen along the wall. The pressure of the blade never relaxed. When Kangen's face was level with his own, Yoshi repeated the question. Kangen could not know the threat was an empty one.

This time Kangen managed an intelligible reply. "They have been taken by the monks of Enryaku-ji," he gasped.

"Why? Where?"

"Before he died, Kiyomori ordered us to kill you. You are our enemy."

"I never acted against the monks. They've made a mistake."

"No mistake. Chomyo, the *gakusho*, has ordered your death. He blames you for Kiyomori's fatal sickness."

"I had nothing to do with Kiyomori . . ."

"Yet Kiyomori felt you were a threat to our survival. You killed many of our Taira allies and caused our temple to lose face."

"I don't understand. I am a representative to the Imperial Council. I have no disagreement with your Tendai sect, yet you threaten me and my family."

Drops of sweat rolled down Kangen's face; his soft moustached lips trembled. Yoshi released his grip; the monk slid to the floor. Keeping Kangen in view, Yoshi stepped back and stamped out the fire that sputtered fitfully behind him.

What should he do? His brows furrowed and a muscle tightened in his jaw. Go-Shirakawa had ordered him to leave Kyoto before dawn. Duty and responsibility to the Emperor demanded that he depart at once. Nami? Lady Masaka? The retainers?

Duty, responsibility, and love of his family demanded he make every effort to rescue them.

If he died in the rescue attempt, he would jeopardize his mission and be a traitor to the divine family. The world would say that his family was not important compared to his obligation to the Emperor. He had been trained in that belief, and once he would have killed the monk and abandoned his family to follow the path of duty; but he could not leave Nami in the hands of the monks. If he died in the rescue attempt, so be it.

The fire was out. The acrid smell was all that remained after he scattered the ashes on the charred wood floor.

Yoshi redirected his attention to Kangen. "It is too easy for a stranger to become lost among the temples of Mount Hiei. Take me to where my people are being held, and when I am convinced you have told me the truth, I will release you."

"Agreed, agreed," blubbered Kangen.

Yoshi used a silken cord to tie Kangen's wrists together, then he led him through the connecting corridors to his uncle's stables. The grooms and cart drivers were gone, but several horses and oxen were in their stalls. Yoshi contemplated carrying Kangen up the mountain in an oxcart. No. There was too little time. Kangen would have to ride.

Yoshi gagged the monk with a *hachimaki*, headband, and attached his wrists to the saddle. His ankles were strapped under the horse's belly. Yoshi led the horse around to the armory, where his uncle stored the finest lamellar armor. Yoshi selected a horned war helmet and a full set of body armor. He adjusted the armor hastily and covered it with his midnight-blue robe. He frowned at the monk's white robe. It would shine like a beacon in the woods. However, there was no time to untie and change the monk's robe.

Yoshi studied the eastern sky. No sign yet of Amaterasu's smile. The trite moon was low on the horizon. He would be able to reach the temple before dawn.

Kangen held tightly to the saddle as the horses pounded through the city. They left by the north gate, riding at a fast steady pace with Kangen leading the way, his white robe fluttering behind him.

The grid of the city fell behind them as they climbed Mount Hiei's slope. They passed through forests of pine, Cryptomeria, oak, and red maple. Kangen motioned with his head to indicate the correct path when they came to a crossroad. They continually circled east, maintaining a steady rate of ascent. Yoshi became aware of buildings in the forest around him. They passed small shrines, large temples, and living quarters. As they came close, the buildings seemed to separate from the forest, and after they passed, the buildings became part of the forest again.

An owl hooted nearby. On their right, Mount Hiei overlooked a sheer drop to the northeast plains. Soon, Lake Biwa and the northern mountains would be visible as the sun rose.

Kangen shook his head and made noises around his gag, frantically trying to catch Yoshi's attention. Yoshi reined in their mounts and leaned over to loosen the gag.

"We are here. Below us, in the hollow, stands the Great Lecture Hall. The main temple is on the precipice above. You must mount the stone steps. At the top, there is a clearing and the approach to the building where the prisoners are being held. You must go on foot; the way is too steep and narrow for the horses."

"How will I recognize the building? We have passed dozens, and it is too dark to differentiate one from another."

"First—when will you release me?"

"When I am sure you did not lie."

"I could shout. The monks would come for me."

"And you would die too soon to see them."

"Hai. I have no choice. So . . . carefully climb the stone steps. The building you seek will be lit by torches. You will see sentries guarding the rear. There, in the kitchens, your family is being held. When you see the torches and the sentries, you will know I told the truth."

"And I will release you." Yoshi dismounted and led the horses to the edge of the forest. He readjusted Kangen's gag and tethered the horses to a tree. "Wait," he ordered.

Yoshi ran for the stone stairway. Strange; there are no sentries, he thought. Another owl hooted mournfully near the top of the stairs. Yoshi moved soundlessly.

As his head came level with the clearing, he saw the torches and the sentries just as Kangen had described. Another owl cried, and Yoshi cautiously backed down one step. His eyes were level with the ground as he studied the undergrowth. He made out a white blur among the trees . . . another white blur. And another.

Satisfied, Yoshi nodded to himself and, as agile as a mountain monkey, raced back down the stairs.

"You told the truth," he said to Kangen. "The building is as you describe it."

Kangen nodded eagerly.

"I will keep our bargain." Yoshi cut the ropes that bound Kangen's hands and feet. "Dismount," he ordered. Kangen slipped from the horse, stretching to return circulation in his arms and legs. He reached for the gag.

"Not yet," said Yoshi. "You are too conspicuous in your white robe. Take it off."

Kangen raised his brows in surprise, but removed the robe.

"Take my cloak to cover your armor," said Yoshi.

Kangen's eyes widened as he realized Yoshi's intent. He shook his head wildly and made small bleating sounds around the gag.

Yoshi slid his sword from its sheath and held the blade to Kangen's throat. He tied the blue cloak to Kangen's shoulders. He took off his war helmet and adjusted it on Kangen's head. Yoshi retied Kangen's arms, this time behind his back.

"Face the stairs," Yoshi said. "I'll be behind you." Yoshi wrapped himself in the monk's robe and pulled the cowl over his head. "March," he said, prodding the monk with his sword until they were near the top of the steps.

"You are free," whispered Yoshi, striking the monk's back with the flat of his sword. Kangen leaped the last step and ran in an awkward crouch toward the main building.

A bell rang.

Yoshi was among the trees before he heard the first bowstring.

seventeen

———————◆———————

Chomyo was first to reach the body, Muku and Gyogi close behind him. "So much for supernatural powers," he said, stirring the corpse with a toe. The body was face down, war helmet knocked askew, robe pinned in place by a dozen arrows.

The light was changing rapidly. The eastern sky had turned pearl gray and wisps of high clouds picked up golden streaks from the horizon. Mount Hiei protected the temple from the northwest wind; the air was still as death. Walls of silent trees surrounded the tableau in the clearing.

One at a time, like white shadows, archers noiselessly stepped from behind the trees and watched Chomyo as he chanted the *nembutsu*. Gyogi sank to his knees and started counting *juzu*, rosary beads, as he intoned the death prayer to help speed Yoshi's soul to the afterworld. "Amida Nyorai, whose light radiates through the ten parts of the world, gather this poor soul who cannot call thy name."

Muku, having lost his chance for personal glory, grumbled and kicked the body with his wooden *geta*.

"Our mission is over," said Chomyo when he finished his prayer. "Let the world know that the Tendai monks did what the entire Taira clan could not do. Gyogi, take the message to the Nii-Dono and return with her acknowledgment within the hour."

Gyogi rose to his feet; he continued to touch each of the one hundred and eight copper beads.

"Now!" snapped Chomyo. "First deliver the message, then count your beads."

The giant hung his head sheepishly. "How can I walk to Rokuhara and return within an hour?"

"Use your head. Yoshi must have ridden here on horseback. Search in the forest. The horse will be tied to a tree somewhere below the steps. Take it. The Nii-Dono must know what happened here tonight."

"And if I can't find her?"

"She will be there waiting anxiously. Undoubtedly she will

90

reward you for bringing such good news."

Gyogi left. He held the double strand of beads in his huge hands, muttering his prayers defiantly as he strode off in search of Yoshi's horse.

The edge of the sun cleared the horizon. Far off, the surface of Lake Biwa turned to molten gold, reflecting the glory of the sun goddess. A flock of blackbirds disturbed the silence with their cawing and the thrum of their wingbeats.

Chomyo motioned to the silent archers. "Two of you bring the body to the temple," he said. "Our goal is won. It is time to release the hostages."

A pair of archers came forward, straightened the corpse, and rolled it over to make it easier to carry.

The sun was now high enough to light the scene clearly. Chomyo and Muku walked away. The archers bent over the body, one at the head, one at the foot. Suddenly one cried aloud, "Kangen! We've killed Kangen!"

Chomyo and Muku spun on their heels, both with their mouths hanging open in shock.

At that moment, there was another cry from the temple. "Fire! Fire!" came the panic-stricken voice of a sentry.

Yoshi blended into the trees. He watched impassively as the *gakusho* and his two companions arrived at the body. By the time Gyogi started counting beads, Yoshi was on his way to the temple kitchen.

The white robe, which would have been conspicuous anywhere else, was a perfect disguise. With the cowl pulled up, in the predawn light he appeared to be another monk. Without drawing attention, he closed the gap from the rim of trees to the rear of the temple and mounted the steps to the veranda. The torches seemed to fade as the dark receded; midnight blue was turning to pearl gray.

There were two pairs of sentries patrolling the kitchen area.

Yoshi boldly stepped up to the nearest pair. "Orders from the *gakusho*," he said. "I am to remove the prisoners."

"Who are you? You are not familiar," said a guard suspiciously.

"I am here on Chomyo's orders. If you want to question him, do so at once. He is waiting in the clearing. The representative is dead, and Chomyo wants the prisoners removed as quickly as possible."

"Only Chomyo can rescind our orders."

"How unfortunate," said Yoshi. He sprang forward, sword in hand. The first sentry died before he could make a move. The second drew his sword and opened his mouth to shout a warning. The shout became a gurgle as Yoshi's blade slipped past his defense; his head lifted and tilted back, held only by a thin flap of skin and muscle. His carotid artery spurted a geyser of red that almost reached the eaves. The monk staggered two steps before he crashed over the low railing. Yoshi had already kicked open the door.

Inside the kitchen, he saw the entire family huddled in groups in the semidarkness.

Nami saw him and rushed to his side. "Yoshi, thank Amida you are here! We have been in terror for hours. I'm all right now that you are here, but take care of your poor mother." She led Yoshi to Lady Masaka, who was crumpled against the wall, huddled in her sleeping robe. Yoshi almost did not recognize his mother; she was not wearing her white powder. How demeaning to make a court lady appear unprepared in front of her staff. No screen of state, no proper makeup.

The grooms, cooks, retainers, and ladies-in-waiting, separated in small groups, averted their eyes from the sight of their helpless mistress.

Yoshi squeezed Nami's hand and, speaking rapidly, told her to lead the lady and the staff to the back door and to wait there until he came for them. There was a covered walkway that connected the back of the veranda to a small storage shed farther up the mountain. Unfortunately, the group would be visible to the remaining guards when they left the kitchen. He needed to create a diversion.

Nami grasped the significance of Yoshi's orders and, as though it were a daily social event, directed the staff to line up at the door. She put her arm around the tearful Lady Masaka to help her.

Yoshi ripped thin wood slats from the cupboards and piled them on the floor. He poured oil from the lamps over the pile and led a trail of oil to the wood and paper wall panels. When he was satisfied with his preparations, he walked out onto the veranda and removed a pine torch from its holder.

"What's going on there?" called one of the remaining sentries.

The sun edged over the horizon. In seconds, the guards would have enough light to see their dead companions.

Yoshi called in a hoarse voice, trying to imitate the dead guard who had challenged him. "I'll explain in a moment," he said. "First I have to see to the prisoners."

Yoshi brought the torch into the kitchen and touched it to the oil-soaked wood. A burst of flame raced along the floor to the walls.

"Quickly. Outside. Through the corridor to the rear." He pushed out the captives closest to the door. They were bewildered but they obeyed, marching in a ragged column to the storage shed at the end of the covered walkway.

"What's going on there?" repeated the sentry.

Yoshi ignored him, helping the last of the captives on their way.

The sun was high enough to make Yoshi clearly visible. Blackbirds circled in the blue emptiness, cawing in the distance.

"You're not Hanshun," said the sentry. He turned to his companion. "He's a spy. Don't let him escape!"

The two monks closed in. Yoshi drew his sword and waited for them to approach.

The closest sentry held his sword firmly in hand and marched directly to Yoshi. "Put your sword down and surrender while you can," he said authoritatively.

Yoshi's answer was to raise his sword in a defensive stance. The monk snarled and swung a wild blow at Yoshi's head. Yoshi side-stepped and sliced across the monk's side, opening him from front to back. The monk dropped his sword, put a hand to his side and looked reproachfully at Yoshi. "Who . . ." he said, and died.

Flames licked through the wall of the kitchen. The second sentry stared at Yoshi, open-mouthed, then he turned and ran toward the front of the temple, screaming, "Fire, fire!"

"Stay until I return for you."

"Yoshi. Please. Take us home now. We are terrified. Your mother is in shock. Forget the monks."

"Dear Nami, there is no choice. The monks stand between us and safety. My mother cannot cross the mountain. To our left is a precipice. To our right, the forest. Only one road leads to safety, and the monks control it."

"You cannot fight them all."

"No . . . there is another way! This *gakusho* they call Chomyo, if I can get to him, we may all survive."

"Then, Amida smile on you. Yoshi, if you do not succeed, know that I love you."

"I will succeed."

The fire blazed, throwing off showers of sparks and clouds of dense smoke. Monks ran back and forth with buckets of water. Despite the appearance of pandemonium, the fire fighters were following an established plan. Fire was so ever present a danger that every temple had its own organized fire-fighting team.

Only Chomyo and Muku ignored the fire. "Yoshi, that damn Yoshi," cursed Chomyo. "How did he escape our trap? Did Kangen betray us?"

Muku said, "Kangen would never betray us. He was my friend. Yoshi will suffer for causing his death."

"What can you do? He escaped our archers. We don't know where he is."

Muku's face turned to stone; his eyes glittered with hatred. "Never mind where he is," he said coldly. "I'll go to the hostages. The entire family of Tadamori-no-Yoshi will die to avenge Kangen's death!"

"You're right," said Chomyo. "Go to the rear. The family will hide in the storehouse; there is nowhere else they can go. Find them and kill them all."

Yoshi saw Muku running along the veranda. Muku had his long sword in hand. His robe was half-open, displaying a full set of lightweight armor. His shins and forearms were covered with layers of iron-hard leather. Plates protected his shoulders and back, while a skirt of leather strips protected his middle. Instead of the comfortable bearskin boots of a warrior, he wore wooden *geta*, the traditional monk's footgear. The *geta* gave him a shambling, clumsy gait that was belied by his speed. He had lived all his life in clogs and was comfortable in them.

Yoshi waited at the entry to the covered corridor. His face was inscrutable. If he lived to rescue Nami and his mother, he would never use his swords to kill again. Calm as a result of his decision, he watched the monk approach. A monk would hardly be a test of his swordsmanship, yet a sword master stayed alive by never underestimating his opponent's ability.

Muku saw Yoshi waiting and stopped short. There was confidence in the way Muku held his sword, both callused hands wrapped solidly on the pommel, the blade extended in front of him, angled up, point level with his eyes. He feinted with his front leg and swung the blade, not in the expected head attack, but at Yoshi's wrists. He was fast, much faster than Yoshi had expected, but not fast enough to penetrate Yoshi's defense. Yoshi parried and took a half step back.

The next pass, Muku used a double attack sequence. Surprisingly sophisticated for a farmer monk. Feint at the head. Strike at the midsection. Yoshi took the force of the midsection blow directly on his blade. The monk was not only fast, he was also strong and experienced. Yoshi took another half step back.

Muku followed like a cat. In close, their blades locked. Muku exerted all his strength; his lips drew back, exposing crooked, brown, gritted teeth. This courtier couldn't possibly match physical strength with him. Yet . . . his sword was being forced down.

Yoshi felt Muku's bristly beard against his cheek; he smelled the hot, sick odor of Muku's breath. He could win this battle of muscle against muscle, but it was taking too long. He disengaged his sword and retreated, leaving Muku momentarily off balance.

Muku quickly recovered. He moved the tip of his sword in a small circle and taunted Yoshi. "This is the great swordsman who bested the Taira's finest? What a poor lot they must have been."

Yoshi did not answer. He was calm. Composed. He felt the wood floor under his boots. His skin warmed to the heat coming from the fire. He was totally aware of the fire fighters struggling against the roaring flames, of Chomyo approaching and signaling an archer to drop his water bucket and come to him. Yoshi's mind was a clear pond reflecting everything around him.

No more time for subtlety, for feeling out his opponent. Yoshi began his offensive. Not one attack or two, but a blinding series of consecutive strikes, no two to the same target.

Muku held his own through the initial phases of the attack. He gave ground grudgingly to the fury that blurred the air with a wall of steel.

As Muku's counter started, he lost his defense for a thousandth part of a second. He would never profit from his one mistake. His eyes bulged, his beard seemed to bristle with an unholy energy, then blood poured from his nose and mouth. His body folded, separating from his head, which fell on the veranda and rolled off onto the ground. The lids blinked once.

Yoshi did not hesitate. Before Muku's head was completely dead, he leaped the rail and reached Chomyo.

Chomyo did not resist. His lids lowered and his lips moved. *"Namu Amida Butsu,"* he repeated.

Yoshi spun the priest around, putting him between himself and the archer. A powerful forearm choked off the priest's prayers; Yoshi's sword point prodded his back.

"Tell the archer to lower his bow," Yoshi said into the priest's ear and released the pressure on his throat.

Chomyo choked. Words did not come.

"Now," said Yoshi. "I do not want to kill you."

Chomyo's voice was a harsh rasp. "Put down the bow," he ordered. Then to Yoshi, "What do you want?"

"Safe passage. Lead my family to safety, and you will live."

Chomyo's confidence returned. There would be another time. Chomyo would avenge the Tendai monks. Yoshi would be repaid for what he had done. "Agreed," he said, his voice now normal.

"Step back slowly," Yoshi told him.

Locked together, the two men marched to the steps, up onto the veranda, and to the covered corridor. Here, Yoshi pushed Chomyo along until they reached the storehouse.

Nami was waiting anxiously. "Praise Buddha, you are alive," she said, and glaring at Chomyo, "This is the man who kidnapped us and brought us here. He must be punished."

"I promised to spare him in exchange for our safe conduct."

"He is treacherous. Kill him, Yoshi."

At that moment, Lady Masaka came forward. "No," she said in a quavering voice. "Let him live. He is a priest, and I do not want his blood on our conscience. If he leads us to safety, he has paid for his life."

"Well said, Mother," said Yoshi. "I have no desire to cause his death." He tied Chomyo's wrists behind him and told him, "We start now. You lead the way. I will be behind you. Order the archers to put down their bows. You will be released when you have reached the safety of the stone steps. At the first sign of treachery, you will die."

Chomyo went first, followed by Yoshi, Nami, the ladies-in-waiting, the retainers, and the grooms. The morning was well advanced; a bright sun shone on the group as they marched.

Monks scurried like white ants on a burning hill. The buckets of well water were slowing the fire's progress. Acrid-smelling smoke rolled over the clearing, billowing up into the morning sky.

Though most of the monks were occupied with battling the fire, Chomyo called, "Safe passage, safe passage," as the group circled the clearing. Two of the archers, arrows nocked to their bows, followed them, keeping pace just out of sight in the thick trees.

Yoshi told Chomyo to order them back. "Safe passage," shouted Chomyo, rolling his eyes at the archers as if to say, *ignore me*.

When they reached the top of the stone steps, Yoshi motioned Nami to lead everyone down while he stayed with Chomyo. When he was satisfied that the last groom was out of sight, he said to Chomyo, "As I promised, you are free to return to your temple."

Chomyo's eyes glittered. He opened his mouth and shouted, "Archers. Kill him!"

The two archers, who had been waiting for the opportunity, raised their bows and let fly. Yoshi shoved Chomyo forward and leaped for the steps. Chomyo stumbled. One arrow flew past Yoshi's ear, the other hit flesh with a solid thunk. Chomyo had fallen forward into the path of the arrow. It sank into his collar, driving down into his lungs and heart, penetrating as deep as his abdominal cavity. He was dead before his knees touched the ground. Grotesquely, the arrow held him upright, kneeling with his head bowed in an attitude of prayer.

Gyogi found Yoshi's sorrel horse, just as Chomyo had predicted. He rode it downhill at a dangerous pace through the dark trees. The left side of the road faced over a precipice; the right side was so thickly forested that the first rays of the sun scarcely shone through the foliage.

Despite his great size, Gyogi had a delicate touch with the horse. He guided and gentled the steed down the mountain, using shortcuts known only to the monks. He rapidly reached the city and galloped across the Sanjo Bridge to Rokuhara.

The Nii-Dono saw him at once. She smiled with bitter satisfaction when she heard the news.

"So Yoshi is dead," she said. "How sad that our friend Lord Fumio did not live long enough to hear of our triumph. Where is Yoshi's head?"

Gyogi apologized that he did not have it.

"I promised to place two heads at my lord's tomb—Yoshi's

and Lord Yoritomo's. The first will be brought to the tomb today. I will not be satisfied till it is done."

Gyogi was upset. The Nii-Dono's bitter smile had turned to raw malevolence. His own cheeks twitched as he apologized again.

"Go back," ordered the Nii-Dono. "If you and your Tendai temple want the support of Rokuhara, you will do what I ask at once."

Gyogi backed away. He doubled his huge body over, bowing obsequiously. He would be glad to be gone. There was something evil, insane, about the old woman.

Within minutes, he was out of the enclosure and driving the sorrel hard. His huge body was an unaccustomed weight, and soon a lather of foam covered the beast's neck and flanks. Gyogi spoke soothingly. He wanted to let the horse rest but he did not dare. It would have to get him to the temple quickly even if it died in the attempt.

Gyogi took a shortcut that led him across the edge of Shimei Peak. The road was narrow; in places, a sheer drop to his right, a wall of stone to his left. The hypnotic sound of the horse's hooves pounding the dirt road made his attention wander.

Suddenly, he saw a group of people walking toward him. Not monks. The hostages! Gyogi felt a small flutter of relief. He was really a man of peace. Although he had been cast in the role of warrior-monk because of his size and ferocious appearance, Gyogi had never wanted more than a monastic life of meditation and prayer. He had feared that the cold, calculating Chomyo would not free the prisoners. Gyogi had no heart for the massacre of innocents. He was so superstitious and sensitive, he even felt qualms at the thought of carrying Yoshi's head to the Nii-Dono.

But Gyogi had done his part. Someone else could deliver the head. Someone like Muku, a bloodthirsty animal who thrived on killing.

Gyogi found a widening in the road where there was a clump of thick trees. He pulled the horse into the undergrowth and patted its flanks comfortingly. He felt guilty for resting, but it would be best if the prisoners did not see him. They had been released; he would let them pass.

They walked in ragged file, women, retainers, the entire staff, some crying, some laughing with relief. Freedom was a heady wine.

When the last person had passed, Gyogi kicked the sorrel's

flank. He felt better now and tried an off-tune whistle as he galloped up the narrow path. The scene to his right was magnificent. He looked down over miles of early green trees and fields. In the distance, the northern mountains were a purple streak painted on the horizon. Lake Biwa glittered even bluer than the sky. Birds circled in formation over the vast reaches. He breathed deeply of the crisp air and smiled to himself. He had done his part.

Ahead of him, a lone figure was approaching at a trot, wearing a monk's robe. Who was it? Familiar, but not one of the brothers.

Then Gyogi knew. He had been right all along. Yoshi was supernatural. A ghost. He had seen the body with his own eyes, crumpled and full of arrows. Yet here he was, on the road, running soundlessly, without a mark on his body.

This contact with the spirit world was too much to bear. Gyogi pulled back on the reins. The sorrel reared, neighing wildly, its front legs waving in space. Gyogi didn't even try to maintain his seat. With an agonized cry that was something between Yoshi's name and the inarticulate howl of a stricken animal, he fell from the horse. He leaped up with surprising speed for so large a man and ran straight into the vast empty space, flailing his arms and legs on his way down to the jagged rocks far below.

BOOK II

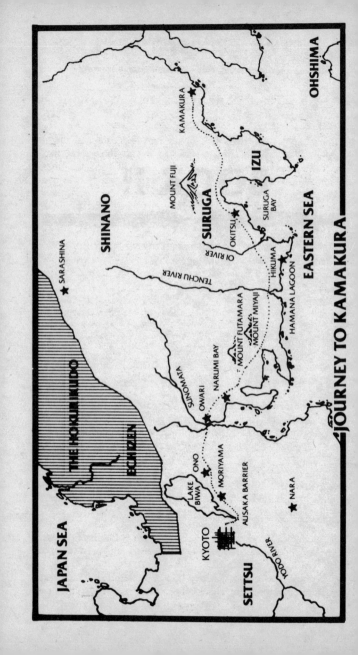

eighteen

Almost twenty-six years to the day before Yoshi and Nami escaped from Mount Hiei, a series of events took place that would radically affect their lives. By the year 1155 the lines of battle between Taira and Minamoto were drawn. As the tide of battle went against the Minamoto, some of them sent their dependents away from Kyoto, hiding them with friends in the surrounding countryside. The Taira soldiers spared no effort to capture and kill members of the Minamoto clan who might eventually do them harm. Lady Senjo, wife of Minamoto Yoshikata, was sent, heavy with child, to hide with a farm family. The farmer served as Yoshikata's retainer, the farmer's wife, Yomogi, accompanied Lady Senjo.

Juro, Yomogi's son, brought word that samurai were combing the area searching for Minamoto refugees. Yomogi, responsible for Lady Senjo, created a diversion to lead the samurai away from the farm.

"Give me the Minamoto banner," said Yomogi.

Lady Senjo knew Yomogi meant well. She protested weakly. "The banner is mine to carry. My lord left it in my care till he returns."

"I will take it to mislead the Taira soldiers," said Yomogi. "You cannot move fast enough to escape them. I can." She stared pointedly at Lady Senjo's huge belly. "The baby is due, and you must escape. If you are captured, you and the child will die."

"But you, Yomogi..."

"I know the countryside well. I will escape with the Taira following me while my son leads you into the hills to safety. In three days, we will meet again at the farmhouse."

"You are good to me. More than..."

"Nonsense. Your husband has cared for my family for years. My husband is proud to be his retainer, and I am proud to serve you. Now, go with Juro!"

Yomogi was a short, heavy-boned peasant. Her face was broad, with prominent cheekbones. She was handsome in a

103

rough, earthy way, not at all like the delicate Lady Senjo. Yomogi might have been of another race with her powerful arms and muscular calves. She had never known perfume or fine clothes, nor had she ever thought of reading or writing, much less of the poetry contests at which Lady Senjo excelled. Yomogi's life was hard and, by many standards, unrewarding, yet she loved Lady Senjo.

Juro led Lady Senjo away from the farm along a trail that went deep into the hills. Yomogi watched until they were out of sight, then she gathered her coarse cotton robe and set off at a slow trot down the gentle slope to the plains below.

The air was fresh in the early evening. Yomogi breathed easily, savoring the perfumes of early summer: the hot, dry smell of the grass, the sweetness of the flowering shrubs, and the tang of the pine forest. Her straw sandals pounded a smooth rhythm as she tirelessly covered distance.

Amaterasu, the sun goddess, had just slipped behind distant Mount Hiei when Yomogi encountered a group of enemy samurai. They saw the flash of the white banner before she plunged into a heavily wooded area.

There were about a dozen samurai, all mounted and fully armored. Yomogi had an impression of riotous color—red, violet, blue, and gold armor; saddles of silver, inlaid jewels, and ornate patterns; red banners, horned helmets, and quivers of black-feathered arrows. Then she was out of their sight.

Armored horses crashed into the woods. The light faded rapidly. In minutes, the last rays were gone and the woods turned black. Yomogi crammed the folded banner into her robe and ran. She heard the horses blundering through the undergrowth and the samurai cursing and striking at branches with their swords.

In an hour, she came to the plain that led to Lake Biwa. Cypress, willows, cedar, and pine grew close to the lake shore. Tsukiyomi, the moon god, shone brightly in a cloudless sky, turning the great lake into a bowl of molten silver. Clusters of fireflies signaled from the edge of the forest. Cicadas rasped messages from the underbrush.

The samurai were far behind. Yomogi smiled grimly to herself; they did not know the forests as she did. She curled up under a willow and was asleep in minutes.

Yomogi awoke at dawn. The sun was just rising behind her. The grass was damp, and her robe was soaked. She removed it and spread it out in a patch of sunlight. She had slept well.

The run and the adventure of the night before had left her exhilarated. She stretched in the sunlight, running her hands over her body, stroking her belly and her breasts. She had spent most of her life working the farm like a beast of burden; this adventure was a welcome change.

She walked to the edge of the lake and waded out into the calm water. It was cold and fresh; her body tingled with energy. Gazing out over the calm blue surface, she saw a fleet of fishing boats moored near the shore about a half mile away. If she could steal a boat, she could row it across the lake. Yomogi was a strong swimmer. She decided to swim out beyond the boats and approach them from the water side, where she would not be readily seen from the shore.

She put on her loincloth, then wrapped her damp clothing in a tight bundle and tied it around her waist. The Minamoto white banner was pushed through her waistband.

Lake Biwa shone warmly in the morning sun. The day promised to be auspicious in every way. Yomogi slipped into the water with hardly a ripple. Strong, sure strokes soon brought her beyond the boats. She turned toward them, swimming mostly under water. As she came close, she saw that they were not deserted. Apparently, some of the fishermen had stayed on board through the night.

The fishermen of Lake Biwa were uniformly friendly to the Minamoto. They hated the Taira and their repressive taxation. Yomogi relaxed. She turned onto her back and drew the white banner from her waistband. In two strokes she reached the nearest boat and held the banner high. "Fishermen, help me aboard," she called, spitting water. "I am running from the Taira samurai."

She stretched the arm with the flag up to the gunwale and tried to pull herself up. A black-bearded face stared down at her. Not a fisherman! Then she saw it: the Taira crest on his cloak. The Taira had captured the boats and stationed their soldiers on them.

Yomogi gasped and tried to push off backward. The warrior's sword hacked into her naked arm, severing it between elbow and shoulder. Arm and flag dropped from the gunwale to sink into the waters of the lake.

Yomogi watched the arm float downward as gently as a falling leaf. The water turned red around her. She floundered back and forth, sinking and swallowing water as she tried to reach her shoulder to stop the gushing fount of blood. The last thing she saw was the coarse face of the samurai pointing and laughing at her.

The Taira troops returned to Kyoto, assuming that Lady Senjo had died. At the end of the fourth day, a farmer who had witnessed Yomogi's death came to tell Juro what he had seen. Juro left for Lake Biwa at once. Although Lady Senjo was close to term, Juro could not stay with her; he had to recover his mother's body, and give her a proper funeral service.

Lady Senjo understood but was afraid to be alone. As a lady-in-waiting at the court, she had few resources to rely on. In her distress, she resorted to her one talent. She dedicated a poem to Yomogi:

> *Ten times ten thousand*
> *Tears form rivers in that world*
> *Where her beloved*
> *Shade lives in eternal joy*
> *Forgetting earth's cruel sorrows.*

Creating the poem distracted her, but she bit her lip in frustration because she had no mulberry paper, no inkstone, and no brush to write out the characters. It was a sign from the Buddha that life was no more permanent than the froth on the ocean.

Juro arrived at the lake at dusk. There were no boats or soldiers. He stripped, then dove to where the farmer had seen Yomogi disappear beneath the surface.

Two hours later, chilled by the cold night air, he found his mother's arm, the hand still clutching the white banner. The arm was almost the color of the banner, pale, bloodless, puffy, and misshapen. He held it to his breast while tears coursed down his cheeks. He thought it useless to search further. The gods would understand. The arm would be brought home, and at the first seven-day ceremony, it would be burned and properly interred.

Juro ran all the way to the farmhouse, the grisly trophy clasped to his chest. He arrived gasping for air, drenched with sweat and predawn dew, to be greeted by the cry of a newborn child.

Lady Senjo was bedraggled, her robe askew, her hair in

tangles, but she smiled and crooned at the baby that suckled at her breast.

She raised her eyes to Juro and smiled a radiant smile. "It's a boy," she said. "A beautiful baby boy."

Her smile turned to a moue of pain when she realized what Juro held in his arms. "Oh, poor child," she said, torn between her selfish joy and the young man's pain. "Come to me." She pressed his head to her breast. The baby suckled and Juro fell asleep, cradling all that remained of his mother.

In the morning, a stranger appeared at their gate. He came quietly, unannounced. Lady Senjo had dozed off, the baby's mouth at her breast. Juro had turned away; he was curled in a fetal position on the floor at her side. The baby gave the alarm: a squawk that made Lady Senjo's head snap up.

"Who are you?" she asked in a trembling voice. This was one of the few times in her life that a man had seen her fully exposed, without proper attire. In the court, she spent her life behind a screen of state. She spoke to visitors through the drapes of cotton and silk that hid her from their gaze. Even in the rough countryside, she remained out of sight of any but the immediate family of the farmer.

"My name is Saito Sanemori," the stranger responded. "I am on my way from Kyoto to the north. I saw the farmhouse and thought I might stop to rest. My horse and I both need water before we can continue."

Lady Senjo was innocent in the ways of the world outside the court. She did not think it strange that a traveler would be so far from the Great Eastern Road. "You speak like a gentleman, yet your garments are plain," said Lady Senjo. She worried that he might be one of the highwaymen who infested the hills and forests.

"I have prepared for a long journey, a pilgrimage to a temple far in the north," said Saito, and made an impromptu poem:

> "Is it but a dream?
> Hear the drab uguisu
> Sing a sweet sad song.
> Though dressed in dull brown plumage,
> He travels uncharted paths."

Lady Senjo found the poem charming. No one without years of training at the court would be able to turn a thirty-one syllable *Tanka* so readily.

The *Tanka* poem was constructed in five lines: five syllables in the first and third line, seven syllables in the second, fourth, and fifth. There were certain conventions that were particularly suited to the language: pivot words, pillow words, and *engo*. The pivot words had double meanings that made the poem ambiguous and capable of being read in more than one way. Pillow words were clichés to express certain emotions: the wet sleeves to represent weeping and sorrow. *Engo* were homonyms that left a subliminal after image.

The ability to create a poem was a talent developed in the court. Everyone of value in society constantly created poems. There were poetry contests for prizes and prestige. The traveler demonstrated his breeding, and Lady Senjo's vague suspicions vanished.

Though the picture of a greenish-brown nightingale singing its sad song hardly fitted the traveler, it did show his wit and charm. Lady Senjo quickly responded:

> *"Drops of morning dew*
> *Stain my sleeve in spreading patches*
> *Amaterasu*
> *Shines to show the dream is o'er*
> *The traveler is soon gone."*

The poem was cleverly crafted, with an *engo* in the first line that echoed her mourning and a conventional symbol of sorrow: the drops of dew that stained her sleeve. Her poem held promise of the future, with Amaterasu suggesting the beginning of a new day and the continuing of the eternal cycle of existence.

The traveler smiled and applauded. "You have a quick wit and a cultured mind," he said. "I find it odd that you live in this poor cabin."

She retorted with another poem:

> *"The wind of morning*
> *Blows its chilly breath across*
> *My path. Far from home.*
> *Yet the same wind blows warm on*
> *Purple mountains, crystal streams."*

The traveler nodded appreciatively. The poem told him that the lady came from the land of purple mountains, crystal streams—Kyoto. His search was over almost before it had begun. This must be Yoshikata's wife and son, the ones he had been sent to execute.

Saito was overwhelmed by sadness. The transitory nature of life was again demonstrated. This lovely, witty, talented woman and her newborn child would be killed as punishment for the actions of their family. He shuddered and turned pale at what he had to do.

Lady Senjo saw his expression and mistook it for malaise, a sickness the gentleman could have caught from his travels. "Please, sir, if you are indisposed, try to make yourself comfortable. Young Juro will fix you a pot of tea." She prodded Juro awake.

Juro rolled over, exposing his mother's pale, shrunken arm. The stranger gasped.

Saito was a courtier and a warrior, not a butcher. He felt strongly attracted to this woman. She and the child would live. He would take the grisly trophy with him and claim it belonged to Lady Senjo. But he had to be sure that the child would not appear in the future to give lie to his claim.

He explained his mission to Lady Senjo and Juro. They were horrified. Finally, Saito convinced them that he meant them no harm. They must disappear into the mountains and forget past connections with the capital. If they swore, by the Buddha and all the Shinto gods, to follow his orders, he would spare them.

Lady Senjo agreed. "We will go far into the mountains of Shinano, to the wild place called Kiso, where primitive mountain men reside. I will raise the child to be one of these men. He will never know the life of the court."

"Then go! Go now!"

Lady Senjo clasped the baby tighter to her breast and said:

> *"In the dark forests*
> *So far from the shining sun*
> *The flower will grow*
> *In the mists on green mountains*
> *Hearing the nightingale's song."*

nineteen

The fourth month of 1181 arrived, bringing a return of unseasonable cold. The weather boded ill for the spring crops; rice paddies had frozen solid, killing the young shoots. Millet and barley fared no better. Farmers and seers alike predicted another famine in the home provinces.

While Yoshi and Nami traveled north to Kamakura, Kiso Yoshinaka, son of Lady Senjo, cousin of Yoritomo, was deep in a war council with his uncle, Yukiie, and his two most trusted aides, Imai-no Kanehiro and Imai's sister, Tomoe Gozen.

Nominally, Kiso was part of Yoritomo's army. Actually, Kiso was in competition with Yoritomo. Under Kiso's command, his army was growing from a motley group of mountain brigands into a disciplined military unit. Although the army's purpose was to harass and eventually overcome the Taira in Yoritomo's name, old habits die hard, and Kiso's tactics were often no different than the tactics of ordinary highwaymen.

Kiso's camp was a conglomeration of thatched-roof barracks, log huts, and crude tents; it was located in the mountains of Shinano province, about 120 miles northeast of Kyoto. A blanket had been spread on the ground under a tall pine. On the blanket, a low lacquered table was set with an earthen jug of sake and a bowl of yams.

It was shortly after dawn, cool and clear, with the sun filtering through the trees. Kiso and the others were seated cross-legged around the table. Kiso wore a jacket of old leather armor over a cotton robe, two swords at his side, straw leggings tied around his shins, and straw sandals on his feet. His hair was ragged, unkempt, pulled away from his face by a rope *hachimaki*. He was a typical mountain warrior, except for his hot, burning eyes, which glared with the expression of one accustomed to command.

Kiso had been born in the mountains twenty-six years before. Though his mother, Lady Senjo, had been a famous court poetess and his father, Yoshikata, a high-ranking Minamoto who had died in battle without ever seeing his son, Kiso seldom used his family name, Minamoto Yoshinaka.

Kiso now felt the pressure of the predicted famine. His military operation had to be fueled with food from the surrounding land. His impatient nature made him eager to mount an offensive before the land became too barren to support his mountain men. He needed more arms and more men, and he had devised a plan that would divide the enemy forces while he foraged for arms and silver.

At this moment Kiso was angry, and when Kiso was angry everyone knew it. Kiso had never developed the courtier's ability to dissemble. He was impatient with diplomacy, which he equated with weakness.

"I will not be contradicted," he shouted at Yukiie, his narrow face contorted with anger. "Only I make the decisions here."

Minamoto Yukiie squirmed under Kiso's baleful glare. His bloated features tried to form an appeasing smile; it came out a strange grimace. He was soft, flesh hanging in pillowy drapes, breasts womanish, hips wide. His knees rubbed together and his feet splayed out when he walked. Yukiie's hair was dyed to hide the first traces of gray, his cheeks were heavily powdered, his teeth blackened in the old style. Yukiie was fifteen years older than his nephew; his character had been formed by his early years at the court. No one liked him, but because he was the brother of Kiso's father, he received grudging tolerance from the samurai of the camp.

Yukiie was trying to listen to Kiso's words. He knew they were important, but he had been dragged out of bed before dawn for this conference and had not yet collected himself. His mind was back in the tent, where he had left his latest lover, a handsome young warrior. It was hard to concentrate on words of war when he still pictured the young man's hardness approaching.

Yukiie pulled his shabby brocaded robe, with its pattern of violet flowers, closer around him as if to ward off a chill. He frowned and made himself focus on Kiso. He would agree to anything to get back to his tent quickly, but he must not make a mistake. Kiso, the dear boy, was really angry.

Kiso continued to glare, waiting for verbal acknowledgment.

"Yes, yes. Quite right, nephew," Yukiie lisped. "You know I leave the planning to you. Yes, yes. If you want me to lead my men to Owari, I shall comply at once. I did not intend to contradict you. Oh no. I merely asked if we could spare the men from our main army."

"We can and will. I want you to lead your troops near Kyoto. Create a diversion to draw Munemori's army out of the city. I want them kept busy chasing your men while I raid for arms and gold along the Tokaido Road. There will be no need for you to fight."

Yukiie relaxed. He understood. There was to be no danger. A week away from Kiso and his infernal foster-brother, Imai. "Of course," he said. "No need to fight. I understand your plan. Yes, yes. Weaken the Taira. Split their forces." He turned to Imai, who was silent. "Your foster-brother is a wise man, a brilliant planner," he said obsequiously.

Imai was a hard-faced young man, slightly older than Kiso. They had grown up together. He was not only Kiso's foster-brother, but also his best friend and retainer. Imai had difficulty concealing his distaste for Yukiie. Yukiie made him uncomfortable.

Imai kept his face in a studied mask of indifference, as if he hadn't heard Yukiie, and reached across the table to pour a generous cup of sake. Imai was aware of the young warrior in Yukiie's tent. Imai was a samurai and had spent most of his life in the field; he had had his share of young warriors too. But . . . Yukiie's womanly manner infuriated him. Whatever one did in the field, one should keep one's self-respect and masculinity. Yukiie was a contemptible toad, pushing his pale, flabby buttocks in everyone's face. Imai gulped the sake and said nothing.

Kiso turned his frown on Imai. "Do you disagree, brother?" he asked menacingly.

Before Imai could reply, his sister, Tomoe Gozen, broke in. Tomoe was small and wiry. Some thought her beautiful, though hers was not a usual beauty; her nose was too bold, her jaw too strong, and her gaze too direct. Tomoe eschewed all makeup and cut her hair as short as a warrior's. She wore the armor and two swords of a fighting samurai; they were not mere decoration. She had gained a reputation for being as fearless and skilled as any male warrior. Tomoe had been watching Kiso impassively, but an emotional current flowed between them. She had been Kiso's lover and confidante for over ten years. She said, "We can spare only three thousand men to Yukiie's command, most of them untrained and un-skilled. They will be within reach of Kyoto's main army, a minimum of, say, twelve thousand of their best . . ."

Imai took another gulp of sake. He nodded. "Tomoe is right. We have to be sure that Yukiie can . . ."

"Then you think my plan will fail?" interrupted Kiso.

"No, not fail. If we can trust your uncle to command his troops well, he may mark the beginning of a brilliant campaign. Yukiie can give us the freedom to gain arms and gold while he extends the Taira forces, gets them into the countryside away from their soft beds . . . but is careful not to face them in direct battle."

Kiso relaxed. He reached for the sake. "Excellent," he said. "My foster-brother shows good sense."

"When shall I instruct my troops to leave?" asked Yukiie, licking his lips nervously.

"Get them started at once," Kiso said impatiently. "I am anxious to begin the action. Let my cousin Lord Yoritomo sit in Kamakura. We will win Kyoto before he realizes what has happened."

"At once. Yes, yes. I hate this dreadful camp. We will battle our way to Kyoto. My men will be prepared to leave at noon," said Yukiie.

"Or sooner."

"At noon, nephew, at noon." Yukiie rose awkwardly and bowed to his nephew before waddling off to his tent. He licked his lips in anticipation; he had at least two hours before he had to begin preparations to leave.

twenty

The horseman was mounted on a powerful sorrel. He wore a cloak of russet-gold brocade over a blue under-robe. Though his clothing and his horse's accoutrements were those of a samurai warrior, he wore no swords through his *obi*, no bow or arrows on his back. He sat tall on a red-and-gold decorated saddle. Even though he was unarmed and followed by only one mounted retainer and a packhorse, he radiated an air of quiet strength.

Ten feet behind him, the traveler's retainer, a slim youth in a cotton robe of unadorned brown, rode a tough mountain pony. The retainer wore a wide-brimmed straw hat low on the face and a short sword at the waist. A *naginata,* halberd, about four feet long, with a fourteen-inch steel blade, was attached to the pony's saddle. The retainer led the packhorse by a short length of rope.

The riders were traveling on the Tokaido Road. They had passed the Ausaka barrier, the first and most important station on the road that led north from the capital. Long ago, the barrier had been built at the southern tip of Lake Biwa to function as a military outpost. The unarmed traveler reined in the sorrel and pointed back to the barrier. "An auspicious sign," he said.

High above them, just visible through the trees, bordering the road, was a plain picket fence. Behind it, the head of a sixteen-foot-high gilded Buddha was visible. The Ausaka Buddha was set on the very edge of the high cliff and looked out over their heads to the northeast.

The afternoon sky was filled with blossoms of cloud; puffs that resembled cherry trees in full bloom. A break in the clouds far beyond the Buddha's head let the sun shine through, haloing the golden head.

The traveler's retainer smiled and nodded vigorously. Buddha's halo was indeed an auspicious sign.

The packhorse was loaded with the samurai's armor and extra clothing. There were blanket rolls and a cloth tent. A saddle bag held extra essentials: ink stone, brushes, powder, oil, and a special case made to hold a secret message. The case was built into the lid of an innocuous box of no apparent value.

Two hours ago, Yoshi, the unarmed traveler, had packed Go-Shirakawa's message into the box lid so it would not tempt the thieves who patrolled the long road to Kamakura. Now, as he guided his sorrel along the Tokaido Road, he reflected on the terrible events of the morning...

When Yoshi led his family and the staff down the mountain to the gates of Fumio's estate, he was greeted by the sight of a stake set before the main gate with a severed head mounted on it...Fumio's head.

There was no sign of who was responsible for the heinous murder, but Yoshi did not doubt that his enemies were involved. But Fumio was a Taira, loyal to their cause. He had never harmed anyone. Then, why?

Yoshi was heartsick. He recalled the life Fumio had given him, the love, the support when Yoshi was a child. A lump formed in Yoshi's throat and he had difficulty restraining his tears. Poor Uncle Fumio had been so enthusiastic at the thought of serving the Taira. How could this have happened? The dam broke and Yoshi's tears poured out. He trembled with a mixture of emotions—rage at those who caused Fumio's death, sorrow for a good man's life ending so horribly, depression at perhaps being the ultimate cause.

Was there a curse that always followed him? Those he loved died violently, in ways beyond his control. "I never want to use my sword again," he murmured brokenly. "This is a retaliation for the evil my sword has caused. I am a *sensei*. I will teach, I will advise, but I will never use my sword to kill again. This I swear."

Nami dissolved in tears at the hideous sight. "You cannot blame yourself, Yoshi," she managed to say between sobs. "Whoever caused Uncle's death will suffer in the Avichi hell for his deed."

Lady Masaka stared dry-eyed at the stake. Despite her sorrow, she stood straighter. Her mouth was drawn in a thin tight line. "You cannot take responsibility for this, son," she said. "Find who killed Fumio and take revenge."

"Revenge will not bring Uncle back, but someday those responsible will be repaid for this deed. Though I am desolate and torn," he said, "I have a duty to act for the Emperor. I must leave within the hour at his command."

The retainers removed Lord Fumio's head from the stake.

Lady Masaka promised to arrange for the proper funeral observances. "Leave at once," she ordered. "And may Buddha smile on you both."

There had been nothing for it but to follow Imperial orders and prepare for the long trip to Kamakura. Go-Shirakawa had given Yoshi a mission of importance. It would be unseemly to delay further.

While Yoshi arranged the secret cache, Nami was busy disguising herself as his retainer. With her makeup removed, her hair hidden beneath her straw hat, and her womanly body swathed in coarse cotton, she felt she could pass as a slim young man.

Yoshi objected at first; he wanted her to ride in a cart with a full retinue of guards in keeping with her station.

"I ride well," Nami insisted. "Though I have given myself to court duties during the past few months, I am still a country girl."

"You will not be safe. We will be riding through mountains infested with highwaymen, and I will be traveling unarmed. There are bands of soldiers who roam the road. If they discover you are a woman..."

"And why should they? Will I be safer if I am hidden behind the lattice of a cart? How many men can we muster in this short time to protect me? Not enough. Remember, the Emperor has charged you to leave at once. You will travel too slowly if we have to stop at every river and mountain to transport the cart."

"Perhaps you should remain in Kyoto. I did not expect to leave under these strained circumstances. Perhaps..."

"Nonsense!" Nami was adamant. "I have done my duty by Lord Chikara; there is nothing more to hold me here. Lady Masaka will arrange Uncle Fumio's funeral services." Nami's voice quavered, and she wiped a womanly tear with her sleeve. "We've suffered enough without each other. I will go with you. If you refuse to take me with you, I will follow... alone."

Yoshi sighed. "What happened to the delicate child I knew on Uncle's *shoen?*" he asked the air.

"She became a woman," Nami retorted.

With a minimum of preparation and the hastiest of leave-takings, Yoshi and his retainer sadly left the capital city to find the camp of Lord Yoritomo.

Now, Ausaka barrier was behind them. The first step of the long journey was taken.

"We will stop at Kagami this evening," said Yoshi, studying the first slight darkening of the sky. The puff-ball clouds were thinning as a strong east wind drove them over the lake and into the mountains. There were no other travelers. Yoshi spurred the horses to greater speed.

Soon the east wind brought the first sprinkles of rain. Yoshi and Nami unfolded and donned straw rain capes. The road became muddy, and the horses' hooves churned it into a thick paste that splashed up to cover their capes. The sky grew darker. Flashes of lightning lit the east. Rain poured onto their heads with unrelenting fury.

They were about six miles from Kagami, on the outskirts of a village called Moriyama, when Yoshi reined in his horse. "We will stay here for tonight," he said.

Nami shrugged and wiped rain and mud from her face. She said:

> *"My sleeves are still wet*
> *With the dew from my old home*
> *Must I now drench them*
> *Further in Moriyama*
> *Where unceasing cold rain falls."*

The poem was a valiant effort at humor, depending on a pun on the name of the town: *moru yama* meant "leaking mountain," and the poem suggested second thoughts about leaving home.

Yoshi responded, reminding her of the temporary nature of discomfort:

> *"Eventually*
> *Even in Moriyama*
> *The damp disappears*
> *From the sleeves of the travelers*
> *Who stop in its floating world."*

He dismounted and pointed ahead to a farmhouse just off the road. "We'll ask for lodging here," he said.

A copper coin bought them lodging for the night, feed for their horses, and two bowls of gruel.

The farmer offered a bed of straw in his shed. The thatch

roof had gaps that let in rain, but the travelers found a dry corner to spread their *futon*. Extra robes would be their bed-clothes.

The farmer watched them prepare their bed, disapproval stamped on his rough features. This samurai, he thought, is shameless, bedding a young boy in a stranger's house.

After the farmer left, shaking his head at the wickedness of the world, Yoshi and Nami, temporarily forgetting the tragedies behind them, dissolved in laughter. The laughter soon changed to an embarrassed silence.

The rain had stopped and the moon shone brightly through the gaps in the roof. They could see each other clearly. The *futon* was in a patch of moonlight. This was far from the romantic dark of the Kyoto mansion. That time, Yoshi had crept behind Nami's curtain and consummated their love in almost complete darkness. This time there was no curtain of state to breach, no screens to remove, and no reason to hasten the act of love.

Yoshi covered them with an over-robe, taking refuge in the darkness of its folds. He reached for her tenderly and held her close, saying:

> *"Wild desolation*
> *Broken roof and straw fill'd floor*
> *And my heart so full*
> *Of moonbeams, the sound of rain,*
> *And vows of eternal love."*

Nami unfolded like a flower opening to the warmth of the sun. Her tiny hands cupped him gently, and she whispered:

> *"Tsukiyomi smiles*
> *Through ten times ten thousand tears.*
> *See his silver light*
> *Glowing through the rough thatch roof:*
> *Desolation turn'd to love."*

Yoshi responded instantly to her touch. Words became un-necessary as their bodies blended and moved as one in an ancient rhythm.

twenty-one

They left Moriyama at dawn. The morning sky was a dazzling froth of glowing pinks and reds. Nami had slept more soundly than she had in years. A night of lovemaking after a day of hard riding had left her pleasantly tired but aching. Yoshi was a tender and gentle lover, patient yet ardent. Though her body was stiff and sore, she had experienced a joy that transported her to another, transcendental, plane of experience. Later she had fallen into a deep dreamless sleep.

Now, rested, she bounced gently behind him. Her pony moved in an easy rhythm. Nami breathed deeply of the grassy smell of morning. Her eyes feasted on the splendid colors of the eastern sky. It was good to be alive and free in these first days of the fourth month of 1181.

Nami reflected on how her life had changed since the beginning of the year. For some, the life of a court lady was glorious. For her, it had been a bore, sitting in semidarkness, always covered by a screen of state, hidden behind bamboo curtains and painted screens. Even when she left her home, she was required to wear veiled hats and travel in latticework oxcarts. Nami had even forgotten her promise to herself. "I will never hide behind a screen waiting for my husband," she had once said, only to find herself in that position as the years passed.

Men complained of their duties. They had no idea how hard it was to be a court lady. The empty hours of waiting, the disappointment when no one visited. No wonder the ladies cried so easily. Their lives were spiraled inward to their emotions. There was nowhere else to turn.

Nami shook her head to banish these thoughts. The court was behind her. She was free.

Above her, the sky opened in bright blue patches. The horses pushed through a sea of tall reeds. The aches of yesterday returned, and the pony's constant motion chafed the insides of her thighs. She tried to ignore the discomfort; it was a small price to pay for freedom.

Nami watched the road twisting its way through the dark pine forests, higher and higher. From time to time, she glimpsed the calm waters of the lake below. She watched Yoshi, lost in his own thoughts, riding tirelessly ahead of her. He seemed so secure, so comfortable with himself. He was so sure of who he was. She envied him.

Her thoughts returned to the court. From the day she had arrived, she had been subjected to a series of assaults on her self-confidence. She suffered the psychic hurt of constant snubs and veiled insults. Ladies born in the Imperial enclosure resented her uncouth provincial background. Yet they thought her secure and confident, even overconfident. If they only had known the terrible doubts that racked her, the innumerable nights she cried herself to sleep, wishing Lord Chikara would deliver her from her duties as a lady-in-waiting to the Empress.

Fortunately, the Empress liked her and supported her. She gave Nami the courage to survive the haughty cruelty of the other ladies. Yes, she had tried to conform, but the ladies had rejected her.

Her thoughts wandered back to her childhood on Uncle Fumio's estate. Reminiscing was a wonderful way to forget the pain of the ride. She remembered demanding that young Yoshi reassure her of her beauty. How vain she had been at fourteen. And how pompous Yoshi had been in his youthful pose of sophistication. How little they had known of life. How innocent they had been. How naïve.

"Yoshi," she called impulsively.

He pulled the sorrel to a halt and looked back. "Are you all right?" he asked.

"Where will we spend the night?"

"It isn't even noon." Yoshi seemed puzzled.

"I know. I just wondered." Actually, Nami only wanted to hear his voice and feel his reassuring strength.

He said, "I would like to reach the town of Ono before nightfall. We'll sleep there. Tomorrow we turn and ride to the eastern coast. There are some rugged hills ahead of us. Do you need a rest?"

"Certainly not," answered Nami, gritting her teeth.

As Yoshi studied her, Nami felt a flutter of insecurity. Her beautiful long hair was tied up under a peasant hat. Her skin was exposed to the air. No bright over-robe. No twelve unlined silk shifts. No colors to show at sleeve and hem. What must he think of me? she thought, dressed in coarse cotton, roughed by the air, and burned by the sun. She lowered her head so all he could see was the straw hat.

To Yoshi, the changes caused by their arduous journey made Nami more beautiful. She did not see his proud smile as he spurred the sorrel and said, "Let us continue."

They reached Ono at dusk. The town was perched on a high cliff overlooking the lake. Cicadas fiddled in the trees. Fireflies spun patterns of light in the darkness of the forest, and frogs boomed and croaked from the lotus pads near the shore below them. Overhead, purple and rose clouds crept westward, soaking up the light of the setting sun.

Nami ached in every muscle and joint. She welcomed the homey luxuries of the small cliffside inn where they stopped. After a modest meal of millet gruel, she excused herself and went to soak in the one-person bath. She had never before appreciated a bath so much. The rigors of the road heightened her perception and made small luxuries great pleasures. She reveled in removing the ugly clothing, releasing her waterfall of hair, washing off the dirt, and feeling her skin soften under the influence of the steamy water.

"Aaah," she said, and smiled.

Back in the room, Yoshi had removed the bamboo curtains, opening the wall to a view across the broad expanse of the lake. As dark cloaked the last purple clouds, Nami could see the far shore in a panorama that stretched from Mount Hiei on the southwest to the far shores of the inland sea to the north.

The night was spent in a continuation of their voyage of mutual discovery. Nami was so deeply involved with Yoshi that her aches and pains were soon forgotten.

The second day, tired but happy, Nami plodded behind Yoshi through flat fields where the miscanthus grass reached higher than their heads.

On the third day, another rainstorm turned the road to impassable mud. The horses waded off the road through miles of watery rice fields. Nami's body was beginning to adjust to the new demands made on it. She grew accustomed to the pain, and the endless miles no longer seemed unbearable. She was able to study her surroundings and see beauty where at first she had been aware only of her discomfort. A flock of the last spring geese crossed the sky, migrating northward. They were no more than black specks, but they filled the air with the sound of their hornlike calls. Yoshi pointed to them and smiled at her.

On the fourth day, they crossed the Sunomata River on a floating bridge; a string of small boats tied together by heavy ropes and covered by rough planks furnished a treacherous but passable surface. Nami was terrified. She had never learned to swim, and the waters were rough and dangerous. But Yoshi watched over her and she did not complain. She tightened her jaw and remained silent as the horses picked their way across the turbulent waters.

The afternoon of the fourth day was spent crossing the cedar forests of Owari province. That night, they stopped at the post station of Orido, where they were informed that the next part of the road was passable only in the early morning at low tide.

In the morning, Nami found herself almost completely over the pains of the first days. Though it was not yet summer, the hours of sun had changed the color of her skin. The straw hat that covered most of her face reflected light and had tinted the pale porcelain of her cheeks and jaws. Her hands had become quite brown, even—and she gasped in dismay when she first noticed—a little callused. She hid her hands from Yoshi's view. What would he think if he saw them? A lifetime of conditioning left Nami unable to conceive of a man of quality loving a woman with work-coarsened hands.

The horses were saddled and on the road by the *ariake*, the moon that shone at dawn. The peninsula of Narumi was clear of water. Nami followed Yoshi down the rolling hills to pure white sand. The beach extended as far as she could see. The road was invisible, but great flocks of plump-bodied, long-legged plovers ran across the beach almost like guides. They left stitch marks in the sand ahead of the horses. Nami felt recovered enough to compose a poem:

> *"Plovers of the strand*
> *Guiding travelers on*
> *With tiny footprints.*
> *Do you sing out of sadness*
> *On Narumi's soft white sands?"*

Yoshi smiled. He appreciated a well-turned poem. Yoshi pointed ahead to where some *miyakadori*, black-headed gulls, with red beaks and feet, took turns swooping down to catch fish stranded in pools of sea water. "Capital-birds," he said, calling them by their nickname. They had been named years ago by a wandering poet who, on seeing them, was reminded of Kyoto.

Yoshi answered Nami's poem:

> *"Miyakadori*
> *Red feet and bills are yours*
> *Bringing home to mind*
> *As we pass the crystal strand*
> *Of Narumi's golden land."*

By nightfall, the lovers sought refuge off the beach and on the skirts of Mount Futamura. Nami helped Yoshi spread a blanket under a gigantic persimmon tree. The sea air made them both sleepy. Nami reached out, held Yoshi's hand to her breast, and immediately fell asleep.

Five minutes later, a cracking sound woke her. She was still half-asleep when Yoshi rolled off the blanket and crouched under the tree.

"What is it?" asked Nami, wide-eyed, brushing the hair from her face.

"I don't know. Be quiet," Yoshi whispered.

No one was in sight. The hill was empty except for groves of trees, silent except for the sibilance of the wind in the branches.

Suddenly, there it was again, the cracking sound. Yoshi leaped to the side. Nami stared in shock. For a moment, Yoshi seemed convulsed with pain. Then . . . she realized it was laughter. She had never heard him laugh like this before. It was charming and before she knew it she was laughing with him, though she did not know why.

"What is it? What is it?" she finally managed to gasp.

"Meet the enemy," said Yoshi. "My sword would not help me against this attack. Persimmons. Falling on my head from the tree above us." He held one out to her. "Try it," he said.

Nami took it. Her laughter calmed. She bit into the pulpy fruit. "I don't think I can go back to sleep," she said with a wan smile.

"Nor I," he answered.

Love was even sweeter than the fruit of the persimmon tree.

In the morning, they set out over a stretch of desolate fields and seemingly endless moors, crossing to the foothills of the Takashi range. Just before they reached the foothills, they came to a field of fringed-pinks, Japanese carnations. The field extended on all sides of them, blending into the horizon in a pink haze. Nami almost cried at the beauty of the vision, and Yoshi was so moved he composed another poem on the spot:

> *"They dwell in the clouds*
> *These fringed-pinks that steal the sun*
> *But morning brings dew*
> *To dampen their soft petals*
> *And they too shall pass away."*

Nami nodded sadly. The poem had many levels of meaning. The opening line could be read literally, or as a metaphor for the court of Kyoto. The name of the flower *nadeshiko* could be read to mean either "fringed-pinks" or "petted children." The last three lines suggested a future of conflict and the impermanence of worldly institutions. The lines seemed to say that the Imperial court would soon be dissolved in sorrow and tears.

Skirting Mount Miyaji, the riders burst out of a grove of bamboo, and once more Nami saw the sea. The horses plodded down Inohana Slope to the water's edge at Takashi Beach. Wind lashed the waves twenty feet into the air. Sand cut into Nami's face. She strained to hear as Yoshi shouted over the roar of the waves and over the cacophony of cries from the thousands of hook-beaked cormorants that searched for food in the boiling surf.

"Put the scarf over your face," ordered Yoshi, setting an example by covering his face with a cotton cloth.

Nami quickly complied. Her delicate skin was beginning to feel as coarse as cotton sacking.

They rode on without speaking, pulling the reluctant pack-horse into the wind. Nami squinted ahead and saw that Yoshi was lost in a world of his own. Nami watched him riding ahead. The sorrel's muscular flanks expanded and contracted rhythmically, like the coiling and uncoiling of huge snakes under the saddle. The white froth and harsh sand beat relentlessly at Nami's face. She kept her eyes closed to the narrowest of slits to keep the sand out. She was overcome by the desolate beauty of the shore. The pulsing roar of the water. The chill damp and the salty edge of the air. She remembered the calm sea of Suruga Bay during her childhood. Could this lashing monster be the same sea? Yes. And could she be the same Nami? Yes again. She trembled at the thought of life's impermanence and change.

Nami spurred the horse until it was abreast of Yoshi's and broke into his reverie:

> *"Takashi's white spume*
> *That lashes the sands of shore*
> *Can this be the same*
> *Sea that nurtured my childhood*
> *With its tranquil blue bosom?"*

The effect was vitiated because she had to shout the fragile poem like a fisherwoman. Even so, Yoshi hardly seemed to hear it. He had been withdrawn since they started out in the morning.

Yoshi stared at Nami as if he did not realize who she was. "I have a premonition. Last night I dreamed we would encounter evil on this part of our journey."

Nami was crushed. The trip had gone so well. For five days they had not met another traveler on the road. The people at the inns and post houses had either helped them or ignored them. But a dream! There was power of evil in dreams. Everyone knew it. Dreams had to be heeded.

"How much farther before we reach our destination?" she shouted.

"Not far," Yoshi responded. "We are doing well. We have come a great distance without incident. Hamana Lagoon lies directly ahead. Just beyond the lagoon is the post station of Hikuma. We will stop there overnight and rest. The post station is near the Tenchu River, which marks the halfway point of our journey. We will cross the river tomorrow morning."

twenty-two

"We'll stop at the stage of Hikuma tonight," said Kiso.

The taciturn Imai nodded imperceptibly in agreement, but Tomoe frowned. The late afternoon sun reflected from her strong features, softening the hard edges and making her appear more feminine than usual. She shrugged her shoulders to her brother as if she were not sure she agreed with the plan. He ignored her unspoken comment.

The horses plodded three abreast down the rocky mountain road. Behind the leaders rode Kiso's lieutenants, Tezuka, Jiro, and Taro, and strung out along the trail for about fifty yards rode the soldiers of Kiso's troop, twenty men on tough little mountain ponies. The horses' hooves pounding rhythmically, the clank and rattle of arms and armor, the sounds of insects, birds, and small animals added to the tapestry of sound in the heavy afternoon air. Far off, a wild monkey screeched a warning from the trees. Mosquitos hovered and buzzed in the ears of the riders. Occasionally, a rider would laugh for no apparent reason, stirred by the nervous humor that surfaces before an engagement.

Tomoe slapped at a mosquito. They had ridden a half mile since Kiso's announcement, and she had spent the time wrestling with the temptation to comment. Though she rode as an equal, she was always aware that to be accepted she had to be braver and tougher than any of the men. She could never give even the slightest appearance of weakness.

Tomoe cleared her throat and said in a disapproving tone, "Kiso, after the past week's rains, the inns will be full. Travelers on the Tokaido Road will be delayed at Hikuma. The waters of the Tenchu will be impassable for at least another day."

"Why should that disturb us?"

"We will have difficulty finding lodging. There are twenty-five of us. An entire inn will be needed to provide us shelter. Unlikely that we shall find one empty at this time. Why not plan to camp on the mountain and arrive at Hikuma in the morning?"

"No! The men need diversion, and I look forward to a comfortable night at an inn. Have no fear, we will find rooms." His voice was abrupt, a trifle impatient.

Tomoe recognized the tone. Kiso was clever and brave, but he was also extremely stubborn. He had made up his mind and further discussion would only make him more determined.

Tomoe was angry. Kiso treated her suggestion as if it had no value. He embarrassed her in front of her brother and—she glanced behind her—Tezuka, Jiro, and Taro. She tightened her lips and stared at the road.

The troop had been riding for two days; one entire day through a soaking downpour and over mountainous terrain. Tomoe recognized that Kiso had a valid point. The riders needed diversion to help them forget their discomfort: wet clothing sticking to their skin under the armor; sweat and itch from the heat of the afternoon; mosquitos and blackflies torturing men and horses alike.

Yes, Tomoe understood why Kiso insisted on stopping at an inn. But she was insulted by his brusque and thoughtless manner. To ride into town in the middle of the night and dispossess a few poor pilgrims might amuse some of the cruder mountain men, but not Tomoe. Acting like common brigands at the inns of Hikuma could mean gratuitous trouble. Their mission was to search for gold and for arms to equip their army, not to antagonize the people of Hikuma. Hikuma, the main city of the Hamamatsu area, was an Imperial outpost. There would be soldiers on duty. Not that she feared the soldiers, for they were a soft lot. No, she simply wanted to accomplish their mission and return home.

"Another hour," grunted Imai, his face impassive. He recognized his sister's anger. She was hot-tempered, and after two days in the saddle she seemed ready to explode. She was glowering at Kiso, who was ignoring her. Imai tried to calm his sister by speaking softly. "Only an hour, no more."

"Brother, I am not concerned with the time. I find it foolhardy for Kiso to harass the travelers when it gains us so little," she said through gritted teeth.

"Except to keep the men from growing restless. Why are you so upset? We have little to fear from the post soldiers. For one thing, we outnumber them. For another, they have no heart to fight. They are southern bureaucrats, looking to live comfortably and garner what they can from passing pilgrims."

Kiso leaned toward the brother and sister. "What are you whispering about?" he demanded.

"Nothing of import, Kiso," answered Imai hastily. "Tomoe has misgivings about tonight."

"She sounds like one of the fat court ladies of Kyoto. Next she'll tell us she had a bad dream." Kiso laughed as if he had told a funny joke. He realized he laughed alone and his hatchet face hardened in a frown of irritation. He turned to Tomoe. "You weary me," he said threateningly. "Maybe we should take your sword and leave you by the road."

Tomoe's anger boiled over. "Don't try to bully me, you bastard," she snarled. "I won't stand for it. Draw your sword or apologize." Tomoe had her hand on the haft of her sword.

She loved Kiso, had loved him since childhood, but she was ready to die at his hand to protect her sense of honor. Her position as a lieutenant was threatened. Who of the men would obey her if they saw Kiso treat her like a silly woman? Tomoe thought Kiso loved her in return, but she knew that would not stop him from killing her in defense of honor.

She sat tensely, one hand on her sword, knees holding her horse in place. She was no match for Kiso, but if she had to, she would give a good account of herself. She glared defiantly.

The seconds drew out to a minute . . . then a minute and a half. Horses shuffled restlessly. The troops stopped and clustered around the two antagonists. It was not unheard-of for one samurai, because of a real or fancied slight, to challenge another and fight to the death. Still, she waited.

Kiso's face was pale. The two onyx pools that were his eyes swallowed the light. The pupils seemed to expand as he glared. Even the cicadas, birds, and tree frogs were silent.

Then Kiso threw back his head and roared, "Where in the ten provinces is there another woman like this? I love her, by the Buddha, I swear it."

The troops chuckled and made complimentary jokes about their leaders. There was horseplay in relief at the averted confrontation. Tomoe was popular with the soldiers. They knew her abilities.

Imai wheeled his horse around. "Enough," he said. "We've wasted precious minutes. Let us ride for Hikuma."

The trees clustered so thickly around the path that the low sun was almost blocked from view. The sky darkened and a cool wind arose to rustle the leaves.

Kiso studied a patch of sky through the branches; he turned to the men behind him. "It will rain again soon. Hikuma is less than an hour away. Does anyone prefer to sleep in the field tonight?"

A chorus of derisive shouts rose from the troops.

"No one?" said Kiso. "Then let's ride as if Emma-Ō himself were on our tails."

"To Hikuma," shouted Imai.

"To Hikuma," echoed Tomoe.

At that moment, Yoshi and his slim retainer were bargaining for the last available room in the largest inn of Hikuma. Few pilgrims traveled the road during this rainy season. However, the Tenchu River crossing was in flood and the one ferry had not been taking passengers. For three days no one had crossed the river, and the inns were filled. There were groups of pilgrims marching steadily toward the Mishima shrine, there were officials in oxcarts wending their way to provincial posts, monks on foot, doing penance, begging bowls in hand. Even the post station was filled. The six soldiers on staff were not above charging desperate travelers for floor space in the decrepit old barrier building. The smaller, cheaper inns ran out of rooms first. The largest and most luxurious inn of Hikuma had only a servant's room available.

Yoshi convinced the innkeeper he could afford to pay the exorbitant rate—in advance—for the tiny room in the rear. A silver coin confirmed the agreement.

The room was barely large enough to spread their *futon*, but Yoshi and Nami were so exhausted they scarcely noticed.

A light rain started falling as the sun went down.

"At least the room is dry," murmured Nami as she loosened her hair and stretched out upon the *futon*. She fell asleep at once.

An hour later they were awakened by raucous shouts and loud noises from the central corridor. Someone ran up and down banging on doors and screens, shouting. At first it was impossible to make out what was being said. Then the words became clear, words that struck automatic fear into every heart. "Fire! The inn is afire! Everybody out. Quickly!"

Yoshi was instantly awake. He didn't hesitate. Leaving everything behind, Yoshi caught Nami's hand and pulled her into the corridor. They joined other confused, sleepy-eyed guests who milled about uncertainly.

"Outside. Everyone outside. This way!" someone shouted. In a panic, half-dressed, tousle-haired men and women pushed and elbowed each other on their way to the main exit.

Yoshi had reacted instinctively to the warning. Then, he hesitated. "Strange, I don't smell smoke," he said.

People pawed at his back trying to get him to move faster. Instead, he flattened himself against a side wall, pulling Nami alongside. "That was not the innkeeper's voice," he said.

"No matter," said Nami. "If the inn is afire, within seconds the entire building will be in flames. Whoever is shouting is a brave man to jeopardize his own life to save us."

"Yes," said Yoshi thoughtfully. He tightened his over-robe around him.

Nami tugged on his hand.

He resisted, saying, "I don't smell smoke. I don't feel heat. Something is wrong. There is no fire. We've been tricked."

Meanwhile, the main corridor emptied. The guests scurried out into the rain.

At the far end of the corridor, Yoshi saw a group of armored samurai marching toward him. "Quickly! Go back to the room. Cover your hair. They must not see that you are a woman. I'll hold them here until you are ready." Yoshi stepped forward between Nami and the approaching samurai.

"Outside, fool," said the samurai leader in a grating voice.

Yoshi instinctively disliked the man. He had a narrow face and smoldering black eyes; the man radiated raw power, a charisma that could not be denied. He was obviously a leader.

"Didn't you hear the announcement? Do you want to die?"

Yoshi thought he detected a slight touch of madness in the man's face. "I don't see or smell fire," said Yoshi. "I wonder why you are not concerned. A group of soldiers marching in the corridors of a burning inn is an unusual sight."

"Enough nonsense," snapped the hatchet-faced man. "Take him!"

"*Hai*, yes, Kiso," the samurai answered in unison.

Kiso stepped aside and six burly soldiers moved toward Yoshi.

The soldiers did not anticipate resistance. Yoshi was half-dressed, alone, and unarmed. As the first man reached for Yoshi's shoulder, he was greeted by a hard-edged palm ramming up into his chin. His head snapped back, his eyes glazed; he dropped like a sack of rice in front of his companions.

Yoshi had sworn not to use his swords. Nevertheless, he would use his hands, feet, and teeth, if necessary, to hold off these brigands long enough for Nami to escape.

Kiso drew his sword and snarled at his men. "Together, you fools. This man is not an ordinary traveler. Capture him alive. We can hold him for ransom."

The central corridor was wide; Yoshi could not prevent the samurai from surrounding him. He didn't try. He hoped to gain time for Nami to complete her disguise and escape in the crowd of hotel guests.

Two samurai grabbed at him simultaneously. With a twist of his upper body, Yoshi avoided the first. Using his arm and extended hand as a sword, he struck at the throat of the second. The man staggered back, making strange gurgling noises as he tried to cry out through a shattered voice box.

Yoshi did not wait; he launched himself at the remaining samurai—four soldiers and Kiso. The sheer weight of the opposition carried him to the ground, but not before he had immobilized two more. One fell with a smashed kneecap, the other held his genitals and moaned as he rolled on the floor.

The two samurai pinned Yoshi to the floor while Kiso towered over him, sword point to his throat. Kiso's black eyes glowed with an almost insane anger. His men had been made fools. "Who are you?" he demanded.

Yoshi's mouth tightened. He said nothing.

Kiso pricked Yoshi's throat with his sword tip.

"You are silent now; soon you will speak," he warned. Kiso held Yoshi in place at sword point and sent one of his men to bring reinforcements. Four came and Kiso ordered them to tie Yoshi securely. "Don't hurt him yet," he said. "Tomorrow we will question him. He will tell us who he is. If he is worth a ransom, we will have accomplished a large part of our mission: gold for arms and armor. Now, there was someone with him. A woman? Tezuka, search the rooms. Find her."

Tezuka bowed and walked down the corridor, kicking open doors. While Kiso kept his sword at Yoshi's throat, the other samurai trussed him. When they had finished, his hands were twisted behind him and knotted to his ankles and his throat. If Yoshi moved in any direction, the rope would choke him.

Tezuka returned from his search empty-handed. "There is no one left in the building," he reported. "Whoever was with him escaped through the rear entrance."

Kiso saw the subtlest light of satisfaction in Yoshi's eyes.

"No matter," he said. "There is no place to hide in Hikuma. Tomorrow we'll find whoever it was and decide on a proper punishment."

"What shall we do with this one, Kiso?" asked one of the samurai, carelessly kicking Yoshi's side.

"Get him out of the way. I think we deserve a celebration for his capture and our luck in finding such fine quarters." Kiso sheathed his sword, then asked, "Is it still raining?"

"Harder than before."

"Good. Take the bastard outside in the rain and put him in a Cryptomeria tree. Hoist him high, and leave him there for the night," Kiso ordered.

The samurai backed away quickly, grumbling at the thought of getting wet. He pulled at Yoshi's bonds, twisting Yoshi's head back from the pressure of the rope.

"Careful, you idiot. We don't want him dead yet. Here, two of you, help haul him out. Tie him safely in the tree. We don't want him to fall out by accident." Kiso's face split in a good-humored smile, the anger of a moment ago forgotten.

One samurai laughed, then another. In seconds, they were all roaring with mirth.

"Be quick," Kiso shouted, "and hurry back. We have sake, women, and warm beds waiting."

When Yoshi sent her down the corridor, Nami instantly understood the situation. If the bandits caught her with her hair loose and recognized her as a woman, they would use her for their amusement. Nami had no illusions about bandits' codes of conduct. From the quick glimpse she'd had of them as they marched toward her, she knew they were the lowest class of samurai, little more than brigands.

She slipped into the room, rolled their gear into the blanket, gathered her hair under her straw hat, and left as quickly as she could. She heard the thrashing sounds of men fighting. Her pulse raced; her lips felt dried and swollen. What were they doing to Yoshi? Amida Buddha help him.

Nami heard a horrid gurgling noise, scarcely human—the samurai whose voice box had been destroyed—then she was through the kitchens and out onto a platform where the food deliveries were made.

The rain had become a violent spring thunderstorm. Flashes of lightning illuminated a scene from hell. The innkeeper, the staff, and the guests milled around aimlessly in the downpour.

Their pale faces were punctuated by the black circles of their open mouths. They were wailing and crying, hands waving shakily in the repeated flashes of lightning.

There were more brigands, dressed in straw rain capes and broad-brimmed hats, riding around the circle of hotel people, harassing them and keeping them in a small area.

Nami immediately reversed direction. Hugging the inn's rear wall, she made her way to a clump of trees. The underbrush was untrimmed, for this was the border of the hotel grounds; she squeezed into the bushes, ripping her clothing on sharp brambles, scratching her face and her hands.

Even the lightning would not reveal her position now. She burrowed deeper, covering the blanket containing the gear with her cloak.

Nami trembled in the cold downpour, not only because of the cold and damp, but also because of her fears for Yoshi. What had happened? Was he alive? Could she help him? How? What if that terrible strangling noise had been Yoshi's death rattle? Amida Buddha, no! Tears joined the rain that fell on her cloak.

The hours passed. Nami heard loud celebration from the inn, drunken voices singing coarse mountain songs. Two samurai, staggering from drink, arms around each other's shoulders, left the back veranda and came within five feet of her hiding place. Her heart fluttered . . . they would see her! She heard their heavy breathing over the rattle of the rain. She smelled the sake and onions on their breath. Lightning flashed, darkened, and flashed again, followed almost simultaneously by a monstrous clap of thunder.

"Did you do that?" chortled a drunken voice.

"No. I thought you did," answered another.

In the momentary light she saw them standing side by side, urinating in the bushes. She could almost touch them. They were laughing uncontrollably at their joke.

"Yomi, it's raining hard."

"Not as hard as I'm pissing." More laughter.

"How do you think our prisoner is faring in this storm?"

"Piss on him, too." More laughter.

"He's a tough bastard. I'm glad I didn't have to fight him."

"Me too. Did you see what he did to Hanazo's throat? He won't talk for a week."

"How about Masakiyo's balls? He won't be using them for a while."

"The prisoner deserves more than he's getting for what he did to our friends. Let's be sure he can't escape."

"I'm wet. To Emma-Ō with him. Let's go inside. I want the fat one you had before."

"Hey, we're so wet now, what difference can a few minutes make?"

"All right." The drunken pair of samurai weaved off around the side of the inn.

Nami's heart raced. Were they talking about Yoshi? She would follow and see where he was being held. She made sure her short dagger was secure in her *obi* and ripped her way through the brambles, wincing with pain but determined not to lose sight of the two men.

Nami inched along the side of the inn. Eaves extended far enough to make a covered walkway. The rain beat a loud tattoo overhead. Except for the two jokesters, the brigands were inside, where it was warm and dry. Laughter, songs, an occasional woman's scream punctuated the steady rattle of the storm.

Apparently, the male guests had been sent away to fare as best they could. Some of the women had been detained. Nami shuddered to think what her fate would have been if Yoshi had not sacrificed himself for her.

There was a flash of lightning. The two samurai staggered in the mud, shouting drunken insults at the branches of a giant Cryptomeria. One threw a rock, laughed, and lost his balance.

In the next flash of lightning, Nami saw the silhouette of Yoshi, trussed and suspended from the branch. The way the rope held him, she could see that his throat was taking a great deal of pressure. If he struggled to escape, he would strangle. Oh, the childish cruelty of men.

The drunks soon tired of their game and wended their uncertain way back to the inn.

Nami was alone under the tree.

"Yoshi," she called up urgently.

"Get away, Nami. Get away while you can. I will live and come after you," answered Yoshi in a harsh gargle. He could barely speak because of the rope.

Nami did not answer. The tree trunk was rough. The men who had put Yoshi there had climbed it. So would she. She grasped the bark, feeling pieces break off in her hands. The rainwater made the trunk slippery. Twice she slid back, tearing her hands and the insides of her thighs. On the third try, she reached the lowest branch. Her hands were bleeding. Incongruously, she thought how unhappy she had been to see them tanned and callused from the ride. Once she pulled herself onto the branch, the rest was easy. She climbed to the branch above Yoshi as he watched her with sorrowful eyes.

"You will fall," she said.

His reply was an inarticulate gurgle. She suspected he was ordering her to leave him. Nonsense, not after having come so far. She stretched down with the dagger and cut the rope that held his hands to his throat. Once the pressure was removed from his throat, he ordered her to leave at once, to save herself. Nami refused to listen; she cut the ropes that held Yoshi's hands and feet together. Now his limbs were free, but he was still attached to the branch.

"Can you hold the branch?" asked Nami.

"I have no feeling in my hands or feet," Yoshi answered in a scratchy voice.

"If I cut the other ropes, you will fall to the ground. Shall I wait for circulation to return? Can you survive the fall?"

Lightning flashed; thunder cracked farther away.

"Now! Cut it now!" said Yoshi.

Nami grimaced. It was about fifteen feet to the ground. There were bushes below, and the ground was soft mud. She would pray this would be enough to break Yoshi's fall.

"Namu Amida Butsu," she said, and hacked the first rope. Yoshi now dangled in space, feet first. Quickly, she cut strands two and three. With a loud crash, Yoshi fell into a mulberry bush.

Nami slid down the tree trunk, tearing her cloak in her haste. Yoshi lay face up with his arms and legs spread in a strange, uncoordinated pose. For a moment, she felt as though her tongue was too large for her mouth; she couldn't speak. Oh, name of the Buddha, he is dead!

Then . . . a moan and Yoshi thrashed over onto his side.

Nami gasped with relief. She knelt down next to him, holding his head to her bosom.

Slowly, he flexed his fingers, his arms, his legs.

"Yoshi. Thank the gods you are alive. Let me help." Nami rubbed his arms and legs to restore circulation. When he was sufficiently recovered, she said, "Please. Let us hide before they find us."

Yoshi made an effort and rose to his feet, staggering much as the drunks had a short while before. Nami slipped her arm under his, supporting him. They made their way along the veranda to the back of the inn. Every step brought more circulation back to Yoshi's arms and legs. A thousand needles pierced his skin as the blood returned to the starving tissue. He was a strange apparition, covered with mud and rain. His throat had a bright red line around it, and his hair tangled wildly around his face.

"Please, Yoshi, hurry," Nami said. "The horses are probably in the barn. Let's go."

"Yes, to the horses." Yoshi sounded strange. His tone was unlike any Nami had ever heard before.

They crept along the rear wall of the inn, past the kitchen and the servants' quarters, over a cobbled yard. Now Yoshi was able to walk without help.

"The samurai are too drunk to know that I am free," Yoshi said as he saddled his horse. Yoshi tightened the saddles; he made sure the Emperor's message was intact in its box; he quickly reloaded the packhorse with their belongings. Then he said, "There is one more thing I must do before we leave."

Nami felt her stomach tighten. She feared he would insist on revenge. Why were men such fools? She pleaded, "No, Yoshi. You have sworn not to use your swords. What can you do without weapons? You must not endanger your life again when we have this chance for freedom."

"Nami. This fellow—they called him Kiso—can't be allowed to escape unpunished. Honor demands he pay for what he did to me." Yoshi's face was carved in granite, an incarnation of the god Fudo, with his glaring eyes, furrowed brow, and down-turned mouth.

"And your duty to the Emperor? You are entrusted to deliver a message to Yoritomo. Would you jeopardize that?"

"Nami, my mission is more than just to deliver a message. I have been commissioned to evaluate the Emperor's possible allies. I suspect Kiso is more than the ordinary bandit he appears. Kiso is a common enough name among the mountain people, and probably, we will never meet this Kiso again, but I must make him respect me. He may be an important ally or . . . a deadly enemy. I cannot leave until I've earned his respect. I cannot afford to lose face if I am to be of value to the Emperor. So . . . no more talk. I'll do what I must."

twenty-three

The sounds of revelry faded as Kiso's band succumbed, one by one, to the influence of copious sake. A pair of sentries had been left to guard the entrance to the inn, but they too had drunk their share. Discipline was not strong in Kiso's troops.

Only Tomoe was relatively sober. She smarted from Kiso's earlier insult, but she held her own with the men through the toasts and dinner. Afterward she retired, shaking her head in disgust when the men fought among themselves over the women captives.

Kiso drank more than anyone else. He prided himself on being able to drink more than his men, as befitted a general. He was considering how to handle Tomoe. He loved her, had loved her for as long as he could remember. Should he leave the men and join her in bed? Tomoe was very independent. Damn her to eternal perdition! Why was she so thorny? His ego would not permit refusal tonight. Better to stay with the men than to chance rejection from her. He could order the men about; they didn't resent him. Why did she? Next to Imai, she was the best, most intelligent soldier in his command. Unfortunately, she knew it. Well, to the Avichi hell with her.

Kiso sat cross-legged in a dark corner of the dining hall behind a low table; he nodded at the troops approvingly as he sipped from a large flagon. He made himself concentrate on the men, but he could not concentrate on them for long. They were going through the same antics they always did, and though he was smiling and nodding, he was also bored. Tomoe kept returning to his thoughts. He wanted to go to her, ask her forgiveness. After the last man had collapsed drunkenly, Kiso swallowed one last sip of sake and uncrossed his legs to get up.

Suddenly, a muscular arm locked around his throat and a voice whispered in his ear, "Don't turn, don't move at all, don't make a sound or you die." Adrenaline shot through his body, burning off the effects of the alcohol. His half-drunken nodding turned to instant awareness. Awareness that besides the arm that cut off his air, a sharp object touched the skin under his ear.

"Hands together in your lap," ordered the voice.

He complied, and a young man, face turned down under a straw peasant's hat, scurried around in front of him, removed the sake, shifted the table, and tied his wrists together with a silk scarf.

"I'm going to release the pressure on your throat," said the voice behind him. "One sound and you die on the spot."

Kiso considered diving forward at the young man. He could shout for help . . . no, there was no one within reach who was capable of helping him. Imai, Tezuka, Jiro, and Taro had disappeared into the guest rooms with women. The few samurai who remained were lying drunkenly around the dais that girded the room. Besides, he saw that the young man with the averted face held a dagger ready to fend him off.

The pressure on his throat lightened.

"Whoever you are, you are a fool," Kiso whispered. "You won't live to see morning."

"Quiet. Speak only when I tell you to. Now get up slowly and walk to the center hall."

The retainer ran along ahead of them. From the run, Kiso judged that this young man would interest Uncle Yukiie. There was a feminine quality in the set of the hips and the movement of the legs. Interesting that the warrior behind him also had a taste for boys. His lips curled in a sneering smile.

Kiso tensed his shoulders. When they reached the entrance, they would encounter the sentries—two were stationed there. Kiso was ready to act the moment the sentries grabbed the retainer.

The youth ran through the front entrance unscathed. As Kiso passed, he saw, to his disgust, that both sentries were bound and gagged. They lay curled up helplessly under cover of the eaves; their unfocused eyes rolled toward him as he was led out into the rain.

Thunder rolled over the mountains, but the rain did not slacken. Wind drove it across the courtyard in sheets. The ground resembled a rice paddy, with only the tips of grass showing above the water. Here and there patches of higher ground stood out, islands in the sea.

"You'll never escape," snarled Kiso as the rain beat on his bare head and ran into his eyes.

"We shall see," was the calm response.

Under the Cryptomeria, Kiso was forced to lie face down in the mud. At one point, he started to rise and felt the sharp point dig into the skin at the back of his neck. He subsided, cursing under his breath. Within minutes, he was tied in the same position that Yoshi had been in. Then he was rolled onto his back, and a soft kerchief was wadded into his mouth.

Kiso saw his captor for the first time—the one who had fought and been captured! The one he had last seen hanging helplessly from a tree branch. How had his victim escaped? Impossible, but here he was. Kiso ground his teeth in fury; the man had only a sharp stick in his hand. No dagger, no sword, scarcely a weapon. The tables were turned. Kiso could expect no mercy. His eyes burned with hatred. He wanted to threaten and curse, but only mewling sounds came through the gag.

Suddenly, Kiso was jerked off the ground and lifted, swaying wildly, toward a branch above. His captor hauled on a thick rope that had been thrown over a branch to act as a pulley. He realized with dismay that he would dangle for the rest of the night with only this one support around his waist.

In the morning, when the rain ended and his men were sober, they would come for him, thinking he was the prisoner. The loss of face when they found him trussed like a chicken would be crushing. Buddha! If they discovered he had been captured by an unarmed man . . . he struggled and succeeded only in tightening the noose around his neck. He remembered his words to the guards who had put the captive in place hours ago. "Don't rush back," he had told them. "Let him hang long enough to learn his lesson well."

Kiso growled helplessly. The rain rattled the leaves and covered the faint sound he made.

No one would hear him. No one would come. Kiso prepared, as a soldier should, for the long wait.

Tomoe was the first to arise in the morning. She had had less to drink and more time to sleep than any of the other samurai. She rose leisurely, took time to dress and polish her weapons. She was surprised that Kiso had not visited her in the night. It was unlike him to bear a grudge. His temper was short, but he usually forgot minor grudges almost immediately. She would find him and make amends. It was foolish to stay angry.

She walked through the dining hall, where she had last seen him. What a sight! Samurai lay haphazardly among broken tables, spilled sake flagons, and torn screens. In the hallway, Imai was slumped on the floor with an overturned flagon near his hand. He snored stentoriously.

Tomoe kicked him in the ribs. "Get up, brother," she said. "The celebration is over. We have work to do."

Imai opened his eyes and looked up at her. He reached for the flagon. Tomoe knocked it out of reach. "All right. All right," Imai mumbled. "I'll be awake in a minute."

To her disgust, Tomoe discovered the sentries bound and gagged. Without sentries, the troop was vulnerable to anyone who passed. Trouble! She had sensed it and she was right. During the night they might all have had their throats cut. She knelt down next to one of the sentries and cut the rope that held his gag in place. He stared at her piteously. He deserved death by any military standard and felt the *kami* breathing on his back.

"We were taken by surprise," he whined. "Treachery. A troop of demons overpowered us."

"Worm. Kiso will handle your punishment."

"Kiso. They took him! I saw him being led away."

"What? Where? Speak, fool, or die where you are."

"I couldn't see where they were going, but I saw them lead him through the gate."

Tomoe was stricken. Her anger of the day before was forgotten. Buddha, let him be unharmed.

Tomoe was up and running through the gate. Though the rain had stopped, the grounds were saturated; tufts of grass showed through pools of water. There were no tracks to be followed. She was frantic. Should she run back and get help or continue to search alone? Then she saw him, suspended by a single rope, ten feet above the ground, twisting in the morning breeze. She was tempted to shout and remind him of her warning, but the wild look in his eyes silenced her. If the men saw Kiso like this, the loss of face would be unbearable. She was glad she was alone.

The rope was wound around the tree trunk. She cut it with her short sword and lowered him as gently as she could, face down, into a pool of water. She cut the tether rope first, then the gag.

Kiso sputtered, unable to speak coherently.

Tomoe rubbed his skin to restore circulation. She leaned

closer and finally made out the words.

"I'll find him. Dying will be too good for him. He will suffer, suffer, suffer!" repeated over and over.

twenty-four

The Tenchu River was in flood. A rushing torrent poured down from the mountains to the Eastern Sea. Yoshi and Nami had been stranded on the bank for several hours. There was only one ferry: a dispirited pair of fishing boats, roped together and joined with crude planking to make a raft. The boatman was an even earlier vintage than the boats. He explained patiently that he had grown to his ripe years by not taking the ferry across when the Tenchu was so high.

Yoshi offered silver. The old man exposed a mouthful of gums and giggled as though the offer were a great joke. "What would I do with so much silver?" he asked. "I am too old to enjoy the pleasure quarter. I have as much rice and millet as I can eat. I have no need for new clothes. No, my young warrior, I cannot be bought."

Yoshi watched the sun rising. Soon horsemen would come from Hamamatsu. He had vowed not to draw his sword against them. Would they show him the same consideration? Of course not! Yoshi knew he could escape by riding north along the river bank, but he feared Nami would not be able to keep up the pace in the mountains.

After what had happened to the women at the inn, Yoshi had no illusions about Nami's fate if she were captured by a troop of angry country samurai and discovered to be a woman. His vow not to use his sword in combat was proving to be singularly difficult to keep. Yoshi had succeeded with the pointed stick to Kiso's throat. The trick was not likely to work a second time. His only recourse was to shun confrontations, which was not in his nature. Yoshi was guilty of pride—pride in his ability with the sword. Pride was a serious fault, but wasn't cowardice worse? Could he spend his life always running from danger? It would be easier to stand his ground and fight back.

Yet Yoshi had seen that violence only begat more violence. He shuddered with distaste as he remembered killing the red-robed children and slaughtering the monks. Where would it end? If Kiso caught them and he did not defend to the death,

Nami would suffer. He could not bear that. If he did fight, how could he face himself and the gods to whom he had sworn his oath? Whatever decision he made, would it be consistent with his mission on the Emperor's behalf? Could he afford to lose face? If he was not respected by the samurai with whom he dealt, would he retain his value to Go-Shirakawa? Yoshi was torn between his vow and his responsibilities to Nami and the Emperor.

During the course of the morning, many travelers came to the ferry only to be turned away. The foaming white waters convinced them that the boatman was right. It would be suicidal to attempt a river crossing.

Yoshi fidgeted, racked by his problem. Nami had stayed in the background during his negotiations with the boatman. After a time she rode close and whispered in Yoshi's ear. At first he disagreed with her suggestion, but after a few minutes of heated discussion he relented. What she suggested might heighten their danger, but if Nami's plan failed, they were both doomed.

Nami, with a last meaningful look at Yoshi, dismounted and went to where the boatman squatted by his mooring rope. The ferry was tied to a tree trunk by a thick rope. The rope was drawn taut as the twin-hulled raft was pulled parallel to the bank by the rush of water.

"A word with you, boatman," Nami said.

"Certainly, young sir, but before you ask, know that I'll tell you what I told your master."

"I understand, good captain. You are a wise and prudent man. No one denies it."

The boatman nodded as if this were self-evident. Nami continued. "We are not what we seem," she said. "My master is a mighty swordsman sworn not to use his sword except in dire emergency. Even then he will do his utmost to avoid sword play. You see, he does not wear his swords. At this very moment, we are being pursued by evil men. My master will be killed if they capture him."

"Not my problem," cackled the boatman.

"I said that we are not what we seem. I am not my master's retainer."

"No?"

"No. Indeed, I am not deserving of the way you addressed me. I am not a young sir. No, indeed. I am a lady of the court escaping from these same brigands. Need I describe what will happen to me if I am captured?"

The boatman's eyes opened wide as he listened to this surprising confession. His stare was glued on Nami's face as she removed her peasant hat and her hair fell almost to the ground. His toothless mouth gaped in astonishment. In his entire life he had never seen a lady without her veils and covers. Her face was unmistakably the face of a court lady.

The boatman was beyond words.

"I am in the service of the Emperor. On a secret mission. If you do not take us across before our pursuers arrive, my mission will fail, and when word is sent back to the Emperor, you will be punished."

"Punish me?" The boatman was in shock. "I've done nothing."

"Exactly." Nami lowered her voice to a confidential whisper. "Because you did nothing, the Emperor's mission will have failed. Imagine the tortures you will suffer before they take your head!"

The old boatman's brow furrowed. "How will they know?" he asked nervously.

"My master's retainer is already on his way back to the Emperor with the message. There is no escape for you. Chance the river or die by torture when the messenger returns with the troops."

"Perhaps the waters have lowered," said the old man cautiously. "I think we should try to cross now." The old man started untying the mooring rope.

"Quickly, then." Nami signaled Yoshi to lead the horses aboard.

Shouts from the far side of the boathouse! Four riders appeared. Kiso, Tomoe, Imai, and Jiro rode like avenging angels, their horses' hooves kicking up clods of mud and sprays of water, as they raced toward the river.

The rope loosened, and the current whipsawed the boat away from the bank just as the riders neared the water's edge.

Kiso jerked his horse to a stop, his face a malevolent mask. He reached over his shoulder and pulled an arrow from his war quiver. In one fluid motion, he nocked the arrow and let it fly. It was a good shot, but the motion and speed of the water caused it to miss Yoshi's horse by inches.

Kiso's obscenities rapidly became inaudible over the rushing river and the increasing distance from the bank. The pursuers now let fly a hail of arrows. All fell short as the boatman poled the raft to the center of the river. They were racing out to sea, making little headway toward the opposite shore. The boatman's skinny, muscular arms pumped at the steering pole, guiding them slowly across. Nami and Yoshi held their horses steady. They could do nothing to help the old man.

The mouth of the river was just ahead. It seemed impossible to prevent being swept out to sea. Suddenly, the boatman's pole hit bottom and dug in, spinning the raft toward the bank. In moments, they were driven onto the sandy beach that formed the north bank of the Tenchu.

Yoshi and Nami led their horses off the boat deck and onto the sand. Before they turned away, Yoshi said to the boatman, "Take this. You've earned it." He handed the old man a bag of silver.

"I took you across for the Emperor," said the old man, but he did not hesitate to grab the bag and tuck it into his loincloth.

Yoshi and Nami mounted their horses and headed away from the river. Yoshi called back to the old man, who was busy mooring the raft to a small stump. "No need to hurry back for the others."

The boatman pulled on his mooring rope. "No need?" His brows raised. "I would be mad to recross again until tomorrow or the next day."

Yoshi and Nami rode hard all that day. They crossed the shallow, mile-wide Oi River late in the afternoon of the second day. On the third day, they arrived at the strand of Okitsu, the small seaside town that was once the site of Lord Fumio's estate.

Yoshi's eyes misted as he looked over the familiar scene. Thirteen years ago he had stood close to this very spot and watched the salt-makers toiling on the sands below. His nostrils quivered at the same scent of wood fires mixed with sea air. It was as though he had never left. He had been so innocent then, starting on a new life, a foppish courtier cast without preparation into the harsh world.

Yoshi watched the women carrying buckets of saltwater on yokes that bent their backs and shoulders. He had once appreciated the aesthetics of the scene without understanding the physical demands of constant heavy labor. He absorbed the scene: the women, small figures moving heavily along the shore under their burdens; the backdrop of Miho in the bay; a curved sword of black sand studded with ancient pines.

It was a picture he had never forgotten. Now he could also sympathize with the hard life these peasant women lived. How many of them were the same ones he had seen then? How his own life had changed, developed, and expanded while they trudged their daily rounds bent under burdensome buckets. They started as children and grew old under the weight of the salt!

Yoshi spoke:

> *"Crescent of black sand*
> *The ancient pines of Miho*
> *Frame a stark picture*
> *Of small figures bent and worn*
> *By the weight of daily life."*

Nami nodded wistfully. She did not have the benefit of Yoshi's experience, but for her too the scene was reminiscent of a more innocent time. As a child, she had often sat on the strand with her nurse and watched such laborers perform their endless daily chores. Though she never experienced labor, she could appreciate their efforts. Yoshi's poem brought tears to her eyes. She had no stylish silk sleeve to dab at them, to make a pose of sorrow. Rather, she wiped her eyes with plain brown cotton and felt cleansed by the coarseness of her garments.

"I want to see Uncle's castle before we leave Okitsu," she said.

"It might increase our danger," said Yoshi. "However, I would feel disrespectful if we did not visit our childhood home."

The old Okitsu castle was situated on a flat area at the top of a small mountain, a mile from the Tokaido Road. The travelers walked up the rocky road, past the Seiken-ji temple, where Yoshi had prayed years before. When they came to the flat clearing, it was early evening. As they rounded the last bend and came in sight of the castle gate, both Yoshi and Nami stopped in wonder. The high protective wall was a pile of mortar and loose stone. The gate was gone. Only the ground beam remained.

The castle had burned to the ground and the forest had regrown around the ruins. Yoshi felt a tightness in his chest as he gazed out over the scene of desolation. Lord Fumio had been so proud of his rural castle. He had built it with loving attention. What had been the first of the modern castles in

Japan was now a rubble that disturbed the serenity of the trees and underbrush that grew around it.

A small campground was set in what once was the front garden. There were wagons and tents in random order; horses and cows moved languidly in the early evening light. As Yoshi and Nami stood silently, overwhelmed by a mixture of emotions, neither wanting to say the first word for fear of losing control, a short fat man waddled toward them.

"What do you want here?" he asked belligerently.

twenty-five

The man was bandy-legged, with a paunch that overlapped his *obi*. His jowly face was round and sported a red nose that spoke of self-indulgence.

"This is our campsite. We want no strangers here," he said. He was unarmed and scarcely taller than Nami. His threatening tone had a hollow ring.

Yoshi, in his mildest manner, introduced himself as a samurai traveling with his retainer. He asked lodging for the night.

"This is not an inn," said the little man. "Down the mountain in Okitsu there are inns where you can find lodging."

"But it is almost dark," said Yoshi quietly, in the face of the little man's bluster. "We would like to camp here. We will not disturb you."

"So you say," said the little man. "How can you judge what will disturb me? Well . . . we shall see." He turned away from them and shouted, "Shite, Shite, come here . . . quickly!"

A tall, well-built young man, the very epitome of his name, *Shite*, which meant "hero," came running from one of the tents. He almost stumbled in his haste to respond to the call.

"Hai, yes, Ohana, *hai,"* he panted as he adjusted his *hakama*.

"Remove these trespassers from our camp," ordered Ohana peremptorily.

"But . . . but, Ohana, it is not ours and . . ." Shite looked askance at Yoshi, his samurai robe, and the armament on the horse at his side.

"We seek shelter, nothing more," Yoshi said. He motioned Nami to stand behind him. She stared at him in surprise, but moved back promptly. Yoshi continued, "We once lived near this castle. We wonder if you know what brought it to this sorry state."

The young man called Shite eagerly responded, "The original lord, they say, fled to Kyoto many years ago. The local peasants took over the castle and the fields. One day when the

148

castle caught fire, they were so disorganized they let it burn to the ground. Most of the peasants have long departed, though a few remain to till the soil in the surrounding fields. We are only a poor troupe of traveling Dengaku players. We use this site when we are in the area."

"Thank you," said Yoshi.

Shite turned to Ohana. "Please let them stay," he pleaded. "They mean us no harm."

Ohana cleared his throat gruffly. He was relieved that there would be no confrontation. Shite was incapable of heroic action, despite his name and appearance.

"They may stay in the field, far from our tents," Ohana conceded. "We have rehearsing to do, and I won't stand for them disturbing us."

Shite was as pleased as a belly-rubbed puppy. "You can stay," he said. "Welcome to Master Ohana's Dengaku Company."

Yoshi and Nami pitched their tent near the rubble of the old boundary wall.

"By avoiding sword play, we achieved our goal," said Yoshi. "If I had drawn my sword, where would we be tonight?"

Nami answered with a poem:

> *"The silvery blade*
> *Of tempered steel hides from light.*
> *The travelers sleep*
> *And dream in peace of lost times*
> *Before steel was stained with red."*

"Yes," said Yoshi appreciatively. "Our days of innocence are truly lost. I can try to regain them, yet I feel that eventually I will have to atone for the deaths I've caused."

"You blame yourself unduly. In the life of a samurai it is often necessary to kill for survival and for honor."

"Nevertheless, I want to try this new way. The old way has always ended in sorrow. I cannot forget the fate of Uncle Fumio."

"You were not at fault. Perhaps one day we will know who killed him and why . . ."

"Do you doubt it was because of me?"

"Yoshi, your enemies were his friends. Why would they? . . ."

"To kill me, they would do anything. Hurt Fumio, hurt my mother, hurt you. Nami, they want my head. I have no fear

for myself and I would gladly give my life for you and my
mother, but I must never forget my mission for the Emperor.
The fate of Japan rests on my shoulders, and I believe that if
I lay down my swords the gods will see that my mission succeeds."

In the morning, Yoshi and Nami watched a rehearsal of the
theatrical company. Nomadic country groups like Ohana's
roamed the countryside entertaining in the rice fields, in the
country lord's castles, and in the pleasure quarters of small
towns. They presented an unsophisticated show: small sketches,
recitations, crude songs, and acrobatic tricks.

At one point, Yoshi whispered to Nami, "I think I could
do as well as that myself."

Nami answered sarcastically, "A fitting career for a great
sword master!"

By midday, they were on route again. Yoshi insisted on a
brief visit to the Seiken-ji temple. The temple at least had not
changed. Yoshi knelt before the Buddha in the main hall and
prayed for divine guidance. He repeated his vow to avoid battle
with the sword. At last, feeling cleansed, he rejoined Nami
and they continued on the path to the Tokaido Road.

Yoshi and Nami followed the shore, skirting the towns and
provincial barriers. They crossed the Izu peninsula in sight of
Mount Fujiyama; the top was white and stark against a deep
blue sky. Gray and white smoke drifted from its summit. The
colors of mourning. Yoshi was moved to compose a poem:

> *"Mount Fujiyama's*
> *White banners of smoke*
> *Remind passersby*
> *Of ephemeral nature*
> *Pale flags forgotten too soon."*

Nami nodded. The comparison of the white wisps of smoke
to mourning and to the Minamoto flag and the reminder of the
evanescence of life, gave her a feeling of nostalgia. She had
been thinking about her life as she rode behind Yoshi's sorrel.
She had left the court she knew in favor of a voyage into the
unknown. True, her life had been restrictive and boring, but
there had been gratification: acquaintances to share her thoughts

with in the lonely hours of night, the warm relationship with the Empress, who had treated her well. Nami had abandoned all this for the uncertainty of a life with her powerful protector and gentle lover.

She loved Yoshi. She loved his strength, the respect he engendered: the most powerful swordsman in the Empire!

But now he was changing. Killing his father, killing the red-robed children, killing the monks, and blaming himself for the death of Fumio . . . these factors conspired to turn him away from the life he knew. From the life she had expected to share.

Nami was uncertain about Yoshi's decision to forego the sword. Her life was at stake, too. A samurai woman had no right to question her lord's decisions, but Nami was not an ordinary court lady. In her early years on the *shoen* she had developed a sense of independence. In Kyoto, she made herself unpopular with many of the court ladies by constantly speaking her mind. Everyone reminded her that she had to obey her lord and remain silent. Nami had not always won her lonely battle against the forces of convention; for a time, she had given in to Chikara's demands and played the role of dutiful wife. She regretted that period lost from her life.

Now, she was with Yoshi by choice. She tolerated the coarse clothing and the difficulties of traveling without amenities because Yoshi treated her as an equal. She felt she had a right to be considered in any decision that might affect the two of them.

Nami was unhappy that Yoshi vowed to abandon the sword without consulting her. He said avoiding confrontations took more courage and strength than fighting. He said many things and she accepted them . . . but this time a small worm of doubt gnawed at her trust.

Had he lost his courage?

She suppressed the thought as soon as it surfaced.

The next three days were uneventful. The horses plodded along the road through the daylight hours. Nami fell into a reverie, closing her mind to the endless hours of travel: fields, moors, pine forests, bamboo groves, and sandy beaches. They spent one night in a poor fishing village immersed in the smell of sea air and dead fish. Another night, after crossing the neck of the Izu peninsula, they stopped at the provincial capital of Izu in a large, well-appointed inn. Nami was bone weary after the day on the road, but Yoshi insisted on making a short pilgrimage to the Mishima shrine, which was just beyond the town limits.

They had their first disagreement. Later, Nami attributed her short temper to the rigors of the road. The day-after-day boredom and physical discomfort from living on a horse were accompanied by an ache in her lower abdomen. She feared that her monthly defilement was approaching. She tried to suppress the feeling of discomfort; if she started to bleed before they reached Kamakura, it would be inauspicious to continue. She would have to retire alone for several days until the period of defilement had ended.

Weary and feeling bloated, Nami found herself unable to accept Yoshi's pronouncement.

"I go to Mishimi shrine to renew my vows to the Shinto god Hachiman," he declared.

"Now the Shinto shrine? You renewed your vows at the Buddhist temple at Seiken-ji. Is my husband to become a monk before we arrive at Kamakura? You spend more time praying to the gods than you spend with me." Nami felt unbidden tears course down her cheeks. What had prompted her to say that? She wanted to bite her tongue, but the words were spoken and the evil *kami* who had said them would not let them be recalled.

The stricken expression on Yoshi's face melted her heart. Then, as she watched him, she noticed his jaw harden in a familiar expression of stubbornness.

"Have I neglected you?" he asked. "I think not. If I find it necessary to renew my vows before Hachiman, it is because the path I have chosen is a difficult one. We are alive. We are safe. The path of peace makes demands on its followers." Yoshi lowered his voice. There was an edge of pain in it. "I must go now. Rest until I return."

Yoshi backed out of the room, unwilling to meet Nami's eyes. She reached out a hand to stop him, to apologize. Too late. Like a shadow, he was on his way into the night.

Nami fell back onto her *futon*. Why had she spoken so thoughtlessly? It was improper. It was unlike her. She stared at the ceiling beams, torn by conflicting emotions.

twenty-six

While Nami tossed, unable to sleep, Yoshi walked thoughtfully toward the Mishima shrine. Small white flags fluttered from five-inch staffs stuck in the ground on each side of the road. The flags were decorated with the name of the deity, Hachiman, and the name of the person requesting divine help.

Mishima shrine was one of the oldest shrines to the god Hachiman; it was often used by travelers along the Tokaido road. The shrine's square Taishi architecture with its large center pillar loomed ahead of him. Dimly, in the moonlight, he could distinguish the woodchip roof and the *chigi*, crossbars, on top.

There was no conflict in Yoshi's mind about visiting a Shinto shrine to pray to Hachiman even if only a few days ago he had prayed to Buddha at Seiken-ji. The court and Yoshi accepted both Buddha and the Shinto gods equally.

Yoshi mounted the unpainted wood steps, removed his boots, and purified himself at the basin beside the portal. Inside, pine torches illuminated the statues of Hachiman and his legendary companion, Takenouchi-no-Sukuna. The shrine was empty except for an elderly monk, who prayed silently in a dark corner. Yoshi was at peace for the first time since his tragic duel with Lord Chikara. Takenouchi-no-Sukuna symbolized long life; his proximity to Hachiman, the god of war, seemed a good omen.

Yoshi had been torn by conflicting emotions since the night he learned of his relationship to Lord Chikara. As he knelt before the altar, he remembered the duel and the events that had transpired since then.

The wheel of fate turned in unpredictable patterns. Yoshi never thought of himself as religious, although Shinto taught him the importance of ancestor worship. Each household was ruled by the ghosts of the family's ancestors; the vast sea of departed spirits controlled the living world: day, night, spring, summer, autumn, winter, rain, snow, earthquakes, avalanches, and fires. So if Shinto ancestors must be propitiated, what crime was worse than patricide? Even the Buddhists considered it one of the five greatest sins. Yoshi had pushed the recollection of the crime into the darkest recesses of his mind, but there was no doubt that it affected his actions. Since the duel he had been uncertain, and convinced that misfortune followed his footsteps. Which way to turn? How to act to prevent the death of his loved ones? He was no longer the confident *sensei* he had been.

Yes... it was the duel that caused his uncertainty. After he killed Chikara, Yoshi had been willing to use his sword as long as he did not initiate the confrontation. Then he had watched Hiromi die and had killed the red-robed children. Although he had killed the red-robes in order to survive, he began to doubt the use of the sword at all. Once started, the path of the sword seemed inevitably to lead to death for guilty and innocent alike.

When Go-Shirakawa had asked Yoshi if he was willing to face deadly danger for the sake of the Empire, Yoshi had unhesitatingly said yes. The mission would be more difficult to accomplish if he eschewed the sword. Nami would have less protection. She and Yoshi would be at the mercy of men like Kiso. Yes... Kiso was a common name. There were hundreds of men from Shinano called Kiso. But what if this man were the Kiso Yoshinaka who was allied with Yoritomo? Yoshi had to evaluate him for Go-Shirakawa. What would he say? Kiso would never reveal himself to anyone but an armed warrior. Could Yoshi report fairly on Kiso or on Yoritomo if they did not respect him?

Kiso had almost caused his death and almost captured Nami. But, the gods seemed to protect Yoshi. He had fought Kiso without his swords and had succeeded in overcoming him.

"I will teach the use of the sword in your name," Yoshi told Hachiman, "but I will no longer wear the swords of my station. I will protect myself and my family, but I will not use my sword to kill." Yoshi pressed his forehead to the hardwood floor.

He continued after a minute of silent prayer. "I may be called a coward. I will swallow my pride. You, Hachiman, will understand that constraint is more difficult than fighting. And if there is a time when I must forswear this oath to accomplish the Emperor's mission, you will send me a sign. Until then, I will serve you as best I can with my hands empty and my mind clear."

Yoshi withdrew from the altar feeling freer than he had for many months. At the portal of the shrine, the monk-guardian offered him an *omamori*. Yoshi paid for the one inch by one half-inch slip of paper inscribed with Hachiman's blessing. The monk who until then had remained silently in the shadows blessed Yoshi verbally, offering peace and a long life.

It was a good omen.

twenty-seven

In the year 1181, Minamoto Yoritomo, leader of the Minamoto clan, was thirty-four years old. Banished from Kyoto as a child, he had lived in the north ever since. In the twenty years since his life had been spared by Taira Kiyomori's whim, Yoritomo swore he would never make the mistake of showing mercy to an enemy. By 1180 he had established a northern seaside encampment at Kamakura and declared himself lord of Kamakura.

Yoritomo was small-boned and not physically strong. He was a withdrawn man who could, when the occasion demanded, exude great charm. Charm was a commodity he used sparingly: mainly to gain political or social advantage. His power as clan leader came from a combination of intelligence, ruthlessness, and dedication to the idea that he would one day unseat the Taira and return the Minamoto clan to its proper place in the court.

He had been fourteen years old when his life was saved and he was exiled. He had put the court behind him. Even at that young age, he had felt that his path to power would come from another direction. His training was supervised by Hojo Tokimasa, an old line Taira lord who allowed him a great deal of freedom. Ordered not to learn the ways of the warrior, Yoritomo took advantage of Tokimasa's kindness and spent his time learning the arts of war and politics.

While still in his teens, Yoritomo's life direction was shaped by a visit from Mongaku, a mad monk who harbored a long-standing grudge against Taira Kiyomori. The monk had devoted his life to undermining the Taira, and in Yoritomo, he saw the instrument of his revenge. He brought Yoritomo a skull that he claimed was that of the boy's father, who had been killed by Kiyomori. He made the boy swear to devote himself to destroying Kiyomori and the Taira clan. It did not take much persuasion. Yoritomo had already decided to try to gain the throne of Japan. Though he was still a youth, he dreamt of controlling the Empire. The monk had sharpened his ambition and from that time Yoritomo's only interest was to regain power for himself and his family, power—as he saw it—to do good for the Empire.

However, Yoritomo had seen the disastrous effects of overprecipitous action. The Minamoto had been virtually destroyed because they did not prepare properly for their attempted revolt during the Hōgen insurrection. Yoritomo was a careful man whose policy was one of patience. He would win by being thoroughly prepared before taking action.

One of his first acts was to court and marry Hojo Masa, the daughter of his guardian and benefactor. With this marriage he accomplished several goals. He gained a power base with Masa's father, and by marrying, he put aside the distractions of romantic love. Masa was taller than he; she was also large-boned, large-featured, heavy, and physically unattractive. Masa was exceptionally intelligent; this was serendipitous but welcome. Gradually, Yoritomo began to trust his wife's opinions on his policies. She was by nature kinder and softer than he, with a streak of sentimentality that occasionally colored her thinking. It served Yoritomo's purpose to cater to that softness. He was wise enough to realize that his cold reasoning was more effective when it was tempered by her sentiment.

Yoritomo had been the moving force behind Prince Mochihito's abortive revolt the year before. It reaffirmed his decision never to act before he was sure of success. Prince Mochihito gave Yoritomo's ambitions the imprimatur of legality, but the Prince had died, betrayed by his foster-brother. Yoshi had almost saved the Prince at the battle of the bridge at Uji. Word of his heroic fight against overwhelming odds reached Yoritomo. Ever since that time, Yoritomo had looked forward to meeting Yoshi and adding him to his formidable force of fighting men.

Now, outriders galloped into camp with the news that Yoshi, accompanied by his retainer, would arrive shortly. It seemed that Yoritomo's plans to use Yoshi's skills would soon be put into action.

Hojo Masa entered the room with a pot of tea and a dish of dried fruits. She wore an unlined over-robe dyed in blue bamboo patterns over eight thin silk shifts ranging in color from pink to dusky orange. She knelt before the raised platform where Yoritomo sat and set a low table for his convenience.

In Kamakura many courtly niceties, such as the screens of state, had been abolished. Most women and men, while not equal—every civilized person knew they never would be—

dressed and lived in a similar country way. Hojo Masa was
one of the few women who preferred to dress in the manner
of the court—she felt it camouflaged the awkwardness of her
body—but she moved about freely without screens or veils.
She considered herself very modern.

Yoritomo nibbled at a piece of dried fruit, then put it back
on the tray. "You have heard? The hero warrior Yoshi will be
in our camp within the hour."

"Yes, one of my ladies-in-waiting brought me the news. Is
this the man who almost saved Prince Mochihito?"

"Yes. However, we must not lose sight of the most important
fact . . ."

"That is?"

"He failed."

"But against insuperable odds. The Taira lord Chikara mus-
tered nearly thirty thousand men against a handful, yet Yoshi
held them for two days at the Uji bridge. We have not rewarded
him for his efforts."

"Reward failure? No matter how valiantly Yoshi fought,
the battle resulted in the death of the Prince and a terrible loss
for our cause."

"You cannot blame him."

"I cast no blame; neither do I offer rewards. We will see
him when he arrives." Yoritomo paused, then added, "Yoshi
has leadership ability; he has proved that. I want him to take
charge of a troop of warriors and challenge the advance guards
of the Taira."

"You have many captains. Why send Yoshi?"

"My spies tell me that young Shigehira leads thirteen thousand men through Mino province. Let Yoshi prove his prowess
against them."

"Yes, my lord. A wise decision, since we cannot possibly
spare even half that many men."

Yoritomo smiled a thin, icy smile and reached into the fruit
bowl. This time he swallowed a half apricot in one gulp and
washed it down with tea.

A bell sounded at the main portal. A visitor had arrived.

A retainer discreetly knocked at the screen. Yoritomo coolly
bit into another fruit, this time chewing it slowly. After a pause,
he said, "Enter."

The retainer scurried in on his knees, head low to the floor.
Yoritomo smiled at Masa, and his lips formed the word *Yoshi*.

"A courier has arrived with a message from Lord Kiso,"

said the retainer. "He demands to see you at once."

"He demands?" Two vertical creases appeared between Yoritomo's brows, a sign of his irritation and disappointment. "Send him in," he ordered.

The retainer hastened out and was replaced by a dusty, armor-clad samurai. The samurai walked forward boldly and gave a minimal bow. "I am Okabe-no-Santaro, lieutenant to the demon warrior Kiso Yoshinaka. I come with a message and a request."

"Speak, Okabe-no-Santaro," ordered Yoritomo.

"I have ridden many hours without stop. First, I would have refreshment to wet my parched throat so I can speak more easily."

Yoritomo frowned so slightly that only Hojo Masa was aware of it. He thought there was something to be said for the strict formality of the court. The new generation of mountain warriors lacked the common courtesies that made the working of authority run smoothly. Yoritomo studied Santaro. He saw a husky, broad-shouldered mountaineer, heavily bearded, crude of speech and manner, yet dressed in well-crafted armor of blue with purple leather trim. The warrior had removed his helmet but wore his animal skin boots, which had left a track of dust across the wood floor. A lout, but a lout with the stance and manner of a fighting man.

Yoritomo motioned with one finger. Hojo Masa hastened to pour a cup of tea for the messenger.

Santaro gulped the tea avidly, then wiped his mouth and beard with one dusty hand. "We have suffered a loss in Owari province," he said abruptly. "Yukiie was to lead a small group of soldiers into the province to divert the main force of General Shigehira's army. He was ambushed at the Sunomata River and his men were forced to retreat into the mountains with heavy losses."

"Yes. Uncle Yukiie is not a general to depend on," said Yoritomo coldly. "Why did Kiso entrust a mission of such sensitivity to him?"

"Lord Kiso did not expect Yukiie to engage the enemy. Kiso thought a diversion would give him time to raid the coast for gold and arms."

"And did it?"

Santaro's face turned red. "Unfortunately, the expedition to the coast was unsuccessful. That is why I was sent to you."

"Yes?" Yoritomo's eyes glazed and he appeared to withdraw. The air of impatience he had shown was gone; it was as if he had forgotten Santaro's presence. This was characteristic of him when he felt the imminence of a request that he did not wish to honor.

"Kiso needs more arms and men. He is preparing an offensive against the Taira during the coming months."

"Why do you come to me?"

"Our men will bear the brunt of the fighting. We are prepared to offer our lives to gain a victory against the Taira that will benefit you as well as us. We want to coordinate our battle plans with yours, and we ask your help with supplies."

"Is this the message from Kiso? I detect a growing taste for power on his part. If I offer my men, if I offer my gold, if I offer my armor, how can I be certain that they will not be turned against me? I will weaken my army while I strengthen his."

"Kiso is a Minamoto and his samurai honor is enough guarantee of his good faith."

"I want more concrete assurances than that before I commit my men, gold, and armor."

Santaro's mouth tightened. "Lord Yoritomo," he said, "the countryside will soon burn in the summer sun and supplies will be scarce. We must begin our offensive while there is food to forage." Santaro waved his hands in the air, outlining the enormity of the problem. He was silent for the time of five heartbeats, then he said determinedly, "I need an answer at once."

Yoritomo grew angrier with every word Santaro uttered. "My dear Santaro, you make outrageous demands and then you have the temerity to ask an immediate answer. Your manner is offensive and your demands insulting. Who are you to speak this way to me? You live only because my cousin and I have similar goals. Mark this well . . . I will take whatever time I need to make my decision." Yoritomo turned to Hojo Masa. "Have someone see to this messenger and his horse. He is not to leave the camp without my permission. Find him quarters, and have him placed under house arrest."

Santaro drew back as though he had been struck. His bearded face darkened with rage. As a high-ranking captain in Kiso's army, he had overestimated the strength of his position. Yoritomo was treating him like a low-born peasant; his honor was insulted. He glowered as he balanced between honor and discretion. Though he had no fear of dying, he had a responsibility to Kiso. He would not draw his sword against Yoritomo. Discretion won.

As Santaro stood motionless, locked in a battle of wills with Yoritomo, Hojo Masa slipped out and returned with a squad of six soldiers.

Santaro broke the silence. "Kiso will not take kindly to the way you have received me," he snarled.

"And he will take less kindly to your return if you fail in your mission." Yoritomo waved at the guards, dismissing Santaro almost contemptuously.

The moment when Santaro might have acted with honor was gone. Now all he could do was try to salvage his mission. He grunted an acknowledgment of his defeat and turned away without bowing. A petty triumph.

He marched out ahead of the guards with his head erect and his shoulders back.

Hojo Masa said, "I think you were unnecessarily harsh with him. We may need Kiso's good will in the near future."

"Kiso needs to teach his soldiers how to show proper respect and not to act like brigands. Our combined armies are not as large as the Taira's. If we do not maintain discipline, we are lost. This man is a lout. Coming into my quarters with dusty boots, not kneeling as he should. Making demands! Giving orders! For Kiso's good will, I spare his life."

"Will you honor his request?"

Yoritomo thoughtfully munched on an apricot half. "I will give it deep thought," he said. "I do not trust Kiso, but I need him."

Hojo Masa squinted at her lord, deciding whether to speak. Finally, she said, "Kiso's army is an undisciplined rabble, yet at the same time, they are superb fighting men. We must not let personal animosity stand between us and a wise decision."

"My feelings never interfere with my decisions."

"I know. Forgive the unnecessary intrusion."

Yoritomo fixed a cool stare on Hojo Masa's heavy features. Gradually, his face softened. She was not beautiful, not even attractive, but he felt a warmth toward her that few were allowed to see. Even Hojo Masa rarely experienced it.

Yoritomo said gently, "The life of a leader is a difficult one. I wish it were otherwise. I must weigh the advantages against the disadvantages of allying myself with Kiso. On the one hand, Kiso brings an army of fighting men to our cause.

On the other, he is untrustworthy. My purpose is to help our Empire by replacing the corrupt Taira court. I do not intend to turn the government over to my barbarian cousin. My anger with Kiso's messenger suggests an inauspicious period to come. I expected Yoshi to be the first to arrive this morning. Perhaps when he comes, he will change the direction of our Karma."

"The outriders did say he was expected momentarily."

"Let us hope he arrives safely and soon."

twenty-eight

It was ten in the morning, the hour of the snake, when Yoshi was announced.

Yoritomo smiled. Thinly, but a true smile. The omens were changing. After a difficult morning, he could relax and give out one of his few rewards. He would not call it a reward, because as he had stated to Hojo Masa, one did not reward failure. It would be an acknowledgment of his pleasure at greeting the hero of the battle of Uji. Yoritomo was confident that Yoshi would be pleased to accept his generosity: the rank of general and a command in the Minamoto armies.

The bell sounded.

"Enter," said Hojo Masa.

Yoritomo's retainer came in on his knees and waited. Again it was Hojo Masa who spoke while Yoritomo stared straight ahead, his features composed. She asked the retainer to make his announcement.

"I am pleased to report to my lord that the person he is expecting awaits in the anteroom."

"Send him in." Hojo Masa turned to Yoritomo and asked modestly if she could remain. She knew Yoshi's arrival was a special occasion and that protocol might frown on the presence of a woman.

Yoritomo nodded mutely; she was welcome.

Yoshi entered with a firm step and immediately sank to his knees in front of the dais. He bowed his head to the floor, then raised himself to sit on his heels with his back straight. "I am Tadamori-no-Yoshi," he announced, "born to a branch of the Taira clan in the province of Suruga. I am godson of Taira-no-Fumio, who was a brave soldier in the service of the Emperor. I have served my lord Yoritomo on the council at Kyoto and am here to deliver a message from the Emperor and then to pledge my honor and offer myself in Lord Yoritomo's service."

"Well said, well said," declared Yoritomo with an infinitesimal nod to Hojo Masa. The movement was slight, but Hojo

Masa interpreted it to mean, This is a proper warrior, unlike Kiso's loutish Santaro.

Yoritomo cleared his throat. "Where is the message?" he prompted.

Yoshi took the box from his robe and removed the message from its hiding place in the lid. Wordlessly, he handed it to Yoritomo.

Yoritomo inspected the Imperial seal, held it up for Hojo Masa to see, then briskly tore it open. His brows raised in surprise. "Go-Shirakawa offers allegiance if we will march on Kyoto in the next eighteen months." Yoritomo was impressed. He thoughtfully tapped the paper against his elbow rest and added in a low voice, almost to himself, "This means I need alliances with the other families, the Miuras, the Dois, the Ochiais. It will take every minute of the Emperor's eighteen months to bring them together under one flag." Yoritomo hesitated. "Can I accomplish that?"

Hojo Masa said reassuringly, "Of course you can. My father will support you. The great families of the north will be eager to join you once they learn of Go-Shirakawa's assurances."

"This is a most important message, Yoshi. You are to be congratulated for delivering it safely."

Yoshi touched his forehead to the floor.

Yoritomo continued, "We have heard much about your service to the white flag. You claim membership by birth to the clan of our enemies, yet you have repeatedly proved your loyalty to our cause."

Yoshi bowed, accepting the compliment.

"You know I do not give rewards freely. Though this is not to be considered a reward, I do want to acknowledge your services. Tadamori-no-Yoshi, I extend to you a full commission as general of the Minamoto. You will command an army of five thousand samurai. You will train them and lead them into battle against the Taira usurpers. How say you to that?"

Again, Yoshi pressed his forehead to the floor. "I am honored," he responded. "It is an offer far beyond my expectations . . . far beyond what I deserve."

Yoritomo gave a faint indication of pleasure. This was a warrior of the old style, a samurai who understood protocol as much as he understood honor.

Hojo Masa's heavy features lightened in an impulsive smile. She recognized Yoritomo's pleasure and was happy for him.

Yoshi hesitated before he went on. "But though I appreciate

your generosity, I must refuse."

Yoritomo's eyes opened a fraction wider. Hojo Masa's lips separated and she gasped in surprise.

"Allow me to explain," added Yoshi. "I am your most loyal servant and want to serve you in the best way I can. I am a *sensei,* a teacher and master of the sword. The gods have seen to it that I have survived many encounters. However, I have come to believe that my sword serves more evil than good. I have been forced by circumstance to commit grievous sins in the interest of survival. I have killed children . . . holy men . . ."

"That is the lot of the samurai," interrupted Yoritomo. "I know your career. You have always acted honorably, perhaps more honorably than most in the same situation. You should not be ashamed."

"Yet I am torn by guilt. I feel that my selfish love of the sword has caused pain and death to my loved ones."

"That, too, is the life of a soldier," said Yoritomo icily.

"I am a teacher, not a soldier," Yoshi continued inexorably. "I have vowed to Buddha and the Shinto gods that I will not raise my sword against another person unless I receive an unmistakable sign from the gods."

"I, Yoritomo, Lord of Kamakura, now give you that sign. You will lead my men in battle. That is an order." Yoritomo's lips pressed tightly together and he glared at Yoshi.

Yoshi dropped his head until his chin touched his chest. "I cannot accept your order. Ask anything else of me; it will be done. I cannot act against my vows."

Throughout their conversation, Yoshi had been evaluating Yoritomo. Was Yoritomo worthy of the Emperor's trust? Thus far, Yoshi would say yes. Yoritomo seemed a hard man . . . but honorable. Yoshi would wait before committing himself to a final judgment. Did Yoritomo have the power he claimed? Who were his allies?

Hojo Masa interjected softly, "Yoshi, do you realize there is a price on your head? Word comes from Kyoto that the Nii-Dono has offered a large reward in silver and land to the person who brings her your head or that of my lord."

"I did not know, but it does not change my vow."

Yoritomo looked disgusted. "The reward for our heads is the same. The difference is that I will fight that evil woman and the foul court that spawned her. Yoshi, I was told you were the bravest of men. I find you a coward. You ran from your responsibilities by craven surrender."

"I do what I must."

"I despise your attitude. You should be executed to prevent the spread of this madness to others . . . yet I owe you a debt for your past endeavors. I therefore grant you your life and will listen to any request or suggestion about your future."

Again Yoshi bowed his head to the floor, acknowledging Yoritomo's generosity. He felt calm and secure. The vow favored him. The gods, in their mysterious ways, saw fit to spare him from Yoritomo's wrath.

"I want to use my knowledge and abilities to train your samurai. I am an experienced sword master. My school in Sarashina has taught some of the best fighters in the land. Permit me to stay in Kamakura and develop a school of martial arts."

"Impossible," snapped Yoritomo. "I cannot allow a coward to teach my soldiers. That would set a bad example."

Yoshi bowed submissively. There was no hint on his face of the turmoil this announcement engendered. He had not thought of the possibility of Yoritomo's refusal. Where were the gods who looked out for him? He could not respond to the insults that Yoritomo heaped on his head; he had eschewed pride and would accept them. Yoshi knew he was not afraid; he also knew that the course he had set himself was more dangerous than the one he had rejected; he recognized that to some his vow would be evidence of weakness. Yet he had not expected so strong a reaction from the clan leader. Yoritomo called him a coward, and he had to accept it.

"*Hai,* yes," answered Yoshi. "I only wish to serve you in peace."

"What are we to do with you? You refuse our offer of a general's rank and insist on this craven course. To serve me in peace! You are a fool. I don't need men to serve me in peace. I need warriors, fighters, killers, not soft-spoken men of god. Go! Become a monk. Join the brotherhood of Amida and forget the strife of our world. You have no place among the warriors of the white flag."

Yoshi's eyes were fixed on the floor. "*Hai,*" he said.

Hojo Masa interjected once more. "With my lord's permission?"

Yoritomo nodded. He would be overjoyed to find a graceful way out of the dilemma that Yoshi's declaration had caused.

Hojo Masa spoke slowly, thinking as she said, "My lord,

you are faced with two problems that could be served by one solution."

"Yes, yes," said Yoritomo impatiently.

"Santaro came with a request from Kiso. Though you became angry with Santaro, you would like to honor the request if Kiso could be trusted."

"True, woman. Say what you have in mind."

"Use Yoshi to your advantage. He does not want to command the army, yet he declares devotion to our cause. I believe he is sincere. From what we have heard about Yoshi, he cannot be a coward..."

"Men change," snapped Yoritomo.

"I feel that is not true. Yoshi's refusal to fight takes great character. I believe he is as brave as he ever was... and perhaps, as the steel is tempered in a fine blade, he is stronger and more loyal than before."

Yoshi bent his head in agreement.

Yoritomo looked interested.

Hojo Masa continued, "Send Yoshi to Kiso's camp. Kiso fancies himself a fine strategist and in truth he is, but he sometimes lets his personal feelings overrule good sense. Commission Yoshi to act as his adviser, as our representative to Kiso's campaign, and as our spy. Perhaps Yoshi can prevent him from making impulsive mistakes."

Yoritomo rocked back on his heels. He pursed his lips in thought. Finally, he said, "You speak well, honorable wife. I would prefer that Yoshi be an active war leader, but I will not foolishly throw away an advantage out of pique." He stared at Yoshi for a long moment. "What say you to Hojo Masa's suggestion?" he asked.

Yoshi was interested. Whether the man they were sending him to was the same Kiso he had met or not, Yoshi would gain a firsthand opportunity to evaluate Yoritomo's most important ally. And he would have Yoritomo's support. Hojo Masa was proposing an honorable way for Yoshi to serve two masters.

"I will gladly represent you at his camp," said Yoshi. "Before we agree to this course, I ask one question."

"Ask."

"Is Kiso a narrow-faced warrior with deep-set eyes who commands a rough band of mountain men?"

"*Hai*, that describes him well."

"Then I foresee difficulties. Recently, I met him at Hikuma

and . . ." Yoshi briefly described his encounter. He ended by saying, ". . . while I have no animosity toward him, I warn you that he may not accept me."

Yoritomo actually chortled—a rare demonstration of feeling for him—during Yoshi's account. He said with good humor, "Your story confirms my decision. You will certainly remain loyal to me if you can stay alive. And if you were brave enough to face Kiso unarmed, I retract my accusation of cowardice. I will help you as much as I can, because I want you to succeed. You will be a commissioned general in my armies and carry with you a personal brief declaring you my full representative. Kiso will be warned that harming you will be tantamount to harming me. Help him strategically, but never trust him."

"I understand and accept," said Yoshi humbly.

"One more thing," added Yoritomo. "Kiso's weakness is that he often puts personal pride before good sense. He may ignore my edict and have you killed without regard for consequences. Can you accept that possibility?"

"I do accept."

"Namu Amida Butsu," chanted Yoritomo, calling on the help of the gods for one whose soul was close to departure.

twenty-nine

The sixth month had arrived. The first two days were busy for Yoshi. He was responsible for outfitting and organizing a thousand men. Santaro stood by, glowering for a good part of the time.

Yoritomo assigned General Yoshi a small private pavilion near the seashore. Yoritomo also offered a trio of personal retainers, an offer which Yoshi refused, saying, "I have my own loyal retainer. I need no others."

Meanwhile, Nami had started her period of defilement. She stayed in the pavilion, hidden from all eyes. Yoshi spoke to her through the screen that separated their rooms.

On the eve of the third day, Santaro, with no function except to observe Yoshi, spent his time in a tavern, drinking heavily. The camp had two small taverns for the amusement of off-duty soldiers. The soldiers were a rough crowd—more disciplined than Kiso's men when they were on duty, just as reckless and sensitive to insult in their free time. Brawls often ended their periods of drinking. The officers did not interfere. They felt the men needed this release of their energies. Occasionally good men were lost in these drunken brawls, but the survivors became better fighters as a result of the practice. The brawls sharpened the edge of their skills.

Yoshi searched for Santaro, to tell him of the departure plans; the group would leave Kamakura at the hour of the hare, six in the morning. Yoshi was directed to the tavern where Santaro could usually be found. Just as Yoshi arrived, a loud disturbance interrupted the quiet evening. A large armor-clad samurai burst through the latticework wall and fell to the street at Yoshi's feet.

Before the dust settled, he was followed by Santaro, who leaped through the shattered wall and landed in a crouch, with his hand on the pommel of his sword.

The large samurai had already rolled away—quickly, despite his armor—and drew his sword, cursing all the while.

Santaro's sword flashed out of its sheath and he circled the other, looking for an opening to attack. Both men were unsteady, but there was no mistaking their deadly intent.

Santaro snarled as he moved sideward, "You intentionally bumped me, you clumsy ape. Apologize or die."

The other man hissed an answer. "I did not see you, you inconsequential worm, but you will die for taking advantage of me when I was otherwise occupied. You could never have thrown me through the wall if I had not been busy with friends. It is you, O Ainu midget, who will die."

Santaro leaped forward, using his blade crosswise in a body attack. The suddenness of his move might have ended the battle right then except that drink made him miss his timing. His sword glanced from the big man's armor.

With a shout of rage, the other counterattacked with a dazzling display of the classic water-wheel pattern. Santaro fell back against the tavern's support post. The blade barely missed his head and sank into the hard wood.

Again, Santaro had his chance. He was glaring madly at his opponent, a froth of spittle on his beard, his chest heaving with strain. And again, the effects of the liquor took their toll. Santaro launched an attack while the big man's blade was trapped in the wood post. The attack never reached its goal; Santaro slipped on the dusty street and fell forward on his hands and knees.

The big man seized his opportunity and, abandoning his sword, jumped on Santaro's back. There was a loud whoosh of air leaving Santaro's lungs as the man's full weight drove Santaro flat on his face. Santaro was helpless. The big man straddled his back with a knee on each arm. He drew his short sword and pulled Santaro's head back, exposing his throat.

Santaro knew he was done. He gasped, *"Namu Amida Butsu,"* and prepared to die.

At that point Yoshi moved. Catlike, he sprang and locked a muscular forearm around the big man's throat, putting on pressure by flexing his other arm. The man's air was immediately shut off. He clawed at the powerful man that was inexorably crushing his larynx. His sword clattered to the street as he lost consciousness. Santaro rolled out from under him, climbed unsteadily to his feet, and raised his sword.

Yoshi spoke quickly in a tone that brought Santaro to a stop. "No!" he said. "I give you your life as a gift because I need you. This samurai fought bravely and would have killed you if I had not interfered. He will not die because of my action."

Santaro's red-rimmed eyes narrowed dangerously. He was armed and Yoshi was not. He hesitated. His befuddled mind raced; one stroke could remove the man whom he resented so deeply . . . but Yoshi had saved his life. Further, there was something about Yoshi's loose, relaxed stance that made him doubt if Yoshi could be killed that easily. Yoshi had bare-handedly attacked the samurai, who was armed and half again Yoshi's size. He had not been afraid then and he did not seem afraid now. The hairs on the back of Santaro's neck prickled. For the first time in a life filled with danger, Santaro understood the meaning of fear.

Santaro had heard that Yoshi refused to use his sword and therefore Santaro considered him a coward. The night's events changed his opinion.

The glare diminished. Santaro snapped his blade into its sheath and wiped the spittle from his beard with the back of his hand.

Yoshi watched him silently, knees slightly bent, arms hanging easily at his side. "Well?" he asked.

Santaro bowed. *"Hai,"* he said. "I owe you my life. Tell me what you want and it shall be done."

Yoshi returned the bow. "Come," he said. "We have business at camp. A thousand samurai wait to march in the morning. The packhorses are loaded, and every man is outfitted and ready."

"Thanks to your efforts."

"True. I have managed without your help, but now I need you. These men must respect Kiso and his commanders. You are their captain. I want you to take command and lead them to the mountain camp."

"You have prepared them; you deserve the honor of leading them."

"Santaro, I do not desire glory or power. Yoritomo has commissioned me to act as Kiso's adviser. I want nothing more. You will take charge until we reach camp."

"I have midjudged you, Tadamori Yoshi. You are more worthy than I. I am proud to act on your behalf. Consider me your friend and servant from this day on."

"Thank you, Santaro. I accept the honor of your friendship."

On the morning of the fourth day, a thousand mounted and armored samurai set out from Kamakura. They were followed by five hundred packhorses loaded with weapons and armor.

In the vanguard, resplendent in sky-blue armor with purple lacing, rode Okabe-no-Santaro. He rode a sleek white stallion armored and saddled in blue and gold. A white pennant flapped atop a long staff attached to the back of the saddle. Santaro wore a quiver with twenty-four war arrows on his back, two swords at his left hip, and a six-foot-long *naginata*, with its razor-sharp twelve-inch blade glinting fiercely in the morning sun, at his right side.

Yoshi, dressed in a brown hunting coat, without arms or armor, brought up the rear on his sorrel. Close behind him, his retainer led an extra packhorse.

Nami wore her wide-brimmed straw peasant hat and a loose over-robe of a plain dun-colored cotton. For the first few hours she rode silently. By now, the small army had moved far enough ahead to leave the two of them alone on the road. Nami dug her heels into the horse's flank and rode up alongside Yoshi.

> *"From Kamakura*
> *The hosts of Yoritomo*
> *March to Kiso's hills*
> *A thousand horses and men*
> *Bustling multicolored ants."*

Nami made the poem as a peace offering. Her defilement had ended the night before, but she had had no opportunity to communicate with Yoshi. Yoshi and Santaro had spent the night in last minute preparations for the morning march. Neither had slept during the night.

If Nami was to maintain the fiction of being Yoshi's retainer, she had to keep her place while they were in sight of the men. She spent the morning thinking about what she had said to Yoshi prior to her defilement. Yoshi had been so busy since that night, Nami was not sure if he had ignored her out of necessity or out of annoyance. She had recited the poem diffidently, waiting for his reaction. She would understand if he was angry with her, but she hoped her small offering would make peace between them.

Yoshi was lost in his own thoughts. When Nami joined him, he was momentarily startled. He appreciated the poem and Nami's intent. He had not understood her irritation when he went to pray at the Hachiman shrine, but he was happy to welcome back the sweet person he loved. He beamed at her and responded:

> *"The sun shines brightly*
> *In Omikami's heaven*
> *The last morning dew*
> *That dampened the early hours*
> *Evaporates from my sleeve."*

With this poem, he told her he had been saddened at being separated from her and he was happy she had offered her poem. He reached for her hand and squeezed it comfortingly.

"The trip has been difficult for you," he said. "Soon we will rest. Your disguise can be discarded once we get to Kiso's camp. Because I am Yoritomo's emissary, Kiso will not dare harm you."

Nami raised her brows quizzically. "Is this the same Kiso that tried to harm you at Hikuma?"

"Yes. From Yoritomo's description of him, I would say it is the same man."

"Are you sure he will honor Yoritomo's commission?"

"Absolutely," answered Yoshi, though he was not as positive as he tried to sound. He had considered leaving Nami at Kamakura for safety, but rejected the thought. He might be with Kiso for months if the campaign was drawn out. Nami would be safer with him, and anyway, he doubted if she would have obeyed an order to stay in Kamakura. She was tough-minded and independent. A few days ago, he had seen another and thornier side of her personality. He did not realize it was a temporary symptom that sometimes preceded her period of defilement.

"How long will we be on the road?" asked Nami.

"We camp in the foothills tonight. Tomorrow, Shinano province. Then Kiso's mountains. I estimate three or four days."

"I look forward to being with you tonight, my lord. Till then, I shall drop back to my place. The end of the column is in sight."

thirty

On the morning of the tenth day of the sixth month, blackbirds soared in circles through a brassy sky. The air was clear under the cloudless expanse, no breeze disturbed the atmosphere, and the faint calls of the birds were the only sounds. The mountains of the region of Kiso had been dry for over a week; the roads were dusty, and the grass already turned brown in patches.

Santaro's horse was covered with a gray film that rose from the road surface. He had been riding for over two hours with the advanced guard of Yoshi's reinforcement army when he met Kiso's sentries. He was immediately recognized and escorted to Kiso's tent.

Santaro left the quiet of the forest roads behind and entered a camp that was bustling with activity. Since Yukiie had returned in defeat from the battle of Sunomata River, Kiso had been driving his soldiers mercilessly. He realized that without field discipline his army would never achieve its goal.

In spite of early morning heat and oppressively still air, armorers and blacksmiths worked feverishly to expand the arms supply and ready the horses for a long campaign.

On one side of the camp, in a wide, dry field, mounted samurai practiced marksmanship, shooting arrows from the backs of galloping steeds. The quiet air was filled with the roll of hooves beating across the field. Swordsmen sweated in the early sun, dueling with wooden practice swords and exercising with live blades—draw, strike, parry, and sheath. The air was rent with varied sounds: steel on steel, wood on flesh, hooves on packed earth and, behind it all, the susurration of insects, birds, and small mountain animals disturbed by the activity of the camp.

Kiso's tent was large, almost empty of ornament. The main entrance flap opened on a bare, earth-floored area where war councils were held. The area was furnished with a circle of blankets around a low table. A pair of swords hung from a support pole over a war helmet with spreading golden horns.

A plain screen covered a separate section of the tent, where Kiso and Tomoe lived.

Santaro had been warned that discipline pervaded the camp. The informality to which he was accustomed was no longer tolerated. He was annoyed, but remembering his unfortunate experience with Yoritomo, decided to act formally.

When Santaro entered, Kiso was alone, kneeling on one of the blankets. Santaro heard movement behind the screen and assumed it was Tomoe. He adjusted his swords and knelt down across the table from Kiso.

"Okabe-no-Santaro, captain of the guards, reporting on my mission to Yoritomo," he announced.

Kiso nodded. His narrow face was intent as he studied Santaro wordlessly. He was thinking that Santaro had learned formality during his stay with Yoritomo. A good sign.

Though Kiso was eager to learn if Santaro's mission had been successful, he suppressed his impatience. He knew his own reputation for rashness and was acting now in a statesmanlike manner. With Tomoe's guidance, he was preparing himself to be ruler of the Empire. Kiso's ambition was limitless. He wanted to be declared *shogun,* military ruler of Japan, an honor that had not been bestowed on any leader in many generations.

"We had expected an earlier return," said Kiso.

"I was detained by Lord Yoritomo," said Santaro.

"A difficult man," said Kiso, thinking that one day he and his cousin would have a confrontation to decide who would lead the clan into the future. Kiso's voice was a harsh bark. Unable to maintain his pose of calm, he asked, "Did you get the men and arms I requested?"

"One thousand men and five hundred extra horses are on route in the mountain pass two hours behind me."

"Good, Santaro, good. Our campaign is almost ready to start. As soon as these new troops are integrated into our mountaineers, we will begin a drive that will not end till we reach Kyoto itself."

"Yoritomo demanded one condition."

"Condition?" Kiso's voice lowered to an ominous purr.

"He included an adviser with the troops."

"By Emma-Ō, I don't need a damn adviser."

"Yet, that is the condition Yoritomo set. His adviser holds the rank of general in the Kamakura army."

"Adviser is another way of saying spy!"

"That may be, but the thousand men have been directed to refuse your orders unless they are approved by Yoritomo's general."

"That son of a whore goes too far. We could attack the column and take the arms and supplies. We can continue our campaign without his thousand men."

Tomoe entered, stepping silently around the screen. "My lord, with your permission, I would speak . . ." Her dark features were impassive; the bold nose and strong jaw seemed carved of granite. Even in her loose warrior's shirt and *hakama* and with her hair cut short, she radiated sexuality; it stemmed from her direct gaze and the way she held her compact body.

"Not now," said Kiso.

"Now," she responded firmly. "Good morning," she said to Santaro.

"Ohayō gozaimasu," answered Santaro, using the polite form of address.

Tomoe nodded. "Santaro, while we three are alone, let us speak informally. You are one of our most trusted lieutenants. Next to me and Kiso's four kings, Imai, Tezuka, Jiro, and Taro, you are the highest-ranking officer in our army. I suggested sending you to Yoritomo. You are often headstrong and full of pride, but I believe you have the inner steel to be a fine commander."

Kiso interrupted. "Enough! What are you trying to say?"

"Just this. I trust Santaro's judgment. He rode with Yoritomo's general; he has an opinion of the man. Is he a spy? Will he help or harm our cause?"

Santaro bowed slowly. He addressed Kiso in measured words. "I owe the general my life. Through an act of foolishness, I placed myself in a position where I could have died. I would have deserved my fate. This man came forward and saved me by attacking an armed samurai with his bare hands. I tell you this so you will understand my position. My life is his, yet . . . you are my leader. I have sworn fealty to your cause and will serve you to the best of my ability."

"Yes, yes." Kiso was impatient. "Get on with it."

"The man is a spy. He was personally chosen by Yoritomo. His general's commission came only after he accepted the mission. We must accept that. Rumor has it that he is a master tactician and that he has no personal ambition. He can be trusted and will loyally serve you only as long as he believes you serve Yoritomo."

Tomoe broke in, "I think we can accept his being Yoritomo's man."

"Only as long as it suits me to serve Yoritomo. The day our interests diverge, this general..." Kiso sneered, "...will die."

Santaro bowed. He would never allow Yoshi to die at Kiso's hand. He had pledged his friendship and would honor it. When the time came, Yoshi would be warned and given his chance to escape.

Two hours later, the column of reinforcements rode into Kiso's camp. The men had cleared an area of their own and were setting up tents when Yoshi and Nami arrived with the last of the packhorses. A corral was built and the horses unloaded within the hour.

At two in the afternoon, the hour of the sheep, Yoshi was ushered into Kiso's tent by Santaro.

"Tadamori-no-Yoshi, general in the army of Minamoto Yoritomo," he announced.

Kiso was sitting opposite Tomoe, sipping from a flagon of sake. Kiso looked up. His face turned red, then gray veins stood out in sharp relief at his temples.

"You!" he snarled.

thirty-one

Yoshi knelt and touched his forehead to the ground. His manner was calm as befitted a general reporting to his supreme commander, respectful, yet at ease. There was no indication he recognized Kiso.

"I am representing the Kamakura headquarters," he said. "I am commissioned by Lord Yoritomo as general in the Minamoto armies. With me I bring a thousand fully equipped fighting men, plus five hundred horses laden with arms and armor, as a gift from our clan leader to Minamoto Yoshinaka, known as Kiso."

Kiso was speechless during this recitation. He finally managed to sputter, "Hikuma... you! You dare to come here. You..." He had difficulty bringing his voice under control. He glanced at the swords on the post; only Tomoe's restraining hand kept him in place. An inner voice told him it would be unwise to kill the spy now. But was it worthwhile to restrain himself? In time he intended to overthrow his cousin Yoritomo. However, at the start of a major campaign, a dispute with Yoritomo's representative would be ill-timed. To act would be satisfying, but premature.

"You are a spy for my cousin! Why should I accept you in my camp?" he rasped.

"Because I offer the men and arms that you need to further your plans."

"I can kill you and take them."

"As prisoners perhaps, but not as soldiers willing to fight under your banner."

"I will have enough arms to accomplish my purpose."

"You will have arms at the cost of the good will and allegiance of your cousin."

Tomoe held one hand firmly on Kiso's sleeve. She studied him anxiously. Normal color had returned to his face; the veins had subsided. He seemed once again in control of his emotions. Tomoe judged he could be trusted for the moment.

Tomoe remembered the expression on Kiso's face when she

had cut him free from the tree in Hikuma. The moment she heard Kiso say *Hikuma*, she realized Yoshi was the man responsible for humiliating him. She knew Kiso would never forget or forgive that incident. When he had the opportunity, he would kill Yoshi, no matter how much the murder would cost him politically.

Men are children, Tomoe thought. For abstract concepts like honor and revenge they would renounce a kingdom. Well, that was why Kiso needed her: to remind him when discretion was called for. If Yoshi must die, so be it, but he would die at a time and place of her choosing.

She felt Yoshi's questioning stare and returned it. As her dark eyes met his, she felt an emotional attraction she seldom experienced. She broke the eye contact. "I am Tomoe Gozen, aide to Lord Kiso," she said.

Yoshi acknowledged her introduction. "I heard much about your exploits while I was in Kamakura," he said. "Your reputation is widely known."

"Then you know I am to be taken seriously," she said flatly, then added with a note of exasperation, "You came alone to our camp, General Yoshi. Surely you realize we would remember you from our recent encounter. You are either a very brave man or a fool."

"I am neither, Tomoe Gozen. I serve the Emperor and my leader Yoritomo. I come unarmed and will not be a threat. I trust the gods to look after me because I have sworn not to serve evil. I respect your judgment enough to trust you with my life."

Tomoe said, "It may be that you are neither brave nor a fool; the only other possibility is that you are touched with madness." Tomoe shook her head slightly, as though unable to comprehend Yoshi's motives. Perhaps he was not so naïve, she thought. Perhaps, he had a cadre of soldiers prepared at this moment to come to his rescue. She hoped that was the case; Tomoe was drawn to him and did not want to believe he was the madman he appeared. "You came alone?" she asked.

"I have only one other person with me."

Kiso took over. "Another spy!" he snapped. "Who is he? Why did he not present himself to me?"

"Lord Kiso. My companion awaits my command to appear. Send a messenger to my tent and you will have the opportunity to meet with both of us."

Kiso turned to Santaro who had been kneeling silently at

one side. "Go to General Yoshi's tent. Bring his companion to us immediately."

Kiso fell silent, glaring at Yoshi from under knitted brows. Tomoe Gozen tried to engage him in polite conversation. "You were in the capital until recently. How was the political climate of the court?"

"As usual," Yoshi answered perfunctorily.

"Did you attend Taira Kiyomori's funeral?"

"Yes."

"How does Go-Shirakawa regard the new Taira clan leader, Munemori?"

"Munemori is a weakling."

"Without a strong clan leader, how can the Taira hope to prevail? Are they not foolish to allow themselves to lose the Empire?"

"Yes, Tomoe Gozen."

Kiso said impatiently, "Munemori is an empty vessel. His brother Shigehira is young, but he is a soldier. Shigehira will eventually lead their clan. The Taira's only hope is with him."

"Perhaps you are right," said Yoshi.

"Of course I'm right. The balance of power is shifting. The monks are no longer important. Now there are three power blocs in the Empire: me, Yoritomo, and the Taira family. If the Taira are discounted because of Munemori, the struggle to control the Emperor will be between Yoritomo and me."

"An excellent analysis," said Yoshi, and bowed his head.

Santaro pushed aside the tent flap. He wore a strange wondering expression on his bearded face and seemed hesitant about announcing the new arrival. He was almost apologetic as he said, "General Yoshi's retainer requests permission to enter."

Kiso nodded for him to usher in the retainer.

Even Yoshi was stunned. Nami had taken the opportunity to shed her coarse retainer's clothing and dress herself in her finest costume. Her face was powdered white and smooth as the pale moon; her eyebrows floated above her natural brow line in soft painted brush strokes; her long hair was brushed and glossy, hanging straight from a center part to be caught in a mauve ribbon at her back. Nami wore a lilac robe that featured a willow pattern and contrasted with the vari-hued turquoise shifts that peeped out at sleeve and hem. Around her wafted an aura of sensuous perfume, heady yet pure. The diminutive retainer who had arrived in rags at Kiso's camp a short time ago was gone.

Kiso's eyes widened; the tip of his tongue wet suddenly dry lips. He had never seen so beautiful a woman. For years, he had been surrounded by warriors who were more concerned with fighting than with cleanliness or appearance. Even Tomoe Gozen, beautiful in her way, had always been disinterested in the outward aspects of femininity. He loved Tomoe. He depended on her. A feeling of guilt and disloyalty stirred in his breast; he realized Tomoe smelled like the camp samurai, and her strong-featured, unpainted face was coarse and unrefined compared to the beauty that faced him. Nami was a vision of another world, another, more gracious, time and place.

A silence followed Nami's entrance. She stepped forward lightly and stopped at Yoshi's side, about five feet from where Kiso and Tomoe knelt behind the low table. She waited silently for Kiso to speak.

Yoshi, who had not moved from his kneeling position, watched Kiso through half-closed eyes. He had noticed the look of avid sensuality on Kiso's face.

Tomoe glanced sideways and caught Kiso's expression too. Her face showed none of the feelings that tore at her heart. She felt crude and unfinished. She, who prided herself on her femininity, felt dirty and ugly. She was engulfed in a sea of conflicting emotions. Her confusion was compounded by the attraction she felt toward Yoshi. This artificial doll was Yoshi's woman. Though Tomoe had not seriously entertained thoughts of a sexual relationship with Yoshi, she despaired at the thought of Yoshi's comparing her to this woman. She ran her fingers over her rough cotton shirt, over the holes, over the stiffened spots. She wanted to cry. She was dirty!

Without volition, Tomoe felt her cheeks turn red. She fought the rush of blood and ground her teeth in an attempt to maintain her composure. She was a warrior! Damn all men to Yomi! She would not allow them to see her in a moment of weakness.

She managed a tone of scorn in her voice. "Is this your retainer, General Yoshi?"

"This is my retainer, and soon to be my wife. Circumstances have made it impossible for us to complete the formal ceremony," said Yoshi.

Nami's face glowed under her white powder. She spoke in a thin bell-like tone. "I am called Nami. I am honored to greet you in my name and that of my future husband. I must explain that in our eyes we are married. The formal ceremony will come when we are settled."

Indicating Nami's court finery with a deprecatory wave of the hand, Tomoe blurted, "How did you get here dressed like this?"

Yoshi answered proudly, "This was my retainer. She rode with me and acted on my behalf as well as any man. Without her, my bones would be whitening in the forest of Hikuma. Nami, my love, you have already met Lord Kiso Yoshinaka. Now, may I present his aide, the brave samurai warrior Tomoe Gozen."

Nami bowed with heart-stopping delicacy and acknowledged the introductions with a smile that completely captivated Kiso and even made a start toward charming Tomoe.

So, Tomoe thought, this fragile creature actually rode the mountains with Yoshi. And she was the one who foiled Kiso at Hikuma. Perhaps there is more to her than appears on the surface. All at once, Tomoe wanted to take Nami aside and talk with her. She had not talked with a woman since childhood. She wanted to ask Nami about her makeup, her robes, her color choices, her perfume, her life in the capital. These were subjects that had never before interested her, but if Kiso's campaign was successful, the next year would see her in Kyoto. She felt a flutter of apprehension; in Kyoto she would be surrounded by women who dressed and smelled like Nami; she would be the odd one, and the court ladies would sneer and hold her in contempt.

Again, the urge to cry was strong. She had learned to ride and fight like a man; she would now have to learn to dress and smell like a woman.

Until this realization came to her, Tomoe felt jealous and threatened by Nami. Now she perceived the threat was not Nami. Nami seemed pleasant, with a delicate beauty that even Tomoe could appreciate and admire. The problem was Kiso. Tomoe studied Kiso; he was enchanted by Nami! Tomoe recognized blatant desire, desire that would give Kiso one more reason to hate Yoshi and want him dead. Without Yoshi, Kiso would think Nami was his to take.

Tomoe pressed her lips together. She would have to prevent Kiso from having his way. While Nami and Yoshi were at camp, Tomoe would be their protector, and Yoshi would live.

"I seem to have no choice," said Kiso in a hard voice. "My cousin Yoritomo expects me to accept you as an adviser. My better judgment tells me to kill you now . . . however, there are many things to be considered." He stared pointedly at Nami.

"I will try to make use of you, General Yoshi. I'm not sure what value there is in a man who refuses to wear a sword. Captain Santaro says you are brave. Tomoe suggests you are mad. Well ... I am open-minded, and I make you welcome to my camp." He swiveled from Yoshi to Nami to Tomoe and to Santaro, who had remained to one side without speaking throughout the interview. Kiso nodded thoughtfully and added, "Welcome for the time being. Captain Santaro, pour our new general a cup of sake."

thirty-two

On the fifteenth day of the eighth month, the "good people" of Kyoto awoke to find themselves pressed under a blanket of hot moist air. The silver willows that lined Suzaku-Ōji trailed limp green streamers. The soft rustle that usually sounded from the cherry trees of the commercial ward was missing; they were silent without a breeze to stir their branches.

In the older parts of the city, especially along the western wall, heat made the usually faint stench of rotting garbage and old sewage almost unbearable.

On sweltering days like this, people who had no important business stayed in the cool, shadowed interiors of their homes, trying to capture a breeze through wide-open shutters.

There were many in the capital whose duties made it imperative they suffer bravely through the heat. On this day, the dutiful ones included Taira Munemori; his mother, the Nii-Dono; and a large entourage of courtiers, ladies, officers of the Palace Guard, and Imperial councillors. They formed a parade at Rokuhara palace and started out just after dawn. Tsukiyomi's face was visible as a perfect circle in the washed blue sky. The sun was just rising over the eastern horizon as the oxcarts, palanquins, and mounted horsemen rumbled across the Fifth Street Bridge.

The Kamo River was a stagnant gray ribbon that gurgled lazily under the marchers. A dead fox floated directly beneath the bridge, surrounded by an oily film of body fluids. In the absence of current, the fox stayed almost stationary instead of floating downstream. The odor of decay rose strongly enough to make the marchers cover their mouths and noses with perfumed kerchiefs.

This was the morning of the "Great Liberation," a mass release of animals, birds, and fish that had been captured during the year and held for the occasion. The ceremony's origins had been forgotten by most of the court. Only Munemori and a few other highly educated courtiers knew the animals were released as retribution for past excesses of the Emperor's army. Many years ago, the god of the Hachiman shrine at Usa decreed that an annual Imperial procession would travel to the Iwashimizu shrine. There, the courtiers would release captive animals to their natural habitats to atone for the past slaughter of thousands of aborigines.

So every member of the parade—on foot, on horse, or in carts—carried a basket, bowl, or cage. The captives included dogs, cats, foxes, monkeys, nightingales, cuckoos, blackbirds, tortoises, frogs, goldfish, and carp.

Heat waves shimmered from the road as the sun rose higher and the blue sky turned to brassy yellow. The route was eight miles from Rokuhara to the shrine.

Munemori rode in a large palanquin with his mother. He stared sightlessly through the shutters. He was not happy. Why, he wondered, must he be made to suffer? It was not the heat and discomfort of the pilgrimage—bumpy roads through the marshlands south of Kyoto, mosquitos, and blackflies rising in clouds to pierce, suck, and bite. No. The pilgrimage was a duty and he accepted duty without complaint; ceremony was often uncomfortable and inconvenient, but he had been trained for it. Munemori's unhappiness was caused by the demands of his generals...and the threats of his enemies. He was ill-prepared for the problems they offered.

Taira Munemori had been trained to take over the reins of government. Although he lacked a knowledge of warfare and the ability to handle political intrigue, he wrote graceful calligraphy, he composed charming poems, his choices of color combinations were impeccable, and he played the koto, flute, and samisen better than most.

His father, Kiyomori, had been in charge of the martial arts; his mother took care of court politics. If the country had remained at peace, he would not need those barbaric arts. Munemori felt it a personal affront that the gods had not seen fit to maintain the peace.

Why must this happen to me? he asked himself when he received reports of thousands dying of famine, plague, or battle.

And his mother! She constantly harped at him. Her shrill voice reverberated in his head. Was anyone else ever so cursed? Why didn't the old woman know her place? He often thought her quite insane.

Now Kiso, may Emma-Ō claim him, threatened the capital from the north. Reports arrived daily that Kiso was running rampant through the *hokurikudo*, the northern provinces.

Munemori had reached such a pitch of frustration and irritation that he refused to accept any more reports from the *hokurikudo*.

Last night had been the final irony. A spy had reported to the Nii-Dono that the accursed traitor Yoshi was Kiso's adviser. Munemori winced; his mother had been acting strangely since his father's death. When she heard Yoshi's name, she became violent. This was a burden more onerous than any man should be expected to bear.

Munemori became aware that the piercing voice was not in his imagination. His mother was again reviling him for being unable to capture and behead either Yoshi or Yoritomo. The Nii-Dono sat opposite him, her small thin body hunched forward over a wicker basket containing a cat. Hanging over her head was a birdcage too small for its captive owl; a ceramic bowl with a pair of goldfish was at her side.

"Yoshi is Yoritomo's arm," she was saying. "Yoritomo sits safely in Kamakura because Yoshi does his evil work. Your father is unsettled in the afterworld because we have not carried out his death wish. Kill Yoshi and flush out his master. If you bring me the head of one, I predict you will soon have the head of the other."

Munemori did not answer. His soft white face turned to the shutters.

"Have you nothing to say?" snarled the Nii-Dono. Her deep-set eyes had sunk even further into their sockets since Kiyomori's death. That, combined with her powdered white face and blackened teeth, made her resemble a death's head. "The gods have given you to me as my instrument of revenge. Weak as you are, I need you. Listen to me and act!"

"Mother, I have the spy's report. He claims Yoshi renounced the sword. He will not fight. He has lost his courage. Let us forget Yoshi. He is no longer a threat."

"You are even a greater fool than you appear. How is it that I am cursed with so useless a son?" The Nii-Dono's voice rose to a scream of rage. "Yoshi is more dangerous without a sword than with one. When he used the sword, we kept him busy protecting himself. Now he uses his brains and is ten times as dangerous. There are ten thousand swords at his command, and he will see us dead if we do not act promptly."

"Ten thousand? You exaggerate."

"If he had ten swords, ten would be too many. Kiso has already swept Shinano, Mino, and Wakasa. He is moving north through Echizen, and if he is not stopped by our armies, he will soon also control Kaga, Etchu, and Echigo."

"Mother, today is not the day to discuss Kiso," said Munemori, placing a plump hand on his forehead to ease the pain that was starting to pound behind his eyes.

"When then, child? When Kiso controls the *hokurikudo?* When his armies have doubled? Tripled?"

"What can I do?" moaned Munemori.

"While we are alone and before you become involved in today's ceremonies, I want you to make an important decision."

"Yes, Mother. Yes, yes."

"In the palanquin behind us rides Jō Sukenaga, lord of Echigo. He came to observe the liberation and tonight's moon-viewing ceremonies. Kiso and Yoshi are approaching his home province; it will be to his interest to see that they go no further."

"Why tell me this?"

"Foolish one! You will appoint Jō Sukenaga official chastiser of Kiso. Sukenaga controls four thousand skilled warriors in Echigo. We will lend him whatever other troops are available. Send him into Echizen immediately and let him destroy Kiso before he crosses the Hino River."

"Yes," whimpered Munemori. "Of course I will do that. That is what I had in mind. Jō Sukenaga will bring us Yoshi's head."

"Exactly," said the Nii-Dono smugly. She leaned back, disturbing the owl, who awkwardly tried to flutter his wings in the small cage and, failing this, uttered a small desolate hoot.

By midday, the heat was unbearable. Sunshades and portable pavilions had been set up in the fields across from the shrine. Courtiers, officials, and ladies dispiritedly waved fans in front of their faces. Several women who had been forced to sit behind screens fainted from the heat.

Munemori took pride in his ability to perform his state functions without outward signs of discomfort. This was the lot of a clan leader and he bore it bravely.

Munemori joined the priests and led the recitation of the Supreme Sovereign Sutra, then he maintained his position during the counting of the animals to be liberated. As each animal was released, it was announced with the name of its liberator. Panic-stricken birds flew, and animals fled in every direction.

Munemori held his place throughout the ceremony. Four hundred and twelve birds, beasts, and fish were freed under the auspices of three hundred and twenty-seven donors. How could anyone doubt his moral character, strength, or fitness as leader, mused Munemori. His face was as expressionless as that of a wax Buddha as he made the final announcement: There would be a program of dances in the field and, after the dances, a series of wrestling bouts.

A ragged cheer rose from the crowd of pilgrims.

Munemori marched to his palanquin. The moment he was behind the shutters, he fell to his knees and sobbed uncontrollably. He was paying the price for his stoicism in the field.

By the hour of the monkey, the sun was well past its zenith, shadows had lengthened, and a soft breeze stirred the dusty field. Munemori wiped his body with scented cloths and changed his mauve outer robe for one of coral red. He sent a retainer to Jō Sukenaga with an invitation to attend him at the shaded pavilion reserved for the Nii-Dono's family.

Jō Sukenaga was a large, gruff warrior. After having served the Emperor in the field and at the court, he had been granted his estates in Echigo by Taira Kiyomori. During Sukenaga's service at Kyoto, his skills at poetry, perfume-smelling, and calligraphy had won him the court's approval. There was no person in the Empire who spoke ill of him. As lord of Echigo, he had earned a reputation as a hard but fair landowner. As *Daimyo*, he treated his people as fairly as he treated his family. He loved his principal wife, his son, and three daughters, but he maintained a formal presence with them. His children thought him stern and unbending. He accepted that. It was part of his position as *Daimyo* of extensive estates. Sukenaga's soldiers were well trained and among the best in the provinces. Echigo had provided well for him. The fertile protected valleys of the province produced more than enough grain for the local inhabitants even when famine threatened the rest of the country.

Sukenaga was a stern disciplinarian. He set high standards for himself and accepted no less from his followers.

He entered the Taira pavilion as quietly as full battle dress allowed. Despite the discomfort, he had dressed in his green and gold formal armor, as a mark of respect to the clan leader. He held his horned helmet in his hands as he entered the main hall of the pavilion. He was surprised to see the Nii-Dono kneeling on a wooden platform at Munemori's side. His sense of propriety was offended. Surely, he thought, this is no place for a woman.

He glanced at her disapprovingly, then, ignoring her, he

said to Munemori, "I am Jō Sukenaga, lord of Echigo, commander of the armies of the *hokurikudo* by order of the former *Daijo-Daijin*, Taira Kiyomori." With this formal announcement, he bowed and knelt on the earth floor before the wooden dais.

"Lord Echigo, you have served our cause for many years," said Munemori in a whiny sing-song. "My father, before he died, commended you to my attention. 'Give Jō Sukenaga responsibility,' he said. 'He will never disappoint you.' I want to give you more than just responsibility; I want to give you rewards."

Sukenaga raised his brows imperceptibly. He could hear the roar of the crowd outside the pavilion as they cheered their sumo champions to victory. He felt the oppressive heat through the canvas roof of the pavilion. He smelled the odor of sweet flowers wafting from the platform. With all this, he felt silent and alone, cut off from humanity. He thought Munemori and his mad mother could only mean evil to an old warrior. He wished he could have rejected the invitation and ridden off, as his instincts had suggested.

"Rewards?" he asked wryly. "Rewards for what?"

"Yes, yes," Munemori answered. "Ten thousand more *cho* of Imperial lands."

"What must I do for this reward?"

"I ask nothing that is not in your own interests. Kiso Yoshinaka is riding roughshod through the northern provinces. His army is already nearing the Hino River in central Echizen, on the route to your castle. The army is destroying or confiscating everything in its path. I commission you to stop him before he reaches Echigo. Bring us his head and the head of his adviser, Yoshi."

"I have four thousand men in Echigo," said Sukenaga. "A messenger must be sent to warn them. No matter how fast the messenger travels, the trip will take time. My son is in charge of the samurai and will act once the message reaches him, but it will take several more days before he can organize and march the men south to face Kiso."

"We will put four thousand of our own Imperial guards under your command. They are fully trained and armed, ready to march on an hour's notice."

"My duty is clear," said Sukenaga. "I will stop Kiso in Echizen."

"We each have our duty to perform. Yours is no more

onerous than mine," said Munemori. "As men of honor, we accept our duty and do our best."

The Nii-Dono spoke for the first time. "Well said, my son," she said, then addressed Sukenaga in a chilling hiss. "Bring us Yoshi's head. That is the most important part of your mission."

Jō Sukenaga rose and bowed. His face was impassive. Inside, he felt a tremor of fear, of foreboding. He shook off the feeling and backed out of the pavilion. These Taira were right. He had to accept the fact that Kiso was conquering the northern provinces. He had ignored the obvious too long and must now take a stand. As he came to this conclusion, a well-ordered plan came to mind. He, Jō Sukenaga, would lead four thousand Imperial guards against Kiso. They would drive Kiso farther north. Meanwhile, a messenger to his home castle in far off Echigo would alert his son to bring his own troops south. They would crush Kiso between the two forces. If he timed the two armies properly, he could not fail. It would be a simple military operation.

thirty-three

The beginning of the ninth month found Kiso's army camped on the north bank of the Hino River in the province of Echizen. The weather was warm and dry. Crops were dry and dead in the fields; rice paddies were vast flats. If rain did not come soon, the northern provinces would turn to desert before the end of the year.

For two weeks, the daytime sky had been like a bowl of molten metal as the dusty army marched through the *hokuri-kudo*, adding starving peasants to its ranks.

Kiso announced that he now commanded over ten thousand men. Yoshi knew the number was actually less than five thousand and that a thousand of those were untrained farmers and laborers who had joined them on their march.

The army encampment was a disorderly sprawl of tents and lean-tos that extended from the north bank of the Hino River to the shadow of the rocky cliff on the western end of the flat area enclosed by the curve of the river. The blacksmiths had already set up their forges, their fires adding smoke and more heat to the already stifling day. Horses wandered in the underbrush, scraping the ground for sustenance.

Inside his headquarters tent, Kiso knelt on a blanket, facing a circle of his officers; this was Kiso's war council. Tomoe knelt at his left; Imai, Tezuka, Jiro, and Taro were on Kiso's right. The *shi-tenno*, the four kings, as they were called, had served Kiso from his earliest days and were ready to die for him.

Yoshi and Santaro knelt shoulder to shoulder, facing Kiso from the opposite side of the circle. Yukiie and four other samurai officers completed the council.

Kiso spoke. "Scouts report that Jō Sukenaga leads a large force from Kyoto. My spies report he has been ordered to chase and destroy us."

"Do the scouts know how many men Sukenaga commands?" asked Imai.

"They estimate close to five thousand, mostly Imperial

191

guards, plus a few farmers that Sukenaga has conscripted during his march." Kiso paused and added, "They are within two days of our present position."

Yukiie shifted nervously, his obese body quivering as he settled in place. He wiped his brow with a scented kerchief. "Can we avoid contact? Can we continue north until they are weakened by the shortage of food?"

"Uncle," Kiso said, staring coldly across the circle, "they have the Imperial mandate. Jō Sukenaga has more resources than we have. Our troops have been in the field for well over two months. We need rest and time to reprovision. These are good reasons not to run, but more importantly, I do not like the idea of flight."

Yukiie avoided Kiso's glare. His voice was tremulous, his lisp more pronounced than usual. "Nephew, Jō Sukenaga outnumbers us. As you yourself say, our men are tired and hungry. Wouldn't discretion be wiser than bravado?"

"Your defeat at the Sunomata River colors your thinking. We will not be ambushed as you were." Kiso dismissed Yukiie contemptuously. "Imai, what do you think?"

Imai, who had been staring at Yoshi, snapped his attention back to the council. He spoke slowly at first. His voice grew louder and the words spilled out faster as he continued. "You are right, Kiso. General Yukiie suggests flight too quickly. We must stand and fight if for no other reason than our pride and reputation. Our army grows in size as we travel farther north; the men who have joined us would desert if they believed we were weak." By now Imai was almost shouting. "Our strength . . . your strength . . . draws them to our cause!"

"Then you advise a stand on this spot?"

"More than that." Imai's eyes gleamed. "I say we show our true strength. Turn back and attack Sukenaga's troops while they march."

Tezuka, Jiro, and Taro applauded Imai's suggestion, and in moments many of the war council cheered with approval.

"Spoken like a samurai."

"Bravo, Imai. Bravo, Kiso."

"Kill the Taira. Wipe out Jō Sukenaga."

"Face them man to man, blade to blade."

Kiso nodded happily. These were his kind, born warriors. Suddenly, his eyes narrowed and his face hardened. Two of the council were silent. Yukiie and Yoshi. An incongruous pair . . . but maybe not so incongruous? Kiso wanted to believe that Yoshi was less a man than he appeared. If he were, Nami would see that a true warrior, Kiso himself, would make her happier than the man she had chosen. He prepared to relish this moment; Yoshi was showing himself to be a craven coward.

Kiso raised a hand until the generals quieted.

"We have two among us who do not agree with Imai's plan," he said with a sneer. "Two old ladies who fear the power of the sword; who are afraid to face the enemy; who would run and hide in cowardly shame."

Santaro, who had cheered with the others, drew away from Yoshi, looking at him with disappointment.

Imai studied Yoshi with disgust.

Tomoe felt the unhealthy undercurrent of conflict that had rumbled beneath the surface since Yoshi's arrival. Kiso and Imai hated Yoshi; that was obvious. Kiso ogled Nami at every opportunity, and Imai—loyal to his foster-brother—constantly sought ways to provoke Yoshi. Tomoe felt that if not for her presence, Kiso would already have killed Yoshi and taken Nami for his own. Tomoe would not allow that to happen. Though she had become fond of Nami—her first female friend—Kiso was hers and she would not share him. Her mind raced as she tried to think of ways to avoid a dispute.

Yukiie flushed under the goad of Kiso's words. His nephew's slurs were unforgivable, but Yukiie knew where the power lay. He could not afford to openly defy his nephew. He squirmed unhappily.

Yoshi seemed unmoved. His face remained impassive, as though he had not heard the insults.

"I have no need to prove my manhood," Yoshi said slowly into the painful silence that had descended over the council. "I am the representative of Lord Yoritomo. As military adviser, I am charged with the responsibility of helping you to victory." Yoshi paused to see what effect his words had on the war council. He had their complete attention. He concentrated on Kiso and continued. "I applaud the brave intentions of General Imai, but I would rather ensure victory by careful preparation than lose the day out of foolish pride. Jō Sukenaga is an able general, a warrior who has a reputation for bravery and intelligence. To send our men against his superior numbers would guarantee our destruction. Jō Sukenaga can only be beaten by subtlety and tactics." Yoshi paused.

Kiso watched him carefully, weighing every word.

Imai blurted, "We are soldiers. We don't need women's

tricks and 'tactics' . . ." He drew out the last word as though it were an obscenity. ". . . to win. I say—"

Kiso interrupted coldly, "Quiet! Let Yoshi speak his mind."

Imai looked at his foster-brother as though he had been betrayed. His mouth opened in shock. "I . . ."

"Wait, I said!" Kiso glared to silence Imai. He nodded to Yoshi. "Go on," he said. "What is your suggestion?"

"Jō Sukenaga rides from Kyoto at the head of Munemori's soldiers. Do not forget that he is also lord of Echigo and commands almost five thousand more. Your scouts report Sukenaga is two days behind us. My guess is that he is pushing his troops to the utmost in his haste to catch up to us. If we run north, as General Yukiie suggests, we would trap ourselves between the Imperial guards and Sukenaga's own soldiers from Echigo. At this moment, his advance riders must have alerted Echigo that we are moving toward them. If Jō Sukenaga's reputation is to be believed, he plans to crush us between Munemori's hammer and his Echigo anvil."

Yoshi looked around Kiso's war council, studying each in turn. He said, "I estimate it will take at least five more days before the Echigo soldiers reach this camp. If we go north, we will meet them just as Sukenaga overtakes us."

"We agree that my uncle's plan to run north is a poor one, yet I see merit in General Imai's suggestion. What do you offer in its stead?"

"Not to race blindly to destruction in the south. No. I propose that we take a lesson from General Yukiie's debacle at the Sunomata River."

On the twenty-fifth day of the fourth month, Yukiie had been ambushed by a Taira force when he drove his men through the Sunomata River in what he thought was a surprise attack. The Taira had been forewarned and were ready to kill any soldier with wet armor. Yukiie fled back to Kiso, abandoning his troops to their fate. The shame was made worse because Kiso had specifically ordered him not to engage the enemy.

Yukiie took insults from Kiso, but this interloper had no right . . . Yukiie turned red with embarrassment, then purple with rage. His fat face threatened to explode. "How dare you!" he sputtered.

"Keep quiet, Uncle," said Kiso, secretly enjoying Yukiie's discomfort. "You were beaten by an inferior force because of your stupidity in not following orders."

Yukiie rose heavily to his feet. He straightened his robe in an attempt to restore his dignity. "You go too far, nephew," he hissed and waddled rapidly from the tent.

One of the samurai snickered. Kiso's hard glance froze him to silence. Kiso's shoulders tensed and he said in a menacing tone, "Yukiie is my uncle. Regardless of what I do or say, there is no excuse for you not to pay him proper respect."

There was an uncomfortable silence until Kiso nodded to Yoshi.

"We are comfortably camped on the northwest bank of the river. The river bends around us, forming a natural moat on three sides. Consider our position: The hills are almost a quarter of a mile behind us and are steep and rocky; they form an impassable wall to protect our rear; before Jō Sukenaga can reach us, we must move our tents there; and before he is joined by his northern host, we must prepare a series of surprises using the advantages of the terrain."

thirty-four

The next two days were busy for Kiso's men. Under Yoshi's direction, trees were cut down and three-foot-high barriers were built to angle in from the river banks, making a quarter-mile funnel along which the enemy would be guided. The log barriers were disguised with thorn bushes. There was much cursing as well as good-humored joking among the soldiers who uprooted and transplanted the bushes.

The best place to ford the river was at the bend of the U, and anyone crossing there would see a hundred-yard-wide path bordered by low bushes ahead. The path led to a cluster of empty tents set at the foot of a rocky hill. Wood fires sent lazy swirls of smoke up above the trees; the smoke drifted in the brassy sky, a signal visible for several miles. The actual encampment of the service troops was concealed to the right of the thorny barricades.

Santaro worked along with the troops. Sweat ran down his face, soaking his beard. His body was covered with scratches and smears of dirt, but he was happy carrying out Yoshi's orders.

Yoshi was a constant source of surprise. Santaro wanted to believe in him. When Yoshi had saved his life, he had pledged his friendship. Yet . . . after two months in Kiso's camp, Yoshi had made no other friends.

For two months Yoshi had antagonized Imai. That took courage, thought Santaro, but it was a grave mistake. Imai was a deadly enemy to have. And Imai's sister . . . Tomoe. Santaro wondered if Kiso saw changes in her. Santaro had served in the field with Tomoe for over five years and regarded her as another samurai fighter, no different from Jiro, Taro, Tezuka, or Imai. How strange to see her in Nami's tent, wearing a silk kimono, her hair brushed and her face powdered.

Santaro guided the placement of a log, helping balance it in place. As he worked, he saw Kiso inspecting the work. Imai was at his side. Yukiie, attended by a young soldier, walked behind them. Kiso seemed discontent. Santaro thought he

understood what Kiso was thinking: If the plan worked, Yoshi
would get credit; if it failed, Kiso's army and his ambitions
would be destroyed.

Santaro straightened from his task and blew out a deep
breath. He wiped his forehead with a grimy paw and studied
the inspection party as they moved toward the tents and dummy
fires. Santaro's expression was grim. He would have to warn
Yoshi to be careful. Whichever way the battle went, Yoshi had
two deadly enemies in Kiso and Imai. No...three. Yukiie
hated him too; Yukiie accepted abuse from Kiso, but he would
never forgive Yoshi for reminding the council of his disastrous
defeat at Sunomata River. Yukiie was more devious than the
other two, and no less dangerous.

Jō Sukenaga rode astride a black-spotted white stallion. His
armor was decorated in green and gold and laced with leather
thongs. He wore a golden helmet with a flared neckpiece and
spreading metal horns, two swords through his *obi*, and a quiver
of white-tipped arrows on his back. His saddle was gold, with
painted green dragons. Riding behind him, a retainer carried
the red banner of the Taira and Sukenaga's personal banner,
with its white crest on a field of green.

Sukenaga had pushed his troops mercilessly since they left
Kyoto. He had been sure Kiso would continue to drive north
toward Echigo, and his plan had been to engage Kiso's army
two days later and sixty miles farther north than their last
reported camp. Reports from his scouts confused him. Apparently Kiso had decided to make a stand in Echizen. He frowned.
Reinforcements coming from Echigo were three days away.
The more than four thousand top fighting men, under the command of his only son, would arrive too late to join the battle.
However, he felt he had enough Imperial troops to overwhelm
Kiso's badly trained forces without the additional help.

Jō Sukenaga was a professional. Although he had not been
in the field in recent years, he had the professional's contempt
for amateur warriors. Kiso's army was a rabble. He respected
Kiso for what he had accomplished in the *hokurikudo,* and he
had heard good reports about his adviser, Yoshi. However,
they could not have had enough time to turn the farmers and
laborers who joined their army into real fighting men. He was
uneasy because Kiso had not acted predictably. Kiso was hot-
headed. If he did not run from the Imperial forces, he should

have turned toward them and taken the initiative. Something was not as it should be.

Sukenaga squared his shoulders and spurred his horse faster. There was no need to delay. He would teach those mountaineers a lesson. Unfortunately, they would not live to benefit from it.

Part of Sukenaga's confidence stemmed from the Taira's having won almost every major battle in the past thirty-five years. Since Kiyomori's victories in the Hōgen and Heiji insurrections, the Taira had consistently outmanned, outmaneuvered, and defeated their Minamoto counterparts. True, last year's flight of Koremori and Saito Sanemori from Yoritomo was a setback, but even then it had not been Yoritomo who had sent Koremori in flight, but his own inexperience.

Jō Sukenaga would not be susceptible to such foolishness. He was a professional.

"Lord Echigo, Lord Echigo," a breathless voice broke in on his reverie. "Our scouts have sighted smoke from Kiso's campfires."

A vertical line appeared between Sukenaga's brows. How strange that one with so high a military reputation should be so careless in giving away his location. But, he supposed, the carelessness was the result of their being amateurs.

They didn't even seem to have sent out scouts. Sukenaga wrinkled his face in disgust. This battle would not be worthy of his steel.

"How far ahead is their camp?" he demanded.

"About an hour's march, on the other side of the Hino River."

Sukenaga reined in his stallion. He looked up at Amaterasu. There would be no relief from the heat for several hours. The sun blazed in a cloudless sky. Sukenaga was aware of sweat trickling down his back under his armor. He itched. He wished he could tear off the armor and cool himself, but that would set a bad example for his men. Sukenaga's face belied his discomfort as he said, "We will not rush headlong into battle. have the scouts bring me a full report. Meanwhile we will stop, rest, prepare ourselves with prayer, and wait until dusk to attack."

thirty-five

By midday, Yoshi had seen to it that the troops were properly dispersed. The scene was set. The men were to hold their positions silently for as long as necessary. The sun was already lowering. Now they had only to wait for Jō Sukenaga's attack.

The afternoon had been a trying one. Kiso was irritated and lacked confidence in Yoshi's plan. "Why doesn't Sukenaga attack?" he demanded shortly after the scouts informed him the enemy was within range. "He has discovered our plan and is setting a counter trap."

"No," Yoshi said. "Sukenaga is an experienced soldier. He will do what he has been trained to do. If you commanded his forces, would you rush blindly across a river in the hottest part of the day... after a hard march? No! He believes we are trapped with our backs to a high cliff. He thinks we cannot escape. Sukenaga will wait till the sun is down and his men are sufficiently cooled and rested. Then he will challenge us in the formal manner. That is his way."

"And if he doesn't?"

"We must maintain our positions."

Imai, always at Kiso's side, snarled, "I think we should cross the river and surprise him before his men are rested. Why allow him to prepare himself? I say strike first. Yoshi's way is the way of a coward."

Yoshi could not afford to be angry. The coming engagement would be his first opportunity to evaluate Kiso and his men. Kiso had listened to Yoshi's suggestions and wisely followed them. Yoshi disliked the man but conceded Kiso was a fine soldier. Unless his army failed in the battle, Yoshi would report that Kiso had excellent potential as an ally. Meanwhile, Imai's provocative manner reminded Yoshi that the way he had chosen was more difficult than that of the sword. The sword was simple and direct. One did not have to think... only to act. This road was a hard one, and he often felt he lacked the inner strength to travel it. How long could he withstand the constant insults before his pride overcame his principles? Give him a sword!

He would best Imai in battle . . . and Kiso. But he would then have to contend with Tezuka, then Jiro, and Taro. The bloodshed would not end until he and Nami had paid with their lives for his foolish pride, and the Emperor's mission would be doomed.

Yoshi swallowed the bitter taste that rose in his throat. He said, "Imai, your impatience will lead you to the caverns of Yomi. The use of the mind is not cowardice. When I fought with the sword, I learned that a direct attack is not always the best attack, that subtlety is more important than strength. You try my patience, but I will ignore it."

"Don't patronize me, you Taira bastard," Imai snarled. "Find a sword or . . . armed or not, I'll cut you down where you stand."

Kiso restrained his foster-brother. "When the time comes to face Yoshi with swords, I shall be the one to do so," he said softly. "We have accepted his plan, so let's concentrate on beating Jō Sukenaga."

The sun was sinking rapidly; it would soon be the hour of the dog. The hottest part of the day was past. A slight breeze arose to ruffle the pines that hid Jō Sukenaga's army. Frogs croaked their deep-throated songs from the banks of the Hino. In the trees, cicadas were tuning their rasping wings for the evening.

The Hino was a glassy ribbon about twenty yards across; the waters reflected breeze-dappled pictures of the few trees that clung to the banks. The smell of wood fires from the camp wafted across the waters to touch the nostrils of the waiting army.

Jō Sukenaga rode out of the shelter of the trees, followed by his standard bearer and three officers. He stood high in his stirrups to shout a formal challenge. "I, Echizen-no-Sammi-Jō Sukenaga, lord of Echigo, Hangwan of the Imperial armies of Taira Munemori, being loyal to the Taira cause and to the Emperor Antoku, hereby challenge any and all who hear my voice. Is there a samurai among you brave enough to face my champion in mortal combat?"

Sukenaga sat back and signaled one of his officers to shoot the formal humming arrow to begin hostilities officially.

There was a stirring in the cluster of tents that hugged the base of the cliff. A group of five armored samurai emerged from the shadows. Sukenaga realized that he was at a disadvantage with the sun in his face; it was difficult to see the enemy camp. The situation made him uneasy. There should have been hundreds of soldiers frantically scurrying for cover. Instead, he saw only tents, banners, fires, and five men.

The leader of the five announced in a stentorian voice, "Imai-no-Shirō Kanehira am I, foster-brother to the demon warrior Kiso Yoshinaka. All the provinces of the Empire know and fear my name, so send your champion if you dare." With that he sent a war arrow whirring across the river at Sukenaga's flag carrier, missing him by inches.

"One volunteer," shouted Sukenaga, "to face the challenge."

Three officers rode forward as one man.

"Me!"

"Allow me."

"Choose me!"

Sukenaga appointed one, a young officer no more than nineteen years of age, smooth-skinned and clear-eyed. The young man spurred his horse into the Hino. Horse and rider were momentarily immersed in the cold water but were quickly out and up the opposite bank. The officer jumped lithely from his mount and drew his sword as he strode toward Imai.

Imai had placed his bow on the ground and drawn his own blade. He waited while the young man made his challenge.

"I am Ikawa-no-Tokohashi, son of Lord Iga, officer in the army of the Emperor. Though I am but nineteen years of age, I have fought and defeated the Minamoto usurpers in three campaigns. Face me if you can."

Imai sprang forward, his sword a blur as the dying sunlight sent flashing orange reflections from the blade. Imai was quick and determined, but the battle was far from one-sided. Tokohashi had the advantage of youth; his reflexes were more than equal to Imai's attack, and it was the young man who drew first blood.

Imai stared in disbelief at the red stain that spread where his left shoulder plate ended. His pause was momentary, a hundredth part of a second, then he exploded in maniacal fury, lashing out again and again. The attack was too forceful and continuous to be stopped. Tokohashi miscalculated a counter against the water-wheel attack, and the first battle of Echizen ended with Tokohashi rolling on the ground holding his midsection.

Imai leaped after him, grabbed him by the hair, and cut his throat. Blood sprayed up and covered Imai's arms and face as if with red paint.

Less than two minutes had elapsed since young Tokohashi's challenge.

Jō Sukenaga watched with sinking heart; the young man had been one of his favorites. This loss was an inauspicious sign. No time for regret. He raised and lowered his sword, the signal for full-scale attack.

The army surged forth from behind the trees, galloping furiously down the bank, and rode forty abreast into the river. They spurred their mounts directly into the sun, squinting to make out the shape of the enemy. Horses lost their footing on the treacherous rocks that lay under the surface. Riders were spilled unceremoniously as the horses slipped and fell, churning up mud and roiling the waters. The river was shallow enough for most to regain their footing and stagger clumsily in the paths of those who galloped behind them.

Wet horses milled about on the northwest bank while their riders shook the water from their armor. The men were a well-disciplined group; they rapidly reformed their ranks and galloped headlong down the quarter-mile path to the campfires. The first companies led the way, followed by the hundreds of horsemen that crowded up the banks behind them. In the noise and confusion very few saw the host of silent archers rise from behind the walls of thornbushes.

The air was filled with the thrum of war arrows as they flew to penetrate flesh and armor. In seconds, the vanguard of Sukenaga's army was decimated as more waves of horsemen splashed across the shallow river to gallop down the long path to death. The hail of deadly arrows continued from the shadowy figures behind the thornbushes, who let fly, renocked their bows, and let fly again . . . and again.

As dusk settled, Hangwan Jō Sukenaga, riding over the bodies of his soldiers, was the first to reach the tents. The full enormity of the trap struck him with the force of a thunderclap. His eyes filled. There was no returning. Jō Sukenaga was a brave man. He had lived many years in the shadow of death and did not fear it. But the disgrace! The loss of face! He had been entrusted with the lives of four thousand samurai and he had failed. He had been outmaneuvered; his cause was lost.

Tears rolled down his cheeks, not for himself, but for the

disgrace he had brought upon his family. His black and white stallion stamped through the empty camp grounds, knocking banners to the ground. The quarter mile behind him was a scene of devastation and carnage such as no army had suffered in years. Horses screeched and fell. Men groaned and cried in agony, crawling toward shelter, trying to avoid the merciless clouds of arrows that came from the shadows.

A few hundred of the men penetrated the thorny barriers and fought face to face, chest to chest. Steel rang on steel. Steel crunched on leather armor. Steel sliced silently into flesh. It was hard to tell friend from foe in such close quarters, but Kiso's troops were ordered to kill any man whose armor was wet from the Hino.

Jō Sukenaga spurred his horse back into the melee. At least he could die fighting beside the men he had failed. He rode down one archer and slashed at the throat of a second. Then the unthinkable happened. His horse stepped in a hole. The sound of the foreleg breaking and the high-pitched scream of the horse rang in Sukenaga's ears as he flew over its head to hit and roll on the ground.

Sukenaga scrambled to his feet, glaring wildly in all directions. "Show yourself," he shouted. "Face me man to man!"

An arrow penetrated his lamellar skirt, sinking deep into his thigh. He fell onto his side, pulling at the blood-slippery shaft with one hand and waving the other hand, screaming, "Face me, you bastards. Face me!"

A horse pounded past, reared on its hind legs with a nervous whinny, and spun around. Someone bent from the saddle; a strong arm caught him and lifted him across the pommel. It was one of the young officers who had volunteered to open the battle. The young officer dug his heels into the horse's flanks, and they raced toward the shadowed face of the cliff.

Dark settled rapidly over the scene. Small pockets of men fought against an enemy they could barely see. One by one, they went down to bloody death under arrows, swords, and *naginatas*. In the pitch darkness, the young officer reined his horse close to the cliff face and leaped off. He tenderly lifted Sukenaga off the horse and stretched him out on the ground.

"All is lost. All is lost," wailed the general.

"They have not taken your head," said the young man. "Let us deny them that ultimate victory."

"Yes! Thank you," said Sukenaga. "Please help me. Be my second." Despite the blood that gushed from his thigh, he knelt and removed his armor, baring his chest and belly.

"Take my head. Hide it. I count on you," he said stoically.

The officer spread a cloth at Sukenaga's knees to catch his head. When the deed was done, he would need only close the cloth and carry the head away from the searching enemy. At the last, Kiso would be denied the proof of his victory.

Sukenaga pressed the blade of his short sword to his forehead and recited a final poem:

> *"How much I would give*
> *To see the sun once again.*
> *In far Echigo.*
> *But this joy is not for one*
> *Doomed by Hino's dark waters."*

A faint smile twitched his lips. The poem would not be remembered, but he was pleased at the *engo* in the second line. How true, he would never see his son again . . . or his wife, or his three daughters. The smile faded and his eyes misted. It was his Karma to die here far from home, and he accepted it.

No more time to hesitate. The enemy was coming and he had an appointment in the Western Paradise. He quickly whispered, *"Namu Amida Butsu,"* and thrust the blade into his left side, immediately twisting it and wrenching it across to the right.

Almost before the blood gushed out, the young officer's blade arced down and Jō Sukenaga's head rolled onto the cloth spread at his knees.

thirty-six

By midnight, Sukenaga's troops were reduced to a few handfuls of brave men who fought knowing they could not win. Less than five hundred abandoned the battle, to escape back over the Hino and flee to the southeast. Shortly after midnight the battle was ended. The last of the Imperial soldiers was cut down in a pool of his own blood.

Despite an intensive search, Kiso's men could not find Jō Sukenaga's head. It was a small disappointment to Kiso compared to the triumph of Jō Sukenaga's defeat, and he ordered the search abandoned.

At Yoshi's insistence, sentries were posted while everyone else proceeded to celebrate by drinking themselves into a stupor.

Two of Kiso's war council avoided the festivities—Yoshi, thinking about the chaos he had caused, and Kiso, making other plans. The *shi-tenno,* four kings, were particularly boisterous. Jiro and Taro kept pounding each other on the back and collapsing in hilarity. Imai and Tezuka drank flagon after flagon of sake, boasting loudly of their prowess during the hand-to-hand battles. Tomoe laughed and repeated drunkenly, "Did you see my sword slip under the captain's armored skirt? Did you see his face? No one fights better than Kiso and his *shi-tenno* except Tomoe, who fights best of all."

"I saw," shouted Jiro. "His eyes almost fell out when he realized you were a woman."

"Damn right! In the underworld maybe he'll be more respectful of women."

Kiso made a show of drinking and laughing with his men. No one noticed he held the same flagon in his hand and did not refill it. He studied Yoshi, who knelt on the periphery of the firelight with his eyes closed.

"Come, Yoshi," cried Kiso in a falsely drunken voice. "Join us. This is your triumph as well as ours."

Yoshi's lids stayed closed. His high cheekbones threw off flashes of firelight, giving him the look of meditating Buddha.

His lips moved minimally as he answered, "We did our duty. I have no regrets, but neither do I rejoice. Nearly four thousand good men died tonight. I commend their souls to the Western Paradise."

"You are spoiling the festival for the rest of us. Come." Kiso waved his flagon in a parody of drunkenness. "You insisted we set sentries along the Hino. I assign you special duty till daybreak. You shall be master of the guard." He winked broadly. "Maybe you are right. I remember a time when my sentries did not do their duty and you caused us a small embarrassment. *Neh?*" Kiso burst into raucous laughter while warily watching Yoshi's reaction.

Yoshi looked up slowly. *"Hai,"* he said. "I take no pleasure in this party. I will take responsibility for the guards." He smiled grimly. "Rest easy. General Yoshi will look out for your safety."

Yoshi rose smoothly to his feet. He went around the fire to clap Santaro on the back, congratulate him for the brave deeds of the day, and share a sip of his wine. Then he disappeared into the darkness.

Kiso put down his flagon of sake and quietly slipped away from the fire in the opposite direction.

thirty-seven

The day before the battle had been a trying one for Nami. The men had been busy preparing to ambush Jō Sukenaga. Nami had seen Yoshi for a few moments in the late afternoon, but he was busy with the logistics of the coming battle. Nami had also seen Tomoe strutting across the camp in full battle dress, black brows knitted in thought. Nami wanted to call her but bit her lower lip and remained silent. She envied Tomoe's acceptance by the men and wished she were skilled in the art of war.

Nami went back to her quarters in one of the larger tents, which she shared with Yoshi. The tent had screen partitions that effectively divided the space into two separate rooms. Nami had almost as much privacy as she had enjoyed at the court. Straw mats were spread on the ground, though the hot, dry weather made them unnecessary. Nami's *futon* was rolled up near the tent flap so that she could catch an occasional breeze. There was one oil lamp burning on a tripod base; outside, the sun was nearing the west and the interior of the tent was already in semidarkness.

Nami unrolled the *futon* and stretched out. She felt a slight pressure over her left eye. It usually presaged an attack of headache. The oppressive heat made the tent canvas smell heavy and musty. The smell mixed with that of burning oil and the myriad odors of the forest to make her vaguely nauseous.

Why didn't Yoshi come? She had not seen him for more than a few moments in several days. The war council! He was so involved with the council and his plan for the coming battle that he neglected her.

The headache, the nausea, the smells, and the sounds of men busily working outside depressed her. She thought of Uncle Fumio and the terrible sight of his dismembered head that had greeted her and Yoshi on the morning of their return from Mount Hiei. Tears rolled onto her sleeve. She pressed her face into the silk fabric. It was cool against her skin. She wondered if she had a fever and in the same moment told herself to stop acting the fool. There was nothing wrong except boredom and a feeling of loneliness.

Yet there was something . . . an inauspicious omen . . . a sensation of impending doom. The forces of the underworld seemed lined up against her. She trembled.

Was Yoshi avoiding her? No. She knew he had his duty to perform and that his role as adviser was not easy for him. Yoshi loved her, but his duty came first. Nami envied Yoshi the single-mindedness that let him concentrate so completely. And she was unsettled because he did it at her expense. If all goes well in the coming battle, she promised herself, I will not let him ignore me again. I will love him till he cries for rest. We will officially marry, and then he will be with me forever.

Nami's eyes grew heavy. The tent walls seemed to rotate. The sounds of axes chopping into trees, men yelling and cursing, horses neighing, and the clank and bustle of an army preparing to meet an attack all became a blur.

Nami slipped into restless sleep about the time Jō Sukenaga issued his formal challenge.

From the darkness, Kiso watchfully studied the warriors who celebrated in the dancing shadows of the firelight. When he was satisfied that nobody noticed his absence, he turned away and hurried toward the camp area. A young sentry, no more than fifteen years of age, challenged him but turned apologetic when he recognized Kiso.

"Well done," said Kiso. "Maintain your vigil. Loudly challenge anyone who passes. Tomorrow I will reward your adherence to duty. Meanwhile, stay at your post and forget you have seen me."

"*Hai,* General Kiso." The young sentry almost quivered in his eagerness to make a good impression.

Kiso continued on his way. There were few lanterns or oil lamps lit in the camp. Most of the women and retainers had left the sanctuary of camp to join the revelers. Although the hour was late, the celebration around the battle field was loud and boisterous.

Kiso checked several empty tents before he found the one he sought. He paused outside the tent flap and listened. In the distance, he heard drunken shouts piercing the night air. Nature's sounds were closer: insects' strident notes, an owl's mournful hooting, a wild monkey's calling a warning from the cliff. The strengthening breeze stirred the Cryptomeria around the camp. Nothing else could be heard. Even so, he held one hand on the pommel of his sword as he stooped and entered the tent.

The oil lamp had guttered out, leaving a thick smell in the sleeping space. Kiso waited until his eyes became accustomed to the darkness. He made out a dim shape near the entrance. Even if he could not see her, the scent would have told him he had reached his goal. A light, sweet perfume made an almost palpable shield around the sleeper.

Kiso felt a stirring in his loins, almost an ache. He had waited a long time for this moment. He removed his swords, then silently untied his *obi*. He quickly removed his armor and laid it at the side of the tent flap. He was now clad only in a light-weight under-robe and a black silk *hakama*.

No movement from the *futon*. Kiso listened to the sound of her breathing and felt his own breath, more labored, rasping in and out in unison with hers. His heart pounded against his chest wall. Nervous excitement made his hands tremble.

Impatiently, he untied his *hakama* and ripped it off as he stepped toward the *futon*. His male hardness throbbed with every heartbeat. He dropped to his knees, then quietly curled himself against the soft, yielding figure.

Nami had spent hours tossing restlessly in a feverish half sleep. She was dimly aware of the sounds in the distance when the battle began. Sometimes it seemed a dream, other times she cringed inside, knowing the battle was real and men were dying on the battlefield.

Eventually, the sounds of struggle changed tone and became the shouts and songs of the celebrants. She thrashed about, thinking of Yoshi. He had promised he would not fight. Unless Kiso's troops were defeated, he would come to her when he could. She felt heavy and lethargic, wanting to see what had happened, unable to rise.

Shortly after midnight, she fell into a deep sleep.

Nami awoke, feverish with the *kami* that had bedeviled her when she went to bed. She murmured, "Yoshi." For a moment, she thought it a dream when she felt his muscular body pressing against her back. His hand circled her waist, separating her silk robes. She stirred against the callused palm, feeling it touch her soft center. She gasped with pleasure and reached behind her to guide him.

Her hand closed on his hardness and gently drew it toward

her as he helped her squirm her robes upward. His hand gently stroked her thigh, then moved up to cup her breast and gently manipulate it. She awakened as she felt him pressing into her, and she became aware of a strange odor of sweat and blood, a different feel to the hard shape of the hand that stroked her, a strangeness in the way Yoshi was using her.

She gasped.

Instantly, the hand that had helped her raise her robes clasped her mouth with a cruel pressure.

The man wasn't Yoshi!

Amida Buddha, help a believer! Nami tried to scream, but only a thin whistle came from her nose. She smelled the harsh bite of stale sake and an unfamiliar male musk that was at one moment both exciting and revolting.

She struggled, twisting, trying to bite the hand on her mouth, trying to pull herself away from the prying fingers that rubbed and fondled. Against her will, she felt a rising surge of passion.

The *kami* that held her immobile moved faster. The odor was stronger. The hand on her mouth loosened and she screamed and screamed and screamed, knowing it was no use, knowing that her screams would be lost in the shouts of the victory celebration. She tried to beat at the monster, but he clasped her arms to her sides.

Then she felt the hot gush of his passion and she subsided bonelessly in horror and disgust. Nami felt despoiled, marred, violated to the deepest core of her being. The fever and torpor that had made her sleep through a battle was gone and she felt a blazing flame of hate. Whoever this was, he would pay for what he had done. The man withdrew; she heard him fumbling with his clothing behind her back. The darkness was complete. She raised herself heavily on her arms, trying to identify the intruder. No matter how she strained, she could not see more than a dim shadow.

Then the tent flap was pulled aside and for one instant she saw the hatchetlike face in silhouette against the gleam of distant fires.

"Kiso," she hissed through gritted teeth. "You animal! You'll pay for this. I'll . . ."

Kiso was already gone. The blackness descended around her again and she lowered herself to the ground, sobbing uncontrollably. What could she do? What could she do?

thirty-eight

The morning after the celebration, a few drunken samurai remained around the scene of the previous night's festivities, unwilling to lose their moment of triumph. A tang of wet smoldering wood filled the air. A rain shower had dampened most of the fires. It did not last long enough to help the dried fields, but the promise of more rain hung heavy in the clouds above the camp.

The battlefield was littered with bodies of dead men and horses. Most of the dead had been stripped of valuables: swords, armor, bows, saddles, and personal effects. The women, children, and old men of the camp had been busy during the celebration, picking the corpses clean.

Shortly after dawn, Yoshi supervised changing the guard and retired to his tent for a much deserved rest.

He thought he heard muffled sobs from behind Nami's screen, but when he looked she lay quietly, completely covered by her *futon*. He thought he must have imagined the noises or that they were the results of her dreaming. She was apparently fast asleep.

Yoshi wearily untied the bows that fastened the right lamellar plate. He dropped it to the floor mat and followed it with the shoulder plates, the main *yoroi*, which had covered his front, left, and back, and finally the leather-bound plates that made up his protective skirt. The armor formed an untidy pile at the side of his *futon*. He was too tired to care about the disorder. He would clean, polish, and arrange the armor when he awoke. He lay back, thinking that he had spent very little time with Nami since their arrival at Kiso's camp. Tomorrow he would make amends.

Tomorrow...

Yoshi awoke with a start. From the feel of the damp heat, he guessed it was already past noon. He heard the clatter of men at work and realized that while he had slept, Kiso must have ordered the striking of the camp. With last night's victory, the road to Kyoto would be clear. The Imperial guard had been

211

committed and had lost. The Emperor and his family were at
Kiso's mercy.

Yoshi removed the stopper from a bamboo tube and poured
a handful of water; he splashed it on his face, shaking off the
droplets to clear his head. Yoshi had to supervise the disman-
tling of the tents and see to arrangements for the captured horses
and armament.

First he needed to speak to Nami, to ask her to be patient
with him for just one more day.

The tent was empty. The *futon* was rolled up, and Nami
had left. Yoshi's brow furrowed. Where could she have gone?
He was worried but quickly suppressed the feeling. Nami was
probably with Tomoe and there was nothing to worry about.
Life in an army camp was not the life Nami was accustomed
to. She had always been an independent and spirited woman,
more than the court ladies who had been her contemporaries
in Kyoto. Even so, when they lived in the capital, she would
never have left the house alone.

Yoshi had faced this dilemma many times in recent months.
On the one hand, he believed in old-fashioned virtues: a woman
should remain at home and attend to managing the house. On
the other hand, he had encouraged Nami to ride as his retainer
and travel freely from Kyoto to Kamakura to the mountains of
Shinano. Because she once again wore formal clothing could
he demand that she hide behind screens and behave as if there
had been no change?

The world was changing. Yoshi sighed. Indeed, the world
was coming to the "latter days of the law," as the seers had
prophesied.

Yoshi shrugged. He loved Nami and her fierce independence. He would never ask her to change. Of course she had
gone to visit Tomoe. The two women, as disparate as two
could be, had become fast friends. There was no doubt that
Tomoe took much from the friendship. Yoshi worried that
Tomoe gave, in exchange, a certain coarseness of outlook
that he did not think appropriate for Nami.

Enough! There was much to be done. Yoshi would see Nami
before the camp moved to a new location. The heat was already
causing the bodies in the field to decompose. Blackflies made
the entire area unpleasant. The clouds that roiled above pressed
down, making the odor of decay almost unbearable. Yoshi
wrinkled his nose at the scent that wafted as far as his tent,
then he squatted next to the untidy pile of armor he had left

the night before. He hurried to finish the tedious work of polishing and arranging the armor before he left to help dismantle the camp.

The new camp was relocated five miles farther north, in a grassy valley. Scouts reported that Jō Sukenaga's son had turned his army back to Echigo. There would be no concerted opposition to Kiso's advance. Kiso decided to halt his drive through the northern provinces. At the evening's council meeting he seemed in particularly good spirits.

The victory was reason enough for Kiso's jubilation; he was so pleased with himself that he even agreed when Santaro suggested an accolade for Yoshi's planning. Kiso, on other occasions, had shown bad temper when anyone—especially Yoshi—was credited for what he considered his by right. This time his good humor remained unruffled and he complimented Yoshi, albeit in a strangely superior and condescending manner.

Yoshi was uncomfortable. He did not trust Kiso, and when Kiso was friendly, he trusted him least of all.

"Yoshi is not much of a swordsman," Kiso said with a sardonic smile that gave the words the edge of a double entendre, "but his foresight shows him to be a wise man who knows when to avoid a battle."

Imai grumbled, "Yoshi's plan worked because we were the better warriors. My plan would have gained us the same victory with more honor."

"No doubt, no doubt," said Kiso silkily. "But let's give him credit. Yoshi's tactic allowed him to direct the troops safely. That is the prudent way to fight. Am I not right, Yoshi? Am I not right, Uncle Yukiie?"

Yoshi's face was like polished marble, his eyes unblinking as he stared coldly at Kiso. Yukiie did not have the same self-control. He shrugged his fat shoulders and pouted. Last night, Yukiie's men had been the only ones who had not held their line. Some said it was because their leader had not been with them. "Someday, nephew, you will go too far," he lisped angrily.

"Dear Uncle Yukiie," said Kiso slyly. Then, as if tired of play acting, he announced, "We have a camping area large enough to hold us comfortably for many months. There is a pond with enough water to supply us despite the summer's drought. The grass is scanty, but it will feed our horses. We

have done our part in Yoritomo's war. We deserve to rest. I
have decided we will stay here through the winter. We will
spend the time recruiting men from the countryside and training
them to be worthy of us. In the spring, we will march again."

Yoshi said, "We must inform Yoritomo of your decision."

Kiso gave an uncharacteristic chuckle and agreed. "Yes,
very well. See that a message is sent."

That night, Yoshi prepared two messages. One was to Yoritomo, describing the battle against Jō Sukenaga. The message
ended with a cautionary note; Kiso's army was growing rapidly
and the victory over Sukenaga would give Kiso a very strong
power base.

The messenger was given a second message to deliver secretly to the Emperor. The message was concealed in the same
box that had carried Go-Shirakawa's message to Yoritomo.
The messenger was warned that his life was in danger if the
secret of the box was discovered. He would be richly rewarded
when the box was safely delivered. The message assessed the
relative merits of Yoritomo and Kiso. Yoshi told the Emperor
that Yoritomo, at the Emperor's request, was making alliances
with the great families of the north. Yoshi recommended that
Go-Shirakawa ally himself with Yoritomo. The message warned
that although Kiso was a fine general, he was unpredictable
and untrustworthy.

Yoshi's conclusion: "Trust Yoritomo. Use Kiso warily."

The farmers had prayed to the gods for months, asking for
rain. The gods answered with a deluge. The temperature dropped
twenty degrees, the daytime sky was black with clouds and
ripped by jagged flashes of lightning. The valley turned into a
bog, with knee-deep puddles in many places. The soldiers
huddled in their tents; training came to a halt and every tent
was an isolated island in the churning sea of mud.

Yoshi found Nami strangely withdrawn. He had expected
her warm welcome now that he was free to devote himself to
her. Instead, she drew away; she shrank from his touch and
avoided conversation.

Yoshi assumed her behavior signified her coming defilement. It was not the first time he had found Nami difficult to
understand when she was plagued by her *kami*. However, it
was awkward to share a tent with the person you loved when

she would not speak and when she rejected your tentative advances.

With time to think about their future, Yoshi decided to make their marriage official. Nami had indicated many times that she was uncomfortable with her unofficial status. Yoshi was convinced that the offer of marriage would cure her depression.

The rain beat an incessant drum roll on the tent. A full week had passed since the battle of Echizen, and this was the third day of heavy rain. The valley was protected from the high winds that uprooted hundred-year-old trees; even so, occasional gusts slipped under tent flaps, causing havoc in the camp.

Yoshi securely fastened the entrance flap. Nami, seated on the floor matting, gazed out at the rain. She did not move, staring now at the closed flap. Yoshi tried a small witticism. Nami seemed not to react, but she turned her head slowly to study him. Her eyes were dull and opaque. Yoshi was distressed. He feared she was seriously ill and that he would have to call upon the priests and healers to rid her of the *kami* that invaded her body.

"Is there anything you need?" he asked anxiously.

"No," was the heavy reply.

"Do you want me to sit with you?"

"If you like . . ."

The conversation was stilted. It was obvious to Yoshi that Nami was straining to answer his simple questions. Yoshi bowed solemnly and said, "You seem to prefer being alone. I shall retire to the other side of the screen. If you need me, you have only to call."

Nami opened her lips to speak. She made a small uncertain motion with one hand as if to stop Yoshi. Then she murmured, "No . . . no . . . never mind," and turned back to stare at the tent flap.

Yoshi was disheartened. How easy it would be to consider this a personal rejection. But what could be the reason? He had done Nami no wrong. He shrugged. He loved her. Whatever was troubling her would pass.

Yoshi took out an ink-stone, put in a few drops of water, and rubbed in some ink from a *sumi*, ink-cake. He blended the ink with the water until it had reached the desired thickness. Then he unfolded a sheet of his best mulberry paper. He dipped his brush in the opaque pool and wrote with crisp, sure strokes:

> *Let us become one*
> *Before our ancestral gods*
> *My heart will feel joy*
> *When we are tied together*
> *Sleeves dry in tomorrow's sun.*

The implication was clear, the calligraphy sensitive, with just the right amount of dash. "Tomorrow's sun . . . tomorrow's son." Yes, they would have fine children and lead a full life. Yoshi smiled for the first time in days, thinking how pleased Nami would be at his proposal poem.

Yoshi folded it carefully and affixed a colorful ribbon. Then he carried it around the screen and handed it to Nami.

Nami immediately realized what the packet meant. Her heart felt as if it were being crushed. Hidden tears suddenly threatened to burst forth. With an effort she hid her distress and held the paper to her forehead.

"*Arigato,* dear Yoshi," she murmured.

"There is no need to answer at once, my darling," he said. "I know you are not well. Take whatever time you need. I will not press you."

Nami closed her eyes and bowed acknowledgment.

Yoshi retreated around the screen to his own area.

The moment he withdrew, tears came unbidden to Nami's eyes. "Why?" she cried to herself. "Why does he come to me now? Too late. Too late!"

The past days had been a torture for Nami. She was torn between hatred for Kiso and what he had done and self-loathing for not having prevented it. The entire affair was unspeakable. In her distress, she had gone to Tomoe. She could not face Yoshi. But even that had been unsatisfactory. Tomoe wanted to help and perhaps even suspected what had happened. But Nami could not bring herself to tell her the truth. There was no gauging Tomoe's reaction; she was a jealous and violent woman. Would her anger turn against Nami or against Kiso? Nami was afraid to test her friendship to that extent.

What a terrible situation! There seemed to be no answer. There was no one in whom Nami could confide. If she told Yoshi, he would renounce his vows and attack Kiso. Of that she was sure. He might win a battle with Kiso—though she suspected his skills had lost their edge—but their idyll would end. Sooner or later, Yoshi would fall to one or another of Kiso's samurai.

Nami had seen Kiso only once during the past week. He was insufferable, leering disgustingly at her as if they shared a voluntary secret.

What could she do? If she did not acknowledge Yoshi's poem . . . if she refused to answer, indicating rejection of the proposal, he would demand the reason. How could she respond? If she sent him a poem of acceptance, how could she face him with a clear conscience?

Nami had been a woman of the court. As such she had had temporary affairs during the years she was married to Lord Chikara. Affairs were expected of her and the men conducted themselves in a discreet and gentlemanly way, with proper protocol, with poems, and with flowery protestations of love. She accepted the court practice. Though she never really enjoyed the sexual closeness, she enjoyed the flattery and attention. Her husband had neglected her for years and kept a secondary wife quite openly, so there was no blame connected with Nami's actions.

This was different. Kiso was an animal who had forced himself on her and whom she had to face while guarding the secret of the violation. Could she convince Yoshi that they must leave together? Without having a plausible reason? Never! His sense of duty meant more to him than his life.

The rain's unceasing rhythm made her want to scream. If she screamed, Yoshi would come to her. He would cradle her in his arms and . . . would want to know why she cried out.

She chewed her lower lip in frustration. What to do? What to do? The words repeated themselves in time to the beat of the rain. What to do? What to do?

Unable to bear the deadly drum of the rain which accentuated the silence in the tent, Nami opened the drawer of her pillow-box and removed the materials to send an answer:

> *Can you understand*
> *How confusion wracks my heart*
> *And my sleeves are damp?*
> *Falling rain drowns my sad cries.*
> *I fear I am not worthy.*

As if to underscore the pillow words *falling rain* as a metaphor for tears, a drop fell on the page, diluting the ink and leaving a soft blot on the last character. Nami folded the paper and delivered it to Yoshi's side of the screen.

thirty-nine

The second day of the tenth month was *Taian,* a lucky day by the six-day *Rokuyo* calendar. Yoshi had consulted the priests and the Yin-Yang seers. With their help, he decided that this would be the most auspicious day for his wedding.

Nami continued to be quiet and reclusive. She accepted Yoshi's suggestions for the wedding ceremony with an uncharacteristic lack of enthusiasm. It was as though she had no interest in the outcome.

The sight of his beloved sitting silently alone in the tent tore at Yoshi's heart. He remembered years before, when he had been in the grip of evil spirits and Nami had nursed him back to health. He determined to do everything possible to help her.

Yoshi called in the healers. They found nothing. After extensive tests and consultation with astrologic, anatomical, herbal, and mathematical charts, they decided she was being influenced by the ghost world. The diagnosis was familiar to Yoshi. He, too, had suffered from a *mono-no-ke,* an evil spirit, and he remembered his helplessness in fighting it.

Yoshi could call on the priests to perform an exorcism, but the pain and danger would be acceptable only as a last resort. He would use his own strength and love to help Nami fight the evil ghosts.

To combat the inauspicious nature of Nami's illness, Yoshi had chosen the luckiest day of the week for the ceremony. A wedding on *Taian* should assure the success of the marriage.

Tomoe acted as Nami's attendant. She arranged the first part of the ceremony, supervising the preparation of *mikay-omochi,* third-night rice cakes, in honor of the Shinto first gods, Izanagi and Izanami.

On the morning of the wedding day, a small group was invited to the tent to watch Yoshi and Nami share the cakes in public. The marriage was now official, but the celebration was not over: a formal banquet and a *san-san-kudo,* three-three-nine, ceremony would be held in the evening.

A special tent was erected for the feast. Two low wooden platforms faced each other along two sides of the tent. Each guest was assigned a place on one of the platforms with a kneeling pad, an elbow rest, a low tray table, and a lacquered wooden sake bowl.

That night, the samurai officers of Kiso's army knelt in two rows facing each other, each dressed in his finest formal robe. Pine torches lit a scene of riotous color. There were robes of brocaded silk: red, blue, gold, and green. Robes with painted designs: dragons, gods, and scenes of war. Robes of woven patterns: chrysanthemums, moonflowers, and abstract patterns. Every officer wore his formal black hat, as if at court. Each wore his hair in a top-knot, tied with a colorful ribbon. Each carried his swords, cutting edge up, at his side. Never in the history of Kiso's army had they gathered together in such pomp and display.

Nami wore a traditional floss silk cap. This *wataboshi* symbolically suppressed the horns of jealousy that all women were supposed to possess. Wearing the cap proved that Nami was eager to free herself of the Buddhist evil of jealousy. Nami's formal jacket was red, over a series of outer gowns that varied in color from violet to pale green. Under these outer gowns was another silk layered gown that shaded from light red to deep burgundy. Nami's hair was brushed smooth, framing her painted white face. Despite the white makeup, her cheeks burned with fever, giving her a high, unhealthy color. She was nervous and responded with brittle laughter when she was addressed.

Yoshi and Tomoe had spent days making preparations. Nami accepted their efforts passively. Custom called for the bride's family to sit on one platform, facing the groom's family on the other. The head of the family and his wife normally sat the top of each row. Since neither Yoshi nor Nami had family, it was decided that Kiso would represent Yoshi on one side and Tomoe would represent Nami on the other.

When Tomoe told Nami of the arrangements, Nami burst into tears and became almost hysterical. "No!" she cried. "No! Kiso will not represent Yoshi at my wedding."

Tomoe reassured her. "I know they are not friends, but Kiso is our commander. Protocol must be observed. He will conduct himself properly. You have nothing to fear."

"I don't want him involved in my marriage ceremony," sobbed Nami.

Tomoe's eyes narrowed and small knots of muscle tightened

at the corner of her jaw. She had been suspicious of Kiso and the way he watched Nami. Nami's overreaction seemed to confirm Tomoe's suspicion that in some way Kiso had molested her. "You must accept the arrangement," said Tomoe.

"I cannot."

"Tell me why not."

"I cannot."

"Nami, I am your friend. Has Kiso harmed you? Tell me!"

"I cannot discuss it."

Tomoe nodded. Nami's refusal convinced her that Kiso had in some way wronged Nami. Tomoe was also convinced that Nami was not at fault. Kiso must not represent Yoshi at the ceremony. If Kiso was insulted by being asked to withdraw, Tomoe would see that he took no revengeful action.

Tomoe remembered the night of the Echizen victory and Kiso's disappearance during the celebration. Had Nami's change stemmed from that night? It was impossible to be sure, but Tomoe felt in the pit of her stomach that she had stumbled onto the truth. Oh, yes; in time, Kiso would answer for this deed. Meanwhile, the wedding ceremony had to proceed.

"Will you accept Santaro to represent Yoshi?"

"Unquestioningly. He is our friend."

"Done. I will see to it that Kiso does not object."

So it was arranged. Santaro sat at the head of the row representing Yoshi, Kiso in the second place at his side. Tomoe led the opposite platform with her brother, Imai, at her side. The bride and groom faced each other from the foot of the two rows.

A priest marched in the aisle between the platforms, chanting the *norito* rituals, purifying the assemblage with a holy *sakaki* tree branch. When he finished the ritual, he bowed formally and retired.

The *san-san-kudo* began.

Attendants placed a set of three sake cups on the tray before Nami. The top cup was filled in three pouring motions. Nami drank it in three sips. Her lackluster eyes flashed once, when they passed over Kiso's sardonic face. He smiled fleetingly.

Tomoe stretched forward to see what had prompted Kiso's smile. She could not see Nami's expression, but she imagined it was filled with anger. Tomoe adjusted her blue over-robe and settled back on her heels. She would watch Kiso closely. He would not be allowed to interfere with Nami's happiness on this auspicious day.

The cup was refilled and brought to Yoshi. He drank the sake in three quick sips.

The second cup was filled, and this time, it was brought to Yoshi first, then to Nami. With the third cup, Nami drank first. This ceremony of three cups being filled three times each and the sake being drunk in three sips was the final Shinto purification ceremony.

Yoshi and Nami were now well and truly wed. The banquet began.

Attendants scurried up and down the center aisle with huge platters of yam gruel; rice cakes with seaweed; baked, pickled, and broiled fish. Wild fowl was served with fruit and nut cakes, and there was sake and more sake. Santaro roared a toast to the groom. Tomoe responded with a toast for the bride. Even Kiso, caught up in the ceremony, seemed genuinely moved when he offered a toast to the couple.

Food dribbled onto silk robes. Sake spilled onto laps and the floor. Someone called for a poetry contest. The country samurai, unskilled in the courtly arts, booed and hissed. One samurai began singing a faintly obscene popular song, "The Maids of Naniwa," to cheers and jeers.

An hour after the banquet started, most of the guests subsided into drunkenness. Food was scattered on the platforms as a few collapsed into their trays. One guest rose and tripped over his neighbor. He fell heavily into the center aisle and immediately drew his sword, wildly waving the blade, threatening whoever had caused his embarrassment.

Only Kiso and Tomoe noticed when Yoshi led Nami out into the night.

The darkness was almost complete. At midnight of the second day of the lunar month, the thinnest sliver of Tsukiyomi's smile showed in the sky as Yoshi led a compliant Nami to their tent.

Yoshi spread the *futon* and embraced Nami, gently guiding her to the ground.

They had not lain together since days before the battle of Echizen. Yoshi felt an ache in his loins and an even greater ache in his heart as he felt the boneless quality of Nami's response.

"I love you, Nami," he said softly.

Her reply was an almost inaudible "I love you, Yoshi."

He laid his cheek against hers, drawing her close to his chest, feeling her heartbeat against him.

Although it was too dark to see more than shadowy shapes, Yoshi knew Nami was crying. He felt her tears wet his cheek and gently wiped her face with his full sleeve.

"Whatever *mono-no-ke* has you in thrall, we will fight him together and we will win," whispered Yoshi.

Nami sobbed silently, her shoulders quivering.

Yoshi slipped his left hand beneath her robe and rested it on her soft flesh. He felt her tense.

"Nami, we are man and wife at last. I will wait patiently until you are ready. I am not a coarse brute who would force himself on a woman...even his wife."

Nami sobbed aloud. "Yoshi, stay with me. Hold me. Caress me. Perhaps the healers are right that I have suffered at the hands of an evil spirit. I need your love. Help me. Heal me. Whatever I do, don't draw away. I do want you..."

Yoshi felt a tear on the edge of his eyelid. He said:

> "A thin cold sliver,
> Even the moon seemed cruel
> Knowing of my pain.
> Now, I see it was a smile
> Its crescent warming my heart."

Nami rolled toward him, laying her leg over his. She answered:

> "In our floating world
> If your heart still beats for me
> Don't wait. Spread my gowns
> And we will love each other
> While our sleeves dry in the moonlight."

With the recital of the poem, the *mono-no-ke* that had haunted her since that dreadful night retired. She was aware of her quickening pulse and the yearning ache she had always felt before her painful experience with Kiso. The past horror was forgotten. Nami wanted Yoshi. She wanted life.

Nami's slim fingers reached for him, stroking gently until, in seconds, she found him fully aroused. She luxuriated in the tenderness of his hands exploring her body, the soft touch of his palm as it caressed her breasts. Yoshi's hand was on her thigh and she felt her body strain toward him, opening like a flower in the spring sun.

Outside the tent, the camp was in almost total darkness. The drunken sounds of the last few conscious officers faded to silence. Only the locusts of the tenth month could be heard, fiddling in the trees. Their sound heightened Nami's sense of isolation. The transient world could not reach her in this place. She rolled back, enjoying the feel of her silk robes spread around her. She pulled Yoshi up and over, guiding him as he loomed above her.

The world receded. The sum total of all experience was centered on one small area. Nami felt the thrusting, the probing, the building in intensity. A warm glow suffused her. A spark of Amaterasu burned deep within her. Subsided. Burned again. And each time the spark burned, it burned brighter.

In a rush that brought visions of the Western Paradise, of flowers and gardens, temples in the sun, palaces, and a glowing heaven, Nami faintly heard Yoshi cry out. Tightening the muscles of her innermost being, she thrust herself against him and screamed in ecstasy.

BOOK III

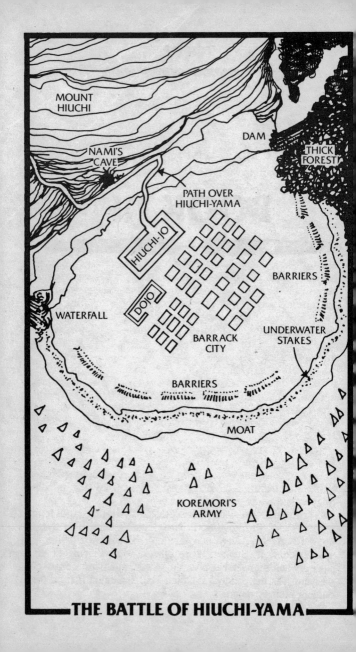

THE BATTLE OF HIUCHI-YAMA

forty

Kiso's camp was set in a flat valley bounded on the north by Hiuchi-yama, the largest in the range of northeast mountains. An ancient forest covered the foothills with gnarled tree trunks and thickly tangled underbrush. The forest enclosed an area of fields and farms over a hundred *cho* square. There was only one road that entered the valley from the east. A half-dozen farms with heavily built main houses were widely scattered through the flatlands.

When Kiso's army first arrived in the valley, they were bivouacked in army tents—comfortable for most of the year, but inadequate in the winter. Kiso ordered his officers to supervise the building of more permanent dwellings similar to the farmhouses. Foot soldiers were put to work cutting down trees. Iron-wheeled oxcarts rumbled along the road all day, carrying logs to the building sites. Women, children, and old men wove thatch for the roofs and filled the chinks between the logs with packed earth.

A site was chosen at the foot of Hiuchi-yama for Kiso's military headquarters. It was called Hiuchi-jo, Hiuchi Fortress, but was actually no more than a large house of logs and earth protected by a tall wooden palisade. Hiuchi-jo was surrounded by a loop in the shallow river that ran along the base of Mount Hiuchi.

Yoshi directed the construction of a drill field and a martial-arts academy. While the army was holed up for the winter, there would be little else to keep the soldiers occupied besides training and drilling. The commanders realized that an idle army would be an undisciplined army.

The martial-arts academy was built in a rectangle, with long narrow sheds surrounding an open central area. The sheds housed barracks, where two hundred soldiers would live in spartan comfort. Shutters were opened to the inside of the square when the weather allowed. At the southeast corner of the yard was the paddock. A high wall separated it from the outdoor archery range.

The rest of the rectangular space was filled with separate sheds connected by covered walkways. These sheds housed an indoor archery range for practice in inclement weather, a section for sword and spear fighting, a center for studying tactics and military history, and a small two-room house that would be Yoshi's and Nami's private quarters.

Kiso's officers made every effort to build a self-sufficient city to shelter their army through the coming winter. The city was laid out in a grid facing Hiuchi-jo, with rough barracks lining narrow streets. Near the headquarters building, storage sheds were stocked with five thousand *koku* of rice, millet, and barley and packed with barrels of sake, dried fish, cured meat, and extra salt. Five thousand *koku* of beans and fodder were stored near the drill field to feed the oxen and horses.

The drought of the spring of 1181 had devastated most of the food crop of Japan, but the valley of Echizen remained fertile. The central lake and the shallow looping river that crossed near the foot of Hiuchi-yama furnished enough water to irrigate the fields, and the farmers were prosperous enough to maintain their herds of cattle.

In the twelfth month, with the arrival of the first snows, hungry farmers from the countryside surrounding the valley flocked to the camp. The newcomers were welcomed and the most promising among them were billeted in the martial-arts center to receive instruction. Yoshi would awake before dawn and work through the day, teaching the men weapons, tactics, and horsemanship.

While Yoshi was occupied giving instruction in the martial arts, Nami suggested that she give classes in calligraphy, reading, and poetry. The war council vetoed the suggestion because the studies were deemed an unnecessary luxury.

Since her official marriage, Nami had recovered from her deep depression. Tomoe was usually busy with the logistics and business matters of the camp, so Nami was mostly alone. She seemed to prefer it that way, spending her time fixing her home and making entries in her pillow-box journal.

By the middle of the first month of 1182, the weather was mercilessly cold, colder than at any other time in living memory. The land, which had dried and burned in the pitiless heat of summer, froze into iron-hard earth, covered by mountainous drifts of snow.

Throughout the provinces, families burned their prized possessions for warmth. Men flocked to the forest, searching for food and firewood. Thousands did not survive the searing cold. Bodies of the poor, the well-to-do, priests, merchants, farmers, and beggars froze and were buried beneath the extreme snowfall. Most would remain undiscovered till the spring thaw.

Kiso's camp was protected from the northeast winds, but there was no protection from the snowfall. Many mornings the camp awakened to a thick silence and found itself buried in snow higher than a man's head. Even the oldest people in the camp were unable to recall ever seeing anything like this winter of 1182.

During the late autumn, Kiso had been pleased to expand his army with peasants. They had come in droves, driven from their farms by famine. It soon became apparent to Kiso that as well stocked as the camp was, it could not house and feed all who came.

With the heavy snows, another thousand men arrived. They earned their keep by shoveling paths through the streets of the camp. This was the last contingent to be accepted. From then on, newcomers were driven away. Sentries were ordered to fire arrows at anyone who came in range of the camp.

Many starving peasants tried. Almost five hundred bodies were packed in the snow drifts near the valley's entrance before the desperate wanderers realized they would not be accepted in the camp.

During the long nights, the lamentations of those denied admittance could be heard from the forest. Small circles of light dotted the darkness as groups of unfortunates gathered, out of arrow range, to build their fires. The fires furnished heat, but no food. As weeks turned to months, the fires gradually disappeared. Sentries reported that frozen bodies were mutilated by desperate men. During the night, they cut strips of human flesh for their cooking fires. Melted snow kept them alive for a while, but in the end, those who had survived by cannibalism were driven away by cold.

The camp had barely enough food for its own people. There could be no charity. No one would survive if the storehouses were depleted.

Yoshi sympathized with the plight of the wanderers. He had not forgotten his two years as a fugitive, hiding in the mountains, living a minimal existence, staying alive by methods so repulsive that he had blocked them from his memory. Sympathy was all Yoshi could spare. Kiso was right to be merciless. He owed the strangers nothing; he owed his troops survival.

• • •

Yoshi closed his eyes and mind to those figures that skulked through the forest, sometimes seen in the distance as fleeting shadows. He was fully occupied with his academy. It felt good to hold a sword in his hand again. He enjoyed teaching; imparting knowledge made him feel fulfilled.

Once more he was called *sensei* and given respect. His skills were again being sharpened and that felt good, too. Yoshi spent long hours with the sword, bow, *naginata,* and the *shuriken,* throwing stars. And he added a new weapon to his arsenal. Eight years ago, as a student under the master teacher Ichikawa, he had studied the use of the war fan. It was a skill he had not developed. Now he had the opportunity to practice the fan against a variety of other weapons. Yoshi did not wear his swords outside the *dojo;* the fan would give him protection in case of a surprise attack.

The fan Yoshi chose to use in practice had eight iron ribs, each pointed at one end. When the fan was folded, the ribs made a thick point at one end and an iron knob at the other. A tasseled white cord was tied in a bow near the bottom. When the fan was spread open, it showed a decorative drawing of a dragon representing the eternal battle between religion and evil. It was the same dragon that Yoshi once engraved on the tang of Hanzo's swords when he was apprenticed to the sword smith.

The war fan was a versatile weapon. With a flick of the wrist it became a solid iron bar to parry a sword stroke, a dull pointed dagger to attack an opponent's vitals, or a knobbed club to strike against joints.

Yoshi spent his leisure hours with Nami, warming the cold center that she had developed after Echizen.

Santaro visited the couple regularly. He was always welcome. Tomoe visited a few times, spending her time with Nami when Yoshi was busy at the academy.

Neither Kiso nor Imai ever came to Yoshi's house, but they frequently visited the *dojo* and watched the training exercises. Imai maintained a seeming disinterest, but Kiso watched Yoshi's movements with calculated interest.

During the second month of 1182, a plague of black-tongue hit the encampment. Soldiers grew listless, feverish, and lost weight. Their tongues turned black and swelled up in their throats. Healers and priests recited incantations to no avail.

Over three hundred corpses were carted the short distance from camp to a deep ravine.

At the beginning of the third month, a warm spell thawed the snow, exposing the bodies of those who had died that winter. The odor of decomposition seemed to affect many of the soldiers, and the incidence of the black-tongue plague increased. Kiso decided to leave the valley before the sickness completely demoralized his men.

A meeting of the war council was called the night before they were scheduled to leave. Yoshi attended. He knelt beside Santaro in the main hall of Hiuchi Fortress. An occasional icy tongue of wind flicked through the earth-packed walls. Braziers burned in the dark corners, and pine torches set in the walls gave a fitful light. It was the seventh day of the third month. Early in the evening the temperature had dropped, refreezing the half-melted snowdrifts.

If Kiso felt the cold, he did not show it. He wore a thin blue robe and jacket as he knelt in his position facing the council circle.

"We march," he announced, "in the morning. North. Our goal is to consolidate the northern provinces before we turn back to Kyoto. We will not wait for my cousin Yoritomo to act. Once the *hokurikudo* is secured, we will take Kyoto in my name. Meanwhile, I have chosen the units that will stay behind to hold Hiuchi-jo until we return."

"How many men will you leave behind?" asked Yoshi.

"Eight hundred samurai—mostly foot soldiers—under four officers, including my uncle, Yukiie." Kiso nodded to Yukiie, who appeared unhappy at being left behind but resigned to what he took to be another insult to his rank. Kiso continued, "Plus families and retainers. That will be more than sufficient to control local problems."

"But hardly enough to hold the fort against a major attack," said Yoshi.

Kiso glared. "What do you suggest . . . master tactician?" he said sarcastically.

"Leave the fort. It has served its purpose as our temporary headquarters. Take the men with us where they can be of use."

"We have made this our valley. It is rich in rice and grain. We would be fools to leave it to our enemies."

"Winter is past. From now on we can live from the land. We cannot garrison every attractive spot we find. When we have won the entire *hokurikudo,* we can return and claim this prize. If we leave eight hundred men, we will lose their support in forthcoming battles and we may end by losing their lives should they be attacked by a superior force."

Kiso's lids drooped; his face hardened in anger. "We will keep the valley," he said. "If you do not think my uncle and his men are sufficient, we can leave you here to help them." He gave a raucous laugh.

"That was not my intent..." said Yoshi.

"I like the idea," interrupted Kiso. "You will remain here. That is an order. You will stay with Yukiie to protect our prize."

"I would prefer..."

"Enough!" snapped Kiso angrily. "I have given the orders. You will accept your assignment and not criticize my decision. You will stay!"

Yoshi bowed his head mutely. Internally, he cursed himself for having put himself in this position. Though he was a general and Yoritomo's representative, he had to accept Kiso's orders.

Yoshi's face was impassive, but he thought Kiso had made the first major mistake of the war. Would Yoshi pay for it?

By the morning of the eighth day, grain, salt meat, dried fish, beans, and personal effects were loaded onto carts and packhorses. The army was ready to march. Before nightfall, Yoshi sent messages, telling Yoritomo and Go-Shirakawa of Kiso's plans. He recommended that Yoritomo send troops to take Kyoto before Kiso grew stronger. In Yoshi's judgment, Kiso was not strong enough to confront Yoritomo...yet. But soon, Kiso would be ready.

Yoshi's message to Go-Shirakawa carried similar information, but was even more critical of Kiso's instability. Yoshi ended by saying, "...Kiso will defy his cousin Yoritomo. Your Highness may be trapped in the battle between them. Place your name and resources behind Yoritomo. Help him crush Kiso before Kiso grows too powerful."

forty-one

It was a month to the day since Kiso's army had threaded its way out of the valley of Hiuchi-yama. In the northeast quarter of Kyoto, shortly before dawn, young General Taira Koremori completed his toilet. Koremori adhered to the old ways: blackened teeth and white face powder. His hair was drawn back in a tight bun and covered by a soft black silk formal *koburi*. His over-robe was brocaded, with a design of crimson horses on a mauve background. The under-robes ranged from warm yellow to deep orange and the colors showed at sleeve and hem. Widelegged trousers of stiff silk rustled when he walked.

Before calling for a cart, Koremori inspected himself in a polished metal mirror. He rubbed a soft hand on his prominent jaw and was satisfied that he had shaved cleanly. Through the white powder, his young skin—he was twenty-one years old—glowed with good health. His classically handsome face was supported by a thick neck and set above meaty shoulders. He closely resembled his dead father, Taira Shigemori, the favorite son of the deceased *Daijo-Daijin*, Taira Kiyomori.

Koremori rang the gong to summon a retainer and order the cart. While he waited for his transport, he ruminated. A year ago, his grandfather had gone to the Western Paradise. In that time, Koremori had hardly advanced his career. He attributed this failure to Uncle Munemori's weakness and to the vile nature of the cloistered Emperor, Go-Shirakawa. Koremori had not forgiven Go-Shirakawa for giving command of the Imperial troops to his young uncle, Shigehira. Go-Shirakawa had insulted and embarrassed him by recalling his ignominious defeat at the Fujikawa River.

Koremori frowned. Shigehira had won great glory defeating Yukiie at the Sunomata River while Koremori wasted his life in the capital with frivolous court intrigues.

A retainer interrupted his thoughts. The cart was in position. Koremori marched on thick-padded soles down the broad steps of his Shinden mansion and across the white pebbled walk to the cart.

Today was the eighth day of the fourth month and the sun shone brightly. The air was crisp, bringing the scent of new flowers. The gardens were just beginning to bloom. Koremori sniffed the cool air appreciatively. He adjusted his two ceremonial swords and his baton of office and regally mounted the steps of the cart for the ride to Rokuhara.

Bumping along the rutted main street, Koremori studied the capital through his shutters. The winter had been cruel. Many buildings had collapsed under the weight of snow; others had been looted and dismantled for firewood. Large areas were burned, leaving black stumps of support columns and a sharp smell that stung the nostrils.

As the cart rumbled along Suzaku-Ōji, Koremori was horrified to see that even the famous willows had been vandalized by desperate citizens, who had stolen branches for firewood. If Koremori had his way, a penalty of death would be imposed on the vandals.

As the cart turned on San-jo, heading toward the Fifth Street Bridge, he espied priests marking the faces of plague victims who had been left dead in the streets. Koremori shuddered. There seemed to be an increasing number of victims as the weather improved. Even the courtiers and nobles were subjected to the horrors of the plague. The gods, indeed, frowned on the "good people" this winter and spring of 1182.

Crossing the bridge to Rokuhara, Koremori gagged at the sight and scent of a mound of partially decomposed bodies. They had been stripped of clothing and valuables and thrown under the bridge without a vestige of decency. Koremori wondered who they were...probably peasants who had starved and froze during the bleak winter. But how could one be sure? Mightn't there be nobles, robbed, stripped, and discarded, among the horrible cadavers? Disgusting thought!

Koremori's cart arrived at the crossbeam and sentry station that marked the entrance to the Rokuhara estates. He immediately forgot the ugly scenes of the city in the anticipation of good fortune. Friends had informed him that he could expect an important assignment after the "Washing-the-Buddha" ceremony. Koremori had waited an entire year for his opportunity while his young uncle gained glory in the field.

His lips tightened and he thrust his large jaw forward as he went to meet his destiny. Informants told him that his Uncle Munemori would announce his assignment after the day's ceremonies. He understood that the assignment would not come from Munemori, who was incapable of making important decisions. Decisions of policy came from the Nii-Dono, who manipulated her weak son behind the scenes.

Normally, the "Washing-the-Buddha" rituals were performed in the Imperial enclosure, but the Nii-Dono's influence was so powerful that when she pleaded a mild indisposition, Go-Shirakawa ordered the priests and nobles to report to Rokuhara instead of the Imperial palace.

The main hall of Rokuhara palace had been converted into a representation of the scene of Buddha's birth. In the center, a twenty-two-foot-high gilt statue of the Buddha looked down serenely on a panorama of pomp and color. The nobles were arrayed in their most colorful formal robes. The colors blended and shifted in the light of a hundred lanterns as they executed stately movements that had been rehearsed with all the care of a theatrical performance.

Nobles of the second rank wore combinations called *fuji*, wistaria, a soft mix of violet or light blue on the outside and light green on the linings and under-robes. The third rank wore the *hagi*, clover, combination: dark red over sea-green. Each rank was resplendent, and the combinations of plum-blossom mixed freely with azalea, yellow rose, and willow. Even the sixth rank courtiers—the lowest rank invited to the ceremony—were handsomely attired in their green jackets and wide-legged trousers.

At one side of the hall, a platform bordered by a low teak railing had been erected. At the corners of the platform, tall celadon vases held arrangements of cherry tree branches. The branches spread five feet across and drooped over the railings to trail their blossoms on the floor.

On the platform, the Nii-Dono leaned on a brocaded elbow rest and watched the proceedings from behind a *kicho*, screen of state, a six-foot-high portable framework that supported translucent drapes. Go-Shirakawa sat on a thronelike Chinese chair, with his grandson, the four-year-old Emperor Antoku, seated on a smaller chair at his side. Munemori, dressed in an ornate robe of brocaded moonflowers on a soft rose-petal background, sat cross-legged on a violet cushion to the left of his mother's screen of state. Behind these royal guests, making a frame for their appearance, was a two-section Korean screen. Each section was ten feet square and dramatically painted; the left screen section depicted the Avichi hell, the right represented the Western Paradise.

Koremori joined the stately dancers. Proud of his knowledge of the traditional steps, he boldly led the others in the dance.

The priests, dressed in white silk, with high hats of gold and white tied with ribbons under their chins, were in stark contrast to the colorful nobles. In a mixture of Buddhist and Shinto rites, the priests—over twenty of them, representing the major temples and shrines of Mount Hiei and Nara—chanted the sutras and intoned hymns of praise for the Buddha.

A high scaffold had been erected behind the statue so that the priests and nobles could mount stairs at one side, pour their offerings of tinted water over the gilt head, and descend the other side. Each priest chanted his own prayer while he ladled colored water from a golden tub. When the last priest had descended, Koremori led the nobles up the steps. The formal dance continued as each made his obeisance, poured his offering of water, descended, and took his preassigned position facing the Emperor's dais.

When the last noble was in place, Go-Shirakawa led the chanting of the lotus sutra. Afterward, the priests solemnly departed, leaving the nobles to their celebration. A samisen player accompanied himself in "Was Ever Such a Day," a pair of dancers swayed gracefully back and forth, interpreting the birth of Buddha. Their red jackets and wide white pants made pleasant rustling sounds whenever they shifted position.

Sake cups were passed freely. Everyone who drank recited a poem. Koremori recited:

> *"Rokuhara's halls*
> *Echo to the holy men*
> *Chanting the praises*
> *Of the great golden Buddha*
> *And his glorious children."*

Of course, the "glorious children" were the court, and particularly the Taira clan. The nobles applauded, and Go-Shirakawa—who had maintained a dour expression through the entire ceremony—nodded appreciatively.

Koremori fixed his eyes on the dais. He drank, recited, sang, and danced, watching for a sign. And finally he was rewarded. He saw his grandmother reach a bony arm through the screen to touch Munemori's sleeve. Munemori pulled away sullenly and sniffed at his perfumed kerchief. With a grimace, he turned to the wily old Emperor and whispered in his ear.

Go-Shirakawa munched on a sweet cake, seeming to ignore Munemori. Koremori held his breath. At last, after Munemori's cheeks had flushed with embarrassment, the Emperor rose and held out his arms to get the guests' attention.

An attendant sounded a Chinese gong until the nobles quieted. They stood in a semicircle around the Emperor's dais, awaiting his announcement.

As an indication of his status as a lay priest, Go-Shirakawa's head was shaved and polished; it glistened in the light of the hundred lanterns. His bold nose dominated his round face, giving him a commanding expression. With his arms extended, his scarlet court cloak opened to reveal dark red damask lining, another white silk under-robe, and loose trousers of deep violet hue. Depending upon the angle of the viewer, the Korean screen backdrop made Go-Shirakawa look either like an incarnation of the Buddha or a demon from the court of the dread king Emma-Ō.

"With today's ceremony, we are absolved of past sins and reaffirmed in our faith in the Buddha," the Emperor intoned, his voice rising and falling in formal cadences.

The courtiers applauded mildly. Go-Shirakawa waited for quiet.

"Our good people have suffered through a disastrous winter," he continued. "I need not remind you; you know those who have suffered from cold and plague in this difficult season. But now..." his voice rose dramatically "...we must forget the winter. Amaterasu smiles and the time is auspicious for us again to take action against the enemies of the Empire."

The applause was thunderous. Who among the nobles was not threatened by the encroachment of the Minamoto? Who had not lost manorial estates in the far provinces? Who would not bravely send his retainers against the enemy to regain lost lands and the revenues they represented?

Go-Shirakawa spread his arms. His red sleeves seemed a symbol of blood and battle. "We will mount an army to destroy Kiso Yoshinaka and regain the *hokurikudo*. In command will be our respected general...Taira Koremori!"

Though Koremori had expected the announcement, he nonetheless felt a rush of blood to his face. He trembled with emotion and pride. He sucked in a deep breath, held it for five seconds, and released it slowly as he listened to the applause of his peers. He could wipe out the memory of the Fujikawa disaster. He bowed to the Emperor three times.

"I accept this sacred mission in the name of the Emperor and my Taira clan," he announced. "Be assured, the traitorous Minamoto will be destroyed before the next year's 'Washing-of-Buddha' ceremony."

Go-Shirakawa sank back on his carved chair and munched another sweet. Although his expression was openly sardonic, the generals and nobles, busy congratulating Koremori, failed to notice. Go-Shirakawa's eyes were half-closed. He thought of the recent message he had received from his agent, Tadamori Yoshi. Yoshi said Kiso's power base was growing; he recommended that Go-Shirakawa support Yoritomo in the coming struggle. Yes, thought, Go-Shirakawa, let Koremori fight Kiso in the northern provinces. Whoever won or lost was unimportant . . . what mattered was that the Taira and Kiso were weakened.

Go-Shirakawa watched Koremori strutting among his friends. The Emperor nodded his shaved head and he smiled cynically. He was sending the right man. A crowd of at least fifteen generals offered to accompany Koremori on his glorious mission. Each of them said variations of the same theme—"The might of the Empire will overwhelm the crude northern barbarians."

The festival continued. The celebrants laughed immoderately as they stumbled between the golden Buddha and the Korean vision of heaven and hell. They toasted victory and became drunk on sake and thoughts of glory.

forty-two

On the day Koremori received his mandate from the Emperor, Yoshi and Nami walked a narrow path that wound along the side of Mount Hiuchi. Several of these abandoned trails led upward for short distances and then disappeared in dense shrubbery. On this eighth day of the fourth month, the crisp air and scent of burgeoning wildflowers inspired Yoshi and Nami to investigate one of the unexplored paths.

The path was unobstructed. Yoshi and Nami congratulated themselves for finding an undiscovered route over Hiuchi-yama. They descended in great good humor, stopping frequently to rest and enjoy the beauty of the day.

"Yoshi, look here," called Nami, who had walked ahead while Yoshi picked blossoms from a campion bush.

Yoshi straightened up and came to her, offering a spray of the pale lavender blooms. "For you, my love," he said.

"You are very sweet, Yoshi," she responded. "But look here! Another discovery!" She pulled at the twisted trunk of a dwarf pine to reveal an opening in the rocks. It was low but wide enough for a person to slip through.

"I think it could be dangerous," Yoshi said. "It may be the lair of a bear or a wildcat."

"It could be, but I don't think so. Stories are told that long ago, when the gods first made our land, primitive people lived in caves like these. I think we've found a cave that has probably been uninhabited for hundreds of years. See how this dwarf pine has grown in the entrance."

"Let's go on. Discovering a path over the mountain is enough accomplishment for one day."

"I want to go inside."

Yoshi's mouth pulled in at one corner. Nami was the most single-minded woman he had ever known. If she wanted to go inside, nothing would dissuade her. "Let me explore it first," he said.

Nami smiled and Yoshi's heart melted. She had rarely smiled since joining Kiso's forces. This past month, since the army's departure, Nami smiled more often and every time she did, it was another transcendental experience for Yoshi.

Yoshi poked at the twisted pine branches with his war fan, pushing his hand into the opening. He listened intently and heard nothing. Forcing the trunk to one side, he squeezed past it and doubled over to get his head in the entrance. There was a musty stillness, as if the years lay heavy in the enclosed space. Then he was inside, inching forward, stretching the fan in front of him. Away from the entrance, the darkness was absolute. He expected to touch rock wall, but there was nothing within reach.

"Nami," he called, and his voice echoed in the darkness. The cave was larger than he had expected. He waved the fan back and forth, moving slowly away from the entrance. His sandaled foot hit something that clattered, a sound like Go stones being dropped in a box. Bending to feel what had made the noise, he felt old dust rising to clog his nostrils. He suppressed a sneeze. Yoshi's hand closed on something smooth, about an inch in diameter, hard, cool. A club of some kind? A human bone! The noise had been caused by a skeleton collapsing on itself.

Yoshi backed away till he was in the dim light of the entrance. He looked out to see Nami peering anxiously through the pine branches. Behind her, the entire valley was visible, the fort of Hiuchi-jo, the water that bounded it, the central lake, the scattered farmhouses with thin wisps of smoke rising from their chimneys. It was an awe-inspiring vista made even more so by the frame of the cave's opening and the sense of isolation the cave engendered.

Yoshi squeezed out from behind the pine. "It is empty of life," he said, then paused and added, "I think you would find it unpleasant."

"But not dangerous?"

"No, not dangerous."

"Then I shall go in."

Yoshi shrugged resignedly and held the pine to one side. He peered in after her, but she was invisible the moment she stepped away from the entrance. There seemed little he could do except wait until she had satisfied her curiosity.

He heard a shriek as she discovered the pile of bones.

Seconds later, Nami tugged frantically at the branches in her haste to get out of the cave.

"I warned you," said Yoshi repressing a grin.

"Let's leave this horrid place," said Nami with a shudder.

As they ambled down the hill to the fort, they stopped frequently to pick flowers from the bushes that bordered the path. Neither spoke, both being content to enjoy each other's company and the crisp fragrance of the mountain air in silence.

In places where the bushes thinned, Yoshi could see the fort and the camp in the valley below. The narrow stream that surrounded the fort was now a deep protective moat. Not a natural moat. Oh no. Labor, hard labor changed the course of the shallow river and built the dam that created the moat.

On this lovely spring day it was difficult to remember the first unpleasant days at Hiuchi-yama...

A month ago, after Kiso marched his army out of the valley, Yukiie and his newest retainer, a limpid youth of thirteen, had chosen the fort as their home. Yoshi and Nami were content to live outside the palisade.

The four units of soldiers were divided so that two hundred were quartered at the fort, two hundred at Yoshi's martial-arts academy, and the rest at the newly abandoned barracks city. Most of the eight hundred soldiers were local farmers who had joined Kiso as an alternative to starvation. With the arrival of warm weather, many wanted to return to their farms and families. Whenever a guard detail was posted at the entrance to the valley, it would return short a few men. Though the punishment for desertion was death, it was almost impossible to apprehend the deserters.

The men who were stationed at Yoshi's academy were generally loyal to him, but the majority at the Hiuchi-jo fortress and the barracks were not loyal to any person or cause.

General Yukiie, in a rare moment of attention, decided to halt the outflow by cancelling guard details. Yoshi objected, pointing out that the camp would be vulnerable to surprise attack.

Yukiie waggled his fat shoulders and said, "Who would attack us here in the provinces?"

"Do you imagine that the Taira will surrender their country voluntarily?" demanded Yoshi, holding back his anger.

"No one will find us here," said Yukiie smugly, stroking the sleeve of his young retainer.

"We are responsible for the troops," said Yoshi. "If you don't value your life, consider theirs."

Yukiie pursed his lips pettishly. "I am very concerned for

my life. I have much to live for..." He turned and smiled
wetly at his young companion. Then his expression hardened
and he added sullenly, "We are safe here in the fortress. I am
as responsible as you are for the men, but I do not care to
explain to my hot-headed nephew why eight hundred soldiers
were reduced to half that number by desertions."

"You are making a terrible mistake. You risk losing all the
men in your anxiety to prevent losing a few."

Yukiie's eyes narrowed to slits, his thick red lips drew back
in a snarl. "I am in charge," he hissed. "You are only an adviser.
I grow tired of your criticism and your insubordination. When
we are reunited with Kiso, I will request your dismissal. If you
wore swords, I would challenge you now!"

Yoshi was thunderstruck, not knowing whether to laugh or
be angry. The idea of this obese monster challenging him was
ludicrous. At the same time, Yoshi read hatred and malice in
Yukiie's expression.

"I am fortunate I do not wear swords," said Yoshi with a
sarcasm that was completely lost on the furious Yukiie.

"Yes, you are."

"Nevertheless, I insist we prepare a defense against attack.
While you have the fortress to protect you, my men and the
four hundred in camp are exposed and vulnerable to an enemy.
If sentinels are not posted at the valley entrance to warn us,
we will be overrun before we can defend ourselves."

"If that is your Karma, then that is what will be."

"I will not accept that. My mission is to help Kiso's campaign against the Taira. That does not permit me to place men
in jeopardy without an attempt to save them."

"I weary of this conversation. You bore me. I want no more
of you." Yukiie signaled his young man to help him rise. As
he ponderously stood up, Yoshi said quickly, "I have a plan
and will need your men to divert the river so that it forms a
deep moat around the camp. The moat will give protection."

"I will never give you my permission. I will not allow you
to make my soldiers into common laborers."

"General Yukiie, may I point out that most of them *are*
common laborers. Those who have achieved a semblance of
military skill are those in my *dojo*."

"Nevertheless..."

"To Emma-Ō with nevertheless! Regardless of what you
say, your men will start digging a moat and building a dam
today!"

"How dare you address me so?" sputtered Yukiie. "You are no more than a barbarian yourself. I know your lineage... bastard son of an unknown father." His face reddened, his expression a cross between anger and embarrassment at losing face in front of his young man. "If you order this dam, I will countermand your orders. The dam will fail."

Yoshi's jaw tightened, he leaned forward and pressed an iron-hard finger into Yukiie's soft belly. "You will not countermand my orders," he said in a flat voice that made Yukiie cringe. "Your men will start digging today!"

So the dam was built. Yukiie disappeared into Hiuchi-jo with his thirteen-year-old boy and Yoshi organized and directed the construction of the moat and the dam. If attacked, the troops could retire to the far side of the moat and be nearly invulnerable.

That dispute had been a month ago. Yoshi was brought back to the moment by Nami. She called him to observe a large butterfly hovering above a cluster of wistaria. "How beautiful," she said and recited:

> *"Silken butterfly*
> *Evanescent red and black*
> *Your throbbing wings beat*
> *Out the measure of your span:*
> *A tear melting on my sleeve."*

Yoshi smiled sadly. There was an undercurrent of pessimism in the poem that touched a sensitive spot deep within him. How fleeting was life. Beauty was temporary, and nothing worthwhile lasted forever.

Yoshi felt a wash of sadness as he looked at Nami's fragile beauty against the purple flowers. She was studying the butterfly with an expression of childish innocence. He had done everything he could to protect her. Was it enough?

Yoshi took her shoulders in his strong hands. He held her close. "If we could freeze this moment for eternity," he said, "then I would be content."

The day had grown cooler as the sun lowered. As Nami nestled against Yoshi's chest, she shivered.

Perhaps it was the cool breeze.

forty-three

Koremori ordered his generals to conscript one hundred thousand men. Imperial guards ransacked the countryside, searching out and drafting every able-bodied man. Threats, coercion, and punishment were the standard; young or old, merchant or farmer, they were summarily enlisted in Koremori's army.

The very old and infirm, who were left behind, sent a messenger with a complaint to the cloistered Emperor. "Is it not wrong to take three men from every four who work the land, who fish the seas, who manage the forest?" they wrote. "Of what use are our young people to your mighty army? They know only the way of the land and sea, nothing of the sword and bow."

The Emperor smiled cynically and sent the messenger back with an answer guaranteed to please no one. "Your suffering brings moisture to the Imperial sleeve. When the battle is ended, your people will gain glory from their service."

A large mass of untrained and ill-equipped men shuffled out of the northeast gate on a gray morning in the second week of the fourth month. Young General Koremori now commanded one of the largest armies in history. Perhaps not quite the one hundred thousand he had demanded, but the largest army ever gathered.

Experienced generals of the Imperial guard served under his command. There was also a large group of generals in name only, men given their rank for service to the throne or for cultural contributions, such as the famous poet-musician General Tsunemasa.

Saito Sanemori, the elderly general who had formerly served Koremori as adviser and whose advice had been ignored at the disastrous battle of the Fujikawa River, added his banner to the great battalions. This same Sanemori, almost thirty years ago, had spared the life of the baby Kiso and his mother, Lady Senjo. Koremori felt Sanemori's presence an affront because of Fujikawa, but Sanemori pleaded with the Emperor for permission to serve against Kiso. He did not explain his reason; he intended never to reveal his secret. Go-Shirakawa had no objection and granted Sanemori's request.

The Emperor and most of the courtiers and ladies stationed themselves along the road in carts and palanquins. They cheered and applauded as officers herded their men through the gate. The spectators applauded loudly whenever a favorite general appeared, colorful in his painted armor. Even the gray skies did not dampen the effect of the officers' brightly hued trappings: green, gold, violet, scarlet, azure, and warm yellows. Each general had his own color combination; each wore his wide-horned helmet proudly as he rode, followed by dozens of banners marked with his family crest and announcements of past triumphs.

The army was complete in every respect...except one. There were very few supply carts following behind the last of the foot soldiers. The city had scarcely recovered from the winter famine, and General Koremori had been ordered to live off the land.

By nightfall, the army made camp eight miles north of the city. After the evening meal was eaten, the supplies were gone. The next morning, the army marched forth on empty stomachs. Scouts rode ahead, searching for food in the farms and villages. They took whatever was available, leaving entire villages depleted. A few farmers tried to hide grain from these Imperial locusts. Those who were discovered were executed on Koremori's orders. On the third day, a ragged and hungry army passed the northern end of Lake Biwa.

Many of the less warlike generals lost their enthusiasm for the march. A group led by the poet-musician Tsunemasa split off to visit the island of Chikubushima, which sat like a jewel in the blue waters of the lake. Koremori was furious. That Tsunemasa should leave to pursue his muse on the famous island was unconscionable, but to take a half-dozen other generals, and their retainers with him, leaving a thousand men without leaders, was treasonable.

Saito Sanemori accompanied Tsunemasa in the boat. He returned with the oarsmen and explained Tsunemasa's dereliction to Koremori.

"Tsunemasa is not a coward. Indeed, he has had no experience to teach him fear. He is a poet who does not understand the urgency of our mission. He is enchanted by the beauty of

Chikubushima. We must understand and appreciate this poetic
impulse or we will be no better than the bestial foot soldiers
we lead."

Koremori was not mollified. He thrust his heavy jaw forward
at Sanemori and glared. "Tsunemasa volunteered to serve with
us and must be responsible for his actions. I accept his desire
to visit the island, but I cannot understand why he remained."

Sanemori's face softened and for a few moments he looked
young again. He explained, "Chikubushima is like the magic
island of ancient China, *Horai*. There he can hear the rapturous
song of the bush-warbler and the *hototogisu,* cuckoo. The giant
Cryptomeria trees festooned with wistaria vines, undisturbed
for a thousand years, add to the enchantment for one as young
and sensitive as Tsunemasa."

Sanemori smiled beatifically at the recollection as he added,
"Tsunemasa stopped at a shrine, and the priest, knowing his
reputation, brought him a *biwa* to play. He played this lute like
an angel, melodies like 'Jōgen' and 'Sekijo' sent notes like
liquid silver flying to the sky. Everyone was lost in the spell
of the music and the island's magic."

"Yet you returned."

"I am older and perhaps not as much of a poet as Tsunemasa."

Koremori, who fancied himself a great poet, understood but
was unforgiving. He drove the men harder as a result of Tsunemasa's defection. When they slackened the pace, Koremori,
on his great gray stallion, was near to reprimand the commanders and inspire the men. This was to be Koremori's time
of glory and he refused to let minor setbacks come in his way.

On the sixteenth day of the fourth month, a week after
leaving the capital, scouts reported that a contingent of Kiso's
men were fortified in a valley near Hiuchi-yama, thirty miles
ahead. They also reported the valley was lush with grain and
livestock.

The army's problems could be solved in one deft stroke—
plentiful food and a skirmish with the enemy. Koremori was
certain his army outnumbered the Minamoto. He called a council of his generals and ordered the drive to Hiuchi-yama to
begin at once.

"There will be reward enough for us," he announced. "And
food enough for our men."

The generals applauded.

There was no rest that night. The men marched until morning. As Amaterasu peeped over the horizon, they crossed the peak between Omi and Echizen. Looking back from the twenty-five-thousand-foot peak, they could see Lake Biwa, with the magic isle of Chikubushima shining in the morning light.

The army was fifty miles from Kyoto and entering the domain of Kiso Yoshinaka. Many of the men secretly wished they could return to the safety of the home provinces. Especially when they looked ahead to see the Kiso-controlled *hokurikudo* spread before them from the far shore of the Western Sea to the threatening mountains of the north.

Koremori, surrounded by retainers, banners fluttering in the morning breeze, raised his sword and pointed it toward the northwest. His thick shoulders were pulled back under his full armor. He raised himself as high as possible in the gray's stirrups and shouted, "There, our glory awaits." He spurred the great horse and raced down the slope, leading his ragged army into the valleys of Echizen.

forty-four

For the entire month since Kiso's departure, Yukiie, with a condescending sneer, had watched Yoshi rehearse his defense plans. Yukiie had relinquished command of the garrison defenses; he refused to consider the possibility of a Taira attack. The first step of Yoshi's plan was the digging of a deep moat around the camp. Before the water was dammed, Yoshi had sharpened stakes set in the bank, where they would be covered when the water level rose. Then barricades were erected, following the technique that had been so successful at the first Echizen battle. Without the moat, the barricades could not have slowed the attackers. Together, moat and barricade could hold off a siege for months. Supplies, sufficient to last through the summer with careful rationing, had been stocked in the inner fortress.

Yoshi and Nami's explorations of the face of Hiuchi-yama had yielded a narrow path that led behind Hiuchi-jo Fortress over the mountain to safety. Yoshi rehearsed the secret exodus of women, children, the old and infirm, by this rear escape route.

Yukiie told his young lover and constant companion, "Yoshi fancies himself a strategist. He is a fool who will one day atone for his insults to me. There will be no attack. His preparations are in vain."

"But, General, the moat does give us a measure of security."

In a fury, Yukiie turned on the boy, his eyes bulging like a great fat frog's. "You dare take his part against me. The moat. The moat! The moat!!" he screeched. "That is all I hear. Safe because of a moat! Ridiculous! If one key stone were removed, the moat would run dry in minutes."

"Yes, my lord," said the boy, his cheeks reddening in distress. He added in an almost inaudible whisper, "The dam wall is hidden deep in the pines at the base of the mountain. Who would think to look for it there?"

"Enough! Who indeed. Say no more. You displease me,

and I am seriously considering giving you to the samurai for their amusement."

The boys cheeks turned ashen gray. He had said too much. He brought every bit of charm at his command to reverse the situation. "I am a fool," he said with pouting mouth and downcast eyes. "I am young and stupid. Of course, my dear general, you are right. Let us retire to our rooms and I will make amends."

Yukiie cleared his throat angrily.

The boy continued in desperation, "There is a secret technique that we have not tried. Perhaps if I had not offended you we might have tried it today. I was told the technique is a favorite in the courts of China."

"Offend me? My dear child, nothing from China would offend me." Yukiie's anger vanished as though it had never been. His frown, which gave his round face a distinctly unpleasant aspect, turned to an even more unpleasant leer. He purred lasciviously. "Let us hasten," he said.

Yukiie waddled rapidly along, leading the boy. They disappeared into Hiuchi-jo, hand in hand. Yoshi, his rehearsals, his moat, and his plans were instantly forgotten.

The nineteenth day of the fourth month promised to be an auspicious day. The sun rose at the hour of the hare. The sky was deep azure; Tsukiyomi, the moon god, was visible as a round white disc overhead, while the orange face of Amaterasu was close to the horizon. Hiuchi-yama's valley lay silently in an enchanted peace. Thin trickles of smoke drifted from the scattered farmhouses. A flock of crows circled noisily near the valley entrance.

Yoshi awakened early and was already at work in the academy. He was explaining the fine points of hand-to-hand combat to a group of twenty ex-farmers, who sat cross-legged in a circle watching and listening intently. These were hard men, men who had lived close to the earth, who had wrested out a meager existence with their hands and their backs. Some were conscripts, some volunteers. Each recognized that through learning martial arts he could move up a social class from the lowly, stagnant category of *heimin* to the expanded opportunities of the samurai class. The sword could ensure each man's future.

For his demonstration, Yoshi chose the largest and strongest man. His opponent held a steel blade, Yoshi a wooden *bokken*. Both men wore padded headgear with an iron grid over the face, slatted bamboo chest protectors, skirts of thick leather flaps, and heavy gloves with wrist shields.

Yoshi said, "To be strong is not enough. Muscle alone will lose to brain. Hold the sword firmly. Two hands on the haft at waist level, blade up at a forty-five-degree angle. Now, relax your shoulders, clear your mind." Yoshi demonstrated. His hard-planed face was clear as still water, his hands held the wooden sword without tension, like a smooth continuation of his arms.

Yoshi continued, "There is only you and the steel extension of your spirit. Focus on your target and when you are ready to strike, do not hesitate. So . . ."

Yoshi leaped toward his opponent, using the power and speed of his hips. His center of gravity remained so low that there was no perceptible jerkiness to the motion. His head maintained a constant level; his eyes held fast to his target.

The farmer reacted quickly but nervously. He swung the blade in a frantic effort to parry; he was too late to stop the wooden blade. There were two cracking sounds as the *bokken* landed on his practice armor, once on the right side, striking his chest under the sword arm, the second strike, almost simultaneously, on the padded helmet that covered his head.

The farmer reeled back as Yoshi followed his advantage with a feint and a figure-eight attack that ended with Yoshi pressed close and holding the wooden edge against the big man's throat. Yoshi pushed him away and stepped back, sheathing his *bokken* with a sharp click.

"You were too tense," Yoshi explained to the disgruntled giant. "Tension made you react slowly. If you had been relaxed, you would have been able to parry my *bokken*. Always, always keep your mind clear and you will never be taken by surprise."

The farmer waited for an opportunity. Thinking he could best his instructor and retrieve his damaged self-esteem, he leaped forward to strike at Yoshi's ribs while Yoshi was involved in the lecture.

Yoshi slipped sideways as lightly as smoke. He drew the *bokken* in a blur of motion. When the farmer's blade passed him, he continued the path of the wooden sword in an unbroken sweep that brought it down sharply just beyond the farmer's protective gloves.

There was a howl of anguish and the sword clattered to the

floor. Yoshi paid no attention to the big man's pain. "So," Yoshi continued, "keep your mind clear and you will never be surprised."

Yoshi signaled two others to stand, one in front and one behind him. "Let us discuss a useful strategy if you are attacked from two sides at once," he said. "Usually the best plan is to move out of the center and force your opponents to face you one at a time, keeping them lined up one behind the other. Sometimes that is impossible, so you must be prepared to use another principle."

Yoshi nodded to the man in front of him. The man stepped forward with gritted teeth and drew his sword. Yoshi did not hesitate. Before his own sword was out of its scabbard, Yoshi stepped toward his opponent with his left knee bent and head ducked low. His wooden blade flicked out and described the famous wheel stroke. Despite his bamboo armor, the farmer doubled over, clutching his midsection. Continuing to spin, Yoshi dropped his right knee to the floor and pivoted on it, using the torso-splitter stroke against the man behind him. The sound of wood striking the bamboo slats resounded like thunder. Yoshi's blade followed through in a continuous arc until he snapped it back in its sheath. His two opponents staggered back out of range. The entire exercise took less than three seconds from the time Yoshi's sword left its sheath until it was returned.

Yoshi's hair was neatly in place. His face relaxed. "Tomorrow," he said, "we will show techniques against more than two enemies, using the peak stroke and the scarf-sweep. Today, we'll concentrate on learning the two techniques I demonstrated: the wheel and the torso-splitter."

As Yoshi dismissed his two opponents and signaled another pair to rise, the gong outside the *dojo* sounded the invasion alarm! He quickly ordered the men to their assigned positions. Samurai and armed farmers rushed about in seeming disorder. The camp was in bedlam. The drills and rehearsals had served their purpose. In minutes, everyone was at his assigned place, prepared for an attack.

Across the moat they saw mounted samurai riding through the fields, banners snapping in the early breeze, armor clanking and rustling, horses' hooves thudding. A vast army covered the new grass, beating it flat as they rode toward the fortress.

Hordes of foot soldiers, armed with *naginata,* bows, and swords, followed the horsemen. Thousands of grooms and retainers darted back and forth among the horses, carrying messages and commands from officers to troops.

To Yoshi, watching from behind a barricade, individuals blended into a mass as featureless as a swarm of locusts. He was aware of disciplined but random-looking movement within the billowing dust clouds stirred by the horses. Yoshi squinted into the eastern sun and revised his first impression. These were not locusts mindlessly covering the earth; rather, they were army ants moving inexorably toward their determined goal . . . his destruction. Thousands of horned war helmets, resembling the mandibles of army ants, added to the image.

The army drew closer, accompanied by the muted thunder of their passage. The vanguard was within fifty yards of the moat. Yoshi watched the leader ride ahead. Yoshi recognized Koremori at once. He knew the worst. Koremori, a stubborn and ambitious young man, would go to any length to advance himself in the eyes of the court. They could expect no mercy from him.

Koremori sat astride a large gray stallion at least two hands taller than the average war horse. The stallion was armored in leather and steel, the saddle covered with mother of pearl filigree. The horse's face was protected by a scarlet steel plate, shaped and painted to resemble the face of a dragon. Its sides and hindquarters were covered by red leather scales to match the dragon face. The stallion stepped forward boldly until horse and rider were at the very edge of the moat.

Koremori rose in his stirrups and announced his formal challenge, "I am Komatsu-no-Sammi Chujō Koremori," he shouted, "son of the famous warrior Taira Shigemori, grandson of the great *Daijo-Daijin*, Taira Kiyomori. I am twenty-one years of age and proud to serve in the name of the Emperor. Come forth any who dare challenge my might."

Yoshi raised and lowered his arm, the signal for his first rank of bowmen to open fire.

A hail of arrows flew around the young general, several bouncing from the horse's armor.

Koremori reddened with anger. This was not proper behavior from the challenged. He sneered at the peasant troop who did not understand the proper form of battle. But he, Koremori, would not ignore protocol. He hastily backed his horse away from the moat and ordered one of his captains to send the humming arrow to officially open hostilities.

There was no response.

Koremori's scouts had reported a small contingent of soldiers holding Hiuchi-jo. There had been no mention of the moat. It was impossible to judge how many men were hidden beyond the barrier. The scouts could have been mistaken. Koremori did not intend to fall into a trap. He called a council meeting with General Michimori and the old man, Saito Sanemori.

The Imperial army shuffled impatiently. Officers held their units in place with shouted orders. The dust settled and the horses quieted, waiting for their riders' commands. The valley was filled with the smell of the mass of men and horses: dung, sweat, and less easily defined odors that overpowered the sweet scent of the valley's greenery and flowers.

"No one has responded to the challenge," said Koremori stiffly. "This is improper behavior."

Sanemori's expression was carefully noncommittal as he shrugged and asked, "What would you have us do?"

Koremori studied the old man for some sign of sarcasm. The wrinkled face was as bland as that of a statue of Buddha. Nevertheless, the question stung. Koremori was unsure of the correct response to unorthodox behavior. He felt impelled to act firmly. "I shall order a mass attack at once," he said.

"No," said General Michimori quickly. He was a seasoned veteran, ten years Koremori's senior. Though he exuded dignity and strength, the Emperor had appointed him second in command to Koremori. "An advance guard should be sent to test the depth of the moat and to discover the extent of their defenses."

Koremori looked to Sanemori. He had learned some humility from his defeat at Fujikawa. He would not lightly disregard experienced advice again.

Sanemori nodded agreement with Michimori. "I agree. Whoever is in charge of their defenses is prepared for us, while we know nothing of him. A squad of ten men can test the moat. They may die, but we will learn something about the people we face."

"Agreed," said Koremori. "We will send twenty men across the moat." By doubling the number of men, Koremori saved face and proved himself master of the situation. His responses would not be timid or hesitant. Koremori felt equal to any sacrifice that might be asked of his men.

"So it shall be," said General Michimori with a slight twist to his mouth that suggested disapproval. He turned his war pony and spurred it toward his troops. Within three minutes, twenty volunteers, who were specially trained in swimming and water tactics, guided their mounts into the moat.

The horses were immediately in over their heads. The riders held themselves high in their saddles to keep their quivers and arrows dry. They were in a group within reach of the far bank when they met the first of Yoshi's surprises...a series of sharpened stakes set in the bank, pointing outward at a forty-five-degree angle. As the horses disemboweled themselves on the stakes, the air filled with their agonized screeches. The waters were kicked into a bloody froth as animals struggled to free themselves from the implacable wood points. Riders dismounted and climbed over their dying steeds only to be greeted by deadly arrows loosed by a hundred archers hidden behind the log barricades. Not one of the twenty reached the far bank. In less than a minute there was no evidence of their passage as some sank and the others were carried away by the current.

forty-five

Koremori's army covered the valley with a multicolored, constantly shifting blanket of men and horses. While Yoshi and his men waited anxiously behind the barricades for the army to attack, the sun crossed its zenith. They maintained their postions, sweating nervously, talking in low voices, encouraging each other, checking and rechecking their weapons. Yoshi was constantly on the move, making sure they were well prepared. When he was satisfied that morale was as high as could be expected among the eight hundred soldiers—there was little doubt that eventually they would be overrun—Yoshi went into the fort to supervise the exodus of the women, children, and old men.

Over one hundred people were ready to leave by the secret escape route, Yukiie and his young lover among them. Yukiie and the boy had preempted places closest to the rear gate of the fortress. They were carrying as many of their personal belongings as they could and had distributed the rest among some women and old men who clustered near them.

Nami, who was with the officers' wives in a group farthest from the gate, hastened to Yoshi's side. "Yukiie took command," she told him. "He intends to lead us out personally."

Yoshi clamped his jaw. He had not anticipated conduct so craven. The leaders and guides for the exodus had been appointed earlier by Yoshi. They had rehearsed and planned the escape for weeks—without Yukiie.

"General Yukiie," Yoshi called. "How generous of you to help these poor unfortunates who are too weak or old to gain honor at our side. We thank you." Yoshi bowed. His face gave away nothing of his feelings. "But now," he continued, "your troops wait for you at the defense line. Koremori may attack at any moment."

Yukiie's face quivered in a mixture of fear and anger. "I have decided to lead these people to safety," he said thickly. "When they are out of the valley, I shall return to lead my troops."

"But, General, the attack may come before you can return. How unhappy for you to miss this chance for glory." Yoshi's tone hardened. "And how unhappy for your eight hundred men if you did not lead them in the fight for your cause."

"That may be, but these unfortunate souls also need my guidance and I have decided to lead them away first."

"Thank you, General. I am sure that your decision has much merit, but our arrangements for escape have been well planned. Your presence is not essential. I suggest you stay with your men."

Yukiie's eyes darted back and forth searching for support. The young boy studiously looked at the ground. The women and old men turned away.

"These people need me," said Yukiie desperately.

"They will have to do without you. The soldiers need you more."

"No. I am going."

"If you do, you are a coward."

"How dare you. You are insubordinate. I will see you punished."

"Will you report to Kiso that I died protecting his fort while you ran?"

"You are insufferable."

"That may be. However, we will return to the barricades together while the women and children escape."

Nami stepped forward and said urgently, "Yoshi, I want to stay behind. Perhaps I can help."

The officers' wives chorused, "We all want to stay."

"Thank you, Nami. Thank you, ladies. I appreciate your bravery." Yoshi glanced at Yukiie, who shuffled about undecidedly. "Your desire should make some of our generals ashamed. General Yukiie . . ." he called, "Nami and the other samurai women want to fight for the fortress. They are perfect examples of bravery and samurai honor."

"They are insane!"

Yoshi faced the women and said, "You must leave with the children, but your bravery will be remembered." He turned to Nami, placed a hand on each of her shoulders, and stared into her sad eyes. "You must go with them," he said softly. "You take my heart with you."

"I want to stay . . ." she pleaded desperately.

"Darling, you cannot help. If you remain, the women will

all remain. The men will worry and be unable to concentrate on their duties. Please . . ."

"Yoshi, don't leave me. Without swords, you are defenseless. How can you help the soldiers? Let Yukiie escape, and you come too. Kiso cannot fault you if you follow Yukiie's example. You are only an adviser."

"Nami, you know that is impossible. Yukiie and I will remain. That is the only honorable course open to either of us."

Yoshi again addressed Yukiie. "Come! Otherwise we shall suffer the embarrassment of placing you under arrest."

"Damn you to Yomi. You'll pay for this insult," snarled Yukiie. His nose and lips twitched in an expression that gave him the look of a cornered rat. He shouted orders to his young companion and the people whom he had burdened with his possessions.

Yoshi watched impassively as the boxes and packages were unloaded. He waited until Nami and the others passed through the back gate. When he was alone with Yukiie and the boy, he said, almost sympathetically, "Leave the boxes. You may not need them again. We have an appointment with our Karma."

A silent Yukiie followed heavily as Yoshi led him back to camp.

It was late afternoon and there had been no overt hostilities from the enemy. As the shadows lengthened, torches were lit and both sides prepared for a sleepless night.

Rations were distributed. Yoshi constantly moved about, cheering the men with advice and good humor.

"The enemy has a hundred men for each one of us, but we are well protected," he told one group. "The taking of our camp will be so costly, they will eventually leave in defeat. Ours is the hope of life and the assurance of glory.

"Our names will be written in history," he said to another group. "Whether we live or die, the price we exact for this valley will earn us eternal fame."

Yukiie hid inside the palisade of Hiuchi-jo. Yoshi took the precaution of leaving a squad of soldiers with him. From time to time, the squad led him around the perimeter. Even when the soldiers cheered his presence, Yukiie's face retained its unhappy expression.

• • •

On the morning of the twentieth day, Koremori attacked. Wave after wave of horsemen galloped into the moat, loosing their flights of arrows at the defenders. The moat turned red as the horses died against the underwater stakes. The defenders, behind the barricades, killed hundreds of attacking samurai before they could climb over the stakes to mount the bank. A few samurai crossed the moat by riding over the impaled bodies of dead horses. On the opposite side, they galloped in circles, looking to engage an invisible enemy. They were easily targeted by the hidden archers.

Koremori watched in fury as his elite samurai were destroyed.

"Halt," he cried, brandishing his sword. "Halt and regroup!"

Before the command was carried out, another hundred men perished in the moat. Most fell victim to the deadly arrows or the underwater stakes, some were trampled by riderless horses, some were unseated and drowned in the bloody water.

The first assault cost Koremori nearly four hundred mounted samurai. The defenders lost twelve men, victims of arrows that blindly penetrated their defenses.

Yoshi's men were jubilant. In the flush of success, they forgot their precarious position. Many of the ex-farmers had never before tasted victory. They had beaten the professional soldiers of the Taira.

Temporarily.

Nami watched the skirmish from her secret cave in the face of the mountain. She had dropped behind the refugee group and made her way to the stunted pine that marked the cave.

Her misgivings arose as the last of the women disappeared along the trail. I am insane, she thought. I cannot help Yoshi. I am torturing myself, watching men die. Eventually, Yoshi too will fall. What could I do then? Do I have the strength to cut off his head to save it from the indignity of capture and display? I don't know.

Her mouth tasted sour, and her belly ached at the thought of what she might have to do. Even if it costs me my life, she decided, I will do what is necessary. But there is a possibility that Yoshi will live. What if he needed me? I could not live, thinking I fled before knowing the outcome of the battle.

She swallowed the lump that had formed in her throat, took a deep breath, and forced herself to look over the valley. An incredible vista brought home the hopelessness of Yoshi's situation. The hundreds of dead samurai scarcely depleted the great Taira horde; their army covered the valley floor in tens of thousands. In contrast, she saw the pitifully inadequate number of defenders below. Eight hundred men were burrowed behind barricades that covered a quarter-mile arc along the inside of the moat. She saw the entire panorama from where the moat started at a waterfall to the southwest to where it arced around the camp to disappear in the thick forest at the base of Hiuchi-yama in the northeast.

Nami studied the camp, searching for Yoshi. Several times she thought she saw him, but the figures were too far away to be certain.

Nami had not seen the first test of the camp's defenses, but she witnessed the most recent attack, an appalling, wanton waste of human lives. Nami was pained to think that some of those she watched die a bloody death were former acquaintances in the Kyoto court. She felt a tear forming at the edge of her lid. Had it been only a few days ago that she had studied the red and black butterfly and composed a poem to it? The lives of men were hardly less ephemeral than the lives of the butterflies.

Nami was observing the bright patch of banners that marked the headquarters of the Imperial army when she saw horses fan out and gallop to the various division heads. Units broke off from the central mass to take up stations around the arc of the moat. Until now, both attacks had been aimed at the central bulge of the moat, where the defenders were concentrated.

Below her, Nami saw Yoshi's men scurry to fortify the flanks. The men were now spread thinly over the entire perimeter, facing the Taira army's solid mass of men and horses.

Koremori signaled and a thousand horsemen leaped into the moat, driving their mounts at the defenders from every side.

Nami grimaced in horror. Could the defenses survive this onslaught? Before the first thousand reached the underwater stakes, another thousand were in the water and still another thousand prepared to follow.

The first horses screeched in pain as the stakes sunk into their withers. They tried to rear up, to pull back, only to be herded forward by those horses scrambling from the rear. Again the moat turned red. The waters were churned by hooves of the second wave. Panic-stricken beasts smelled blood and heard the sounds of agony. They were caught between the unfortunates ahead and the third wave behind. It was a scene from hell as warriors were toppled into the water and forced against the stakes by wild-eyed horses.

Nami covered her ears to drown out the screams of the dying.

Perhaps two hundred men and half that many horses reached the far side. Arrows cut most of them down before they could climb the barricades. Nami saw about two dozen samurai scale the walls to meet the defenders in hand-to-hand combat.

The samurai were more skilled swordsmen than the farmers. Their years of experience were used to good effect. They killed twice their number before the last attacker fell.

The moat was so full of bodies, the current was unable to clear it. Over a hundred horses and men were left impaled on the stakes. They rolled back and forth languidly in the current, streamers of red flowing from their eviscerated bodies.

Koremori's commanders gave orders to withdraw. They had lost a substantial army of their best men. The defenders had lost an ill-afforded fifty, making the defense perimeter even thinner.

The skirmish had been a victory for Yoshi, but Koremori could afford to lose a hundred men for each one of theirs. The fort was doomed. Of that there was no doubt.

forty-six

Yukiie watched the last onslaught from behind the heavy defensive slats of Hiuchi-jo Fortress. Though he cringed in fear, with trembling hands and quivering chins, he managed to avoid a complete breakdown because he had the inner palisade and the heavy shutters to protect him from the enemy. His vision encompassed the wide spread of battle and he knew that the encampment would fall.

After Koremori's men withdrew and the agonized cries of the wounded subsided, Yukiie left the shutters to sit cross-legged in a corner, staring wild-eyed at his young companion. The boy shifted uneasily under Yukiie's gaze; he had gladly accepted the favors bestowed on him, but now he was fearful of the fat man.

Yukiie was deeply disturbed, ravaged by his fear of the enemy, consumed by his hatred of Yoshi. He sat in sullen silence, then suddenly started muttering to himself: inarticulate sounds, loud curses, hisses of rage, and whining lamentations.

The boy drew farther away. The guards, stationed at the portal, observed Yukiie with thinly veiled contempt.

Shortly before the battle, Yoshi appeared and demanded that Yukiie leave the shelter to join his men. Yukiie wept shamelessly, pleaded sickness, and finally collapsed on the floor, wetting himself. Yoshi's sympathetic pat galled Yukiie more than the looks of frank disgust he received from the guards. And the boy had shunned his touch as if ashamed of him. They would pay. They would burn in the hottest of the underworld hells.

Yukiie turned his attention to himself. His violet robe was askew and stained; his black silk hat was shapeless and dusty; his wide, sea-green court trousers were damp and wrinkled. Yukiie considered himself a fastidious man, careful of color combinations and sensitive to perfumes. He flushed at the terrible picture he presented.

Vanity overcame fear. Battle or no, he could not remain in this sorry state. "You . . . soldier!" he called the head of the guards. "I need a change of clothing."

The guard smiled nastily. "We are under orders to keep you here unless you intend to join your troops."

Yukiie sank back in his corner. These barbarians enjoyed his discomfort. He had to save himself; he had to find a plan to turn the tide of his fortunes. If the present situation continued, it could result in eventual disgrace, more likely in his death. He had to overcome his fear or he would die because of it.

Then . . . a plan came to mind. A plan that would avenge the wrongs he had suffered at Yoshi's hands and would conceal forever his disgraceful conduct. He addressed the guard again. "Call General Yoshi to my side! I have decided to give him my full support. However, I must change my clothing. I cannot appear before my troops in this condition."

The guard exchanged glances with his companions. "Call General Yoshi." As an aside, he whispered, "Enough of this demeaning duty. If Yukiie takes his command, we will be released. I, for one, want to join my companions on the field of battle."

The guards agreed. None of them wanted to guard Yukiie; all looked forward to a chance at glory, fighting Koremori's army. One was chosen to search for Yoshi. He found him near the barricades, helping the wounded. Yoshi motioned him to wait until he finished the task before him.

Yoshi wore the full battle dress called *rokugu*, six articles of arms. The armor was made of lightweight metal and leather strips. It included the *yoroi*, chest protector; *kabuto* and *ho-ate*, helmet and face mask; and the *kote*, *sune-ate*, and *koshi-ate*, arm, shin, and loin guards. In place of the usual two swords he carried a war fan, which he used to direct the activities of the unit around him. "Build a shelter by those trees," he ordered, pointing with the fan. "A heavy roof will protect the wounded from Koremori's arrows." Tomorrow all might die, but while they lived, Yoshi felt responsible for the care of every man under his command.

As soon as the construction was under way, Yoshi turned to the guard and nodded for him to speak.

The guard bowed respectfully. "Sir," he said, "General Yukiie requests your presence at the fortress."

Yoshi answered impatiently. "I cannot spare time for his foolishness." He immediately regretted his snappish tone. He was tired from the strain of the day. The soldier was not at fault. Damn Yukiie! "All right," he said more calmly, and wondered what Yukiie wanted of him.

"He wants to join his troops," the guard volunteered.

Yoshi had been ashamed of Yukiie's behavior. The man was a samurai, the uncle of Kiso and Yoritomo. Yoshi was obligated to give him the respect due his family. Under the pressure of battle, Yoshi found himself hard pressed to remember his obligation to the Emperor. The hope that Yukiie would play his proper role greatly relieved him. Yukiie's help would free Yoshi to concentrate on survival. Yoritomo and Go-Shirakawa should be informed about the battle at Hiuchi-yama. Yoshi's brow smoothed and he felt his tension ease.

"Tell General Yukiie that I cannot leave the men. Another attack is expected. Send the general my compliments and see that he joins his men at the barricade."

"Sir, he requests permission to change his clothing first."

Yoshi, remembering the pitiful sight of the obese man crumpled on the floor, his clothing stained with urine, said, "Of course. I am pleased to honor his request. When you get back to the fortress, release two of the guards for line duty. You and one other will be sufficient to accompany Yukiie now that he has agreed to cooperate."

"Yes, sir." The guard hurried to Hiuchi-jo with Yoshi's instructions.

Yukiie could hardly conceal his satisfaction at Yoshi's orders. From a cringing shell of a man, he became a pompous bully. "Follow me closely," he hissed at the boy, who was thoroughly confused by the change in his master. "You, soldier, bring up the rear. And you..." he turned to the remaining guard. "Bring me the red lacquered pillow box and the bamboo trunk from my belongings at the rear gate."

The guard hesitated. Yukiie snapped, "Immediately. I am commander here. You have your orders."

The guard shrugged in bewilderment and left, relieved to be away from the odor that surrounded Yukiie.

When the box and trunk were in hand, Yukiie went behind a screen and removed his soiled robes and trousers. "Come here, boy," he said loudly. "Help me dress." The boy turned red at the snickers of the guards but went dutifully behind the screen. Yukiie was rubbing his pallid body with a scented cloth. Without clothes, he resembled a fat white slug, amorphous in shape, with rolls of pasty white flesh concealing his bone structure. His belly made three folds and the bottom fold covered his genitals like a soft dewlap. Thick thighs of doughy consistency and splayed feet angled out from under the gross body.

The boy was handsome in an androgynous way. His soft, delicate features had recommended him to Yukiie's attention, but he was slow-witted and weak. However, looking at his master, he was embarrassed. How he must appear to the guards! Yet the boy did not dare ignore Yukiie's orders. He handed Yukiie a lined white silk *fundoshi*.

"Dress me, stupid boy!" ordered Yukiie.

Over the *fundoshi* a white kimono was draped, which the boy secured by winding it twice around Yukiie's belly and tying a bow in the back.

Yukiie indicated which garments he wanted. The boy wrapped him in several *hitatares* of different shades of pale green, sky blue court trousers instead of the traditional warrior's *hakama*. Then Yukiie had the boy pull on his brocade-lined bearskin boots—his one concession to his military rank. Yukiie checked to be sure the boots were well fitted and well secured. He would need them later.

"There is an inkstone, a brush, and a sheet of fine mulberry paper in the pillow box. Bring them to me," he demanded loudly. "I would write a poem to honor my troops and their fine showing in battle."

The guards exchanged glances. Though these ex-farmers regarded the ability to write poetry with respect, they found it a strange preoccupation under the circumstances.

"I can't compose with you barbarians hovering over me," Yukiie said peevishly. Then he softened his tone, and his voice was almost friendly as he added, "The sooner my poem is written, the sooner I will join the troops. Have no fear. I cannot run away." Yukiie indicated his corpulence self-deprecatingly. His face creased in a smile of good humor. The guards did not notice that his eyes did not smile; they remained flinty and watchful from their pads of fatty tissue.

The guards nodded in unison. True, the general could not run far. Leaving Yukiie alone seemed a small price to pay for his cooperation.

"Yes, sir. We will be within earshot. When your poem is finished, call out and we will escort you to General Yoshi."

The moment the guards left, Yukiie prepared his ink and brushed a message on the paper. He folded it carefully and held it up to the boy. "Listen carefully," he said. "And follow my orders exactly."

The boy took the message and nodded unhappily. He was frightened of what he saw in Yukiie's face—a raw, blazing malevolence that bore no relationship to the poem he was supposed to have composed.

"The guards will return for me when I call. Meanwhile, you will keep my message concealed in your *obi*. The guards are not concerned with you. When I leave with them, you will do as I order." He fixed a baleful glare on the boy.

"You will slip out the back gate, where our belongings are stored. Follow the palisade to the northeast . . . your right hand," he said impatiently when the boy looked confused. "When you are deep in the woods, find the path across the dam. I have heard it is narrow, suitable for one person to cross at a time. When you have found the path, wait till nightfall, then walk to the other side."

"But if the enemy captures me . . ."

"Nonsense, boy. Trust me. Offer the message to anyone who challenges you on the other side. Tell him it is important and must be delivered to General Koremori at once. The message will be your passage to safety. You will live and I will join you. Do you understand?"

"Yes, sir. What is the message?"

"Yours not to ask, lad. Remember it is your safe conduct and our revenge for the insults we've suffered."

"I'm afraid . . ."

"Enough. You will follow my orders, or you will die a horrible death before the enemy breaches our defenses. I have the power! Remember that."

"Yes, sir. I'll go . . . at once."

"Quickly. Wait and cross after dark."

Yukiie raised his voice for the guards. "I am ready," he told them in as dignified a tone as he could muster. His knees trembled as he thought of the ordeal he would soon go through.

"What about him?" said a guard, indicating the boy who cowered in a corner.

"What about him?" echoed Yukiie. "He is of no further use to me. Leave him. His presence offends me."

The guards conferred. There were no instructions about the boy. Only Yukiie. One less to worry about, they decided. As they left, one of the guards kicked the boy contemptuously. He whimpered, and Yukiie's lip curled in a snarl. For a moment Yukiie actually forgot his fear.

• • •

Yukiie maintained his composure with difficulty. He did not enjoy the rough camaraderie of the soldiers. When he visited the groups along the barricade, they quieted down respectfully and seemed genuinely pleased at his presence. To the ex-farmers and professional samurai, Yukiie represented another world. Whatever Yukiie's personal weaknesses, the men saw no deeper than his formal costume and his rank.

Close to evening, Yoshi and Yukiie started their inspection. Except for an occasional stray arrow, there was little activity. Torches were being lit on the far side of the moat, tens, then hundreds, then thousands of fireflies as darkness cloaked the valley.

With the darkness, activity came to a halt. Sentries remained on the alert, but no full-scale attack was imminent. The soldiers huddled around small fires and told stories to keep their minds from the attack that was sure to come with the new day.

Yoshi invited Yukiie to join him at the academy. Yukiie demurred. He was unusually friendly in a way that made Yoshi uncomfortable.

"You must forgive me," said Yukiie. "I was not feeling well and I acted badly." He continued after a short pause. "The strain has been great, and I am very tired. I think I shall retire. I want to rise early to join the men."

Yukiie seemed contrite, but Yoshi was suspicious of this sudden change. "I'll send a man to stay by you while you sleep and to awaken you on time."

"I would appreciate that, General Yoshi, yet I would feel guilty if the soldier lost his much needed sleep. He will need his rest. But since my young retainer seems to have disappeared, I will need someone to wake me. Send a sentry to my quarters at the hour of the tiger. That will allow me time to prepare myself and join you before dawn."

Yoshi was thoughtful. Yukiie, even when friendly, was an unpleasant fellow. Was Yoshi being too hard on him? The man had visited the troops, nervously but willingly. He now gave every indication of trying to atone for his earlier cowardice. And where could Yukiie go in the dark?

"General Yukiie, it shall be as you request. Tomorrow will be a day to try the strongest of men. Your thoughtfulness is appreciated. I will see you in the morning."

As Yukiie bowed and turned away, Yoshi thought he saw

a flash of malice in his eyes. Or was it a reflection of the firelight?

Yoshi attributed his suspicions to fatigue. He was very tired and tomorrow could be their last day on earth. Let Yukiie be alone in these final hours to make peace with himself.

Yoshi bowed. "Good night, General Yukiie," he said. "Until tomorrow."

forty-seven

The river had been blocked across a narrow pass where it cut into the face of Mount Hiuchi. Thick forest came to the edge of the rock and earthwork dam. The boy found the crossing without difficulty. It was a narrow and precarious path, passing over tumbled rocks and rushing water. The builders had not concealed the entrance from the camp; they had never considered anyone leaving from their side.

A sentry was always on duty at a small lean-to that had been constructed as a sentry station in the thick woods at the far end of the dam. It had been carefully camouflaged so that Koremori's men would not accidentally find it. The sentry was not allowed to make a fire; it could mean disaster if he were seen by the enemy.

The boy almost bumped into the sentry in the dark. The crash of water on the rocks behind him covered the sound of his movements and prevented the guard from hearing him. The boy pressed his body against a tree trunk in terror. If he tried to pass the station, the sentry would be sure to see him in the pale moonlight. How could he explain his purpose? He trembled. If he returned to Yukiie having failed in his mission, he would be punished. If he went forward and was caught, he would be killed.

The sentry stirred. The boy heard him move about in his shelter. They were within ten feet of each other, and the boy felt his heartbeat must be audible over that distance. He controlled his breathing with difficulty as panic overcame him. He was going to vomit, defecate, scream. He gritted his teeth and clutched the tree to keep from falling.

A sound from the sentry, a grunt followed by a loud passing of wind. The sentry came out of the shelter, looked around, and stomped deeper into the woods.

The boy tried to move, but was frozen in place. Now! he told himself. His legs would not obey. He was stuck to the tree. Then a strong odor hit his nostrils; the sentry was relieving himself in the woods on the far side of the shed.

Now!

The boy scurried across the clearing and into the thick underbrush. Twigs snapped under his feet, brush whipped and stung his face. He made so much noise it seemed impossible not to be heard. But the roar of the water and the preoccupation of the sentry saved him. He burst out of the woods undetected.

Ahead, he saw thousands of fires. Koremori's army covered the valley as far as the eye could see. He was safe. He had done it. He had crossed the dam and reached his goal. It was time to put distance between himself and the woods.

He ran toward the fires.

Yukiie slipped out of his quarters. He carried a small bundle of extra boots, a robe, some silver coins, a bamboo tube of water, and a packet of rice cakes. He had considered wearing more practical clothing but decided against it; whatever he wore would be inadequate for his coming ordeal. He would have to make do. Ideally, a horse would be helpful, but unfortunately the road before him could only be traversed on foot.

Stealthily, Yukiie left the rear of Hiuchi-jo Fortress. He threw a last wistful look at his precious belongings stacked near the gate. No matter. His life was more important than these few paltry things.

A quarter moon floated among scattered clouds, enough to see his way along the escape path. Free of the camp, Yukiie had time to wonder if the boy had reached Koremori with his message. Well, he had to trust the boy. Sweet child. Not too bright, but willing, and with a certain shrewdness when it came to survival. Yukiie licked his lips, thinking of the Chinese variation the boy had recently demonstrated.

Yukiie panted from the unaccustomed exertion. His fat legs shook, and though his boots were the best available, his feet suffered from the rough ground. Sweat soaked through his robes, making them cling uncomfortably to his back. He had to rest. He had come a long way. He sank to the ground and looked back at the camp he had left—it seemed hours ago. Shock! He had hardly made any distance at all. The camp below and the campfires across the moat seemed close enough to touch.

Yukiie whimpered. He had to move on, but his body refused.

Then he heard noises coming from the face of Hiuchi-yama. Someone or something was directly behind him. His heart thundered in his breast. A thick taste of bile filled his throat. He had to move...had to move! Panic gave him strength to get to his feet and lumber ahead. He forgot his packet of food and supplies, dropping it as he stumbled higher and higher up the cliff face.

Nami froze in place.

Hunger had driven her out of her secret cave. She was picking berries from a nearby bush when she heard a thrashing on the trail above her. She tried to see what had caused the noise, but the moon covered its face with a rag of cloud and she could only make out a large lumbering shape.

In terror, she squeezed behind her dwarf pine into the cave mouth. It must have been a mountain bear, she thought. They were scarce close to human habitation, but she had heard stories of their occasional forays and of their ferocity.

The handful of berries would have to suffice. She could not risk going out again. Nami peered out of her cave at the panorama of fires and wondered where Yoshi was and if he thought of her.

Tsukiyomi's face came out of hiding again as the cloud drifted past. Nami was beset by doubts. Why should Yoshi think of her? He thought she had left with the others. Perhaps she was wrong to remain in the cave. Was it too late to go on alone? She thought of the bear on the trail ahead. No, she would have to stay, at least until daylight. She settled down to wait the night, eating the meager handful of berries one at a time.

Just as she finished the last berry, she heard a keening scream from far off. It sounded like the cry of a wild beast, but somehow she knew it was a human in pain. She shuddered.

The boy was halfway to the closest fires when an armored soldier loomed out of the dark.

"Halt," ordered the soldier. "Who are you? What do you want?"

"I am General Yukiie's retainer. I have an important message for General Koremori. You must take me to him at once."

"I must, must I?" The soldier came closer. He was thick-chested, heavily bearded, and wore the minimum armor of the *ashigaru*, the lowest warrior rank. The *ashigaru* were often little more than peasants. Their name meant "agile legs," because they were foot soldiers and spent much of their time in battle running between the higher-ranking men on horses. The rank was one that offered a chance at promotion and many of the *ashigaru* were extremely sensitive about their rank, acting more samurai than the true samurai.

"You are a pretty lad!" smirked the *ashigaru*. "Maybe we should forget the message and..."

"This message must reach Koremori at once," said the boy in a quavering voice, "or it will go badly for you."

"Ho? Badly for me? You haven't the balls to make it go badly for me. In fact, you may not have any balls at all." The *ashigaru* leered. "Take off your clothes, little butterfly. I want to see if you're a boy or a girl...not that it makes much difference."

The boy was near tears. "Please, sir. I have orders from my master. The message must get to Koremori before daybreak. I will answer with my life if it doesn't."

The *ashigaru* frowned. He was new to the rank of *ashigaru* and took his status seriously. His sense of self-esteem was tenuous and any threat caused an overreaction. This was a clear case of *kirisute-gomen*, disrespect. How dare this little pimple insist on his orders? It was clearly the *ashigaru*'s duty as a samurai to cut down this pretty boy on the spot. He hawked and spit at the boy's feet. His sword had not tasted blood since the beginning of the campaign, and he had his newfound status to maintain. Who would respect him if his blade remained unbloodied in the face of an insult?

He worked himself to a point where good sense no longer mattered. Without warning, he drew his sword and slashed across the boy's abdomen with all his strength. The boy's eyes bulged. His mouth opened and an unearthly scream issued from it as he sank to his knees, holding his middle with one hand and proffering the message with the other. The *ashigaru* flicked the blood drops from his sword and sheathed it. He spit again, this time barely missing the lifeless hand holding the message.

"To Yomi with you and your 'important message,'" he said contemptuously. "I am a samurai. No one denies me and lives." Since he did not know how to read, he could not conceive of a written message as being important. The importance lay in properly punishing the person who insulted his status. *Ashigaru* he might be, but he was a samurai. He stalked away arrogantly, leaving the boy's body and the message lying in the field.

• • •

Yoshi heard the scream and wondered what it meant. He supposed it was a disagreement in Koremori's camp. As a precaution—the sound seemed to come from the hidden dam— he sent a soldier to check the sentry.

Yoshi reflected on the situation. In a matter of days, Koremori could discover the dam and attack it. The sentry must have time to warn the defenders. Yoshi's troops had been drilled in tactics necessary to protect the dam and would make Koremori pay dearly for the attempt to breach it.

The pass was easy to defend. A squad of archers could fend off an army as long as they had sufficient warning.

Yoshi believed the dam was safe for the time being. However, despite the almost impregnable nature of the moat, tomorrow would assuredly bring another mass attack. Yoshi's troop would be ready.

Thank the Shinto gods and the Buddha that he had convinced Nami to leave with the women. Did she think of him? He peered at the moon. Did she watch the same moon tonight?

Yoshi was overcome by sadness. This could be the last time he saw Tsukiyomi in the night sky. The camp might possibly hold for another day, perhaps two. But if Koremori was willing to sacrifice a hundred men to his one, Yoshi would eventually lose.

The soldiers' morale was high. Yukiie's presence helped. Yoshi's mouth twisted. What a strange man, Yukiie. Repulsive. Loathsome. But his family name and court connections brought him wealth and power. It was easy to question the ways of the world when one thought about people like Yukiie.

If Yoritomo won out in the battle for power, would the Yukiies of the world be deposed? So Yoritomo seemed to promise. Yet Yoritomo, from his safe haven in Kamakura, used Yukiie as an ally. Where was the justice in that? Was expedience more important than justice? Yoritomo would never depose the Taira if he did not use every advantage, including Yukiie and Kiso. Certainly, Go-Shirakawa understood that and, indeed, used both Taira and Minamoto to maintain stability in the Empire. Was Yoshi's mission complete? He had warned Go-Shirakawa. He had made his recommendations.

Yoshi sighed. If he had not spoken out at Kiso's war council, he would not have been left to die at Hiuchi-yama. He had spoken out of pride and because of that pride his mission might fail. He had learned an important lesson at Hiuchi-yama. Without diplomacy and patience, the most careful plans could fail.

Would he benefit from what he had learned? He composed a poem:

> Tsukiyomi hides
> His face behind rags of cloud
> Solemnly winking,
> From the night sky, at striving
> Armies, dying for a dream.

What was the dream? The Western Paradise, for some? For others, a return to higher station on the cycle of Karma? An honorable death? Fame and renown in this world? The knowledge that one's duty was done?

Would he die bravely tomorrow? There had been no sign from the gods for him to take up the sword. He would face the enemy with the war fan in his hand. He would not break his vow. He would not wear swords.

What would be the difference if he died fighting an army with a sword or a fan? He was doomed unless the gods intervened.

It was late when he finally fell asleep, three hours before dawn.

On the other side of the moat, the *ashigaru* told two of his companions about the boy on whom he had bloodied his sword. "I left the body lying where it was cut down," he said proudly.

"Did you take the head?" asked one of his listeners.

"I don't need the damn head," he said, bristling angrily. "Tomorrow there will be more heads. This was an exercise to warm my blade. The boy was of no value. The head would add nothing to my name."

"What about the message he carried?" asked the other.

"To Emma-Ō with the message! It could have been a trick to get the boy into our camp. I can't read, can you?"

"A little."

"Where would a whoreson learn to read? You are trying to insult me!"

"No insult was intended. I was retainer to a warrior-scholar, who taught me a little of letters. I do not demean you; we are only *ashigaru* here. Let's not fight among ourselves."

The bearded man grudgingly agreed.

"If the message is important, it could mean immediate rewards and promotion."

"Maybe you are right. Come, I'll lead you to the body. Prove you can read."

The three men marched off toward the woods at the cliff face. The body was where it had fallen. The major arteries in the trunk lay open and the ground around the corpse was dark and boggy with blood.

The bearded man squished through the bloody earth and pulled the message from the dead boy's fingers.

"This is fine paper," said the reader, unfolding it. He peered closely, turning the sheet so it could catch the feeble rays of the moon. "These are instructions addressed to Koremori . . . the secret of the dam's construction."

"Yes?"

"The message explains how they built the moat, so Koremori can destroy it and their defenses will be gone."

The bearded samurai started to take offense, then he grabbed at the message. "I'll take it," he said with a curse. "It's mine to deliver."

"I thought we . . ."

"I don't care what you thought. It's mine." He had his sword half pulled out.

His companion stepped back. "Of course it's yours," he said placatingly.

Koremori resented being awakened. General Michimori came himself to see that Koremori understood the import of the message.

"I want the man who insisted you wake me," snapped the sleep-addled Koremori, thrusting his jaw at Michimori. "How can I command when I am not allowed to sleep?"

"Punish him by all means," said Michimori calmly. "But read the message. It seems General Yukiie has betrayed his army."

"Wha . . . what?"

"The message from Yukiie tells us how to destroy the dam and empty the moat."

"Can we trust Yukiie?"

"We must investigate. If this is true, a squad of men can infiltrate the woods at the base of Mount Hiuchi and dismantle the dam before daylight."

"And if the message is false?"

"We will lose a squad of men." Michimori studied Koremori's sleep-swollen face thoughtfully, then he added dryly,

"We can easily afford one squad after the numbers we've sacrificed attempting to cross the moat by force of arms."

Koremori glared at his second-in-command, then turned away from him and shouted for a retainer to help him into his armor. He suddenly realized that triumph was within reach. There was every possibility that Yukiie had delivered his army into Koremori's hands.

"We'll leave at once," he told Michimori. "Prepare a squad of our finest warriors and breach the dam before the sun rises. And," he added as an afterthought, "discipline is to be maintained among our troops. They must learn their proper ranking. Kill the man who had the temerity to have me wakened."

forty-eight

Horns blared; gongs reverberated in the darkness. It was the hour of the tiger, two hours before dawn. The sentry at the dam had spotted Koremori's invaders and given the alarm. The sleeping troops were instantly awake. Men poured from the castle, from the academy, and from the separate barracks buildings. Foot soldiers and mounted officers, many without armor, raced to their assigned positions around the dam site.

Within five minutes, a hundred bowmen were stationed at their emergency posts, prepared to draw aim on anyone who approached the dam from the other side.

Koremori's surprise raid failed due to an alert sentry. Only a few of Koremori's samurai reached the dam before the bowmen stopped them. The dam suffered no substantial damage.

During the next hours, the dam was under constant siege. Koremori was in a rage. His vast army was held in place by a handful of irregulars. He called a war council with Michimori and Sanemori. "We must destroy the moat," he shouted, the veins standing out on his thick neck. "A traitor in their midst gave us the secret and we failed. General Michimori, I hold you responsible for this fiasco."

Michimori's hard soldier's face froze. He was furious, knowing he had done his best. He was being blamed for events beyond his control. If only Go-Shirakawa had placed him in charge instead of Koremori! Young Koremori had presence, but he lacked a true soldier's knowledge and experience. Michimori reined in his anger and bowed fatalistically. He wondered why the Emperor had chosen the least experienced general to command. It was as though the Emperor wanted the Taira defeated.

Koremori turned to the old man. "Sanemori," he said grimly, "once you gave me sound advice and I refused to listen. This time, I promise to heed your words." His voice took on a whiny note. "What can we do? I am feeding a hundred thousand empty bellies and am accomplishing nothing. The army is laughing at me."

Sanemori's brow wrinkled thoughtfully. "We need to create a diversion," he said.

"What kind of diversion?"

Michimori, sulking, but hiding it well, said, "'Fire' arrows! Burn their barriers. Fire their camp."

"Yes," Koremori said. "That might be the diversion we need. If we can keep the Minamoto busy fighting fires, we can take the dam."

Sanemori bowed to Michimori for making the suggestion and again to Koremori. He studied the general shrewdly. Whatever was said about Koremori's youth and inexperience, at least he was able to make a quick decision and take necessary action. "Well put," Sanemori said at length. "Though the range is long, we do not need accuracy. Set the brush afire. Panic their horses. Make them draw men away from the dam. We can keep them busy fighting in three directions at once: at the dam, at the fires, and at the moat."

"Agreed," said Koremori quickly. With the resilience of his twenty-one years, he changed smoothly from depression to ebullience. "General Sanemori will arrange to attack the dam. General Michimori will command the archers and the 'fire' arrows. I will lead the frontal assault on the moat."

By late afternoon, the dam was taken. Sanemori lost five hundred men to the defenders' fifty. Michimori's fire arrows did extensive damage to the camp. The barriers smoldered in dozens of places, the underbrush was burned to black skeletal fingers. Koremori, who lost a thousand men trying to cross the water for the third time, called another war council.

"We have the dam," he said. "We must plan our next move carefully. Though I am willing to commit our men regardless of casualties, I do not want to sacrifice them needlessly. I have stormed the moat three times and have been turned back by the sharpened stakes each time. There must be a way..."

Old General Sanemori interrupted, "I have an idea that may..." he went on to describe a plan that brought smiles to the faces of Koremori and Michimori.

Yoshi was smudged with soot from hours of battling brush fires. A messenger from the dam site reported the dam was already partially dismantled and a small army of Koremori's laborers were breaking away the mortar and removing the stones.

The water level in the moat was dropping. Wooden points

were visible above the water line, and as Yoshi watched, the water continued to recede.

Across the moat, Koremori's army cast long afternoon shadows as they waited out of range of the bowmen. Yoshi saw a large group of foot soldiers detach themselves from the main body. They wore no armor. Without the weight of armor they would make vulnerable targets, but they would be able to swim easily, and once the stakes were exposed, they could slip between them.

Yoshi hurried from unit to unit, ordering a steady barrage of arrows the moment the unarmored men appeared within range.

Yoshi studied the opposition, attempting to fathom their plan. These unarmed men were to be sacrificial lambs. There had to be more to Koremori's tactics than was obvious. Yoshi saw the banners around Koremori's headquarters flutter in the afternoon breeze. A banner was lowered in a signal, and immediately, thousands of men advanced toward the bank; they halted, packed sixty deep around the quarter-mile arc of the moat, just out of range.

Yoshi watched the water level continue to sink. Now a full three feet of wood was visible above the water line.

Another banner dipped and a horn sounded. The men in the vanguard—there must have been five hundred of them—stripped to their breeechclouts. As they jumped into the water, Yoshi realized their intent.

Each man carried one end of a coil of rope. The other end was attached to a horseman's saddle. When a swimmer reached a stake and looped his rope, his mounted partner would bring tremendous pressure to bear from the opposite shore. The stakes would be ripped from the muddy bank.

No moat? No stakes? The camp's six hundred soldiers would not live fifteen minutes against Koremori's horde.

"Pick them off before they reach the stakes," shouted Yoshi.

The first swimmers appeared near the defense line. Yoshi's archers rose behind their smoking barriers and let fly black clouds of war arrows. The moat again ran red as men fell, pierced in a dozen places. Most died before they reached their goal, but over a hundred snared the sharpened stakes, which were now completely exposed.

Yoshi watched helplessly as the horsemen slowly uprooted the stakes from their mud bases. Those set deep and anchored with rocks resisted. Additional horses were harnessed to the ropes, and the stubborn stakes popped out with loud sucking sounds. The defensive line was as jagged as teeth in an old beggar's mouth.

Few of the five hundred swimmers survived the arrows; these managed to attach their ropes and swim away under water.

Still, the water receded.

Again the horn sounded and Koremori's command flag dipped. A great roar rose from the throats of the mighty host as the first rows charged into the ditch.

Yoshi's archers held fast, sending arrows as fast as they could nock and release them. The arrows were as effective as mosquitoes stinging the hide of an ox.

The roar of the men, the jangle of armor, splashing of mud and water, and the thin screams of the dying blended into a cacophony of sound. Yoshi shouted orders. Nobody heard him. Yoshi leaped atop a barricade and directed the archers to close the widest gaps in the line. Yoshi made a heroic figure in full battle armor, his blue and red armor smudged with soot, his horned helmet gleaming gold in the late sun. He seemed a divine spirit come to earth.

Koremori's horsemen spotted Yoshi as the leader and drove their mounts in his direction. They released arrows from horseback, miraculously missing him.

Yoshi waved a prearranged signal and his pitifully small band of horsemen galloped from behind the barriers to engage the enemy before they established themselves on the bank.

A handful against five thousand. Yoshi's horsemen were brave, reckless, but the results were foreordained. They expected no mercy from Koremori and received none. In minutes, Yoshi's horsemen died and the camp lay helpless before the mightiest army of all time.

The sound of Koremori's advancing army roused Nami from a dream-filled sleep. She had slept the day in the timeless blackness of the cave. She awakened, hungry and confused. The hard floor and the utter darkness disoriented her. Then she remembered.

Filled with dread, Nami hurried to her vantage spot at the cave mouth. She looked out over a vast panoply of banners and men converging on the moat. She saw how the waters had receded and knew with certainty the camp was doomed.

And Yoshi? Was that he? Yes. She saw his golden helmet with its spreading horns. He was alone on the barrier, running surefootedly from group to group, directing the bowmen to the most important targets.

She sucked a short breath and held it in horror. Yoshi was an exposed target. His life seemed charmed by the spirits of the underworld, how else could he have escaped the clouds of arrows directed at him?

"Yoshi. Yoshi," she cried to herself. "Why didn't you leave when there was a chance?" In her heart she knew the answer. Honor. Duty. Responsibility. What meaning did ephemeral life hold compared to those eternal values? Yoshi's values were his life. But decisions were not easy to make. Yoshi's honor and his responsibility for his men were at odds with his duty to serve the Emperor. If Yoshi died, what of his duty to Yoritomo and to Go-Shirakawa? She was only a woman. How could she be expected to understand?

Nami felt a wave of revulsion. Damn them to Emma-Ō, these men who fancied they could separate the important from the unimportant. They were wrong! They had always been wrong. And she, a mere woman, knew the true values. Love. Home. Family. She felt her cheeks flush in anger and said aloud, "Your life is being wasted . . . for nothing."

The anger quickly passed. Her shoulders convulsed in a sob. There was no one to hear her, no one to see the tears roll down her cheeks.

Nami wiped her cheeks with her sleeve and strained to distinguish the details of the battle; difficult because of the smoke, the distance, and the darkening afternoon sky. She saw Yoshi balanced on a barrier, engaged in hand-to-hand fighting with one of Koremori's officers. The officer's sword against Yoshi's war fan. Time after time, Yoshi's speed and skill equalized the sword's advantage and saved him.

The officer was a strong and competent swordsman. He drove Yoshi farther back with every assault. Nami's heart lifted when she saw Yoshi upset the swordsman. Yoshi struck the man's wrist with his fan, and for a moment, it seemed he had succeeded in disarming the man, but the stroke was deflected by the officer's *kote*, wrist guard.

Yoshi tried to press forward before the officer recovered his equilibrium, but the man dropped back with catlike speed and sliced at Yoshi's throat with a well executed wheel-stroke. Nami screamed silently as Yoshi dropped under the blade. The blow caused no serious damage; it caromed off Yoshi's horned helmet, dislodging one of the metal horns, which flickered in the dying light as it turned end over end to the ground.

Nami's gaze was glued on Yoshi and his opponent. Although other men were locked in mortal combat, she was oblivious to them all.

The officer reversed his blade, cutting backhandedly in an unorthodox stroke. It went wide and Yoshi seized the opportunity to step inside the blade's arc, block the sword arm, and simultaneously strike at the officer's face plate with the club end of the fan. The man's face spurted blood as he fell backward like a felled ox.

Another swordsman waited to take his place.

Nami left the security of her cave entrance and crept to the edge of the path to see more clearly. A handful of defenders fought on valiantly, but she watched them succumb to superior numbers.

The sky darkened rapidly. Nami hoped Yoshi could escape in the twilight. She had lost sight of him. Her heart leaped. Was he heading for safety? No. There he was, surrounded by two swordsmen. He dropped to one knee under the blade of one, striking up with the pointed end of the fan into the man's throat. Even though she was far above them, Nami heard the gargling scream of the mortally wounded swordsman over the grisly sounds of the battle. And . . . saw the second samurai's blade smash into Yoshi's helmet.

The helmet was torn from Yoshi's head to spin off into the growing darkness. Time stretched for Nami. A second became an hour as Yoshi twisted around and toppled off the barrier, his face a red mask of blood.

Nami clenched her fists and screamed.

forty-nine

With the coming of night, the last defenders of Hiuchi-yama died, fighting valiantly against insuperable odds. The camp belonged to Koremori.

The councillors suggested an immediate respite and a celebration. The huge army, held at bay for three days, had suffered five thousand battle casualties. The survivors who had fought all day were too exhilarated to sleep. The councillors advised Koremori to let them relax before the next stage of the campaign.

Koremori agreed. Troops were assigned to collect heads in the morning. They would search for the leaders; perhaps Kiso or Yoshi had fallen defending Hiuchi-yama. There was time for bodies to be counted and separated, trophies taken, rewards given. The foot soldiers who survived the swim across the moat would be promoted to full samurai. And a morning war council would decide the army's next move.

Michimori cautioned that the army should march by the following afternoon; nothing of value was left in the valley and the food supply was dwindling.

"Field officers will meet in Hiuchi-jo Fortress," Koremori announced. "Samurai horsemen will use the martial-arts building. *Ashigaru* will stay in the camp and the surrounding fields. Tonight we celebrate our first great victory with sake and extra rations for all!"

The council cheered almost to a man. Only Michimori and Sanemori refrained. They exchanged significant glances, understanding each other perfectly. Great victory? One hundred thousand needing three days to overcome eight hundred. Extra rations? There wasn't enough food in the supply carts for normal daily rations!

Koremori noticed their expressions. His brow lowered and his nostrils pinched. He angrily signaled them to join the applause. Reluctantly, they obeyed.

Word spread quickly through the camp. Sake! Carts, brought up from the rear, delivered the barrels to the celebrants. Shortly afterward, the men were singing, dancing, and laughing. The ardors of the day were forgotten as they reeled from the effects of the wine. Before midnight, most of the victors had fallen from fatigue and drunkenness.

Nami's duty was clear. All too clear. Yoshi had died bravely. Nami must deny his head to Koremori and the Nii-Dono, who manipulated him. She would have to descend into the enemy camp to remove and hide Yoshi's head.

Her stomach heaved at the thought. Warriors decapitated their enemies as an afterthought. She, with no experience and no sword, would have to sever her beloved's head with the small dagger she concealed in her robe.

Impossible!

But there was no other way. There was no one to help. The burden was hers and hers alone.

Her traveling coat was sturdy but too colorful; it would be conspicuous in the camp. Nami wished she had dressed in the plain robes she had once worn as Yoshi's retainer. It was too late to think of that. She improvised by turning the bright orange coat inside out, exposing its darker burnt orange lining. In the dark it might pass.

It would have to pass!

Nami gathered her under-robes and pulled them through her *obi*. They made a rough but acceptable *hakama*. Although her feet were tender, she would have to leave her feminine shoes and go barefoot. It would be a small penance to pay for living when her husband was dead.

She would take Yoshi's head back and hide it in the cave. It was their secret and would serve as a memorial to their love. Once she had completed her horrid task, she would follow the path away from Hiuchi-yama to find Yoritomo's camp, tell him of Yoshi's heroic end, and offer her services to unseat the Taira. There must be some way she could serve the Minamoto cause. Yoshi's death made her realize she was no longer a creature of the court. She would never return to that life. Someday she would return to Kyoto to see Yoshi's mother, Lady Masaka. She would tell her how heroically Yoshi had died. Until then, Nami was determined to work toward the Taira's downfall.

The sounds of revelry diminished. Occasional bursts of drunken song, boastful shouting, and horseplay among the soldiers became sporadic with the passage of time. The moon, in

its last quarter, gave a fitful light, making it difficult to see.
Nami barely distinguished the shape of the barricades in the
faint glow of embers and the light of scattered campfires. She
had made a mental note of the place where Yoshi fell. Locating
him in the welter of bodies would be difficult in the darkness.
It would also be difficult for Koremori's sentries to identify
her.

Yin and yang. For every advantage, a disadvantage. For
every disadvantage, an advantage.

Nami left the cave when she judged it to be midnight. The
trip down Hiuchi-yama was uneventful. Koremori's men had
not yet discovered the paths that laced the mountain. Before
she reached the fortress's palisade, she removed her shoes and
hid them in the branches of a pine. Time to be careful! She
skirted the palisade, scurrying from shadow to shadow. She
heard officers celebrating inside the castle. They would cause
no problem. It was the hundreds of soldiers in camp that she
had to fear; many were noisily carousing, others had already
collapsed in drunken stupors.

Once, Nami was challenged. She went on as if she didn't
hear. The challenger followed. A companion called him back,
"Have some more sake, tomorrow we will be dry," he shouted
in a slurred voice. The challenger hesitated, followed again,
then shrugged his shoulders and retraced his steps to join his
friends.

Nami was rigid with fear. She hid behind an overturned cart
ten feet from where the challenger had changed his mind and
turned away. She heard him tell his companions, ". . . something strange about the one that passed. I could have sworn it
was a . . ."

The other soldiers laughed and cut him off with cries of,
"Have some more." Nami released her breath and slipped away
quickly.

She was more careful when she came upon the piles of
bodies, soldiers from both sides, heaped in mounds along the
perimeter of the barricades. The bodies lay in patches of shadow
and Nami found it almost impossible to differentiate one from
another. The smell of burnt brush blended with a distinctive
odor of death: a combination of sweat, blood, urine, and feces.
She tried to feel for the features of a corpse only to find she
felt a dismembered arm or a headless torso.

Nami's insides shriveled at the horror of her task. Once,
she thought she had found Yoshi, and as her hand felt for his

face, it sank to the wrist in a gaping wound. Her hand touched a cold, viscous shape. Heart? Lungs? She could not hold back the revulsion; she heaved, vomiting bile. She forced herself to continue. She was sure she was in the exact spot where Yoshi had fallen. There were too many bodies! She sobbed in frustration and disgust.

Suddenly a voice shouted from the surrounding darkness. "Who goes there? Speak up!"

Nami stretched out along a body and lay as still as a ghost.

"Damn grave robber," shouted the voice. "I'll find you in the morning."

"Come away. Join our celebration," said someone else.

"Bastards can't wait to steal from the dead," muttered the first man. "Tomorrow we'll share the spoils fairly, but there's always someone who has to be first." He raised his voice. "You out there! If I catch you, you'll be one more body."

Nami did not move. Her legs quivered and she nearly threw up again. The moon shifted. The shadows left her in a patch of light. She lay face to face with a corpse. The face was covered with blood. She recoiled, trying to sit up and pull away simultaneously.

Buddha! It was...it was Yoshi! She had found him and, not realizing it, was locked in an obscene embrace with his corpse.

Nami trembled uncontrollably. It was time to perform her grisly duty. She drew the dagger from her robe. Her hand shook so badly she could hardly hold it. "Great god Fudo give me the strength, great god Hachiman give me heart to do what I must," she sobbed.

Gradually, her shaking lessened and her body came under her control. When she was able to hold her hand steady, she steeled herself for her task.

"Oh, Yoshi," she sighed before she put the blade to his throat. "You thought by disavowing the sword you would gain a life of peace. Beloved, there is no peace in this world. No peace and no justice. Perhaps you will find what you sought in the next cycle of existence. Wherever you are, know that I love you."

With these words Nami leaned forward to kiss the cold lips for the last time.

They were warm!

Yoshi had been dead for over six hours, yet his lips wre warm. Was it possible?

Nami tore off a piece of her robe and wiped the bloody face. She pressed her ear to his chest. She heard no heartbeat through the leather armor. She touched his throat, applying a slight pressure under his jaw.

Was it imagination? There seemed to be the faintest of pulses.

Nami's heart raced. How long had she searched? How many hours were left till the first streaks of dawn?

"Buddha, help me," she pleaded and tugged at Yoshi's body, moving it a few inches.

The last campfires died out. The last revelers fell silent. The night was filled with the rasping song of cicadas. Nature continued as though no battle had been fought, as though no men had died. The moon floated among scattered clouds, alternately hiding and coming forth. Peace returned to the valley.

Nami started the long ordeal, dragging Yoshi past a sleeping army and up to their secret lair.

fifty

Over and over, Nami doubted her ability to drag Yoshi up the mountain of Hiuchi-yama. Was she dragging a dead man? Was her effort in vain? Adding to the impossibility of the task was the need to bypass the soldiers and carry Yoshi without harming him. One careless move and she might sever the tenuous thread that was keeping him alive. The path uphill! Her body cried for rest.

When the first light crept up the eastern sky, Nami was at last able to maneuver Yoshi and herself into the cave. Inside, she collapsed at his side and fell into unconsciousness.

Nami awoke in pain, her feet torn and bloody, her body scratched and abraded in countless places, her muscles aching from the unaccustomed strain. She lay still, delaying decision and action, feeling her heart beating like a captured bird. After the hope of last night's discovery, she was afraid to find her efforts had been fruitless.

The cave was in darkness except for faint light near the entrance. Dim rays haloed Yoshi's head against the surrounding black. Nami studied his pale face and wondered how long he had lain unconscious. Was he alive or dead? She couldn't tell. She scrambled to her feet in sudden panic. She had to know.

She knelt at Yoshi's side, hesitantly feeling for a pulse, afraid to not find it. But . . . she thought it was there. Weak, erratic . . . so faint she couldn't be sure.

Nami had had more education than most women. She had learned the rudiments of the Chinese classics, including the Book of Documents and the Book of Changes. She was trained in calligraphy, composition, rhetoric, poetry, astrology, and music, and she had lived on a country estate, where life was closer to nature than it was in the capital. With all those advantages, she did not know how to help Yoshi.

Nami had seen healers work with herbs and incantations. She had been present at exorcisms and rites. None of those experiences were helpful in her present situation. Anything she did might extinguish the small flame of life. She began to shake

287

at the responsibility. Panic would be harmful; Nami forced herself to breathe slowly till her pulse slowed down. Think! she told herself.

The moment she was under control, her course of action became clear. First, she would remove Yoshi's armor and look to his wounds. The armor was complex and had to be removed in reverse order to the way it had been put on.

Nami slid Yoshi into the light and proceeded by trial and error. What did a woman know of armor? She wished she were Tomoe, a woman who knew the facets of war as well as a man. No use wishing; she had her job to do. She untied the lacings of his *yoroi*, chest protector, and found it interlaced under the shoulder and back plates. She removed his *kote*, wrist guards, then the arm guards, and the *haidate*, lamellar skirt. There were so many ties!

At last, Nami had him stripped down to his long *fundoshi*, the undershirt that covered him from throat to upper thigh. She searched his body for wounds and found nothing more than scratches and contusions. Wryly, she thought she had suffered worse on route to the cave.

Nami had wiped most of the blood from Yoshi's face before she moved him. Now, she inspected his head and immediately discovered the cause of his unconsciousness: a thick flap of skin had been lifted just above and behind his left ear. Blood had seeped out and formed a thick scab. The sword stroke had been partially deflected by his steel helmet, but the impact was strong enough to cause a concussion and a great loss of blood.

Nami tore another piece from her under-robe and gently wiped the wound. She pressed the flap of skin back into place, wishing she knew how to mix the poultices that healers used in such cases.

Yoshi groaned!

Nami's pulse raced and a rush of warmth flushed her cheeks. Her hands trembled. Yoshi *was* alive. She removed her travel coat and folded it to pillow his head.

What else could she do? Water! She needed water to wash the wound. There was nothing more she could do until she had it. A small stream ran close to the mountain path. She gathered her robes and slipped out past the dwarf pine.

The sun was well past its zenith. In the valley below, Koremori's army was on the move. Nami heard the sounds of horses, carts, and men, saw clouds of dust. She hunkered down to observe the departing soldiers from behind a bush. The ground was trampled flat where they had been; grass, brush, flowers, and grain were stamped into a brown sameness. The moat was a muddy ditch much like the fields around it. She looked for the martial-arts academy where she and Yoshi had spent a happy month; it was gone, razed along with the barrack town.

Great long mounds of turned earth covered the thousands of Koremori's dead who lay buried in communal graves. High piles of defenders' corpses were carelessly thrown near the flattened barricades. Nami shrank back when she realized she watched dozens of decapitated officers being pulled helter-skelter from the mounds of foot soldiers. She imagined Koremori's consternation when the head of the leader was not found. No Kiso. No Yoshi. Well . . . perhaps Koremori would be content with the head of Yukiie. She hoped it would be scant comfort. Nami's lips tightened grimly. She had contributed to making Koremori's first major engagement a failure.

Nami plodded on with aching legs, searching for the stream. Ahead, she spied a bundle abandoned on the trail. She opened it hastily and almost sang with joy. There was a stoppered bamboo tube of water and food in the package, real food. There was also a change of men's clothing. Feminine colors. Not what Yoshi would have chosen, but if he recovered—please Buddha—he would need clothing more comfortable than his armor.

Nami did not know that last night, Yukiie, in his panic at hearing Nami behind him, had dropped his supplies and thus contributed to Yoshi's salvation.

Nami took the pack and hurried to the cave. She poured a few drops of water onto a rag and sponged Yoshi's wound. He groaned in pain, a sound that gladdened her heart. He would recover.

Nami tried to pour water into his mouth, but most dribbled from his lips. She would wait; it would not do to waste the precious liquid. She took a small swallow herself, then ate a portion of the leaf-wrapped rice cakes.

"*Amida Butsu,* light of the Western Paradise, come to one who needs your aid." Nami knelt beside Yoshi's form and prayed. Several times in the past, she had maintained a vigil at Yoshi's bedside when he was at the mercy of the spirits. Now she watched him, stretched out in a small patch of light, a pitifully small form in the vast cavern, and felt unseen forces surging around her. Centuries of silence, crumbled bones of long dead ancestors, and the palpable darkness combined to give her the sense of powers struggling in the nether world.

Hours passed in prayer and meditation, Buddha, Hachiman, Fudo . . . the gods of the Shinto and Buddhist religions rewarded Nami. Yoshi opened his eyes. His mouth twitched in a tiny smile of recognition.

fifty-one

From the moment he regained consciousness, Yoshi was eager to return to his duties in the service of Yoritomo and the Emperor. His Imperial mission was incomplete. He would not be satisfied until he was assured that Go-Shirakawa had received his message and accepted his recommendations. Nami tried to convince him to rest at Hiuchi-yama. With Koremori's army gone, the valley was at their disposal. Yoshi was not convinced. "Duty," he answered when Nami asked why he insisted on leaving. Nami could not deny him, remembering her own vow to put forth every effort toward the downfall of the Taira.

However, Yoshi's first efforts to leave ended in failure; he was too weak. No matter how strong his spirit, his body refused to obey. Nami found the next few days among the happiest of her life. They were alive, together, and Yoshi was completely dependent on her.

As Yoshi regained his strength, Nami became more withdrawn. His eagerness to report to Yoritomo and to rejoin Kiso filled her with dread.

On the bright morning of the twenty-fifth day of the fifth month, some thirty miles north of Hiuchi-yama, Koremori won another victory against one of Kiso's garrisons at Ataka in the province of Kaga, a minor victory that gave Kiso intelligence about Koremori's movements.

On the same day, Yoshi and Nami, clad in a strange assortment of rags and luxurious court robes, set off in search of Kiso's headquarters. Three days later, under a blazing sun, Yoshi and Nami found Kiso's camp on the border between Echizen and Kaga.

Yoshi was fully recovered from his scalp wound. The only indication of his brush with death was a livid scar above his left ear.

A sentry escorted Yoshi to Kiso's command tent. Kiso's greeting was less than cordial. "Scouts reported the loss of the garrison," he said coldly after they had settled the formalities. "How is it that you survived?"

As Yoshi explained, he read expressions of disbelief and contempt. Kiso and Imai exchanged pointed glances; it was obvious they had already drawn their own conclusions about how Yoshi had survived Koremori's massive attack.

"Yukiie died bravely, fighting to the death, while the great General Yoshi hid," said Kiso when Yoshi ended his tale. "You are still the representative of my cousin Yoritomo, and as such I must accept you." Kiso's eyes glittered with malice.

Imai interrupted. "I am a warrior," he said. "This man's escape while his men were left to die is impossible to accept. He should be executed at once as an example of our treatment of cowards."

Kiso nodded thoughtfully. "I am not yet strong enough to defy my cousin. But . . . someday soon . . ." Abruptly, he changed the subject and asked in an offhand manner, "Did your wife die at Hiuchi-yama? She was not among the women who escaped."

Yoshi explained that Nami had saved his life.

"A remarkable woman," said Kiso. "Where is she?"

"She stopped at Tomoe's tent."

"I see," said Kiso enigmatically. There was a hint of something strange in the hatchet face. Malice? Satisfaction? Yoshi was confused. "You join us in time for the next stage of our campaign," Kiso added. "Our scouts keep us informed about Koremori's movements. His army is dwindling. Conscripts desert in droves. He hasn't the supplies to feed those that remain. However, he did win a minor skirmish against a handful of my men at Ataka, and he will undoubtedly march through Shinohara in the next two weeks. Are you too frightened to face him again?"

Yoshi had maintained an inscrutable calm through Kiso's and Imai's insults. His face remained impassive as he said forcefully, "I will be close by your side, and you will see my bravery or cowardice."

Santaro welcomed Yoshi openly despite the frowns of other officers. Yoshi reflected that it was impossible to guess who would stay a steadfast friend and who would desert in times of difficulty. Santaro proved his loyalty many times, and although the pressure to renounce Yoshi was great, he never wavered. The gods repaid good deeds in their own way. When Yoshi had saved Santaro's life, he had no advantage in mind, yet he had been compensated many times over for his action.

Tomoe was overjoyed to welcome Nami. She received her

without question, protecting her from Kiso. For all of Tomoe's bravado and rough ways, there was a streak of sentimentality in her character. She was capable of facing down a formidable opponent with a masculine curse and, if necessary, with her sword, yet she could also register affection and love without shame.

Three weeks later, on the twentieth day of the sixth month, the two armies met. Amaterasu's rays burned mercilessly on the plains of Shinohara in the province of Kaga. The early summer grass wilted in the heat. Soldiers scratched uncomfortably, sweating beneath their armor.

Kiso's army had gained volunteers from all sides; Koremori's army had visibly shrunk. Withal, there were less than twenty thousand with Kiso against fifty thousand with Koremori as they came face to face on the plain.

Yoshi was in the vanguard at Kiso's side. The *shi-tenno*, four kings—Imai, Tezuka, Jiro, and Taro—and Tomoe flanked them. They rode six abreast, surrounded by white banners and flags proclaiming past triumphs.

This was to be a traditional battle, and the humming arrow was sent toward the red banners of the Taira to deliver the challenge.

It was accepted by the old general, Sanemori. "I cannot announce my name," he proclaimed. "But I have served the Emperor longer than any other soldier. I have returned to Echizen and Kaga, the provinces of my youth, to defend the Emperor's cause with my life."

This was a moment Sanemori had simultaneously anticipated and dreaded for many years. When he was in Kyoto, he had gone to Munemori, the acting *Daijo-Daijin*, and begged to be assigned to Koremori's northern campaign. His reason was to atone for the secret he had kept for thirty years, the saving of Lady Senjo and her infant son, Kiso. He had saved them because he was swayed by the woman's beauty and her poetry. Sanemori had helped Lady Senjo and her son survive in the wild mountains. He had visited regularly throughout the boy's youth. At the time, he had thought, How can a poetess and her newborn son harm the Empire? And he had disobeyed his orders. The result was Kiso Yoshinaka smashing through the northern provinces, threatening the fabric of the Empire.

Sanemori had decided to die as an atonement for his sin, to die in the northern provinces, where he had been born.

Munemori had been touched by Sanemori's bravery and granted a tearful permission, knowing the old man intended never to return.

Now, Sanemori issued the challenge without using his name. He believed Kiso would spare him if he were identified, and Sanemori could not accept that dishonor. He was determined to die in the service of the emperor.

On this twentieth day, Sanemori's bold challenge reverberated in the hot, damp air.

Imai accepted and returned the challenge, at which Sanemori signaled his men and several hundred chosen troops rode forth in a wide line.

Imai tilted his white flag and an equal number of horsemen thundered out from Kiso's ranks.

"Let me join them," Yoshi called to Kiso.

"No. You are useless without swords. Stay by my side and observe how brave men fight. There is no better soldier than my foster-brother, Imai."

As he rode forward as second-in-command to Imai, Santaro waved to Yoshi. His face was flushed with excitement and anticipation; his beard virtually bristled with energy. Yoshi envied him his single-minded devotion to the art of war. Santaro accepted his role as a samurai officer and was content to do battle for its own sake.

The horses pawed at the ground, nervously holding their places, as Sanemori and Imai each sent five champions to open hostilities.

There was a crash of metal on metal, the lonesome shriek of a wounded horse, and shouts and curses as two teams smashed into each other. One man toppled from his horse, cut almost in two by a wheel-stroke. Another slumped in his saddle, spurting a fountain of blood from a severed arm. In two minutes of battle, one man remained. He was Kiso's lieutenant. Unhorsed, he stood in the middle of the field, legs widespread, teeth flashing in a smile of triumph, holding aloft his enemy's head.

The opening gambit had gone to Kiso, but the battle had scarcely begun. Sanemori dispatched his entire group. They galloped full speed toward Kiso's soldiers, shouting war cries.

As they rode, one of Sanemori's officers stretched out and decapitated the lone survivor of the opening battle with a stroke. His headless trunk staggered two steps, then fell over his recent victim, twitched once, and was still.

The two groups crashed into each other and all became

confusion as everyone searched for a foe worthy of his steel.
Men screamed in pain, horses ran out of control; in the midst
of this pandemonium, samurai were announcing their pedi-
grees, seeking their chance of glory.

After gaining the initial advantage, Sanemori's soldiers lost
ground to the tougher mountain men.

Sanemori himself was in the middle of the fray, directing
his men. He was an awesome figure on his black-spotted gray
horse, sitting straight and high on his gold-ornamented saddle,
his wrinkled face hidden by a mask and helmet of gold inlaid
steel. Over green laced armor he wore a crimson brocaded
hitatare and wielded a gold-mounted sword. On his back he
carried a quiver of twenty-four arrows with black and white
feathers and a bow of black lacquer with red rattan trim.

The tide swung strongly to Imai's forces as more units from
both sides rode out to engage each other.

Kiso's men were tough veterans whose future depended on
victory. Sanemori's men were soft-living Imperial guards or
farmers unwilling to die for the abstract idea of duty. The
conscripts broke first. When the Imperial guards saw their
support troops run, they abandoned the fight, spurring their
mounts in panic-stricken flight. Their panic communicated itself to the main body of Koremori's army. Thousands of horsemen and foot soldiers abandoned the field in hasty retreat.

Sanemori held his ground, racing from one attacker to another, giving his men a chance to escape. Of Koremori's vast
army, only Sanemori was left on the field.

Taro, one of Kiso's *shi-tenno*, recognized the warrior who
had refused to give his name. He motioned his samurai to hold
back while he advanced toward Sanemori.

"You fight well, samurai of the red brocade," he shouted,
"yet we do not know who you are. Before I kill you, declare
yourself, for you are obviously a brave and worthy opponent."

"And who are you to ask?"

"I am Taro Kanesashi-no-Mitsumori of the mountains of
Shinano, one of the trusted four kings of the demon warrior
Kiso Yoshinaka."

"Then you will suit me well, and though I cannot declare
my name, we shall battle man to man. See if you can stand in
the face of my strength." Sanemori spurred his gray and black
steed at Taro, waving his golden sword in a flashing figure
eight pattern.

One of Taro's men raced between them, thinking to protect

Taro from the onslaught. Hardly slowing down, Sanemori leaned over, caught him against the saddle and, with a twist of his blade, cut the man's throat.

In that fraction of an instant, Taro kicked his horse around and slipped in at Sanemori's left. He pressed his blade under Sanemori's armored skirt and stabbed upward into his vitals not once but twice. Sanemori reached beneath his armor for his belly. He lowered his blade and stared at his red-covered hand.

As Sanemori toppled slowly from his saddle, Taro leaped to his side and caught him. He tore off the mask and looked with surprise into the dull eyes of a wrinkled old man, whose hair was as black as a youth's. Old as he was, he had fought valiantly. Taro drew his short sword and with two powerful slices removed the old man's head.

The battlefield grew silent, except for the buzzing of black-flies clustered around the dead. Taro climbed back into his saddle and guided his mount toward Kiso's command post. The dark-haired head hung from his saddle, trailing blood.

"Ho, Kiso," called Taro when he was opposite his chief. Taro's face was red and sweaty from the excitement of the fray. "I have a mystery here."

"And what is this mystery?" asked Kiso, humoring him.

"The warrior who challenged us, the one who would not reveal his name, I have his head." Taro lifted the head by the hair. "Despite his raven hair, he is an old man. Today he fought with the strength of youth. I might not have prevailed if my retainer had not sacrificed himself."

Kiso studied the head with a puzzled expression. "The face is familiar," he said.

Yoshi turned sadly to Kiso and said, "I know this man. I saw him frequently at the court in Kyoto."

"You know him, do you?" said Kiso. He was annoyed that Yoshi recognized the man when he had not. "Who is he?"

"A brave soldier. A poet. Saito Sanemori of Musashi."

"Impossible! I know Sanemori well. His hair is white as the northern snows. He is near seventy. This man is much younger. You need only look at his hair."

"Yet this is the same Sanemori."

"There is a resemblance. I've seen Sanemori many times through the years. He visited my mother regularly until her death, but his hair was white."

"Take the head and wash the hair," said Yoshi sadly. "And

you will know a great poet died on the battlefield today."

Kiso waved a hand brusquely at Taro to follow Yoshi's suggestion.

Taro turned his horse and rode toward a nearby creek.

During Taro's absence, Kiso and Yoshi sat their horses stoically, ignoring each other.

Tomoe edged her horse close to Yoshi's. "You've angered him," she whispered. "Kiso doesn't like to be contradicted."

"My intent was not to contradict him. I spoke the truth."

"Perhaps you weren't aware that Kiso felt strongly about Sanemori. He often spoke of him. When Kiso was younger, the old man took the place of his father. I suspect he denied the head as being Sanemori's because he could not accept the poet's death. He will not thank you if you are right."

Yoshi studied Kiso's hard-planed face and wild eyes. He doubted Kiso's deep feelings...especially about an old man who served his enemies.

Taro raced up and reined his horse to an abrupt stop. His eyes were open in wonderment as he held up Sanemori's head by its long white hair.

"It was dye," he said.

Yoshi studied Kiso and was surprised to see the narrow face turned down. Kiso averted his eyes, but not before tears rolled down his lean cheeks.

Yoshi had never before seen Kiso display an emotion other than anger or scorn. A surprise and a lesson. All humans had a well of feelings they drew on from time to time, and even the worst of them were sons, friends, or lovers to someone.

While he considered that perhaps he had misjudged Kiso, Kiso's head lifted, his lids opened, and his wild dark eyes stared at Yoshi with an expression of absolute hatred.

fifty-two

―――――――――――◆―――――――――――

After dark, Santaro surreptitiously approached the entrance of
Yoshi's tent. He stood in the shadows for several minutes,
waiting to be sure that no one saw him. When he was satisfied
he was alone, he rapped on the tent pole.

Yoshi and Nami had just finished a late meal and were
looking forward to spending a quiet evening together. Yoshi
was not pleased at the intrusion. His first instinct was to ignore
the knock. Nami made a disapproving face and opened the tent
flap.

"Santaro! What brings you here at so late an hour?" asked
Nami.

Santaro glanced swiftly over his shoulder. "Let me in,
quickly." He was extremely agitated.

"Come in, then," said Nami, surprised at Santaro's tone.

"I can't stay more than a few minutes. They'll notice my
absence." Santaro lacked his usual confidence. He sounded
concerned.

Yoshi motioned Santaro to join him at the low table, where
some dried fish and a flagon of sake remained from their repast.
Santaro refused the food with a wave of his hand. He knelt
beside Yoshi and spoke breathlessly. "You must leave tonight.
At once if possible."

"I don't understand . . ."

"There is no time for long explanations. You know that
Kiso and Imai hate you."

"*Hai*. Their hate stems from my first day in camp."

"They intend to kill you tonight."

"Ridiculous. For what reason? Do they hate me more tonight
than last week or the week before? Kiso respects and fears his
cousin Yoritomo too much to do me overt harm. Why do you
tell me this?"

"Yoshi, you saved my life when we were in Kamakura. I
have not forgotten. I pledged my aid and I want to help you.
I want you to flee to safety."

"Why tonight? There have been other opportunities to kill

me. Why now, in their moment of triumph?"

"Yoshi, today Kiso was so angry he lost regard for the consequences. I, too, thought he would rejoice after our victory, but he returned from the field in so black a mood he was unreachable. I have never seen him so angry and distraught.

"The troops celebrate our victory. Sake flows freely. Yet Kiso storms about his tent like a madman. None of us know the cause, but we know it concerns you. He swears to kill you."

Yoshi remained silent, remembering the day. He had seen Kiso cry at Sanemori's death. Was that the reason Kiso could not forgive him? But people cry when they are deeply touched. In the court, men cried at the beauty of a flower or of a well-brushed piece of calligraphy. How sad if men can not demonstrate honest emotion without feeling demeaned.

Or was it Sanemori's death? No. Sanemori's death was a blow, but one Kiso could accept. It was a samurai's lot to fight and die for the cause he believed in.

The brief moment that Kiso's defenses had been lowered and Yoshi had seen behind them must be the cause. To a man as rigid as Kiso, this would be an unforgivable sin. How strange the workings of the human heart. Yoshi almost liked Kiso in that moment, the same moment that fueled Kiso's hatred beyond control.

At last, Yoshi said, "Kiso must consider Yoritomo's orders. He wouldn't dare ignore them."

"Not so. With today's victory, Kiso believes the balance of power has shifted. He believes he is stronger than Yoritomo and no longer needs his cousin's support."

"He is wrong. The Minamoto can win control of the Empire by presenting a unified force to the Emperor. Without cooperating with each other, they will lose Go-Shirakawa's support and neither Kiso nor Yoritomo will have power enough to succeed."

"I agree. I have discussed this with the others. Tomoe, Tezuka, Jiro, and Taro agree with us. Only Imai thinks Kiso right. Imai is a hot-headed fool for all his bravery. He cares only to die honorably in the heat of battle."

Yoshi sighed in resignation. "It is impossible to reason with madness," he said. "We must wait. Kiso will return to sanity and calm tomorrow. He will realize his best interests lie in maintaining the alliance with his cousin . . ."

Santaro wiped a big hand through his beard and snorted. "There will be no tomorrow for you. I overheard his plans.

Tonight! When the camp sleeps, he will come with Imai and kill you."

Nami listened silently to this entire exchange. Her pale face betrayed a mixture of emotions on hearing Santaro's story. She could not contain herself any longer and burst in, "We must leave at once. Kiso is a madman."

Santaro studied her sorrowfully. "That would be unwise. You would slow Yoshi's escape."

"I've ridden with Yoshi before. I will dress as his retainer and we will flee within the hour. I will not stay behind. I do not trust Kiso."

"You will stay with Tomoe. You have nothing to fear. Tomoe will control Kiso. But Yoshi must leave immediately. He will have to bypass the sentries and travel on foot through the mountains. Kiso's mountains! That will be a monumental task for one man alone, impossible if you accompany him."

"I will not stay. I would rather die with Yoshi."

Yoshi interjected. "Santaro is right. I must go alone. You will be safe with Tomoe. I think Kiso will change his mind before he acts rashly, but if he intends to kill me when I sleep, I am at his mercy. If he fails tonight, he will try again and again until he succeeds."

Nami bit her lip in frustration. She was tempted to tell Yoshi about Kiso. She resisted the temptation. If he knew about the assault, Yoshi would confront Kiso and that might mean his death. She pleaded again, "I must go. I want to be with you."

Yoshi nodded thoughtfully. "If we had only ourselves to think about, I would take you," he said. "However, it is my duty to inform Yoritomo of Kiso's new attitude. It will change Yoritomo's strategy."

Nami hung her head sorrowfully. Yoshi had to put duty first and could not jeopardize his mission for selfish reasons. But . . . if he knew her fears? Her lips tightened. She held her peace. Nami turned to Santaro. "Because Tomoe promises to protect me and will allow me to share her rooms, I will stay."

"Agreed. There is no more time for discussion. My life would be forfeited if Kiso thought I warned you. I must return before they notice my absence. Nami, I will send Tomoe as quickly as I can. Be ready. Given Kiso's rage, even Tomoe is not beyond his wrath if he believes she conspires against him. Go with her as if on a friendly visit, a mere coincidence that it comes at this time."

Yoshi rose to his feet. "Enough," he said. "You must leave

now." Yoshi clasped Santaro's shoulders warmly, then stepped back and bowed. "Amida be with you," he said. "Thank you for the warning."

Santaro peered outside. There was no one in sight. He whispered a farewell and disappeared without a backward glance.

Nami hastily packed. As Santaro promised, Tomoe arrived, her dark features flushed with distress. "Why are you here?" she asked Yoshi. "Didn't Santaro tell you your life is in immediate danger?"

"I waited till you came for Nami," Yoshi told her. "You are a true friend."

Tomoe seemed abashed at Yoshi's words. She flushed and said, "I would be less than human if I did not protect Nami." She turned and, putting a hand on Nami's sleeve, said, "You have been kind to me and generous. I am a simple country girl. Without you, I would have known nothing of the life that awaits me when we reach the capital. You helped me unselfishly and I will never forget."

Nami interjected, "And without you I would never have adjusted to life in the camp. You befriended me." The two women embraced. A strange pair: one, an educated woman of the court, pale and delicate; the other, unlettered, dark, intense, a woman of the rough northern mountains. Withal they shared a common bond, an unusual bond... both were fiercely independent women who had thrown off the shackles of conformity.

The women parted with moist eyes. Tomoe brushed her cheeks with her sleeve and turned to Yoshi. She cleared her throat and said brusquely, "May Hachiman protect you as I will protect your Nami. I must be certain that we can reach my quarters undiscovered. Take this time to say goodbye, then go swiftly." She rose and bowed as one samurai to another before she slipped out.

"Oh, Yoshi," cried Nami. "Why does fate separate us whenever we find peace?"

"There is no answer, beloved. Such matters are in the hands of the gods. We must be brave, do our duty to ourselves and those we serve, and we must never forget our love."

Nami was tearful at parting. She offered a poem:

> *"The sweetest music*
> *Will bring me tears and sorrow*
> *When you are away*

*In the far northern mountains
And I cannot hear your voice."*

Yoshi embraced her sadly. "I will not be gone too long," he said, knowing he spoke a lie. "Promise you will remain with Tomoe till I return. She is your true friend. I trust her. She is strong and will protect you."

"I promise," said Nami. Her eyes glistened with unspilled tears. "I will wait forever if I must."

"Let us pray we will soon be together. Now . . . you must be ready to leave the moment Tomoe returns."

Five minutes later, Tomoe ducked through the tent flap. "Hurry," she said. "Kiso and Imai will be here soon." Again she bowed to Yoshi and added, "Go now or our efforts are wasted."

Yoshi closed his eyes as Nami followed Tomoe into the night.

Then he made his own preparations.

The victory celebration ended near midnight. The myriad sounds of a hot summer night filled the hot plain. Bullfrogs sang in the rushes, wild monkeys, owls, and the ever-present cicadas made riot in the woods. The air was suffused with the sweet scent of grass combined with lilac, flowering paulownia, gentian, and moonflower. Since it was close to the middle of the lunar month, Tsukiyomi was in full face, beaming peacefully on the landscape below.

Two figures, cloaked in dark cotton, came silently along the dirt path between the tents. They were intent on their mission, oblivious to the sights and sounds around them.

Kiso and Imai!

Kiso held out a hand. "Stop," he whispered. "This is the tent. I'll go first. Follow closely. Remember, spare the woman. Kill the man quickly." He lifted the tent flap and ducked under it. He stayed motionless, hardly breathing. The tent seemed strangely silent, devoid of life, as though it was a passing stage on the way to the Western Paradise. A fitting setting, he thought.

Imai joined him and they waited while their eyes grew accustomed to the dark.

Kiso whispered in a hardly audible voice. "There." He pointed to a huddled shape wrapped in a *futon* near the back wall. They moved toward it, eyes and ears straining for the slightest disturbance.

Nothing!

They took up positions on either side of the *futon*. There was the faintest sibilance as their swords were drawn in unison.

Kiso raised his blade overhead and hissed, "Die!" as he smashed downward at the bulky *futon*. The *futon* shredded.

"Wait."

"What is it?"

"Light the oil lamp."

In the lamp's guttering light, Kiso and Imai stared at a pile of demolished bedding. Cotton wisps floated as high as the top of the tent. Some landed on the men's heads and shoulders.

Even in the semidarkness, Imai saw Kiso's face darken. The narrow features distended in an unnatural expression. The mouth opened and emitted an animallike scream barely recognizable as human speech. "He has made fools of us again," Kiso howled.

fifty-three

Near the end of the eighth month, the heat and humidity made everyday living unbearable. The people of Kamakura were more fortunate than most; the eastern ocean, lapping at the edges of their rough city, cooled the air and allowed them to breathe by day and sleep by night.

The shutters of Yoritomo's quarters were open to catch the sea breeze. Painted screens and tall vases with sprays of flowers decorated the corners of the large room. On the polished wood floor, a bright new straw mat was spread before a dais. Visitors knelt on the mat when granted an audience with Yoritomo and Hojo Masa.

This day, Yoritomo wore a cool white glossed silk robe over wide-legged blue-gray trousers. He constantly waved a paper fan. Hojo Masa was at his side. Her bulky body was covered by a thin robe of dark orange over multiple white shifts. She cooled herself with an orange-colored fan that matched the over-robe. The low table before them was set with a blue ceramic vase containing red flowers and a bowl of fruit. Despite the fans and open shutters, both Yoritomo and Hojo Masa were covered with a thin film of sweat. The scent of the flowers could not completely mask the faint odor of perspiration that surrounded them.

Yoshi had waited outside their quarters, frustrated by the formal procedures required by protocol. His report was important and he was impatient. Now, at last, he knelt in front of the dais, telling Yoritomo the details of his assignment with Kiso. He finished with the account of Kiso's treacherous intentions.

Yoritomo received Yoshi's news calmly. "I was warned many months ago and expected this to happen. That is why I sent you to him. I am surprised you escaped with your life." He hesitated, then added, "I am pleased."

Hojo Masa's heavy features warmed in a smile. In the short time she had known Yoshi and Nami, she had grown to admire them. At Kamakura, there were few people to match her culture and intelligence; she valued those she found.

"With your permission, my lord," she said to Yoritomo. He nodded for her to speak. "I am pleased you are with us again, though I am sorry you had to abandon your charming wife. You must be suffering at having had to leave Nami behind," she said to Yoshi. "I'm sure you arranged for her comfort and safety while you are away from her?" Her voice rose in a questioning inflection at the last.

Yoshi bowed his head. "Kiso was my enemy before I arrived at his camp. That situation never improved. However, he has no quarrel with Nami. Tomoe will protect her from his reprisals. With her support, Nami is safe from harm. If I had thought otherwise, I would not have left her." Yoshi spoke boldly, with confidence in his voice, though underneath he suppressed a feeling of unease. Kiso was unpredictable. There might be a time when even Tomoe could not restrain him.

Hojo Masa said, "I'm sure you have taken every precaution. I understand how difficult this parting was for you."

Yoshi inclined his head in acknowledgment.

While Hojo Masa spoke, Yoritomo studied Yoshi. He saw a hard face, the features even and strong; the overriding impression was of inner calm.

In the months he had served Kiso, Yoshi had come to an understanding with himself. He no longer questioned his decision to forego the sword. The gods had protected him at times when a sword would not. Yoshi's feeling of rightness communicated itself to Yoritomo.

Yoritomo bit into a piece of fruit and spit out the pit. "You escaped immediately after the battle of Shinohara?"

"That same night."

"What did you hear on the road?"

"Sir, I avoided human contact. I thought Kiso might send assassins after me, and my first duty was to reach you with my report."

"Well done." Yoritomo pursed his lips thoughtfully and leaned toward Yoshi. He stabbed out a finger. "Since you left Shinohara, Kiso rides a wave of success. He won a decisive battle at Tonami-yama. Koremori's army is virtually destroyed. Whether we like him or not, trust him or not, Kiso has proved himself a brilliant strategist."

"I never doubted his ability or his bravery."

"He apparently respects your ability also . . . almost as much as he hates you. Kiso has posted notices on public boards in every town offering rewards for your head."

"I know of his hatred. As to the reward for my head, the Nii-Dono offered one first and no one has collected it."

"Your head seems to be more wanted than mine," said Yoritomo with a mirthless smile. The smile disappeared quickly as he continued, "You say Okabe-no-Santaro warned you of Kiso's assassination attempt?"

"Yes, Lord Yoritomo."

"I remember him as a loutish country brute who was held in custody. Yet you saw qualities in him you admired and you found him cooperative in organizing the reinforcements I provided to Kiso's army."

"He is a good soldier, and we are trusted friends."

"Then I give you sad news."

Yoshi felt a weight sink in his belly, a sudden rush of apprehension. His mouth tasted of cotton.

"I'm sorry," Yoritomo said. "Spies inform me that Santaro was put to death shortly after you escaped."

Then I am at fault for his death, was the thought that flashed through Yoshi's mind. A curse follows me. Santaro was my friend and he died because of that friendship. A lump rose in Yoshi's throat and tears welled up. Unashamedly, he wiped his eyes with his sleeve. "Tell me how it happened," he demanded.

"Kiso claimed Santaro was a traitor and had him publicly beheaded."

Yoshi's heart sank. Poor Santaro. Loyal soldier. Loyal friend. To suffer this final indignity!

In spite of the events at Hikuma, the insults in the mountains of Shinano, at Hiuchi-yama, and at Shinohara... in spite of all these provocations, Yoshi had not fully hated Kiso until this moment. If Kiso were before him with a sword in his hand, he would forego his vows. The calm demeanor Yoshi had so carefully cultivated fell away. Beads of sweat burst forth on his forehead, a muscle twitched at the corner of his jaw. He struggled to regain his composure.

At last he spoke. His voice was flat and cold as he repeated, "He was my friend."

Hojo Masa murmured sympathetically.

Yoritomo cleared his throat. "Santaro's death was unfortunate," he said, "but it is only one of a series of events that could have far-reaching effects. If you had been able to reach us sooner, these events might have taken a different turn. However, we cannot change the spin of the wheel of life."

Yoshi bowed, waiting. His mind churned angrily, but outwardly there was no evidence of his turmoil.

"While we were on the road, I received a message from Go-Shirakawa. He decided to cast his lot with us. If you had been here, I would have sent you to him as my emissary. You would have been able to bring him to us in safety. The man I sent failed in this mission. Go-Shirakawa fled to Mount Hiei to hide with the Enryaku-ji monks."

Yoshi was startled by Yoritomo's news. Yoritomo did not realize that Go-Shirakawa's decision was due to Yoshi's report. Yoshi's message had been delivered. Yoshi, as Go-Shirakawa's emissary, should have been the one to bring him to Yoritomo. Perhaps there was still time! "Can I go to Mount Hiei to arrange for his safe passage?" Yoshi asked.

"It is too late! Too late. This morning I learned that Kiso arrived at Enryaku-ji over a week ago and took the Emperor prisoner. By now, Kiso and Yukiie have probably entered Kyoto with the Emperor at their side."

Yoshi's disappointment at this political setback was offset by his surprise at hearing Yukiie's name. Yukiie? Yukiie alive and with Kiso?

"Yukiie is dead!" said Yoshi. "He died at Hiuchi-yama."

"Not so. My spies inform me that after you left, Yukiie reappeared, claiming you had deserted Hiuchi-yama and that he had been wounded in battle and escaped into the mountains before Koremori's troops found him."

"Lies!" said Yoshi, stunned by the news. How unfair, he thought, that a good man like Santaro dies while a swine like Yukiie lives on.

"Lies, of course lies. I doubt that Kiso believes his uncle. He accepts the story because it is convenient; there are troops foolish enough to follow Yukiie, and Kiso wants them under his flag."

"Then we have lost. If Kiso and Yukiie control Kyoto with the monks and the cloistered Emperor as their allies, they will be invincible."

"Kiso's power will be limited because Go-Shirakawa lacks the official symbol of the ruling family, the Imperial regalia. Without the official mirror, sword, and jewels, he cannot claim the throne. The boy Emperor, Antoku, has the regalia and remains sovereign of Japan."

"Where is the boy?"

"In the confusion that accompanied Kiso's entrance to Kyoto, he escaped with Munemori and his grandmother, the Nii-Dono. The Taira family, with the child Emperor and the loyal members of their court, fled Kyoto in the eighth month. Munemori's weakness and the Nii-Dono's evil are amply repaid by the pain of their banishment. Their lives are miserable, they are like *eta,* non-persons, without a roof over their heads.

"They earned their pain, yet . . . how can we not sympathize with them, the mighty cast into the world, blown about as dust before wind."

Yoritomo paused before he concluded, "The Taira are no longer a force in the Empire. Though they harbor the regalia, they flee from hamlet to hamlet in fear of their lives. The final battle will be between my armies and Kiso's."

"Even without the regalia, Kiso will have enough support to make his the stronger force."

"In Kiso's strength lies his weakness. He will destroy the remaining Taira for me and will in turn be destroyed by Kyoto. He has no inner resources to fight the corruption of the capital. He is uneducated and lacks the discipline to control his men. I predict that soon after they conquer the city, Kiso's men will destroy themselves."

Yoshi nodded. He knew Kiso's weakness. Not the weakness that allowed him to weep at Sanemori's death, but the weakness of being unable to admit to his own humanity.

"I agree," said Yoshi. "Kiso is naïve and inexperienced in court intrigue. Kyoto will corrupt him. The citizens of Kyoto will join Go-Shirakawa in begging our help."

"And now . . . I have a mission for you."

"I am at your lordship's service."

"I want you to go to Kyoto . . ."

"Into Kiso's territory?"

Hojo Masa demurred. "Oh, no!" she said, apologetic at interrupting, but with deep concern in her voice. "Reward notices with Yoshi's description are posted at every approach to the city. Yoshi will never enter Kyoto alive."

Yoritomo shook his head in irritation. "Do you think I am unaware of the danger?" he said to Hojo Masa. He leaned toward Yoshi. "You will not be recognized. You will be disguised as a farmer, a merchant, an indigent monk, any disguise you choose. Grow a beard. Change your hair. Take the necessary time to build a new character for yourself, one that Kiso will not recognize. I trust your ingenuity."

"And how much time do I have?"

"Kiso's control of Kyoto has undermined my position. I will need about eighteen months to reunite the major northern families under my flag. You must be in Kyoto by the second new year celebration."

"And what is my goal if I succeed and reach Kyoto undiscovered?"

"Locate Kiso. Get close to him. By the time we are ready, I judge his power will be weakened by his corruption and the court's greed. Send me word when you reach him. My men will be at your command. You will capture Kiso while I march on Kyoto. You must not fail. Our success depends on you."

BOOK IV

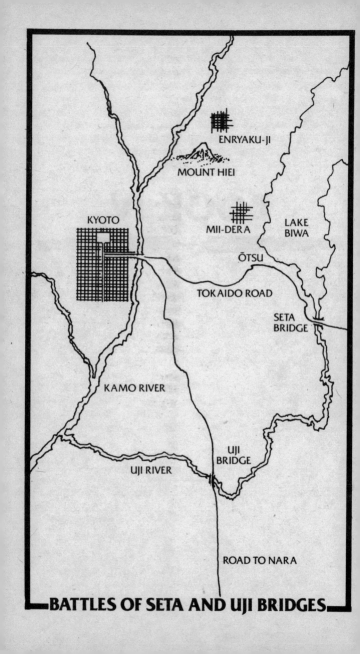

BATTLES OF SETA AND UJI BRIDGES

fifty-four

On the twentieth day of the ninth month, morning light turned the sky into an azure sea with tiny wave crests of cloud. Yoshi was awakened by a flock of crows disturbing the morning with their raucous, "Caw, caw, caw."

He lay on a pile of straw behind a storage shed. The straw was moldy and rotted from time and weather. The shed was earth-walled and straw-thatched, once used as a stable, now empty and neglected. A faint odor of horse and cow manure clung to the walls. He thought wryly that he had spent more comfortable nights in his lifetime. Yoshi had traveled the back roads dressed as a vagabond, avoiding people, since he had left Kamakura three weeks earlier. People could mean trouble.

Yoshi became conscious of noise from the other side of the shed, a clanking of metal mixed with animallike grunts. He leaped to his feet, feeling a tension between his shoulder blades. Quickly brushing loose straw and dead insects from his rough clothing, Yoshi stepped to the corner of the shed and peeked around it.

In the open yard that had once been a corral for cattle, two men were dueling. What swords! To Yoshi's ear, trained to the sound of fine steel, they sounded like children's tin toys. In spite of the poor weapons, the men were obviously serious. Sweat ran down their naked backs. They grunted with effort, made angry faces at each other, and staggered back and forth in a clumsy parody of attack and defense.

One of the swordsmen was a fine-looking young man a few years younger than Yoshi. He looked familiar, but Yoshi could not recall where he had seen him. The young man was getting the worst of the battle from the other swordsman, a sinister-looking older man whose lip curled nastily with every clumsy stroke of his sword.

Yoshi felt an instinctive desire to help the younger man. He wished he had some kind of weapon. Without one, it would be foolhardy to step in even against a bad blade.

The sinister man was driven toward Yoshi's hiding place.

Seizing his opportunity, Yoshi picked up a small stone and threw it at the swordsman's back. The result was completely satisfactory. The man cried out in pained surprise and dropped his sword. There was a sudden silence broken only by a flock of sparrows fluttering in panic from under the eaves of the shed.

Instead of finishing off his opponent, the young man dropped his sword and ran to him, saying, "Tsure, what happened? Did I cut you? I'm sorry. Terribly sorry. What can I do?"

"It wasn't you, you ass. Something hit me from behind. Owwwww!" The pained cry resulted from the younger man feeling the older man's bruised shoulder. "By the Amida Buddha, Shite," he shouted. "Leave it alone."

"Let me call Ohana. He will massage it for you."

"Be quiet a moment." The sinister man turned warily around, searching the field.

Yoshi had pulled back behind the earthen wall. His surprise at the fighters' reaction left him confused until he realized the truth. Now he remembered the young man. They had met about a year ago, when he had camped with Nami at Okitsu. These men were strolling players, practicing a mock sword battle for a theater entertainment.

Yoshi had seen many groups of acrobats, dancers, musicians, and actors in the past. Usually ragged, ill-disciplined, and badly rehearsed, these groups eked out their living by performing their shabby little programs for country folk. Most of the groups were composed of *hinen,* people of low caste. Their performances were called *Dengaku,* rice-field music, because they played at farmers' festivals for spring rice-sowing and autumn reaping. More professional troupes were sponsored by the Buddhist temples and Shinto shrines; it was these professional groups that Yoshi had seen during his court stay.

Yoshi was relieved. There would be no danger from this group of semi-outcasts. He chuckled softly at first, then broke into laughter. How ridiculous the situation was. Toy swords! The swordmaster taken in by toy swords!

As he leaned against the rough-textured wall laughing, the two duelists came around the corner and stared at him, one in open-mouthed amazement, the other in anger.

"Well, peasant, do you always throw rocks at honest working folk?" demanded the sinister one.

The seriousness of the man's expression sent Yoshi into another paroxysm of laughter.

"There's something wrong with him," said the younger one nervously.

"Nothing that a good kick in the bottom wouldn't cure."

"Hold on, hold on," said Yoshi. "I mean you no harm. I'm laughing in relief. I thought you were fighting to the death and I wanted to save you from yourselves." Yoshi exploded again as he watched their startled faces.

The actors looked at each other. One smiled, the other snickered, and in seconds, they joined Yoshi and were pummeling one another on the back and laughing hysterically.

"What in Amida's name is going on here?" boomed a deep voice behind them.

This sent the three off into even wilder extravagances of mirth.

"I send you two off to practice for the sword dance and find you either drunk on sake or insane. Who is this vagabond? What is he doing here? And why are grown men howling like mad dogs?"

Shite, the handsome young man, managed to catch his breath first. "He thought we were dueling," he said. "Can you imagine? We actually fooled him. Ohana-san, he threw a stone at Tsure to save me."

"Then he is more of a fool than you are. Your rehearsals are worse than your performances. You can't deceive a blind deaf cripple with your sword dance. Get back to work. Tomorrow we appear before the *Daimyo*." He turned to Yoshi, who had finally subsided. Ohana saw a muscular man with ragged hair tied with a dirty *hachimaki*, dressed in rough cotton, a straw cloak, and worn straw sandals. Possibly a poor traveler. More likely, a cutpurse and a thief.

His voice took on the pontifical tone of a great man addressing an inferior. "If you can talk at all, I'd like an explanation. Who are you and what are you doing here?"

Yoshi in turn assessed Ohana as a pompous blowhard who was undoubtedly trespassing on this deserted farm as he had trespassed on Fumio's land in Okitsu. Behind Ohana's commanding voice was a small man who stood with his chin raised and his weight back on his heels. Thin, bowed legs under a large paunch made him look like a bandy-legged rooster. The effect was heightened by heavy jowls that quivered when he spoke. Ohana had been a handsome man, but his features, once classic, were blurred by years of indulgence with the sake bottle. Yoshi remembered the distinctive red nose that gave him his name. The little fellow obviously did not recognize Yoshi. As uncomfortable as Yoshi found the dirty clothing, he was glad he had chosen it.

Yoshi had dealt with this type of provincial before; he thought he knew how to deal with him. Yoshi used his most cultured accent, speaking with the lilt of the Kyoto court. "My dear sir," he said. "You may call me Suruga, though I really don't believe an answer is due you."

Most men not of noble birth used names taken from physical traits or their place of birth. Yoshi had decided to use Suruga, the name of his home province. He leveled a cold stare at Ohana and said, "Your people have no more right here than I, an innocent traveler strayed from the road. Do you know whose land you are on?"

Ohana was awed by the soft educated voice coming from this muscular vagabond. "Certainly," he blustered. "It is the *shoen* of Lord Hachibumi, *Daimyo* of Okabe, ally of Lord Kiso Yoshinaka, and employer of my band of players."

Yoshi silently cursed his bad fortune. Hachibumi was a staunch supporter of Kiso and Yukiie. Though several months had passed since Yoshi had escaped from Shinohara, he was sure Kiso and his friends continued to search for him.

Yoshi's description had been posted in every town. Okabe would not be an exception. If the little man had not recognized him—after having met him before—in all probability Hachibumi's men could not identify him either. Yoshi decided to take the offense and bluff this big-nosed fellow. "In that case," he said. "I shall not register a complaint with Hachibumi's samurai. They are famous for their lack of patience with trespassers."

"We are not trespassers. We are to appear tomorrow night at a special victory celebration given by Lord Hachibumi in Kiso Yoshinaka's honor."

"That might be hard to explain to the samurai. They are known to strike first and ask questions later." Yoshi thought he detected an edge of nervousness in Ohana's manner and hastened to add, "But enough! I see that you have a legitimate right to be here."

"Of course we do," said Ohana too quickly.

"I have a suggestion that might be to our mutual benefit."

Ohana studied the straw-covered robe and stained *hakama* with disdain. "I doubt you have anything we want," he said.

Yoshi continued as if he hadn't heard. "If I joined you, I

could contribute to the skills of your two swordsmen. I am a trained swordsman and it would suit me to travel with your group."

By this time, Ohana was hopelessly confused. He didn't know what to believe. Between the ragged clothes and the reference to swordsmanship—an attribute of the samurai class— he couldn't place Yoshi in any category. Was he merely a liar, or was he a *ronin* who had run into a streak of bad luck? Did one speak to him as to an inferior or as to a superior?

"I find that interesting." Ohana kept a purposefully non- committal tone. "My swordsmen need help. If you join us for morning tea and a little dried fish, we can discuss this further. I may be able to use someone in my company who speaks well and knows the sword." Watching Yoshi's reaction from the corner of his eye, he boldly added, "If you really know how to use it as you claim."

"It would be my pleasure," said Yoshi, ignoring the probe.

Shite and Tsure had stood silently through the conversation. Now Tsure broke in. "I'll be damned to Yomi if I need some ragged stranger showing me how to handle a sword. I've done this sword dance for almost twenty years and no one has com- plained."

"Then you've done it for fools and farmers," said Yoshi coolly. "If you want to play for people like Hachibumi, your performance will have to be better."

"I'd like to learn," said Shite, his handsome face puckered in a frown of concentration. "If we improved, we could get more work and more money. Why not let the stranger teach us?"

"Well, I'm against it. Everything has been working smoothly. Why do we need change?" grumbled Tsure.

"I'll decide that," said Ohana imperiously. Lifting the hem of his robe, he led the way back to the players' encampment.

There were two oxen and a sad-looking horse tied next to a mountain of bags, sacks, and boxes. The camp was near an old well behind the deserted farm building. Yoshi later dis- covered that the original tenant-farmer had been executed for withholding taxes. The land lay fallow while Lord Hachibumi decided how to distribute it to his best advantage.

The three animals were accompanied by four muscular ac- robats; a dour-faced little man, who was the company musician; two attractive young women, who were eating rice and fish; and an older woman, who spooned the rice from a large iron pot. Three men of varied ages and sizes made up the rest of the theatrical troupe.

No wonder the oxen and the horse looked sad, thought Yoshi, carrying the effects of fourteen people plus the paraphernalia and props for the acrobats and actors. He was later to discover that the two young girls were Aki, the daughter of Ohana, and Ume, sister to one of the acrobats. The older woman with the rice bowl was Ohana's mother, Obaasen, and the musician who played a four stringed lutelike *biwa* was his cousin, Ito. A family enterprise!

The fire sent spark showers and clouds of aromatic smoke that brought Yoshi pangs of hunger.

"I've invited this stranger to join us for morning tea," said Ohana.

The two girls seemed interested. Ume lowered her eyes; Aki stared at Yoshi with frank appraisal.

"If I may wash first?"

"Of course. Use the basin by the farmhouse door."

Yoshi borrowed utensils and a clean robe from one of the acrobats. He went behind the farmhouse, stripped his filthy clothes, and bathed himself thoroughly. He combed his hair, changing it from his usual style, and shaved his beard.

A more presentable traveler sat beside the fire a few minutes later. His borrowed robe was admittedly theatrical: bright red and embroidered with dragons. Yoshi felt the robe changed his appearance even more than his ragged traveling clothes. It also had a great advantage . . . it was clean.

Yoshi ate rice and fish with as much restraint as he could manage. There were certain penalties in disguising himself as a vagabond. Though he had two coins hidden in his *obi* for emergencies, he could not demand or purchase food at will; this was his first meal in twenty-four hours.

Were there possibilities in the theatrical company? Yoritomo wanted Yoshi established in Kyoto by the end of the next year. Could this primitive troupe be used to get him to the capital? From what he had seen, that was questionable; the troupe was too crude to appear in Kyoto. On the other hand, they would furnish an excellent disguise. Who would suspect a lowly member of an acting company to be a famous *sensei?*

If the company did not eventually appear in Kyoto, Yoshi would have lost valuable time. Yoritomo needed Yoshi to help him further his plans against Kiso. It was imperative that Yoshi reach the capital.

On the whole, Yoshi decided, the acting company would make a good choice. He would put his effort into joining them and seeing to it that they reached Kiso . . . and Nami.

fifty-five

The sun rose in the east, burning the rice fields and bamboo patches that spread across the plain from the river to distant mauve hills. Clouds of dragonflies glinted over patches of scattered purple thistle. It was a peaceful scene.

Yoshi listened idly to the incomprehensible professional jargon of the acrobats as he sipped his tea.

"Horses are coming. There, across the river bed," said one of the actors.

Everyone snapped to instant alert. A cloud of dust rose in the north; moments later, the low rumble of horsemen became audible.

Ohana, remembering Yoshi's warning about Hachibumi's samurai cutting first and questioning afterward, said, "Shite, you talk with them before they reach here. Tell them we camp here by Lord Hachibumi's invitation."

"Ohana, I'm not the one to tell them. Perhaps Tsure should go."

Tsure looked contemptuously at the handsome young actor. "You speak well enough when it is about yourself. Are you afraid, hero?"

"I'm not the one to talk with them," repeated Shite.

"Shall we send Obaasen or the two girls?" asked Ohana sarcastically.

Shite was sheepish but stubborn. "Maybe women would calm the warriors and convince them of our good intentions."

Yoshi, seeing that the argument would continue till the horsemen were upon them, saw his opportunity to ingratiate himself with Ohana. He said, "Wait, stop arguing. I have handled situations like this before. I will meet them, but on one condition..."

"Hurry, man," said Ohana. "They are almost upon us. What do you want?"

"I need employment. Decide now and I will speak as a member of the troupe."

"Granted. Now, hurry before they get here and take our horses and women."

". . . and lives," added Shite.

Yoshi, resplendent in the embroidered red robe, strode purposefully toward the rapidly approaching horsemen. There were twenty-five of them, each dressed in battle armor. Lord Hachibumi's crest flew at the front and back of the formation. The leader raised a hand to signal a halt.

"Who are you?" he demanded.

"A band of players engaged by the great Lord Hachibumi to perform at his castle tomorrow night." Yoshi reminded himself to keep his inner thoughts dampened. His role demanded an obsequious air that was more difficult to maintain than his physical disguise.

"How long have you been here?"

"Two days, sir. Practicing and rehearsing to please his lordship." Yoshi's voice quivered. He carefully stared at the ground under the horse's belly, afraid his eyes would belie his voice.

"Have you seen any stranger pass this way?"

"Stranger, sir?"

"Yes, stupid, stranger."

"No, sir, I don't think so, sir."

"You don't think so, you idiot? Think harder. We're looking for a man about your age, a sword master. Have you seen anyone like that?"

"Definitely not, sir. Some pilgrims passed on the road two days ago, but they were women and old men."

"Fool! I told you he is a man about your age. Lord Kiso himself instructed us to search till we find him. He could have passed your company any time in the last several weeks. Think again!"

Yoshi's brows raised in evident puzzlement. "I don't remember anyone like that, sir."

The samurai glowered. "If you see a person who answers this description, find us and tell us."

"Gladly, sir." Yoshi kept his eyes focused on the ground. "May I ask what crime this person committed?"

"No, you may not ask . . . but I'll tell you anyway. He is wanted for deserting Lord Kiso's army and for traitorous acts against Lord Kiso and Lord Yukiie. When we find him . . . and, in time, we will . . . he will die. Now, enough talk. Pack up your band and move on."

Yoshi reached under his fancy robe for one of his emergency gold pieces. "Sir, I am sure Lord Hachibumi would want us to stay and perfect the performance in his honor. We would be pleased to pay rental as a sign of good faith. We are not vagrants. We are employed by his lordship."

"A single gold coin?" The samurai sneered.

"Oh no, captain! I was merely giving you one coin at a time. We are a poor group, not yet paid by his lordship, but we insist on your taking our gold." Yoshi took out his last gold coin.

The samurai shoved both coins under his sash. "You will leave immediately after tomorrow night's performance. Woe betide you if I ever see you on Lord Hachibumi's land after that." He signaled the horsemen, and kicking up clouds of dust, they rode back toward the river.

Yoshi walked back to Ohana's group, dusting himself off.

"What happened? What did he say?" they asked anxiously.

"I've taken care of everything. We can remain till the performance tomorrow night."

"What did you tell him?" asked Ohana.

"That we are employed by Hachibumi."

"And he believed you?"

"I was very persuasive," said Yoshi dryly.

"Yes, you have a way..." Ohana gave him a thoughtful look.

"They could have killed you," said Shite.

"No great loss," said Tsure.

"Let's finish our tea," said Ohana's mother, ending the conversation on a practical note.

The dust and clatter from the samurai band were gone. The sun was directly overhead and it was quite warm. Yoshi sipped more tea. He was sweaty and uncomfortable under the red robe. Dealing with samurai was a perilous business for an unarmed man.

Many samurai would cut a man in half merely to test the edge of a blade. Theirs was the freedom and the duty to cut down anyone whom they thought acted disrespectfully. *Kiri-sute-gomen* it was called. Dressed as a vagabond or an actor—and unarmed—Yoshi had no recourse against their whims. He could not afford to forget that to samurai he was little better than the *eta*, slaves, who did the menial, dishonorable chores of life. That was a sobering thought. Any misstep could mean death, and his death would have no more meaning than that of a swatted fly. For a man of his accomplishments, this was difficult to accept. A lesson in humility.

However, Yoshi could not forget the importance of his duty. He had to stay hidden. For that while, he would put the time to good use and work at becoming the best of traveling players. The troupe was uneducated and coarse; he had the advantage of years of studying poetry, art, aesthetics, and the martial arts. Most important, Yoshi was intelligent, capable, and accustomed to command. He would learn their craft and, in turn, help them to become professional enough to appear in Kyoto.

Whatever his assigned task, whatever his outward appearance . . . he was *sensei*, teacher and sword master.

fifty-six

The acrobats spent the afternoon practicing their routines in the open field. Except for signals, grunts and shouts of encouragement, they did not talk. Yoshi watched in fascination. First they did a series of warm-up exercises and stretches that extended their spines and hip joints beyond what Yoshi imagined was possible. Even the largest of the acrobats—who generally supported one or more of the others—was capable of bending over backward to put his hands flat on the ground. All four in unison stretched their legs to the sides and, in this unnatural position, leaned their upper bodies forward to press flat on the ground. They did sit-ups, push-ups, and all manner of exotic variations. They exercised in bare feet and loincloths, their rippling muscles shiny with sweat.

Once the exercises were over, they practiced the program. Yoshi noticed that the moment they were aware of him they worked harder, as if it were a performance instead of a rehearsal, each man trying to outdo the others. With a shout, and in unison, they turned themselves in cartwheels. Then one threw himself in the air and dove headfirst at the ground. At the last instant, his head ducked to his chest and he rolled on the ground, unharmed. Another leaped backward in the air, landing on his feet in a series of somersaults.

The largest one, a muscular giant, was called the "understander." He supported one man on each shoulder and one, upside down, on his head. They performed intricate combinations, contorting themselves in weird, loose-limbed positions, and ended with a final series of cartwheels and multiple dive rolls.

Yoshi decided to ask them to teach him some of their stunts. He noticed that the lightest and most daring of the four was the organizer and leader. While the acrobats took one of their few rest periods, Yoshi spoke to him. "I've never seen acrobats practice. Do you do this all the time?"

"Every day," the acrobat answered politely but with little interest.

"My name is Suruga," said Yoshi. "I suppose you know I'll be joining the troupe."

"Yes. I'm Koetsu, brother of Ume." Koetsu introduced himself while he guardedly studied Yoshi.

"The girl who was seated next to Ohana's mother?"

"Yes. Ume was one of us, but she injured her knee. Now she sews the company's costumes." Koetsu was ready to end the conversation, but Yoshi pressed on. Yoshi was finding in himself a chameleonlike ability to adapt to the ways of those around him. His eyes were being opened to another mode of life. A far cry from the rigidity of his early upbringing in the court.

"Perhaps one day you would allow me to exercise with you. I would like to learn to do some of the stunts," Yoshi said.

"Too hard! It takes a long time!" Koetsu changed abruptly and said, "Maybe we can make a trade."

"What can I trade? I have nothing of value."

"You are educated. Can you read and write?"

"Yes, I can."

"You will teach me, and I will teach you." Koetsu nodded, satisfied with his decision.

"Agreed," said Yoshi, bowing formally.

While this conversation was going on, the *biwa* player uncased his instrument. He sat with his back to the farmhouse, playing musical scales. The plangent notes rose like colorful jays into the hot yellow sunlight. The *biwa*'s four silk strings vibrated softly, resonating from the tear-drop shaped body, as the player stroked them with a large plectrum.

Koetsu returned to practice with his group, while Yoshi wandered back to sit near the *biwa* player. Just as the acrobats had extended themselves when Yoshi watched them, so the dour-faced little musician came to life. Deserting his exercise scales, he started to play his music.

This was Yoshi's first day with the entertainers and he had already noticed two important things. First, all of them, whatever their art, spent endless hours in practice. He had watched acrobats, musicians, and actors at the court; he took their abilities for granted, never thinking about the work hidden behind the professional performance. The second was that they performed for one stranger in an empty field with the same intensity as they performed on the stage.

Now that no one watched, the acrobats worked mechanically on their routines, but the musician played as though it were for a grand audience instead of one attentive stranger.

"I am Ito, cousin to Ohana," said the little man, putting his *biwa* aside.

"I am Suruga, a new member of the company." Yoshi bowed.

"What do you do, young fellow?" Two raisin eyes peerèd speculatively at Yoshi.

"Why, I'm not sure," answered Yoshi as he ran a finger on the *biwa* strings and smiled at the discordant result.

"Can you read and write?" Ito gently placed the instrument out of reach.

"Yes."

"Paint, draw?"

"Yes."

"Do you know music and dance?"

"Some."

"Then my cousin will find much work for you to do." Ito smiled ironically, then continued in an amused voice. "You see, Ohana barely reads or writes. He knows little of painting or drawing, and less of music and dance."

"Then what does he do?"

"Ah, I've often wondered."

"I don't understand."

"You are new to our business. You will find that entertainers are like children. They need a parent to look after them, to tell them what to do. This parent is in charge of the company and is called the manager or producer. He takes care of collecting and distributing the money we earn."

"Why can't one of you do that?"

"Ah, you still don't understand. Each of us has a talent, therefore we are the slave, the servant, the supplicant of that talent. We spend our time and energy tending what we have. We need someone else without that handicap to deal with the lords, priests, and townsmen. This Ohana does well." Having said that, Ito picked up his instrument and began to play.

The music was soft, with dark overtones that suggested the liquid melody of the *uguisa,* a nightingale that sings in the deepest shadows of the bamboo forest. Gradually the music changed. Ito plucked bright single notes of a different melody in counter harmony to the bass accompaniment. Sitting on the dry brown earth in the blazing daffodil sun, Yoshi closed his eyes and pictured plum blossoms scattered in a field of powdery snow, sparks of color on a crisp white mountainside.

Yoshi marveled at what a talented musician could accomplish and, caught in the magic melody, he wanted Ito to teach him the *biwa*.

Yoshi's reverie was broken by Ohana, standing over him. "Time to earn your keep. The duelists are ready to rehearse. Let's see how much you can help them."

Yoshi scrambled to his feet and, with a bow to Ito, followed Ohana to where Shite and Tsure were preparing for their sword dance. The three other players sat and joked as the swordsmen took up their tinny swords and, with snarls and grunts, dueled in mock battle.

Knowing it was a theatrical show, Yoshi was embarrassed that he had thought it real. If they knew he was a *sensei,* a teacher of the sword, how they would laugh.

Shite was a model of ineptitude. Yoshi shuddered inwardly at the thought of his appearing in front of knowledgeable swordsmen with so amateurish a performance.

"Is this all right?" asked Shite, executing a maneuver of startling gracelessness.

"Perhaps we can improve it a little," said Yoshi tactfully. He took the sword and showed Shite how to hold it properly. "If you keep your body straight instead of bending forward, you will be better balanced and able to move more quickly."

Shite tried the suggestion, and to his surprise it worked. A pleased smile lit his face.

"Tsure, you handle the sword quite well," said Yoshi aloud. He paused and added in a low voice so the onlookers would not hear, "If you keep your knees bent and your weight lower, you will look stronger."

Tsure snarled but followed the suggestion, as if he had been doing it all along.

"I'll leave you to rehearse," said Ohana, bowing minimally; it was hard to tell if he was pleased at Yoshi's directions. Ohana was in charge of the actors and of the skits and dances. While he wanted Yoshi's help, he would suffer a loss of face if the stranger improved too much on his handiwork.

Yoshi worked with the swordsmen all afternoon. The three extra players wandered away to practice the farcical sketch they would do tomorrow.

Shite proposed a rest. Tsure sheathed his sword and walked away without a word.

"Did I offend him?" asked Yoshi.

"No. He is always angry because he plays second to me. Tsure wants to be the hero, but Ohana says he looks wrong for the hero parts, so he is unhappy." Shite shrugged and smiled without malice.

Yoshi agreed with Ohana. Tsure looked evil, while Shite was a model hero. In actuality, Shite was timorous, clumsy, ineffectual, and a little stupid. Withal, Yoshi found him a likeable and good natured "hero."

"Will my sword dance improve?" asked Shite eagerly. "You know they laughed and threw things at me when I did it at the rice festival last month."

"It's already much better," said Yoshi.

"Do you really think so?"

"Absolutely. Soon the audience will applaud your sword play."

Shite was like a kitten with its stomach being rubbed. Yoshi was to find that all performers reacted the same way to praise. They existed in a half-world where they came alive during performance or when flattered about their abilities.

"What do you think of Aki?" asked Shite, changing the subject now that he had been reassured.

"I don't know. We haven't spoken. What does she do?"

"She is beautiful. She can do anything. She acts both male and female parts, paints scenery and . . . she does more to get us work than her father does."

"You admire her," Yoshi said.

Shite lowered his eyes and spoke quietly, but with great intensity. "I love her," he said.

At the evening meal, everyone talked about the day's re-hearsals except for the acrobats, who sat to one side and scooped great quantities of rice into their mouths. Aki watched Yoshi warily as Shite told how the sword dance had improved. Shite spoke at great length, showing his good nature, his generosity with praise, and his measure of stupidity. As Shite rambled on, Ume gazed at him shyly from behind the rice pot.

Ito, the little *biwa* player, saw that Yoshi noticed Ume's interest. He leaned close to Yoshi and whispered, "Yes, she loves the fool. Will man ever understand the ways of women?" When Shite stopped talking, Ume immediately refilled his bowl.

The evening grew quiet; the company broke into small groups. Smoke spiraled from the cooking fire in ghostlike waves, carrying a scent of burnt cedarwood. The distant hills turned deep brown and the lowering sun turned patches of purple bell flowers into mysterious oases in the sea of grass.

Ohana furnished Yoshi with a rough quilt, and soon the murmuring voices of the actors made him sleepy. He spread the quilt behind the farmhouse, pulled the red robe to his chin, and lay reviewing what he had seen and learned on this eventful day.

How different the players were from the way they had seemed when he and Nami had watched them in Okitsu. He had said he could do better than they. With the sword, yes. The acrobats! The musician! These people had developed skills he could not approach. He wished Nami were with him to share the experience. At last, he had found a way to use the sword without causing pain.

Yoshi smiled, remembering Nami's sarcasm when she had said, "A fitting career for a great sword master."

"Buddha! Hachiman! Let her be well and thinking of me as I think of her." His mind wandered groggily; the actors' voices lulled him. Aki's oblique glance was the last thing he remembered before he fell into a dreamless sleep.

fifty-seven

The following morning, the troupe was in controlled bedlam, packing, moving, and dressing in preparation for the evening performance.

The castle of Lord Hachibumi was two miles north of the town of Okabe, less than twenty-five miles from the abandoned site of Lord Fumio's *shoen*, where Yoshi first saw Ohana.

The company was far from Kiso in Kyoto, yet Lord Hachibumi's troops actively sought Yoshi. Kiso seemed to have unlimited resources since becoming the power behind the throne. Yoshi wondered if Yoritomo would be successful against an enemy so strong and implacable. *Shigata ga nai*, there was nothing to be done about it. Yoshi would try his utmost to be in place on the day of reckoning.

Ohana arose before dawn, organizing the march through the town. A mauve sky hung clear over the plain. Tiny birds darted in and out of the bamboo brush that patched the uncultivated rice fields. Chirping, calling, and trilling, they added their noise to the clatter of horses being loaded with pots, pans, costumes, and background screens. Ohana unpacked masks from the baggage and assigned them to each of the actors. The acrobats would lead, performing cartwheels and somersaults, then the masked actors would follow, and finally, Ito, beating a drum for the occasion.

Yoshi was assigned to guard the luggage along with Aki, Ume, and Obassen.

"Ohana, wouldn't it be helpful if I, too, wore a mask?" Yoshi asked.

"What for? You are to tend the baggage." Ohana was too busy to spend time with the newcomer.

"If I wore a mask, the townfolk would think me an actor. They would believe your company was bigger than it is."

"True, but wearing a mask is hot and uncomfortable." Ohana eyed Yoshi suspiciously. Why would anyone want to wear a mask?

"I'll gladly suffer the discomfort in the interest of helping your troupe," said Yoshi diplomatically.

"Very well. Wear this demon mask."

"I'll wear it gladly," said Yoshi. There was now no possibility of recognition. No one would ever associate a muscular actor with Tadamori-no-Yoshi, *sensei* and sword master.

The troupe breakfasted on bitter green tea and rice cakes. When the sun grew warmer, they left the deserted farmhouse and headed across the plain to the mountain that overlooked Okabe. Dust rose from the rice fields, stirred by animal hooves, marking the caravan's progress toward town.

By noon they reached a narrow path at the base of the mountain and rested under a wild pomegranate tree. Stands of birch rose like pale sentinels on both sides of the rocky path, casting welcome blue shadows.

"Who *are* you?" asked a voice. Yoshi was startled. He turned to see Aki, sitting a few feet away. She was looking at him calculatingly.

"Were you talking to me?" asked Yoshi, giving himself time to collect his thoughts.

"Yes. I think you are hiding something. Be warned. You cannot keep a secret from us. Our troupe lives in close quarters. Eventually we will know all about you."

"My name is Suruga," Yoshi lied. "I have no secret that concerns the troupe, only a desire to be of help and earn my way." Yoshi studied Aki against the green background. She was a beautiful woman made artificial by heavy cosmetics. The slope of her face gave her the look of a clever mountain fox, a look accentuated by her habit of turning sideways and looking out from the corners of her eyes as she spoke.

Whatever her imperfections, at this moment she was lovely.

Aki bent toward him conspiratorially, "That is good, if true. The more open we are with each other, the better for us all. Some of the group spend their time gossiping." She paused for breath, then asked quietly, "What have you been told about me or my father?"

"Nothing at all," Yoshi answered, surprised to find that behind her mask of calculation she sought reassurance. He was touched by this evidence of insecurity. "Those to whom I have spoken remark on your talent and beauty."

"Do you find me beautiful?" she asked.

"Yes. Very." The heady odor of the pomegranate tree, the dappled light shining through the leaves, and Aki's proximity made this easy to say. Yoshi felt a twinge of guilt. What would

Nami think if she could hear him complimenting a low-born actress? Yet . . . his mission was to blend in with these *hinen*, to become one of them. The duty would not be unpleasant; the girl was undeniably attractive.

On the spur of the moment, he said, "I'd like to compose a poem for you."

"You compose poetry? I hardly believe that possible . . . you are a man of many talents." Aki's cool control snapped back in place. Her tone was sardonic, even unpleasant.

"Why, do I seem uneducated?"

"On the contrary. You speak well, too well. I wonder about your background. Who are you?"

Aki turned back to Obaasen and Ume, leaving Yoshi alone with his thoughts. Yoshi felt he had been graded and found unsatisfactory. Aki was a young person accustomed to having her way. On the surface, headstrong, independent, and taken with her own beauty, beneath, a reservoir of vulnerability that made her curiously appealing. It was easy to understand why Shite found her so attractive. Yoshi would have to be careful; she resented his education and that could cause him problems. If Yoshi was to succeed in his mission for Yoritomo, he could not afford gratuitous enemies among the company.

Ohana was up. The rest period was over.

The path up the mountain was long and narrow. A sudden drop on one side made the passage dangerous. The caravan crept slowly up the precipitous slope, hemmed in by a pine forest above and a sheer drop below.

Yoshi helped the three women, carrying Obaasen over the worst spots. Ume hung her head submissively and followed instructions, but Aki shook off his hand and tartly told him she was capable of going herself. She seemed to regret having revealed so much of herself to a stranger.

The troupe descended into the main street of Okabe without incident. Before they entered the town, the actors donned their masks, the acrobats warmed up by the side of the road, and Ito tightened his drum. When they were ready, Ohana led the way into town, holding aloft a banner inscribed with the announcement of the evening festival. He was followed by the acrobats, kicking up dust clouds as they slipped and spun to the beat of the drum. The masked actors marched in single file, Shite and Tsure waving their stage swords while the others sang a martial song about the exploits of Lord Hachibumi.

In the rear with the women and horses, Yoshi watched the

awestruck townspeople, lining the street in a solid wall of humanity. Where did they come from? In such a small town? He was learning his next lesson in the art of entertainment. People would travel miles for a free show. They seemed to sprout from the ground. Most of the townsfolk saw a complete festival only twice a year, at the new year and at the rice harvest. The entertainment today would last them for months.

In the center of town, Ohana stopped to post the festival announcement and laboriously read the other notices . . . items for sale, items to exchange, to buy, rewards for information. One notice caught his attention—a deserter wanted by Lord Kiso.

There was no doubt about the description. So the stranger had deserted in the middle of a battle. No wonder he was willing to join the troupe without regard for payment.

The situation could be used to Ohana's advantage. If he turned the man over to the samurai for the reward, he would receive one payment . . . if he collected it at all. Ohana knew the samurai were just as likely to take the information and kill the informer as to reward him. However, if he kept the knowledge to himself, there could be a time in the future when it would be worth more than the doubtful reward. Besides, Ohana could always report the man; he need only say he had not recognized him at first.

Should he discuss this with Aki? No. He would save the information until a more propitious time. She was clever, but she was only a woman. It would be better if he kept his own counsel. There were many possibilities to consider. Ohana was thoughtful as he returned to lead the company through the town to Lord Hachibumi's castle.

fifty-eight

The festival was in full swing. Flutes, bells, lutes, and zithers could be heard in every corner of the castle yard. Ladies and gentlemen from as far away as Kyoto drifted serenely over the greensward. Some of the men played instruments borrowed from the musicians while others sang or danced.

An artificial lake filled with water lilies sported small boats that raced each other across the blue-green water. Guests competed in different sports. The gentlemen were followed by their entourages of squires and assistants. Their clothing made bright patterns against the green earth. There were Chinese jackets decorated with rich brocade, elegant riding outfits, and kimonos of every hue. The colors mixed with the ladies' robes of leaf-green, peach, plum blossom, and soft shades of violet and rose.

Ohana's company was ushered in by the majordomo. They were led to a pavilion, where they were left amid a rabble of grooms, maids, and bearers who waited for their masters to finish the revelry.

Yoshi had attended dozens of these festivals in Kyoto and he knew how sophisticated the audience could be. He feared that Ohana's troupe would be booed off the grounds, if not executed on the spot. Their third-rate travesty of entertainment could not compete with the guests' dancing ability or even costuming. Yoshi glanced at the shabby finery of the actors and compared it to that of the least important guests strolling on the lawn. He winced at the comparison.

The actors removed their masks and laid out their costumes for the performance. Ito put aside the drum and tuned his *biwa*. The acrobats were exercising, and Shite and Tsure ran through a last-minute rehearsal. Yoshi, wearing his mask, helped Ume and Obaasen unpack the background screens for the farce.

Aki was applying heavy makeup for her part. Close up, Yoshi thought the makeup execrable. He had not seen Aki in rehearsal, so he had no idea what she would do.

The company milled around the pavilion for almost an hour before the majordomo told them they would not perform till after the sun set and the flares were lit. They were to start immediately after the grand concert band played their cue.

Ohana called Yoshi, Shite, and the acrobats to help him set up the stage. Yoshi was again struck by the crudity of the backgrounds. The stage was a raised platform approached from the front by a ramp and backed by painted flats of a forest filled with garish flowers.

Behind the stage, Yoshi sat next to Aki, earning angry stares from Shite and Ohana.

"You seem withdrawn. Are you nervous about performing?" Yoshi asked Aki.

"I'm not at all nervous," she snapped, and turned away.

"I apologize. I hope my question did not offend you," he said.

"The question was nothing, it is your attitude toward us that does offend me," she said coldly.

"Why do you say that?"

"You think you are above us. The vagrant, who sleeps in haystacks and claims to read and write poetry, thinks we are crude creatures beneath his high station."

"No! You are mistaken. I admire the company's talents and abilities. I don't feel that writing poetry puts me above you; writing poetry is a small talent compared with yours. A poem is only the expression of the writer's sentiments. Here..." Yoshi's brow furrowed. "I promised you a poem, and I have written it." Yoshi hesitated. "Of course, if you don't want to hear it..."

"Well...if you've already written it."

Yoshi recited:

> "Sun, gold in the west
> Moon, pale light in cobalt sky
> Only your shadows
> As your beauty radiates
> Evanescent as a tear."

"You wrote that for me?"

"For you."

"Perhaps I misjudged you." Aki smiled. When she smiled, she was beautiful. Yoshi felt the attraction again. He was drawn to her despite her erratic behavior; perhaps it even lent piquance to the way he viewed her.

The courtyard turned dark. Flares and paper lanterns were

lit around the lake; the guests were drifting toward the makeshift theater. The sounds of the musicians brought a nostalgic tear to Yoshi's eye. The music reminded him of Nami. Where was she tonight? What was he doing here? He stared at Aki, unable to understand the attraction he had felt only minutes before. Yoshi was confused. The life of the theater was not at all like the simple life of a warrior.

"Hurry, we are going on." Ohana's voice interrupted his thoughts.

fifty-nine

From his vantage point in the pavilion, Yoshi was far enough away to see the reaction of the audience, but not too far away to see the program. The performance was saved from disaster by Aki and the acrobats.

The acrobats delighted the lords and ladies with their daredevil routines. No matter how sophisticated an audience, the sight of a man defying nature by standing upside down on another's head is entertaining. The ladies waved their fans in approval and the gentlemen gave vocal encouragement. It looked as though Ohana's ragged band would take the honors of the day.

Next came Ohana, with a long dissertation on the hundred-year-old campaign against the forces of Sadato and the Abe family. In the flickering light of the flares and lanterns, he made a rather heroic figure, though the effect was spoiled by his coarse manner and his ill-chosen subject. The courtiers had little interest in past military adventures. The ladies stirred restlessly and many engaged in conversation. The gentlemen listened for about one minute, then, ignoring the speaker on the stage, moved around, joking about the afternoon's sporting events and engaging in horseplay.

Ohana gave up the stage to Aki who, to Yoshi's surprise, mounted the ramp with great flair and grace. The makeup, which looked so overdone from close up, was perfect from the distance. Aki had presence, the quality that makes some stand out even when they do very little. In a clear voice—liquid tinkle of distant temple bells—she recited a short poem. Slowly, Aki lifted an arm; her kimono sleeve draped in a graceful curve. She danced with subtle sinuous movements, changing her position from one breathtaking pose to another.

The audience loved her and Yoshi was proud that he was part of her world. What a magical talent . . . to be able to move people to such emotional heights. The audience cheered for minutes after Aki's departure. In such a good mood, almost anything would please them.

Almost anything.

Three actors leaped onto the stage and acted out a farce. It might have pleased the country folk at a rice-field festival but was too leaden and crude for the courtiers and ladies. As they lost their audience, the actors grew broader, widening the rift. The audience hooted with derision. Compounding the problem was the busy backdrop, which confused the image of the players. What worked well for one solitary actor was now a disadvantage. The quick-moving actors in their varicolored costumes were nearly invisible at times.

The farce ended, leaving Shite and Tsure to their sword dance, the mock duel. The lords laughed and jeered. Even the carriage attendants and ladies' maids, in the pavilion with Yoshi, found the swordsmen ridiculous.

The acrobats could not save the day. Before the program ended, the audience dispersed. They divided into small groups and ignored the grand finale on the stage.

Ohana was paid by the majordomo, who told him to leave the grounds as soon as possible. There was nothing extra, indicating Lord Hachibumi's disappointment with the program.

The actors were hungry after their efforts and wanted to sit together to discuss the evening's program. The majordomo grudgingly brought them to a table at the rear of the pavilion.

"What did you think, Suruga? Did you like my handling of the sword?" Shite asked Yoshi while stuffing a handful of rice in his mouth.

"Your sword play needs more work. I think we could improve it if you used a better blade. I'm afraid the lords recognized it as a toy."

"If we could only afford real swords," mumbled Shite, looking to Ohana to see if he had heard Yoshi's comment.

"The audience was insufferable," said Ohana, ignoring Shite. "I find no excuse for their bad behavior. We have performed hundreds of times, but never to such a boorish reception."

"Have you ever performed for this type of audience before?"

"What do you mean?" Ohana drew himself up and glared at Yoshi. He resembled an angry rooster, an effect heightened by the few grains of rice that dribbled from the corner of his mouth.

"Ohana, these are aristocrats. One wonders what incentives Lord Hachibumi offered to make them travel so far from Kyoto. They are *yoko-hito*, persons of quality, most from the fifth rank. Tonight you played to as sophisticated a group as any you would find at the Emperor's palace."

"You suggest they found us wanting?" Ohana angrily brushed rice from his jowls.

"Frankly, yes. I may be the lowliest member of this troupe, but I've had experience with these people," said Yoshi. If Yoshi could convince Ohana that the company's future success would be helped by taking advantage of his background, he could be instrumental in eventually leading them to Kyoto.

Ohana and Aki exchanged glances. It was obvious there had been some conversation between them. Ohana's raised eyebrow said, *You see. I told you there is more to him than he's told us.* And Aki's look said, *Perhaps he can do something for me.*

Shite pouted and Tsure grumbled, "We were considered good enough till you came. Now you say we are found wanting. What would you have us do?"

"Nothing, if you want to play for farmers. If you want to play for gold, there are changes that must be made," said Yoshi.

Ohana's expression cooled. "This is my company," he said. "I will decide if changes are to be made."

Aki interrupted with a rustle of her kimono sleeve and a flick of her hand. "Of course you will decide, dear Father. We love and respect you and know you will listen to suggestions from the group. If we can earn more gold by making minor changes in our program, we will make the changes."

"I have an open mind, anyone will tell you that. But what are the 'little changes' that will undoubtedly take us to the Emperor's palace by the new year?"

Yoshi ignored Ohana's sarcasm. "The new year is too soon," he said. "But in time, we will play in the Emperor's palace if we work hard and polish every part."

"Where would you start?" asked Shite.

"With Ohana's permission, I would change the backdrop."

"The backdrop! It has been in my family since I learned the trade from my father," said Ohana indignantly.

"Then it's time to change it. The audience cannot see the actors because of the garish colors."

"What would you do?" asked Aki.

"A painting of a pine tree, to symbolize the unchanging qualities of simplicity and strength. I would have no color but the green of the tree. Nothing will interfere with the purity of the actors' movements."

"Who would paint this new backdrop?"

"I could repay your kindness by painting it myself. I have some skill with the brush."

Ito, who had listened silently through the conversation, said, "He is right, Ohana. I have felt a confusion of the spirit with our backdrop. If people of rank strive for simplicity, we should do the same."

"Yes, our new man has many talents," said Aki, studying Yoshi with an expression between mockery and admiration. "Let him paint the pine tree, then my father will decide if we are to use it."

sixty

———————◆———————

Months passed. Yoshi was busy every day from the temple bells at dawn to the wooden clappers that signaled all's well long after dusk.

The caravan camped outside the town of Shimada, ten miles from the castle of Lord Hachibumi. It was an important town, because of its location on the Oi River. Processions of all kinds passed through or tarried there. Food and lodging were readily available, and there were fields outside of town where a caravan could stay undisturbed for a small price.

When Yoshi had volunteered to paint a new backdrop, he had started a chain of events that led to responsibilities far beyond his original expectations. He took upon himself the task of preparing the company to play in Kyoto, remembering Yoritomo's admonition to be there by the following year. When he thought of Nami, virtually a prisoner of Kiso, the following year seemed forever.

The painting was the first of his suggestions. As the days became weeks and then months, he took on more of the company management. Ohana was loath to give up his authority, but laziness and pressure from his ambitious daughter made him withdraw from decision making.

Ohana drank while Yoshi finished the backdrop to enthusiastic comments from Ito and Aki, who wholeheartedly supported Yoshi's plan. They were quick to recognize Yoshi's ability to better their condition.

Filling the vacuum left by Ohana's withdrawal, Yoshi made suggestions to the actors; at first he worked with Shite, who was malleable as soft clay. Shite soon came to follow Yoshi like a pet dog.

One day, after a long, wearisome rehearsal, Shite confided in him. "I love Aki," he said. "I want to marry her, but she says I am stupid and uneducated. If you help me, maybe I can learn the ways of a gentleman and she will come to love me as I do her."

Yoshi was uncomfortable with Shite's request. He was attracted to Aki himself. There was nothing to prevent Yoshi from taking Aki as a mistress. This was customary. Many men in the court had four or five mistresses; often they were given official status as secondary wives. Indeed, Chikara had kept another wife while married to Nami.

Would Nami understand? Yoshi reasoned the arrangement would not affect her standing as principal wife.

An alliance with Aki would increase the security of his disguise, give him more power in the company, and hasten the process of reaching Kyoto.

Patience, he told himself, patience.

Aki was not to be manipulated so easily. She was shrewd and cunning about her career. She would decide what she wanted to do. Poor Shite, so handsome and well meaning, but Aki was right . . . so stupid.

Yoshi liked the hero and had no wish to hurt him. Putting Aki out of his mind, Yoshi worked harder to help Shite improve the delivery of his lines and to better his handling of the sword.

The effort met with mixed success. The lines stayed wooden, while the sword dance bogged down in Shite's lack of coordination.

"Will I ever learn?" asked Shite during a particularly trying session.

"Good enough for the theater," answered Yoshi, a little out of patience.

"Someday I will wield a real sword and be a real hero instead of only an actor. Then Aki will be impressed with my bravery."

"That is possible, Shite, but there is a long path ahead of you before you are ready."

"Can we try again?"

"Tomorrow, Shite. Working with these toy blades is frustrating. You'll never be a real hero while you use a toy."

"Suruga, don't you think a real hero is in the heart; that he can transcend toy swords because of his inner spirit and bravery?"

"A great hero, yes. But Shite, you are not a great hero. You are an actor in a *Dengaku* company."

"If I were a real hero, Aki would love me."

"Maybe that will happen," said Yoshi, looking at the naïve "hero," knowing there was little chance Shite's wishes would ever come true.

"You're a wonderful friend, Suruga. How did I manage

before you came? Next to Aki, I love you more than anyone else in the world."

Shite grew up in a small town. His parents were peasants who tilled three *cho* of second-rate land for a local lord. From earliest childhood, Shite was different from the other children of the village. Where they played games in large noisy groups, he dreamed of the time when he would be a warrior.

Ohana, passing through the town where Shite lived, saw him and recognized his potential; his handsome appearance and unathletic movements made him an ideal choice for a theatrical hero rather than a real warrior.

It did not take much persuasion to convince the country boy his future lay in the theater. Shite's only other choice was to be a farmer as his parents and grandparents had been before him. He took the name Shite, hero, and embarked on a new life, leaving his family for the life of the road. It was a decision he never regretted. The company was exactly suited to his needs. He could dream of himself as a hero and act out the dream in front of the world.

And the people of the theater were so much smarter and more sophisticated than the country folk he had known as a child. There was no happier life than to be with a beautiful actress like Aki or an obviously high-born man like Yoshi.

Soon Yoshi wrote the lines the actors delivered. Crude farce, he told them, was satisfactory in the rice fields; subtlety was needed for Kyoto.

One day, Ohana announced an engagement for the following week. They were to appear at the local Iris Festival. Yoshi remembered the Iris Festival in Kyoto, a gala time when houses, palace, and people were festooned with leaves of iris and branches of mugwort, a time when leaves were made into pillows, hung on swords, and worn as garlands, when competitions in horse racing, fencing, dancing, and archery were avidly attended by the court.

"We leave tomorrow at the sound of the temple bells," Ohana announced.

The troupe was excited by the prospect. Lords and ladies from the castle of the local *Daimyo* would attend. Many came from families with ties in the capital. The engagement was for three days. And more important, this audience would test Yoshi's suggestions.

sixty-one

The first night was a triumph compared to that at Okabe. The acrobats drew their usual applause. The new backdrop was received enthusiastically; a single green pine limned against sky-blue lent an air of elegance to the performers. Ohana was more imposing than ever. Even the crudities of his speech and movement were provided a new vitality by the starkness of the scene.

Aki sang in a voice that charmed the spirits from the air.

The actors spoke their material flawlessly and were heartily applauded. Only Shite failed. His sword dance drew snickers from the ladies and a few rude guffaws from soldiers sprinkled throughout the audience.

After the performance, Yoshi expected euphoria from Ohana; instead, he received silence and a glum stare.

"Pay no attention to him," said Aki, who was in a world of self-satisfaction. "He is jealous because our success is due to your efforts."

"I do not want him to be displeased."

"Say nothing. I know my father. When he loses face he is angry, and whatever you say will anger him more."

"Yet..."

Aki put a soft hand on Yoshi's sleeve. "Suruga, I advise you well. Stay away from Ohana for a while. You and I need to discuss the company and tonight's performance." She gave him her sideways glance. This time the glance communicated something enigmatic. "Would you join me later tonight? We can talk privately."

"I would be honored," said Yoshi, suddenly breathless. She was beautiful!

Yoshi had thought little of sex since leaving Nami; he controlled his sex drives by turning them to work. Alone with Aki, he felt the stirring of passion.

Aki closed the tent flap and tied it down as soon as he came in. She obviously was experienced in the arts of love. Every

344

movement of her body was suggestive. As she poured a cup of tea, her mauve kimono, embroidered with colorful birds, rustled and swished. She calculatedly exposed a bit of leg, a bit of arm, an edge of breast. Her sinuous body performed a sensual dance meant to arouse Yoshi. It succeeded. He tried to put his teacup down and spilled the tea on the floor. His hand trembled with suppressed excitement.

Aki smiled and stretched out on her floor quilt, letting the kimono fall open to expose her inner thigh. She had dispensed with under slips.

"Are you nervous?" she asked slyly.

"No . . . yes . . . I mean . . ."

"I think I know your feelings. I like you, Suruga. You have accomplished wonderful things for me and for the company. I want to show my appreciation. Come closer, where you can be more comfortable." There was none of the insecurity Yoshi had detected in the past. In this situation, Aki was in complete control.

Yoshi pressed himself against her, feeling her body yield to his masculinity, feeling her warmth and smelling her sensuous perfume. There was no need for subtletly with Aki. He reached under the kimono and stroked upward along her thigh. How long a time it had been . . . too long! His breath came in short gasps as he ran his tongue along her throat. Aki's back arched as she pressed against his groin. A soft moan escaped her lips. His mouth found hers; he forced his tongue between her lips, tasting her sweet breath.

Quickly, without removing her kimono, she opened the way and led him into her warmth and wetness.

The full moon hung low in the sky. It was after midnight when Yoshi parted the tent flap, ready to leave. Behind him, Aki, her kimono in disarray and her hair hanging free, gave a tiny shriek of dismay.

"What is it?" asked Yoshi, startled into immobility.

"Shite! He was standing in the shadows." Aki was distraught. She stared wildly.

"Nonsense. There is no one there." Yoshi strained his eyes in all directions. He saw no one.

"I tell you I saw him. He was spying on me," hissed Aki.

The encampment was quiet. Nothing moved except the animals. They shifted uneasily. The horse whinnied in a small thin voice, as if something had passed.

"You must be wrong. Everyone is asleep," said Yoshi, his heart beating faster. Was it Shite who had disturbed the horse?

"I saw him. I saw Shite."

"If he was here, I'll talk to him in the morning."

"To say what?" Aki's voice was shrill.

Yoshi liked the poor romantic fool, but Shite and his problems were far away. He could not contend with them tonight. His new relationship with Aki was enough.

After moments of passion and exhilaration, Yoshi was tired and depressed. Aki must be stopped before she woke the entire camp. His voice was sharp as he snapped, "I'll decide tomorrow. Good night!"

"Good night." Aki dropped the flap, upset as much by Yoshi's brusque tone as by her view of Shite's pale face ...watching!

sixty-two

———————◆———————

While Yoshi and Ohana's troupe prepared for the Iris Festival, Kyoto celebrated. The Imperial Palace was a scene of intense activity as servants hung *kusudama,* decorated herb bags, from shutters and eaves. Courtiers wore sprigs of iris on their head-dresses; ladies festooned it in their hair.

Common folk covered their roofs with branches of iris and mugwort. *Kusudama* tied with long silk threads of five colors were displayed at building entrances; these were known to ward off the *kami* of sickness and ill luck that ran rampant on this day.

Later that day, Go-Shirakawa would offer *kusudama* to his high officials. They would toast with wine cups containing soaked iris leaves to give them extra protection from the *kami.*

This year had not been auspicious for the capital's residents. Many nobles had left the city before the arrival of Kiso and his rough mountain men. In the eighth month of the previous year, the child Emperor, Antoku, had ordered Rokuhara burned to the ground and fled Kyoto with his Uncle Munemori, his mother, and the Nii-Dono, his grandmother. Antoku carried with him the Imperial regalia, a black and gold chest containing a bronze mirror, a sword, and the Imperial jewels. The regalia was a gift from Amaterasu, the sun goddess, to the first Emperor of Japan. By possessing the regalia, Antoku was honored as the true Emperor and Go-Shirakawa was prevented from naming another to the throne.

Go-Shirakawa controlled the Imperial Palace, while Kiso Yoshinaka thought he controlled Go-Shirakawa from his head-quarters in the rebuilt Rokuhara palace.

In this inauspicious year, Kiso's mountain men had wreaked havoc on the court and the citizens. They were beyond the law, taking what they wanted, terrifying those too frightened to protest. The samurai conquerors considered the sophistication of the citizens of Kyoto a personal affront; they reacted with a frenzy of destruction. Pillage, rape, and murder became everyday occurrences.

347

At the hour of the snake, ten in the morning, Nami hung iris from the eaves of Yoshi's house.

Yoshi's small estate was typical of those in the northwest quarter. The main house had a bark shingle roof supported by red lacquered pillars. A broad stairway of natural wood led to the main level, set a foot above ground to avoid the damp that plagued the western city. The main house, where Nami stayed, was connected by covered passageways to two subsidiary houses, empty except for the one occupied by Goro, Yoshi's aged retainer.

Today, the shutters of the south wall were open, bringing the interior and exterior together in harmony. As Nami pinned up iris, she could see into the cool interior. A rich, sparse room; bare polished floor, lacquered chest, vase of camellias, raised sleeping platform, and a round brazier for heat.

Nami was followed by old Goro, who carried a wicker basket of assorted branches. He handed them to her as she placed them at the intersections of crossbeams and pillars. Nami should have been happy with her task, but instead she was thoughtful and withdrawn. She had been living in Yoshi's house for nine months with no one but Goro for company and had developed the habit of talking aloud to herself. As she pinned up a branch, she murmured, "Oh, Yoshi, where are you?"

"Did you say something, my lady?" asked Goro, who was slightly hard of hearing and tried doubly hard to pay attention as a compensation for his defect.

"No, Goro. I sigh from loneliness. I miss your master."

"Yes, my lady. I miss him too. I spent many years as retainer to your Uncle Fumio and then as retainer to Yoshi. I am pleased to serve you, but I miss the master."

"I understand."

Nami had come to Kyoto as a prisoner when Kiso and Go-Shirakawa took the city in the eighth month of 1183. Tomoe had arranged for her to be released to Yoshi's house, but she was only allowed to leave the grounds when invited by Kiso or Tomoe.

While Goro was not much company, the house and grounds kept Nami occupied. She had been accustomed to a host of servants as Lord Chikara's principal wife; this solitary existence was a complete change. To forget her loneliness, she fell to domestic chores with a will. Goro cared for the heavy work while Nami busied herself with the flower garden and the house management.

This day, the garden was a burst of harmonious colors and scents. It should have lightened Nami's spirit, but it did not. She thought of Yoshi and what might have happened to him. Tomoe had told her that Yoshi was alive and the object of a relentless search by Kiso.

Tomoe! Praise Hachiman and the Buddha for her friend Tomoe. Nami frowned, thinking of the march to Kyoto and Kiso's constant advances. If not for Tomoe... Tomoe had faced Kiso and told him that his choice was fighting her to the death or leaving Nami alone. Kiso chose the latter, though Nami thought she detected a smile that said he had not yet given up.

Kiso lived in the Rokuhara palace, nightly gorging himself on white rice and sake. Nami heard that the courtiers and ladies found Kiso a ludicrous figure because of his bullishness. They smiled to his face, treated him royally, and snickered behind his back.

Tomoe, on the other hand, had been accepted by the ladies of the court. Without Nami's help and coaching in the proper way to dress and speak, Tomoe would have appeared even more of a fool to the court than Kiso. Tomoe insisted on her right to visit Nami; Kiso did not dare deny her.

After hanging the iris, Nami retired to the open front room. She was prepared to spend the day alone, thinking of Yoshi and offering prayers for his safety.

She thought of the evanescent quality of life. Uncle Fumio gone. Her former husband, Lord Chikara, gone. Yoshi's mother far away in exile with the child Emperor. Nothing stayed the same. Last year she had been with her lover and today she was alone, a prisoner in the great city. Where was Yoshi today? And why did she sense that all was not well? There was a heaviness in her breast, a sadness that the sunlight and the flowers could not dispel. Nami looked out over the garden at the brilliant flowers... recently bloomed and soon to wither. She was older and had not provided an heir. She had disappointed Lord Chikara, and it seemed she would also disappoint Yoshi. She did not have many child-bearing years left.

"Oh, Yoshi," she said aloud to the open room. "Beloved, where are you?" She bit her lip in frustration. She needed news of the outside world. If Yoshi's whereabouts were known, Tomoe would tell her.

"Goro," she called.

• • •

In the late afternoon, Goro announced Tomoe's arrival. Nami received her in the open south room. This was a different Tomoe from the country warrior of the previous year. Instead of galloping up on a war pony, Tomoe arrived in a palanquin carried by eight bearers. Instead of rough clothing and armor, she wore an over-robe of cherry-red silk and an assortment of under-robes colored in shades ranging from cream to coral. Her hair was longer and combed back from a center part, clasped at the small of her back with a stiff white bow.

Only Tomoe's face and movements were the same, the same intense features and smooth dark skin, the same samurai walk, a slight strut that was out of place with her feminine clothing but was natural to her.

"Tomoe, how glad I am to see you."

"Dear Nami, I am pleased to be here. I've missed you."

"And I you. The days hang heavy on my heart. In my isolation I fancy terrible happenings outside my gates."

"You are not far from the truth. We were mistaken, Kiso, Imai, and I. We should have stayed in the field and left Kyoto to Yoritomo. We are soldiers and know little of court life."

"Kiso wanted to rule."

"He wanted power and thought this the right path. He was wrong. He flounders. A sense of doom surrounds the court. An unhappy Kiso is an irrational one. The courtiers live in fear of his violent moods. He was never prepared for the rich life of the court."

"No one born outside the court is prepared."

"True. Yet you helped me. Without your friendship and advice, my life would have been intolerable. Kiso, as uncaring as he is, knows the courtiers laugh behind his back. He is driven mad being unable to respond without looking a further fool. Sometimes I understand what he feels, when I think the court does not truly accept me."

"They do accept you. You are a lady."

"Thank you for saying that, but I believe I serve best in my role as a samurai and my place is with Kiso and my brother . . . in the field."

The women spent an hour together. Nami reveled in Tomoe's companionship. She had needed to loose the emotions she had bottled inside while alone.

After the last of the tea and cakes disappeared, Tomoe's face took on a serious expression. "I would like to discuss the happenings at the court," she said. "I did not intend to burden you with my problems, but I need your advice."

"If I can help, you have only to ask," said Nami humbly.

"Kiso and his captains are not prepared for the subtle intrigues of court life," Tomoe continued. "Go-Shirakawa is a crafty fox. He moves Kiso like a stone on a Go board. Kiso believes he is in control, but he is manipulated by the cloistered Emperor."

"What about Go-Shirakawa so disturbs you?"

"Go-Shirakawa has convinced Kiso to find the Taira and regain the Imperial regalia. Go-Shirakawa would then be officially sanctioned to choose a new child Emperor and he would continue to rule the throne."

Nami, remembering her determination to fight the Taira at every opportunity, said, "Where is the harm? Go-Shirakawa is accustomed to power and understands the way of the court. If Kiso destroys the remnants of the Taira, the country will be unified under the banner of the Minamoto."

"Nami, you have been isolated too long. You have not seen the power shifts that have occurred. When Kiso brought us to Kyoto, he defied Yoritomo. Now Yoritomo is amassing an army to march against Kyoto. The Taira are less the factor. Today, it is Minamoto against Minamoto."

"Then Kiso will fight his cousin?"

"He would if he were not being duped by Go-Shirakawa. Go-Shirakawa wants the Imperial regalia. He offered Kiso the title of *Shogun* if he retrieves it."

"*Shogun*? There has been no *shogun* for a hundred years."

"Kiso aspires to the title." Tomoe paused. When she continued her voice was heavy. "I am convinced Go-Shirakawa will betray us. When Kiso recovers the regalia, Go-Shirakawa will renounce him because Kiso's men have caused so much grief in the city. The courtiers and citizens demand that Go-Shirakawa stop them. Go-Shirakawa hasn't the power without Yoritomo. He will betray Kiso to Yoritomo, given the chance."

"And you, Tomoe? If this comes to pass, you will suffer because of Kiso's excesses," Nami said thoughtfully. Change! Everything was change. Life was lived on a bed of quicksand. *Shigata ga nai,* there was nothing could be done about it.

At last, Nami asked Tomoe for news about her beloved. "Yoshi?" she said raising her eyebrows questioningly. "Is he with Yoritomo's forces?"

"There are rumors. A spy reports that Yoritomo ordered him to kill Kiso."

"Impossible! Yoshi took a vow not to kill. Do you believe he would break it because of Yoritomo's orders?"

"I don't know . . . Kiso believes it. Since the death of San-taro, Kiso is obsessed with thoughts of Yoshi. Another reason I came here today was to warn you that Kiso has placed a permanent watch on this house. Kiso is certain that if Yoshi reaches Kyoto he will search for you here."

"If that were only true."

"Fear of my anger and Yoshi's vengeance keep you safe from Kiso's lust. He waits until he has Yoshi's head." Tomoe's forehead wrinkled. "Kiso is convinced that his life depends on Yoshi's death. He has continued the search for Yoshi since we left Shinohara, a fruitless search since Yoshi seems to have disappeared."

"Yoshi must be in hiding. I fear Kiso is right and Yoshi will come here when he can."

"Can you stop him?"

"I don't know where he is, and though I long for his presence, I would do everything in my power to prevent his falling into a trap."

"If there is news I will bring it to you immediately."

"Thank you, dear Tomoe."

"I must leave." Tomoe rose and adjusted her robe. She clasped Nami's hands in hers and said, "Be careful. Remember, if Yoshi comes here, Kiso's men will be waiting."

sixty-three

━━━━━━━━━━━━◆━━━━━━━━━━━━

The troupe's encampment was just outside the town limits, in a flat field of goose grass. It was surrounded by berry bushes on three sides and a stand of cherry trees on the fourth. Morning light picked out pink wood berries, moist with dew, shining like stars against a dark green leafy background.

The nine tents of the company were spread through the clearing. Shite's tent was near the one Yoshi shared with Ito. Ohana, Aki, and Shite each had small private tents; the other tents were larger and shared by the rest of the company.

The morning after Nami's conversation with Tomoe, Yoshi rose with the ringing of the town's temple bells. The night had been a restless one for him. Dreams had become nightmares of Fumio, the Nii-Dono, Santaro, Kiso, and Tomoe. Worst of all, Nami appeared in ghostlike form, as though accusing him of unspeakable deeds.

Yoshi was glad to leave his guilt and open the tent flap to another day. His mood soured as he looked pensively at Shite's tent. Had Shite been watching him last night? That would not be a surprise, since he constantly followed Yoshi about the camp.

Like a wet-nosed puppy, Shite was a creature of foolish emotion; he played the part of hero, knowing he fell far short of the ideal.

Yoshi told himself, "This problem cannot be solved easily. Though Shite will be crushed, I must face him and explain." Yoshi walked across the damp grass, feeling the leaves rasp against his bare feet. He knocked on the wooden tent pole.

No answer.

"Shite." He scratched his nails on the flap.

No answer.

"Shite, wake up! It's Suruga."

No answer.

"Come, Shite. I have to talk to you."

No answer.

Yoshi slipped his hand inside the flap, straining to reach

353

the tie cords. The fabric stretched enough for him to get his fingers on the knot and undo it. He thought Shite was behaving like a child in not responding. Would that unpleasantness could be avoided so easily!

The sun brightened the morning and the contrast inside the darkened tent blinded Yoshi for a few seconds. Then he saw . . .

Shite, stripped to the waist, half covered by his hero's costume, lay sprawled before a small altar. The scent of incense lingered in the corners of the tent. Shite had fallen forward, half on his side. His intestines hung from a ragged wound that ran across his belly and up into his ribcage. Torrents of blood almost completely soaked the coverlet on which he lay; embroidered red flowers blended into the wetness, showing their shape only at the edges of the material.

The weapon was still in his hand. The toy sword!

Yoshi's eyes filled. He couldn't swallow; his hands were hot and swollen. He backed out of the fetid tent into the cool morning air. *Amida Butsu Nyorai!* Poor Shite. What had he felt to make him rip himself with so miserable a sword. Where had he found the strength to force the dull blade into his vitals. Hero or fool?

And his friend Yoshi was the cause!

Yoshi found his voice. "Ohana. Come quickly," he cried. "What is it? Who calls?"

Voices came from every tent. The pain in Yoshi's voice alarmed the entire company.

Ito was first to reach him. One glance told the story. The musician placed his arm around Yoshi's shoulder and led him away.

The company was in shock. While life and death meant little to the warrior class, to simple actors it was an uncommon thing. The consensus was that Shite had died like a hero, though only Aki and Yoshi guessed why. Those two, lovers so short a time before, kept apart. They did not speak, holding their thoughts to themselves.

Ohana led the acrobats to a far side of the field, where they buried Shite's mutilated body with a brief Shinto service, asking the sun goddess to commend him to a hero's heaven.

Yoshi spent the rest of the morning searching his soul. His action had caused the death of another good man. His vows did not prevent the death of an innocent. Yoshi shed bitter tears over Shite. Many men had died, some at his hand, but none touched him as deeply as this young actor. Why?

In the past year, his uncle had died at the hands of villains; recently his friend Santaro had been executed for helping Yoshi. He had faced their deaths stoically. Why then did Shite's death affect him so strongly? He analyzed his feelings. He felt guilt! Aki's physical attraction had led to his betrayal of Shite. Shite died because of that betrayal.

The longer Yoshi thought, the unhappier he became. Perhaps his best course was to leave the troupe and pursue Yoritomo's mission alone. Although the time allotted to reach Kiso was short, Yoshi could fulfill his task without involving or causing pain to the company.

That afternoon, Ohana sought out Yoshi. Ito, who had played mournful songs while Yoshi sat with his thoughts, put aside the *biwa* and tactfully left them alone.

"We are sorry about the death of so fine a young man, but it is done. We must take up our lives and continue," said Ohana.

Yoshi said nothing.

Ohana waited a few moments in silence, then added, "Come, Suruga. Enough mourning. No one can help the dead, and we have important matters to discuss." His tone was impatient.

"There is nothing to discuss. I shall be leaving the troupe tomorrow." Yoshi turned away, dismissing further conversation.

"Nonsense! You feel shock. It will pass." Ohana tried to force warmth into his voice. "We understand. The two of you were good friends. Shite loved you."

"I know," said Yoshi sadly.

"Stop sulking. Shite chose his death. He fancied a hero's death . . . he chose that of a coward. He could not face reality. You are ten times as brave as he was. Stop acting the child." Ohana's voice was suddenly harsh.

Yoshi's jaw tightened, his eyes drilled into Ohana. He said grimly, "I am not ten times as brave as he was. His deed required tremendous courage. Shite became the hero of his dream. I warn you, Ohana, do not belittle Shite."

"I have nothing further to add about the boy, but I have responsibilities to those who remain and . . . I might point out, so do you."

"I have no responsibilities here. I earned my board. I will leave as I came." Yoshi was getting angry.

"You will not leave. You must play Shite's role until I find a replacement."

Yoshi was taken aback. "Ohana," he said, "you have taken leave of your senses. I am not an actor and I have no intention of making myself a fool."

"There is no danger of that," snapped Ohana, his jowls wobbling agitatedly. "You can play the part better than Shite. Admit it. You coached him daily and you know every word and every move."

"I can't do it, and I won't." How could he step into Shite's place? Ohana did not realize Yoshi felt responsible for Shite's act of *seppuku*.

"Yes, you will." Now it was Ohana's turn to level a threatening stare at Yoshi. "Listen to me. I am not stupid. You came from nowhere in ragged clothes, dirty and hungry. An hour later, soldiers appeared looking for a person who fitted your description. And you, who speak like the son of an Emperor, accepted employment without asking for payment. Why?"

Ohana paused, waiting for Yoshi's answer. When none was forthcoming, he continued, "A poster in Okabe described the fugitive; a substantial reward was offered. I was tempted, but being good-hearted, I held my counsel. You are free, thanks to my generosity."

Yoshi's cheeks colored. "Do you threaten me?" he demanded.

"Not at all." Ohana was obsequious. "And there is no reason to be abusive. I have your interests at heart. I am convinced you will make a fine actor and will never forget my kindness."

Yoshi's stomach churned. But . . . there was some truth in Ohana's words. Yoshi *could* play the part better than Shite. In spite of himself, he was at once flattered and challenged. He thought again of Yoritomo's admonition: Be patient, but reach Kyoto by the coming new year. The acting company was a perfect disguise and an excellent vehicle for getting him to Kyoto undiscovered.

Ohana was a hypocritical oaf, but he offered an opportunity that Yoshi could not ignore. The question was, Could he become an actor?

"The ability to turn a phrase or direct a movement does not make me an actor," Yoshi said. "You are making a mistake."

"Actor or not, you are what I have. Only you know the part well enough to play it tonight." Ohana stabbed a finger at Yoshi's chest to emphasize his point.

"Tonight? You are mad! I couldn't prepare in time. I would need rehearsal."

"You must! Rehearse this afternoon. Tonight you will perform or my good nature will disappear and you will be in the hands of Hachibumi's samurai before morning."

"You are threatening me again. You bastard!"

"Now, now, Suruga." Ohana became unctuously paternal. "That's an ugly word. Let us be polite? I bear you no grudge for what you've done here."

"Grudge? I have worked like a salt farmer to improve your company and you repay me with threats."

"Suruga, I need you. All of us need you. You turned my daughter against me and usurped my position as leader of the company, but I forgive you. Without the hero we have no performance. It's that simple." His voice turned, wheedling. "Will you do it for the company?"

"Tonight, yes," said Yoshi with hatred in his expression.

sixty-four

Having made his decision, Yoshi threw himself into preparations. There was no time for guilt or remorse. Aki tried to talk with him, but in his concentration on the task at hand, he paid her scant attention. The insecurity that Yoshi had originally found so attractive became seething fury under what she took to be a personal insult. How dare he ignore her? Her pride could not accept Yoshi's neglect. No one, she told herself, could use and forget her.

The company returned to their rehearsals; only Ume grieved for the sad departed Shite. To the others, it was as though he had never been.

In rehearsal, Yoshi was excellent. He had coached and prepared Shite so often that without the pressure of an audience, he was secure in the role.

Even Tsure admitted, "Suruga makes the play easier. For the first time, my partner is dependable." The other actors, too, were enthusiastic.

Aki, who watched the rehearsal with her father, said, "We'll see if he can perform as well in front of an audience."

Ohana's nose was redder than usual from an early beginning with the sake. His voice was blurred, his expression unhappy. "He must do well tonight. His life depends on it," he said.

Aki dismissed her father's comment with a shrug of irritation. "Letting him appear tonight is unwise," she said. "You feed his arrogance."

"Don't worry, my dear. Suruga is on a tight rein. He will serve us well while we need him. Then . . . we shall see."

Yoshi applied his makeup in front of a small glass that had belonged to Shite. He was careful to use it heavily, changing the appearance of his features. He contemplated playing the entire program in a mask, but decided that would be too conspicuous. He drew thick black eyebrows, changed his mouth to a heroic slash of red, and rearranged his hair by pulling a forelock over his brow and brushing the sides back, exaggerating the style of a warrior.

"Do you think you will deceive them?" Aki watched from the tent entrance, a sneer marring her carefully made up face.

Yoshi was startled. Had she read his thoughts? "Deceive whom?" he asked as calmly as he could.

"The audience, of course. You have no experience on the stage. You will make an ass of yourself and bring shame upon us."

Yoshi was relieved. Apparently, Ohana had not exposed him. He said firmly, "I have rehearsed the part many times. I will not shame you."

Yoshi's apparent confidence irritated Aki. Had he so quickly forgotten their night together? If Yoshi would only talk to her as a man to a woman ... if he would look at her, if he would remember ... but no! Not he. She turned away angrily, dropping the tent flap with a clatter.

Yoshi felt much less confidence than he showed. He did not want to alienate Aki, for he would have liked her support, but his guilt about Shite's death and his preoccupation with his coming performance prevented his asking for it.

Yoshi closed his mind to everything but the work ahead. He spread Shite's costumes around the tent. They were a poor lot, with holes in awkward places, the embroidered designs pulled loose, and seams carelessly sewn. There were four brown over-robes with embroidered flowers in circles on a leaf background. He chose the least shabby, hoping the pattern would hide the holes. The *hakama* would be covered by the robe except for a few minutes during the climactic sword dance. The costume would have to do.

Ohana's mother, Obaasen, scratched his tent flap to announce that it was time to leave for the theater.

A strange sensation: walking through the woods in full costume. An artificial construct in a natural setting. The berry bushes were already in shadow; only an occasional glint of red flashing from their depths.

The theater was set in the garden, fronting the main house of the mansion. The lord and his entourage sat in a row on the open veranda. Iris leaves dangled from the dark beams over their heads. It was a small audience on this second night of the festival.

Yoshi waited in the pavilion with the rest of the troupe. He grew more nervous with each passing minute. How strange that a sword master who had fought to the death against as many as ten opponents with hardly a trace of nerves was anxious about reciting a few lines.

Ohana's troupe would perform after the five musicians finished their concert. The haunting wail of the flute wove a filigree against the five-beat rhythm of the small drum and the countertempo, seven beat, of the large drum. The strings filled in with an improvised harmony.

The music almost made Yoshi forget his growing nervousness. Almost!

Yoshi tried to go over his lines in his head. It was no use. He had forgotten everything. How was he supposed to start? His palms were wet, his forehead dripped sweat on his makeup, yet simultaneously, his hands and feet were cold and he had lost feeling in his fingers.

Then . . . the concert was over and the acrobats were spinning, jumping, and diving across the lawn to applause from the veranda.

Too soon it was time for Yoshi's entrance. He was unconscious of walking onto the stage. He heard his cue and a stranger answered. Was that he? He went through the beginning of the program in a dream state. Suddenly, he peeled off his outerrobe and was in the middle of the sword dance. Dimly—it seemed so far away—he heard Ito play the sword-dance music and was aware that he was turning, thrusting, and parrying in time to the *biwa*. Then it was over.

Applause!

Yoshi had never been applauded before. It came in great waves and bathed him in a sea of warmth. Yoritomo, Kiso, and Shite's tragedy were forgotten. The rest of the company was forgotten. This was Yoshi's triumph. His alone.

Later, at the encampment, he sat around the fire with the others. Even Tsure congratulated him. Everyone except Aki and Ohana praised his performance.

"It was never better," said one of the actors. "I was drawn into the story as I haven't been in years."

"The sword dance was marvelous."

"You handled the sword as if you were a real sword master."

"Everything was on cue."

"Did you hear my second speech?"

The conversation went around in circles. Now Yoshi understood why actors could not sleep after a performance. His time on the stage had gone by seemingly in seconds. He wanted to recall it, to hold it once more to his breast and swirl again in the sea of applause.

A bottle was opened and passed around. Ohana, jowls quivering, proposed a toast. "To my discovery," he said in his blurred voice. "The man I found in a field, whom I trained and developed so that on this night he would bring us fame."

There were several raised brows. The company members were well aware of Ohana's growing jealousy of Yoshi's success and his fury at the loss of face it entailed. The silence that followed the toast was broken by Yoshi, who raised his cup in response. "Thank you, Ohana. I have followed your example since you were kind enough to employ me. I offer a toast in appreciation."

There was an audible, "Hmphh," from Aki.

"And," continued Yoshi without smiling, "in appreciation for the support and encouragement of your charming daughter."

Everyone sipped at their cups except Aki. She glowered at Yoshi, thinking he was being sarcastic and laughing at her in front of the entire company.

Later, Aki confronted her father in his tent. "Father, you are giving Suruga too much power. He will take your company if you are not careful."

"My dear Aki, you must believe me. I watch him carefully. He will take nothing from me." Ohana took a swallow of sake.

Aki peevishly retorted, "He is making a fool of you."

"You insult me, daughter. I told you, he does what I want. I control him. Now you must trust me a while longer. We will use the man's talent to improve and strengthen the company. Perhaps with his help we will play for the Emperor one day. I am ready to be patient. I suggest you be the same." He reached for the flask to refill his cup. He shook it angrily when he found it empty.

sixty-five

The next few months slipped by quickly as the company worked its way down the coast along the Tokaido Road. Each month brought them closer to the capital. Their fame grew with every performance, and in the towns along their route the new "Shite" and the lovely Aki were eagerly awaited.

Shite's death greatly influenced Yoshi. Where the company had been merely a way station on his road to a confrontation with Kiso, now it was his way of life. Not that he hated Kiso less. He blamed Kiso for the recent sorrows in his life—Santaro's execution, his separation from Nami, and even Shite's death.

Meanwhile, Yoshi worked diligently and the company prospered. Gold jingled in Ohana's purse. The more Ohana depended on Yoshi, the richer he became. As Ohana relinquished his control of the troupe, he found solace in wine; he changed from an overbearing blusterer to a sake-sodden figure who inspired derision from the company. Ohana was the nominal head, but Yoshi made the decisions; Yoshi filled the vacuum left by Ohana's abdication. Although Yoshi was officially an apprentice, he managed the company's artistic and internal affairs. Ohana handled the contacts with their employers, who now included not only local lords, but also the great Shinto and Buddhist temples. Ohana made the outside arrangements and collected the gold to pay the troupe. Yoshi, as an apprentice, was paid nothing but was given board and expenses.

"We will need new costumes before the next *Tanabata Matsuri*, Weaver Festival. I plan a new production based on the weaver story," Yoshi told Ohana one morning.

"We had new costumes made last month. The gold is not unlimited."

"Nevertheless, you will have to spend more."

"You press me too far."

"Not far enough. You must invest to become worthy of the Emperor's Palace."

"You have already hired two more musicians and another

actor, with costumes for all and new swords for the sword dance." Ohana was furious, his voice cracking with anger.

"No matter. We will need costumes for the Weaver and the Herdsman. You will play the heavenly Emperor. I have something special in mind for your costume."

"My costume? The heavenly Emperor? Well, I suppose if we must . . ."

Two approaches worked with Ohana—appeals to his greed or his vanity. Though Ohana had never again mentioned Yoshi's fugitive status, Yoshi knew he held it close to his breast, nurturing it as the weapon he would use when greed and vanity were no longer served.

When others rested from their rehearsal schedule, Yoshi worked on his first original production.

Historically, the Weaver Festival was inspired by an ancient Chinese story of a love affair between a herdsman, represented by the star Altair, and a weaver, represented by the star Vega. Because of their love, the weaver lost interest in her work for the gods and the herdsman neglected his herds. Discovering their dereliction of duty, the heavenly Emperor banished them to opposite sides of the heavens. They could meet once a year; if the night of the seventh day of the seventh month was clear, a band of heavenly birds would form a bridge so Vega could cross to meet her lover. If it was cloudy or rainy, the meeting would be postponed till the following year.

The festival was an important event; poems were written for the star-crossed lovers, and women prayed for skill in weaving, sewing, and the arts. This was one of the five most important festivals of the year.

Yoshi created his version of the story in a combination of verse, prose, and song. Yoshi would play the herdsman. Aki would play the weaver. Ito composed a special score. Nothing like it had ever been done before. The story and action would be performed in a symbolic manner to appeal to the most sophisticated audiences.

Since Yoshi had joined Ohana's company, he had made many artistic changes. They were no longer mere *Dengaku* players; they had reached a new level of artistry and were the forerunners of a new kind of theater, the theater of *Noh*.

Aki's fame grew as Yoshi expanded her roles. The quality he had seen in her developed with every performance. Success and recognition should have made her happy. It didn't. As her father's increasing success made him more grasping, she became more demanding as her name became more widely known.

Aki avoided Yoshi, thinking to punish him for ignoring her. She refused his company and spoke to him only about her new roles.

Yoshi noticed the distance Aki kept between them; it would have been impossible not to. He had meant to apologize for his seeming coldness, but the time was never appropriate. When he attempted to speak of personal matters, Aki withdrew or company business interfered.

Koetsu, the leader of the acrobats, asked Yoshi for more articulate outlets for his talents. In the early mornings, Koetsu coached Yoshi in basic acrobatic movements. In exchange, Yoshi taught him reading and writing and how to play small supporting parts. Yoshi found the stretching and flexing exercises gave him more fluidity and balance on the stage. The strength he had developed earlier as a sword master was channeled into a fuller use of his body. As Koetsu had a flair for acting, Yoshi had a flair for acrobatics; he sensed his body's relationship to the space around it.

In the evenings, Yoshi practiced sword play with Tsure. Tsure improved under Yoshi's tutelage. With the new blades that Yoshi purchased, the sword dance was more realistic and exciting. Although Tsure was not a great swordsman, he was useful to practice against. Yoshi found the acrobatic exercises with Koetsu increased his speed, while the daily sword practice with Tsure kept the edge on his skills.

Yoshi was alone in his tent, making revisions in the script of the weaver play. The lamp flickered overhead, casting heavy shadows that danced across the paper. His brush moved deftly from inkstone to paper, economically calligraphing the characters onto the page. The play was ready, except for these last changes. The cast knew their roles. The new costumes were finished; even Aki and Ohana were pleased with them. Ohana would wear a full court costume, as befitted the heavenly Emperor. He would carry a golden sword especially made to go with his costume.

Aki, as the weaver maiden, would wear a peach-blossom Chinese jacket over her robe and a long-trained skirt embroidered with patterns of the celestial sphere.

Yoshi was pleased with the preparations. Today's rehearsal had gone well. Ito's music was a triumph. The cast and the audience would be happy with the result.

Across the encampment, in Ohana's tent, Aki berated her father. "This should be your triumph, yet you sit like a sodden lump watching Suruga take your company away from you."

"He takes nothing," Ohana muttered, then his voice rose shrilly. "I am in charge. He listens to my instructions."

"He does what he chooses and gives you a new costume to keep you from questioning him. Don't you see that?"

"I tell you, I am in charge. I paid for the costume, not he."

"All the more fool you."

Ohana's voice shook. "Be quiet!" he ordered. His voice was harsh as he pulled himself upright with an effort. "I've listened to enough, now listen to me. Because I control him, we have more gold than ever before. Soon we will perform in the capital. When we have established ourselves in Kyoto, our use for Suruga will be over. Then I will decide what to do with him." Ohana dismissed his daughter with a peremptory wave of his hand and turned back to his cup.

sixty-six

The first performance of *Chih-nu,* the stylish Chinese name for Yoshi's original production, created a minor sensation. This was particularly important to Yoshi because among the guests of the *Daimyo* was the *Kurodo,* the chamberlain to the Emperor and his palace. The *Kurodo*'s approval could well speed them on to Kyoto and the completion of Yoshi's mission.

There was one sour note in the otherwise auspicious evening . . . Aki was not at her best. Everyone else in the company surpassed themselves. However, Aki even not at her best was impressive enough for the chamberlain to send her an invitation to supper.

"Aki did not seem herself. Is she unwell?" Koetsu asked.

"She was beautiful!" said Ohana, glowering at the acrobat.

"Beautiful, yes. She sang like an angel, but it was as if she were unhappy."

"Why should she be?" said Ohana disdainfully. "The chamberlain didn't consider her lacking."

Yoshi was disturbed by Aki's absence. "It is unwise for Aki to accept an invitation from a member of the audience, whoever he is," he said.

"You may have the honor of telling her that. As her father, I am proud that a man of such high rank desires her company . . ."

"Nevertheless, she should have refused."

Yoshi was in conflict between being elated with the success of *Chih-nu* and irritation with Aki's social insensitivity. He had written a splendid role for her. The company had performed successfully. Now, Aki's decision to join the *Kurodo* could have unfortunate repercussions. Yoshi felt that *Chih-nu* was the vehicle that would bring the company to Kyoto. Aki's actions could exert a negative effect.

Ume and Obaasen spooned out rice and vegetables to a thoughtful Yoshi. The gay mood of the rest of the players was enhanced by the passing of the sake cup. They sang in execrable harmony, and Yoshi quietly slipped away to his tent.

The night was hot and still. Each leaf etched a black unmoving shadow in the moon's white light. Horses, oxen, and
players slept heavily. The snores of the exhausted troupe mixed
with the high fiddling of cicadas and the bass rumble of tree
frogs.

Yoshi was awake, writing a poem, waiting for Aki's return.
The airless night found him restless and unfulfilled. He had no
one to share his feelings about the success of *Chih-nu*. He had
been away from Nami for almost a year. Many nights he stirred
restlessly, unable to sleep, thinking of her, wondering when
they would be together, and worrying about her safety.

This was a night for such melancholy thoughts. He lived a
lie, unable to talk freely. Ito and Koetsu were friendly acquaintances; he needed more. His thoughts drifted to Aki. He
remembered their one night together, the night of Shite's death.
It was sad to contemplate. Life: temporary as foam on water.

A small sound from the road.

Coming down the silver-lit path was a royal palanquin borne
by six silent bearers. It stopped at the edge of the field and
Aki descended, laughing with someone behind the curtain.
Yoshi couldn't hear what was said, but Aki covered her face
with her fan and hurried to her tent.

The chamberlain! Yoshi doubted they had spent the night
in innocent conversation. It really was not his business to interfere; Aki was a grown woman, capable of managing herself.
Ohana was right; it was flattering for a woman of low social
caste to be invited to share an evening with an Imperial func-
tionary. Yoshi asked himself why he was annoyed. Was it
because Aki's behavior threatened the success of his mission,
or was it the loneliness of the night, the lack of a woman to
share his triumph?

The palanquin left. Yoshi waited until it was out of sight.
He scratched on Aki's tent flap.

"Who is it?"

"Suruga," answered Yoshi.

"What do you want at this hour?" Her tone was cool, indifferent.

"I want to speak with you."

"Very well. Come in. Say what you must quickly. I am
tired."

The tent was lit by one small lantern. Aki's quilt was spread
on a sleeping platform. A faint odor of perfume and theatrical

makeup pervaded the air. She was prepared for bed, her toilet articles arranged in order, her robe neatly folded on a lacquered chest. Her hair was brushed out, and whether from familiarity or contempt, she made no effort to change it.

A warmth suffused Yoshi's cheeks. The dimly lit tent appeared domestic and charming and he was made more conscious of his loneliness. In an effort to contain these unwelcome emotions, his voice sounded unintentionally harsh. "What happened tonight?" he asked.

"I was invited to dinner by the *Kurodo*."

"I mean during the performance."

"Is that the important matter you wanted to discuss?" snapped Aki.

"Yes. It is important. You jeopardized the entire play by not doing your best."

"It pleased the audience and pleased the *Kurodo*." There was a sarcastic edge to Aki's voice.

Yoshi said, "I don't understand your tone. Are you angry with me?"

Aki's face hardened. "How dare you ask me that? You who made love to me one night and then ignored me! Am I so repulsive in the act of love? Did I offend your gentlemanly instincts? Even in the court, a gentleman sends a next-morning poem to a lady whose favors he enjoyed . . . but not the great Suruga!"

"No, no. Amida be my witness. I worked for your glory. I write to make you famous in the home provinces. When Shite died, I felt I had betrayed him. Can you understand and forgive that? He was my friend. I could not approach you with Shite fresh in my mind."

"How can I believe that?" Aki was suspicious, but she listened.

"I wrote another poem for you." Yoshi pulled a parchment from his sash and read:

> *"The end of summer,*
> *And where are the sweet blossoms*
> *That bloomed in green spring?*
> *Gone like withered memories*
> *Of when we two were lovers."*

"A trifle late . . . but it is beautiful. You wrote it for me?" Her mouth softened.

"For you." He came closer and put his arms around her, feeling her softness. His nostrils quivered to the scent of her perfume. Aki slowly yielded, her eyes deepened with emotion, her mouth swelled with passion.

Yoshi's body responded of its own volition. He pressed her backward toward the spread quilt, opening her robe at the same time.

"Shall we be lovers again," she murmured just as the tent flap opened and Ohana staggered in.

"What in the name of Buddha . . ." he mumbled, looking at Aki, with her hair loose and her robe open, in Yoshi's embrace. "What in the Avichi hell are you doing here? How dare you! Suruga, I took you in, protected you from those who seek your head, and you repay my kindness by seducing my daughter. I've harbored a serpent." Ohana blubbered drunkenly between anger and tears of self-pity. "Speak up! Have you no shame? You've betrayed me."

Yoshi was embarrassed, but his desire to assuage Ohana's anger gave way to resentment. He said, "You are a worse fool than I thought. You would be grubbing for coppers in the rice fields without me. I've worked to make you rich and yet you believe I've betrayed you. Yes! I am attracted to your daughter. You need not worry, Aki will come to no harm through me. Rather I will make her a famous performer and guarantee you both a prosperous life. Are you too drunk to understand?"

Ohana burst into drunken tears; he had been supplanted as head of his company, and now the upstart was stealing the affections of the daughter. He sank to his knees, mumbling, "Betrayed, betrayed by my own flesh."

sixty-seven

The coming of winter, which had been a hardship for the nomadic company in the past, was eased by their moving into an inn not far from Kyoto. As was expected, Ohana complained of the extra expense, especially since these new accommodations were in addition to Yoshi's hiring three more actors and buying more oxen and carts.

Through the fall and early winter, suitors followed Aki from town to temple to castle—wherever she appeared. She seemed content with Yoshi's attentions and held them at arm's length.

Yoshi's only public appearances were onstage in full makeup. No one had recognized him in the year he had been with Ohana; he decided he could safely appear on the streets of Kyoto. There was little resemblance between the brash, muscular actor—his hair cut in theatrical fashion, his clothes, flamboyant—and the dignified sword master of the year before.

He went to Kyoto alone. His first stop was at the home of Yoritomo's agent, a courtier of the fifth rank. The agent was pleased to receive Yoshi's report. "I will send word that you will be established in Kyoto and ready to carry out your orders before the new year," he said.

"Tell Yoritomo that I hope to use my disguise as an actor to catch Kiso off guard," said Yoshi.

"I will report that to my master. Until we hear from him, continue with the theater troupe and report back to me within a fortnight for further instructions."

Yoshi agreed. Before he left, he asked for news of Nami's whereabouts. The agent was sympathetic, but not helpful. "She is secluded somewhere in the city," he said. "Kiso's men guard her around the clock."

"Is she safe and well?"

"To the best of my knowledge," was the answer.

Yoshi was disappointed at not having more definite news. At least the agent was optimistic. Yoshi would search for Nami at his first opportunity. Meanwhile, the theater in Kyoto would be his first step toward accomplishing his goal. He spent the rest of the day searching for a suitable location. His plan was to develop the theater on a permanent site where the company would present different plays each night. They would schedule daily performances for those who could afford the price of admission.

The theater would be his gift to Ohana's troupe for providing him with a vehicle to reach the capital. When Yoritomo's plan was formulated and the time was right, Yoshi would act. A little more than a year had passed and Yoshi was in sight of his goal.

He thought about Nami being in Kyoto. Was she a prisoner of Kiso at the Rokuhara palace...at the Imperial enclosure...Fumio's old house...Lord Chikara's, or Yoshi's home in the northwest quarter? There were so many possibilities. Kyoto was large; Yoshi would need to start a systematic search. It would be dangerous; an unarmed actor in a city under siege could attract unwanted attention. He must not jeopardize his mission. Yoshi was impatient, but inner discipline would keep him concentrated on his goal.

As he walked down Suzaku-Ōji, the broad main street, Yoshi listened to the strident cries of the street vendors, the clatter of hooves, and the rumble of oxcarts. He smelled the horse dung, ox flop, incense, and all the odors of urban life. He absorbed the energy of the capital, so different from the somnolence of the provinces.

But there was a pall over the city. Energy was there, but it contained an undercurrent of fear. Yoshi stopped at a small inn on one of the side streets. A group of local shopkeepers buzzed excitedly, discussing recent news. Yoshi eavesdropped. Their talk centered on a double defeat Kiso had suffered in recent days.

Kiso had made a tactical error, dividing his army to battle the Taira in two places. Though the Taira were weaker than they had been a year earlier, they rallied and routed one segment of Kiso's men at Mizushima. Kiso's other segment, under Yukiie's command, fled when Yukiie deserted them at Muroyama. The angry and beaten remnants of Kiso's once-proud army returned to Kyoto to avenge themselves on the hapless citizenry. There were signs of angry occupation within the city. Shopkeepers cowered from the rowdy groups of samurai. Only old and unattractive women appeared on the streets. The palanquins of royalty were guarded by armed bearers. Citizens hurried to their destinations casting furtive glances behind them.

The city was in a state of siege. The people of Kyoto lived in fear of the rough mountaineers who took what they wanted and killed those who objected.

As heartless as the Taira Imperial guards had been, Kiso's samurai were worse.

At first Yoshi had breathed the atmosphere of the city with all the pleasure of a prodigal returning, but as he listened to the shopkeepers, he experienced a feeling of depression. Beautiful Kyoto belonged to his enemies.

sixty-eight

Kyoto basked in an unseasonably warm fall and early winter. The days were short and mild, the nights long and cool. To the northeast, Mount Hiei showed a mantle of velvet white on its highest peaks. The white was visible behind the rich green shoulder of Higashiyama. After three consecutive years of brutal winters, the weather was so pleasant that even Kiso's samurai could not completely dampen the spirits of the good people as they went about their daily business.

Yoshi returned to Kyoto several times during the first part of the twelfth month. The company believed he was searching for the theater he promised them. He was. He also waited for Yoritomo's orders and cautiously asked about Nami's whereabouts.

A theater in the fashionable northeast would be the ideal site—close to the Imperial Palace and within reach of the courtiers Yoshi wanted to attract. The northeast was also the safest part of the capital for Yoshi, far from Kiso's headquarters at Rokuhara.

Yoshi carried a war fan for protection. It was not incongruous with his theatrical clothing; for an actor, wearing a sword was a crime punishable by death.

Yoshi spent the daylight hours scouting a theater location. After dark, he planned to cover the city, starting with Fumio's and Chikara's estates. If Nami was not there, he would work his way west, combing the Imperial grounds, then his own estate—he wondered briefly how Goro managed without Lord Fumio. Yoshi would save Rokuhara for last.

The first night's exploration found Yoshi at the former home of Lord Chikara. The once proud mansion was in shambles. The main gate was torn from its hinges; fire had destroyed many of the buildings; looters had removed everything of value.

Yoshi left, depressed at the transitory nature of man's accomplishments. Lord Chikara had been proud of his splendid estate, and now it was an abandoned shell. Obviously Nami had not lived there recently.

A week later, Yoshi found the theater location he wanted. During the day he made arrangements for construction, then he sent word to Yoritomo's agent, giving him the theater address. He decided against telling the company until the theater was near completion.

That night he inspected Uncle Fumio's former home. It was occupied!

The first light dusting of snow of the year touched the city in the late afternoon. The mild weather melted it almost as quickly as it fell. By evening the ground was boggy and dotted with puddles of muddy water. Yoshi's boots sank into the earth as he walked, leaving prints around the perimeter of the white stone wall that girded the property.

There was no sentry at the gate, but smoke, rising in the moonlight, indicated people in residence.

Yoshi's pulse raced. He might be within fifty yards of Nami! Yoshi studied his trail of footprints; it would not do to march through the gate leaving so visible a sign of his passage. The wall was in good repair, and no one was on duty. Yoshi pushed his war fan into his *obi* and climbed a cypress that overhung the wall. He dropped into a wide puddle with a splashing sound . . . and froze against the wall as he heard a thick voice from close by say, "Rokuro, did you hear something?"

"No. Come back and eat."

"I heard something."

"Probably one of the wild dogs that roam the neighborhood. Come in. The food will be cold."

"We're supposed to be on watch. I'm going to investigate."

"Go ahead, play the fool. The rest of us will eat."

"All right," mumbled the first man. "But I think you are wrong."

So, thought Yoshi, there were several of them. He silently worked his way around the main building. If Nami was within these walls, she would be living in one of the outer buildings.

Yoshi completed his search after a tense half hour. There were signs of occupancy in most of the buildings; an entire company of samurai were distributed throughout every part of the *shinden*, mansion. The condition of the rooms showed that no women were in residence.

He was exiting the last portal when he heard a shout.

"Someone is here!" It was the same thick voice he had heard earlier. "There are footprints along the wall."

"Where?"

"What?"

"Who?"

A dozen voices took up the cry.

"Fresh footprints! He must be inside the walls. Rokuro, guard the gate. Two of you start a search of the grounds. The rest will check the buildings. Hurry!"

Yoshi's mind raced. He was trapped. There were four gates to the estate and three were permanently sealed. The front gate was the single means of entrance or exit.

Yoshi pulled the war fan from his *obi*. He would try to escape without a fight, but he would fight to the death if he had to. He had heard the man's name, Rokuro. The leader's voice was distinctive . . . and Yoshi was an actor.

The night was dark. Only a few pine torches lit the grounds. He marched toward the gate boldly, shouting in a passable imitation of the leader's thick voice. "Rokuro!" he cried. "Quickly, the intruder is hiding behind the bushes near the lake. Run! Take him from the right, I'll go to the left."

Rokuro did not question the order; drawing his sword, he ran toward the artificial lake.

Within seconds, Yoshi was out the gate and down the narrow street that fronted the estate. Behind him he heard confused shouts from over the wall.

sixty-nine

On the cold, clear twentieth day of the twelfth month, Yoshi spent the daylight hours supervising construction at his theater site. Carpenters were building a stage with a broad entrance ramp. Special backdrops were being prepared, and a balcony was being erected behind the open gallery.

While the carpenters did the manual labor, Yoshi was thoughtful, reviewing the results of his search for Nami. Lord Chikara's estate was an uninhabited ruin, and Uncle Fumio's was an army barracks. Three major possibilities were left: the Imperial enclosure, his own estate in the northwest quarter, and Rokuhara.

Tonight, he planned to investigate the Imperial enclosure; it was the closest to the theater site. The last time he had visited there had been for his clandestine meeting with Go-Shirakawa. That time he had slipped in disguised as a fishmonger. He remembered the smell of rotting fish and smiled wryly; finding entry would be difficult enough without that handicap. Nevertheless, he was determined to enter the enclosure.

A chance conversation with the head of his construction crew solved the problem. These same carpenters were working at night to repair the areas of the Imperial Palace burned out by Antoku and his retinue the year before. Yoshi would go with them into the enclosure. When asked the reason he wanted to go, Yoshi hinted at a liaison with a court lady. The head carpenter nodded understandingly. "It will be dangerous for you," he said. "The grounds are patrolled by Imperial guards and Kiso's samurai. We can help you to get in, but we cannot guarantee you will get out safely."

"That will be my problem," said Yoshi. "Just find a way to get me in."

The enclosure held over fifty buildings and pavilions. Once inside, Yoshi's search for Nami would have just begun.

Yoshi came through the Suzaku-Mon, the southern gate, shortly before midnight. He carried planks, as did the two carpenters he was with. They were passed through without question; easier and more pleasant than arriving as a fishmonger.

Inside the gate, Yoshi thanked the others and headed briskly for the women's pavilions located behind the *Dairi,* Imperial Palace. He was alert to the possibility of meeting Kiso's men; they were known to prowl the women's quarters, terrifying the court ladies.

Yoshi wore his most conservative brown over-robe to appear as inconspicuous as possible while he searched the grounds. Without swords or marks of rank, he was a commoner and would be severely punished if he was discovered wandering in the enclosure. He reached the women's quarters without incident. If Nami was there, finding her would be difficult. The ladies occupied twelve large pavilions. Each had a private screened cubicle protected by heavy wooden shutters. Yoshi moved from shadow to shadow; the sight of a strange man in common clothing might cause the ladies to panic.

Yoshi squatted behind a thick row of privet hedges and took stock. He wished he knew more about the current political situation. Being part of an acting troupe had its disadvantages. Yoritomo's agent had told Yoshi that Go-Shirakawa was Kiso's prisoner. When he had met Go-Shirakawa a year ago, the Emperor had desired an alliance with Yoritomo. But there was no guarantee that the situation was the same. Go-Shirakawa might have to betray Yoshi to save his own life if Kiso demanded it.

Several times, groups of samurai passed Yoshi's hiding place. They shouted coarse remarks, sang in drunken harmony, or laughed at each other's coarse jokes. He saw few Imperial guards. The grounds seemed to be controlled by Kiso's mountaineers.

Streaks of light appeared in the east. Yoshi was ready to give up and return the following night when he had a stroke of fortune. A courtier was leaving one of the lady's rooms. As the lady stepped to the portal, a beam of light touched her face. Yoshi recognized her. Lady Shimeko! He had met her at court. She had been a lady-in-waiting to the Nii-Dono, and rumor had it Taira Kiyomori once fancied her. Yoshi remembered her pale beauty and hair that reached the floor. Some said she had served the Nii-Dono unwillingly and had feared Kiyomori.

Yoshi had spoken to her several times, always through her screen of state . . . she was an extremely proper and modest young lady. Yoshi had actually seen her only once, when she appeared with Nami at a court function. Her beauty was not easily forgotten. She had been a friend to Nami, and Yoshi was confident she would help him.

When her male visitor was gone, Yoshi climbed the veranda rail and silently approached the closed shutters of Shimeko's room. He tapped lightly on the wood.

Shimeko, thinking her lover had returned, flung open the door. She saw a strange man, a commoner, and before Yoshi could say a word, she screamed wildly.

Shutters banged open, lanterns were lit, and dozens of startled voices filled the air.

Yoshi leaped the rail. He landed . . . facing a squad of Imperial guards, who seemed to have appeared from nowhere.

"Take him," shouted the leader, brandishing his sword.

Yoshi pulled the folded war fan from his *obi*, as the half dozen men leaped toward him. He spun, striking behind him with the dull end of the fan. There was a meaty thud, and one attacker fell. Yoshi dropped to one knee as a sword blade whizzed over his head. He struck upward into the guard's solar plexus and was rewarded with a howl of pain as the man doubled over.

The remaining guards paused: they were face to face with a commoner armed only with a fan who moved with uncanny speed. With a roar of rage, two stepped forward simultaneously. Yoshi blocked one man's blade with the iron fan ribs and continued the motion into the face of the other. The man's nose erupted in a flood of red; his sword fell as he tumbled to the ground, holding both hands over his destroyed face.

Yoshi flipped backward, in a move he had learned from the acrobats. He landed in a crouch, straightened, and simultaneously lashed out with a foot that caught the second assailant in the chest. The battle lasted less than a minute, and four guards were incapacitated.

The guard captain misread the situation. He thought Shimeko and Yoshi were lovers. He caught Shimeko in the doorway, pulled her head back by the hair, and placed his blade to her throat.

"Halt. Drop your weapon or your woman dies," he shouted.

Yoshi was torn. Shimeko was a means to locate Nami. If he surrendered to save her, he would undoubtedly be executed. His mission would fail, and his search for Nami would have been for naught, wasted because of a virtual stranger. Yoshi ground his teeth in frustration. He couldn't allow an innocent woman to die.

The guard captain pulled Shimeko's hair tighter and moved his blade threateningly. "Now!" he snarled.

Yoshi straightened and dropped his fan. He held out empty hands. "Let her go," he said. "She is not my woman."

The guard captain released the trembling girl. "Take him. Tie him securely," he snapped. "This commoner will pay for his actions tonight."

seventy

A bright winter sun lit the sky as Yoshi was taken to the Emperor's palace. Despite the sun, the palace reception hall was dimly lit by oil lamps. Copper braziers hardly warmed the great cold room. It was cavernous, almost empty, with ceilings that receded into absolute darkness far above the small cluster of people below.

Yoshi was surrounded by a dozen Imperial guards. He was on his knees, his hands cruelly tied behind his back. His hair was disheveled, bruises visible on his cheek and brow. The guard captain had exacted his revenge.

Yoshi remembered the smell of burning oil and old ashes. He faced a dais with a thronelike Chinese chair in its center. Screens with painted scenes of ancient Chinese cities backed the throne. Go-Shirakawa watched him coldly; his mouth was twisted in irritation. Yukitaka, Go-Shirakawa's wrinkled old retainer, had placed a bowl of candied fruit at his side, and Go-Shirakawa's pudgy hands constantly dipped into the bowl, sampling its wares.

Go-Shirakawa said petulantly, "You must have been very persuasive to have convinced the guards to call me." He pulled his robe closer around his chest and sank lower in his chair. "Who are you? What do you want? Speak!"

Yoshi touched his forehead to the wood floor three times. Despite bruises, Yoshi's face was composed, strong, and dignified.

"Your Highness, I would speak with you alone. I have information for your ears only."

"I admire your audacity. You, a common trespasser who deserves no consideration." His voice took on a biting edge. "I should have you summarily executed."

"A moment alone, Your Highness, and I will explain."

Go-Shirakawa squinted at Yoshi, his shaved crown furrowed thoughtfully. "There is something familiar about you, commoner," he said. "Where have I seen you before?"

"I will explain when the room is cleared," said Yoshi coolly.

Go-Shirakawa ordered, "Guards, wait outside the doors." He lowered his gaze to Yoshi and added, "My retainer will stay."

Yoshi nodded, "I trust Yukitaka," he said.

The old retainer looked puzzled. "You know me?" he said, then echoed Go-Shirakawa. "Who are you?"

The guards marched out, suppressing their annoyance at being ordered about by their prisoner. They left Yoshi, hands bound, on his knees before the dais. Yoshi raised his head proudly and caught the Emperor's eye. "I am Tadamori-no-Yoshi. You sent me..."

The Emperor interrupted. "Yoshi?" He turned to Yukitaka for confirmation.

The old man studied Yoshi closely and said, hesitantly, "I think it is he. Changed. Different..." His voice became firmer. "It is definitely he."

Yoshi nodded.

Go-Shirakawa relaxed and lifted another piece of candied fruit to his mouth. "Yes, it is you. I recognize you now." He smiled slyly and added, "You smell much sweeter than at our last meeting."

"Thank you, Your Highness."

"Enough!" Go-Shirakawa bit into the fruit. He ordered Yukitaka to untie Yoshi's hands. Yoshi rubbed his wrists to restore circulation. When he seemed ready, Go-Shirakawa said, "Tell me about your mission."

"Your Highness, you sent me to report on Yoritomo's suitability as your ally. You received my reports. That mission is complete. You ordered me to work on Yoritomo's behalf...I do so." Yoshi leaned toward the Emperor and asked, "Are you still interested in an alliance with Lord Yoritomo?"

"More than ever."

"Yet despite my recommendations, you are allied to Kiso, whom Yoritomo considers his enemy."

"My allegiance to Kiso was forced upon me," said the Emperor bitterly. "My interest is in the welfare of the Empire. When Kiso met with me on Mount Hiei, I thought he and Yoritomo were allies. Once under Kiso's power, I had no choice but to accept him. Kiso's rule is disastrous. Kiso and his men are destroying my capital and terrorizing my people."

Go-Shirakawa sighed wearily. "Yoritomo will have my

wholehearted support if he can rescue me from the city. I am virtually a prisoner in my own palace. Tell that to Yoritomo when next you see him."

"I haven't seen Yoritomo in over a year. I will not see him before my mission for him is completed."

"What is this mission?"

"To capture and punish Kiso!"

The cloistered Emperor sucked air through his teeth. "I wish you good fortune," he said, "but yours is an impossible task. Kiso is never without his bodyguard, the four kings, and his woman, Tomoe. They are sworn to defend him to the death. How could you get close enough to capture him? I know Yoritomo wants his head to show the people, but he will not have it unless Kiso's men are defeated in battle." Go-Shirakawa motioned Yukitaka to his side and whispered a question. Go-Shirakawa nodded at the answer.

"Yoshi, we trust you and will help you. Yukitaka tells me that Yoritomo is gathering an army to attack Kyoto. Kiso's forces were weakened when they were defeated by Koremori at Mizushima and by Shigehira at Muroyama."

"I heard gossip about that defeat. Kiso has always been a good tactician. Why did he split his forces?"

"I suggested it," said the Emperor smugly.

"He agreed? It seems suicidal."

"Kiso committed his men in exchange for a reward; a reward he wants more than anything else in the world. At the next promotion ceremonies, he will be declared *sei-i-taishogun*, the third *shogun* in the history of the Empire!"

"The title and your official recognition will strengthen his political position."

"He will have the title but will lack the strength to keep it. His army was weakened by his recent losses. Kiso considers himself betrayed by Yukiie's cowardly desertion at Muroyama; he has foolishly divided his men again, sending part of his army to capture Yukiie. Troop morale is at a new low. His men will fight, but they can no longer win against Yoritomo."

"If I could reach Kiso first and capture him, his men will surrender without fighting," said Yoshi.

"If? . . ." Go-Shirakawa's brows rose.

"I will succeed," said Yoshi confidently. He abruptly changed the subject. "Your Highness, may I ask a personal favor?"

Go-Shirakawa waved a languid hand, giving Yoshi permission.

Yoshi paused, then plunged in with the question uppermost in his mind. "Do you know the whereabouts of my wife, Nami?"

Go-Shirakawa and Yukitaka exchanged significant glances. The old retainer stepped forward and spoke in a faltering voice, "Be warned, young man. She is being used as bait in a trap. She lives in the northwest quarter on Sanjo Street..."

"My estate?"

"Yes. The grounds are patrolled by Kiso's samurai. Kiso speaks of revenge against you. He says one day you will come for the woman and will be captured."

"I know my estate well enough so I can enter undetected to free her," said Yoshi, ignoring Yukitaka's comments.

"If you are seen, Kiso's men will hold her hostage. You will either surrender or she will be killed. My guards told me you withdrew when Shimeko was threatened. Would you fight if it caused your wife's death? I doubt it. Stay away from Nami!"

"I must know if she is well."

The Emperor said sadly, "Except for her loneliness. Like me, she is a prisoner. She is allowed one retainer and one visitor, Tomoe. She is well."

"Then Nami never leaves the estate?"

"Only by my direct invitation," said Go-Shirakawa.

Yoshi said softly, "I think there is a way to free you and Nami and deliver Kiso into my hands."

"Speak!"

"I am established in the northeast quarter and, through an agent, communicate with Yoritomo. Before Yoritomo besieges Kyoto, he will infiltrate samurai to help me. When I am ready, I will send for those men and..."

Yoshi described the theater company, the new theater he was building, how they could be used to further his plans, and how Go-Shirakawa could help.

When he was finished, Go-Shirakawa made additional suggestions. Yoshi agreed to their wisdom. "I have been patient a long time, and will be patient longer." Yoshi again touched his forehead to the floor three times.

His course was clear.

seventy-one

Yoshi considered various approaches to Nami and decided to make a direct approach on his own. Despite Go-Shirakawa's warnings, Yoshi was confident that he could see Nami without alerting her guards. It was his home they were guarding, and he knew it better than anyone. He would wait for the cover of darkness.

Yoshi spent the day at the theater site. After dark, he changed into clothing that was inconspicuous—dark-colored and un-patterned. He concealed his war fan in the jacket and he was ready. Yoshi walked across Nijo Street at a brisk pace. The night was cold and clear; Tsukiyomi was at three quarters, casting harsh shadows from trees, fences, and walls. A flurry of snow had come during the afternoon; most of it was gone without a trace, but small drifts, driven by the biting northeast wind, clung to walls and tree trunks along the way. After sunset, the temperature dropped precipitously and Yoshi found the cross streets deserted. In the half hour it took to walk across the city, he passed several groups of samurai. They sounded less boisterous than when he had first arrived in Kyoto. Perhaps it was the cold, but more likely, their dampened spirits came from knowing Yoritomo would soon be at the city gates; their year of tyranny was coming to an end.

During the hour of the bird, about seven in the evening, he came near his small estate. A lump rose in his throat. Had he ever expected to see it again? Under such circumstances? He wished he had built a solid wall instead of the wooden fence and evergreen hedges, but it was too late for misgivings. At least he did not have to scale a high wall.

Yoshi slipped from shadow to shadow, inspecting the perimeter. He concentrated on his task, but thoughts of Nami continually intruded. He was aware of every stir of wind, every shadow that moved, every branch that creaked. Knowing that he was walking into a trap gave him an advantage. The guards didn't expect him. They had no reason to remain silent or to work at staying unseen. Half-disciplined soldiers could hardly be expected to remain constantly alert. Time made them careless.

There were two sets of guards outside the boundaries of the estate, one group across the street on the south, the other on the east. Because much of this old quarter had been leveled and not rebuilt after the earthquakes and fires of previous years, the guards had built temporary shelters for protection from the weather.

Yoshi moved like a wraith, soundlessly approaching the southern watchpost. Four men huddled around a fire; they grumbled, the typical complaints of soldiers relegated to unpleasant duty. Yoshi heard that one man was supposed to stay on watch at all times. After a year of fruitless sentinel duty, none of the guards wanted to be the one to stand in the cold. Yoshi nodded to himself. As long as no alarm sounded from the estate, these men could be ignored.

Opposite the east border hedge, the scene was similar; there was a full squad of six men standing in front of a roaring fire. They passed a flagon and wolfed food from a common pot.

Yoshi skirted their shelter. With ghostlike silence, he appeared at the northern perimeter. It was as he remembered it—there was a narrow space between the hedges where a north gate had once been set. He was quickly inside, facing the back of the guest house.

It was occupied.

He studied the sky. Cloudless. There was no hope that Tsukiyomi's face would be covered. He would have to cross the open ground in bright moonlight. So be it.

Yoshi raced for the veranda, diving for its shelter as he waited for an alarm to be sounded. There was nothing but the murmur of voices from inside. He raised himself slowly, then silently climbed over the low rail. Here, on the veranda, he pressed against the wall in the shadow of the eaves and listened.

Inside, two men were talking. Confident that they were alone, they made no effort to mute their voices. One said in a bitter tone, "This assignment is fruitless."

"I agree, Ichijo. We've been quartered here over a year. If Yoshi is alive, he must be with Yoritomo's army."

"No question. Kiso should order the woman and the old man executed; then we could join the hunt for General Yukiie. I didn't join Kiso to spend my life on guard duty. Now that winter is here, there isn't a chance that Yoshi will come for the woman."

"What are you suggesting?"

"I'm going to an inn to find some warm companionship."

"That's desertion. If Kiso finds out, he will have your head. Remember Santaro."

"He won't find out."

Inside, there was a loud crash. Yoshi hugged the wall.

"You seem nervous tonight," said Ichijo bitterly.

"I am. I don't like being on watch alone."

"I'll take your turn tomorrow night."

"No. My head is too valuable to me. I couldn't enjoy myself thinking what might happen if I were discovered."

The guards continued their discussion while Yoshi considered what he heard. Two men. If he was patient, perhaps only one . . . a nervous, alert one! Should Yoshi bypass them while they were embroiled in their discussion, or wait for one to leave?

He decided to wait. If the bitter-sounding Ichijo left the other alone, Yoshi could stop him before he sounded the alarm. One man should be easy to handle with the advantage of surprise. When the deserter reappeared to find his companion bound, he would have to keep silent. Otherwise, both guards would lose their heads. Yoshi smiled grimly; it was worth the discomfort of waiting in the cold.

Yoshi climbed over the rail and rolled under the veranda. The earth was cold and damp. As he lay soundlessly, time stretched without end. Far off, bells and clappers announced the hour of the dog. Another infinity passed before the hour of the boar, two more hours until midnight.

Yoshi shivered. He lay less than fifty yards from Nami and she didn't know. His desire to see her kept him from freezing. He felt his blood heat up at the thought of her closeness. He couldn't wait much longer. The guard was not going to leave. The man was full of bluster but afraid to desert his post. Yoshi would have to circumvent them.

Yoshi was just rolling out from his hiding place when he heard feet stomping on the veranda overhead. He rolled back, thanking Hachiman and Buddha for having saved him from moving ten seconds earlier.

"I'll be back before dawn," said Ichijo, directly above him.

"You'd better or we'll both end up with our heads on poles."

Feet clattered down the three steps to the ground.

"I don't like this," muttered the nervous guard to himself. Yoshi waited to be sure Ichijo would not change his mind and return early. The nervous energy and desire for Nami were cancelled by the increasing cold of the night. He prayed to Buddha and the Shinto gods for strength to maintain his vigil.

It seemed as though years passed before the temple bells rang from Mount Hiei. Midnight, the hour of the rat. The guard had been silent for an hour. Yoshi crawled from his cramped hiding place. He had difficulty getting to his feet. He stretched his muscles and joints. When he was satisfied that he had regained his flexibility, he vaulted the railing and glided to the shutters. A faint sliver of light where two slats did not fit tightly gave him a narrow view inside. The usually bare guest room was heaped with soldiers' gear and the detritus of a year of careless occupation. The guard was hunched over a copper brazier, his back to the door. His swords were on the floor by his side. He had wrapped a bulky blanket around his shoulders for warmth.

Yoshi crept away from the slit and tried the door. He cursed silently. It would have been so easy if the door had been unlatched. It wasn't. The guard must have relatched it after his companion left. There would be no surprise from behind.

Yoshi took the war fan from his jacket and used it to rap loudly on the door.

"Is that you, Ichijo?" asked the nervous guard.

In a fair approximation of the missing guard's bitter tone, Yoshi snarled, "Yes. Open up. Quickly! I'm freezing out here." The latch lifted. The man inside was saying, "I'm glad you decided to return. I told you . . ." when the door slammed into him. His mouth dropped open; he staggered back, too stunned to shout. Yoshi's weighted fan caught him on the temple as he desperately scrabbled for his swords. His breath expelled from his nose in a thin whistle and he dropped, unconscious, to the floor.

Yoshi's heart was pounding. He had come close to failing. If the man had shouted instead of leaping for his weapon, the other guards would have swarmed to his rescue. In reaching for his sword, the guard had given Yoshi his chance.

Rummaging through the scattered gear, Yoshi found rope. He securely tied and gagged the unconscious guard.

Now, if Ichijo did not return early, Yoshi had five hours to spend with Nami. He boldly walked along the covered corridor to the main building. It was dark and silent. He tried the shutters; they were latched. He tried the door: latched.

Yoshi scratched on the shutters. "Nami, Nami," he whispered urgently. He heard someone move inside and had a sudden doubt. What if it wasn't Nami? He was committed. "Nami," he repeated. "Open. It's Yoshi."

He heard a loud intake of breath and the click of a latch being lifted.

The door opened and Nami's pallid face appeared in the moonlight, her eyes wide with shock, her mouth open in disbelief. "Yoshi," she gasped. "You will be caught. Run!"

"No! I am safe. Let me in. Quickly!"

Nami stepped aside like a sleepwalker, unable to believe Yoshi was really there. Inside the room, Yoshi said, "Close the door. Light the oil lamp. I want to see you." Nami snapped the latch in place. With the closing of the door, the room was in absolute darkness. Yoshi swam in the sweet scent of her familiar perfume. "Nami, where is the light?"

"We mustn't. The guards..."

"Are taken care of. Nami!" Yoshi forgot the light in the rapture of her embrace. They clung to each other in the darkness while Nami sobbed with joy and Yoshi trembled with emotion.

"How did you find me? Where have you been? What are you doing here? The guards?" Words tumbled breathlessly from Nami's lips as she held Yoshi tightly to her breast.

Yoshi crooned wordlessly, caressing her hair, kissing her forehead, nose, lips. Finally, he murmured, "Nami, Nami. So long a time. Too long. Beloved..."

Nami responded to the urgency of his body. She whispered, "Hold me close, love me." She led Yoshi to her *chodai*, the curtained sleeping platform, and pushed the drapes aside. Together they sank down to her *futon*.

"My dearest." Yoshi nuzzled his face into the hollow of her shoulder.

"So long a time... do we dare?..."

"Yes, yes." Yoshi undid his *obi* and reached inside her sleeping robe.

"How I've missed you," she sighed.

Then they loved each other as if they never had before and never would again.

Sated with love, they rolled apart and Yoshi tenderly responded to Nami's questions. "I cannot come here again until my mission is fulfilled," he said in conclusion. "Soon you will receive an invitation from Go-Shirakawa. The invitation will request your presence at a theater party given in honor of Kiso and Tomoe. You will accept..."

"I can't accept. I can't be near Kiso."

Yoshi detected a strange note in Nami's voice. He said placatingly, "Of course you can. I hate Kiso more than you and with more reason . . ."

Nami interrupted in a flat, dead voice. "No . . . no you don't!" In the dark, Yoshi could not see that she had turned away and was fighting to control her tears.

"You will come because you love me," said Yoshi.

In the aftermath of their love, Nami could not hide the truth. She couldn't bear the thought of Yoshi sending her to Kiso. She had to tell him of her shame, of the secret she had held to her bosom since Hiuchi-yama.

Nami erupted in tears, sobbing wildly, crying for Yoshi to hold her and to understand.

"What is it, my beloved?" he asked again and again, unable to hear her sobs through the sobs.

Finally, Nami told Yoshi how she had been tricked and raped. Her voice broke as she sobbed and moaned in the horror of her words.

Yoshi was silent.

When she stopped at last, she waited for Yoshi to respond. Silence!

Nami touched his face and felt hot tears wetting his cheeks. Her fingers brushed his jaw. He flinched, but not before she detected a twitching lump of muscle at the corner of his mouth and cords straining at his throat.

"Oh, Yoshi. Forgive me," she cried.

His voice was infinitely strained, infinitely patient. "You are not at fault, beloved. It is Kiso's evil, his fault. His fault! Now I understand your sadness and withdrawal before our marriage." Yoshi's voice rose in a fury. "Kiso must die!"

"I tried to spare you, to protect you. I know your vow and respect it. I cannot be the cause of breaking it."

"My vow is broken," said Yoshi in a voice strangled with emotion.

"No, beloved Yoshi. Your vow is more important than revenge. You have told me that a hundred times. Your vow is to the gods and means more than worldly matters. What's done is done. I don't love you less. My love for you is stronger than ever before."

"And my love for you," said Yoshi in a wondering voice. "How much it must have cost you to remain silent . . . to protect me from myself."

Yoshi swallowed. He had come close to losing his control, the control of a master. He was the *sensei,* and no matter the provocation, he would not use his sword to kill . . . unless there was an unmistakable sign from the gods. So he had sworn, and so it would be.

Was this the sign? His heart, his rage, his disgust wanted to say yes. His mind refused. He had accepted Santaro's death without renouncing his vows. His heart cried, *This is worse,* and his mind replied, *No. Not so.* He had made love to Aki. Was this so different? Yes. Yes! Aki voluntarily shared her bed, while Kiso had forced Nami to submit to his will.

Yoshi turned back to Nami and pressed his cheek to hers, feeling her tears mix with his own.

"Kiso has to die," he muttered. "But his death will not be at my hand."

Nami held his face against hers and repeated his name, "Yoshi. Yoshi. Yoshi," with such tenderness and understanding that fresh tears ran down his face to stain his robe.

seventy-two

After that night with Nami, Yoshi found it hard to stay away from his estate. He was torn by his desire to see her again—she was so close!—and his need to follow the plan he had arranged with Go-Shirakawa. He concentrated on the theater construction, making small improvements as the work continued. A few days after his capture by the Imperial guards, his bruises had healed well enough for him to be able to face the company, and shortly before the new year, he returned to the inn.

"We have a theater," Yoshi announced at dinner. The entire company was gathered in the dining area. The smell of smoked fish and green tea filled the air. "At this moment, carpenters are completing the stage, artists are painting a new pine tree backdrop, and all will be ready shortly after the new year ceremonies."

The company burst into excited discussion.

"What about space for us?" asked Ito, including the musicians with a wave.

"There will be room on this stage for the musicians to sit comfortably. The lanterns will provide enough light, and I have placed large jars under the stage for greater resonance. You will be able to play without strain; every note will be heard." He turned from Ito to smile proudly at the others as he went on, "Actors and singers, you may speak and sing more naturally because of the resonating jars and the solid screen backdrop."

"And what of us?" asked Koetsu, speaking for the acrobats.

"You have not been forgotten. You will be the background chorus in the play and . . . I have prepared a special part for you."

Before Koetsu could ask about this special part, several people interrupted with the same question, "When can we see the theater?"

"Soon, but first we have to learn an entirely new production. With Ohana's help, I have written a play with rich parts for everyone."

Ohana looked surprised, waiting to hear what Yoshi had done in his name.

"Tell us the story," shouted one of the actors.

Yoshi rose to his feet and spread his arms. In a loud voice, he proclaimed, "I will play the god Haya-Susa-no-wo. Returning to earth after being exiled from heaven, I find an old man, played by our leader, Ohana, and an old woman, played by Ume . . ."

"Oh no, I couldn't." Ume hid her face.

Yoshi ignored the interruption and continued, "They are with a beautiful maiden, played by Aki. The old man and old woman cry because the eight-headed serpent of Koshi has, over the years, eaten their other girl children; the serpent is due to come for this last child. The old man tells Haya-Susa-no-wo that he is Ashinadzuchi, son of the god of the mountain, and he sings a song describing the eightfold monster. Its eyes are winter cherry-red; its body, with eight heads and eight tails, extends over eight valleys and eight hills and is covered with pines and cedars."

Yoshi took a deep breath and raised his voice dramatically. "With Ashinadzuchi's permission, Haya-Susa-no-wo takes the daughter and turns her into a comb, which he puts in his hair. He tells the old couple to brew sake of eightfold strength and fill eight tubs to be placed in the eight doors of a great fence. Then they are to wait.

"The serpent comes and drinks from each tub, becomes drunk, and lays down, whereupon Haya-Susa-no-wo draws his sword and kills it. Cutting the serpent open, he discovers the great sword called *Kusanagi,* the herb-queller, and reports his discovery to Amaterasu, the sun goddess."

The company was silent, stunned by Yoshi's vision.

Koetsu was the first to speak. He had waited anxiously for his opportunity. "What is the special part for the acrobats?" he asked.

"You will be the eightfold monster of Koshi, moving together as one man."

Koetsu's face broke into a radiant smile as he visualized the effect. Ito leaped to his feet. "Brilliant," he said. "I shall compose music at once. Already I hear a special theme for the monster to be played on the bass drum and *biwa* and a counter theme for Haya-Susa-no-wo to be played on the flute."

Yoshi said, "Tomorrow we prepare for our coming triumph in Kyoto. The capital is within our reach, and if we do well, we shall soon play for the Emperor." As the company cheered these enthusiastic words, Yoshi told himself: And I shall be close to the completion of my mission. Kiso will pay for what he did.

The acrobats went into the capital a week before the scheduled opening. They put up handbills describing Ohana's company and the repertory program to be offered. The rest of the company arrived on the evening of the final day. They came quietly, settling into the quarters Yoshi had prepared behind the theater. Their unannounced entrance to the city caused a bitter quarrel between Yoshi and Ohana.

"We have always announced our arrival with a show of acrobats. How else can the people know of us?"

"This is Kyoto. Our handbills have been posted for a week. The capital has seen little entertainment since the arrival of Kiso's army. They will be waiting."

Yoshi's face was expressionless, but it took him great effort to hide his impatience with Ohana's lack of foresight. The man's stupidity and greed could jeopardize Yoshi's plans. He wondered if his attempts to repay the man were worthwhile. Perhaps he should exact his revenge on Kiso and let the pompous Ohana sink with his company. No! He had no quarrel with the actors. They were his friends; he must maintain his patience.

"How can you be sure the people will be waiting? There is time to send the acrobats in first. I am paying them," Ohana whined.

"Ohana, trust me. Your way would offend the court people. We must appeal to their sense of the aesthetic in a gentle way. This approach will earn us an appearance before the Emperor... and win us fame and riches."

"But a small taste of the acrobats to whet their appetites?"

"No acrobats!"

"Father, Suruga is right. We must believe in him." Aki was so thrilled with her new role and the dances Yoshi had choreographed, she was ready to accept anything he said.

Ohana also was being congratulated by the company, but it rankled that he was treated as if he were a mere actor and not the man whose name appeared on the handbills. He realized unhappily that Yoshi was in complete control, using the company for his own purposes.

seventy-three

The opening presentation of *Haya-Susa-no-wo* came on the second night of the new year. Despite the cold, the theater was full. Oil lamps cast fretful shadows on the black rafters over the stage. A ramp led from the center of the audience to the front of the stage; the actors entered and exited by this route. The musicians, sitting cross-legged, played their accompaniment in front of a pine tree backdrop. The chorus, in costumes and masks, lined the open sides of the raised wooden stage.

The general audience sat under the stars in a half circle facing the actors. Lords and ladies of the fifth rank and above were in a special, second-story, covered gallery. The rustling of winter robes and kimonos blended with the droning choral voices:

> *"As for Haya-Susa-no-wo*
> *As for Haya-Susa-no-wo*
> *He comes from the heavens*
> *With the sword of a god*
> *Haya-Susa-no-wo*
> *From the heavenly skies*
> *With the sword of a god*
> *With the sword of a god."*

So sang one half the chorus while the other half repeated the line, "Oh, how I wish for the sword of a god," in counterpoint.

The voices echoed through the theater, projected by the reverberating jars under the stage.

Koetsu sang from behind a *hannia,* demon mask, as befitted the eightfold dragon. Ohana wore the mask of an old man and Ume, an old woman. The others appeared in stage makeup. Yoshi, who acted as *kimi,* lord of the chorus, wore full battle dress for his role as Haya-Susa-no-wo.

Ohana shivered behind his mask, more from nervousness than from the dry cold of the night. The opening was, in his eyes, doomed to disaster. He was accustomed to a noisy crowd full of boisterous humor, encouraged by the acrobats to laughter and horseplay. This audience, sitting silently, with only the swish of brocaded silk to signal life, presaged failure.

Haya-Susa-no-wo stepped forward and drew his sword in a sweeping gesture. He stamped his right foot to the stage, lowering his body in a powerful stance, legs apart, knees pressed out as though sitting on a mighty steed:

> *"When began the earth and heaven*
> *By the margin of the river*
> *Of the firmament eternal*
> *Met the gods in high assemble ..."*

The performance started. Ohana trembled at the silence. Oh, unhappy day when he had let this vagabond into his company. To come so far and have everything destroyed by too much ambition!

Ohana played out his part, and the despair he felt at the failure of the production made him more effective as the tragic Ashinadzuchi.

When the acrobats appeared as the eightfold monster, the audience gasped, and when Haya-Susa-no-wo, in a flashing display of sword play, finally cut off its head, they broke their silence with enthusiastic applause.

The mask saved Ohana from embarrassing himself onstage. He stood dumbstruck, mouth agape, unable to speak. They liked it! The play was a success! He was saved!

Afterward, the worm of jealousy writhed inside the nominal leader of the Ohana *Dengaku* Company. The company clustered around Yoshi and Aki, ignoring Ohana. He hid his feelings, laughing when he caught someone looking at him.

"A toast! A toast!" he shouted, trying to regain his position as leader.

"Quiet, everyone," said Yoshi. "Our leader wishes to propose a toast."

Someone snickered. The derision was not lost on Ohana, who found bitter bile in the back of his throat.

"I took in a stranger and taught him well. Much of my success tonight belongs to Suruga, who has worked hard under my guidance," he declared pompously, looking more the ineffectual rooster than ever.

"Your success?" shouted a drunken actor.

Yoshi interrupted quickly. "This is the night of Ohana's greatest triumph. Without him there would be no Ohana company. We owe everything to him."

"To you, not Ohana," hooted one of the newly hired musicians.

"Enough," said Yoshi. "I propose a toast to the leader of the greatest acting company in the ten provinces. To Ohana and his beautiful daughter, Aki." He raised his cup and drank. The company whistled and cheered.

Another toast was proposed to the acrobats, and then another and another. Yoshi was not a devotee of the sake bottle, but he could not graciously refuse. He drank... and drank.

Yoshi opened his eyes from a dream. He stared blankly at the bamboo slats rattling against a latticed shutter. The cold breeze that shook the blinds brought a faint odor of green tea from the next room. He was aware of the sounds of horses, oxcarts, and people on the other side of the shutters. Slowly he focused; the dream of Nami slipped from his mind, leaving a bittersweet tinge of something lost.

Yoshi was back in his rooms at the inn. He remembered the celebration. How could he have forgotten? His head throbbed and his tongue tasted like a sumo wrestler's breech-clout. He groaned.

"Ah, the great Suruga is awake at last," said Aki from the other side of the screen.

"Amida! It must be noon. What happened to me?"

"That is what I asked myself. I thought we might celebrate privately last night. I have not been alone with you since you first went to Kyoto. I came to you... but the iron-hard Suruga was soft as a silken *obi*. Nothing I did could wake you."

Yoshi thought of Nami and their wonderful night together... only a week before... and was glad he had not responded. What made him feel revulsion at the thought of lying with Aki? He wanted his own wife... he had waited so long... one night was not enough.

Yoshi changed the subject abruptly. "Give me tea. I have work to do."

"No work today. We need a rest more than rehearsal." Aki poured a cup. Yoshi took it greedily. He swished it around in his mouth to kill the terrible taste.

"I suppose you are right. We need a few hours off. The company performed well last night. They seemed happy."

"Except my father," said Aki dryly.

"I thought he was happiest of all."

"I know him better than that. He is torn between enjoying the success you've brought him and jealousy because he couldn't do it himself."

Yoshi frowned, holding his throbbing head. "I give him more credit than he deserves."

"Exactly why he is angry."

Aki poured more tea. She made a little ceremony of the process. As she handed Yoshi the cup, she said, "Forget my father. Let's take advantage of our freedom." She smiled suggestively.

Yoshi grimaced. "I cannot," he said. "Why not join the others and tour the city while I rest?"

Aki's mouth tightened. "Since your first visit to Kyoto, you have been too tired, or too busy. Are you angry with me? Have I done something to offend you?" Her voice grew shrill.

Yoshi hastened to reassure her. She had done nothing. He couldn't tell her about a wife whom he had never mentioned and that he felt guilty at having made love to her while Nami was a prisoner. There was no social reason why he should not have lain with her . . . only the reasons of his own heart.

Aki watched him from the corners of her eyes, a look of dissatisfaction marring her foxlike beauty. She was being neglected again, and she didn't like that. She was sought after by men of the highest rank. How dare Suruga treat her so cavalierly?

seventy-four

On the fifth day of the first month of 1184, the bestowal-of-rank ceremony took place at the *Seiryo-Den,* the Emperor's residential palace. It was held in the Great Hall and was presided over by Go-Shirakawa and the assembled Ministers of the Left and Right. Go-Shirakawa was seated on his Chinese throne, dressed in a royal-blue court cloak lined in aqua silk. His wide-legged trousers were of apple green. His round face, with its commanding nose, was carefully noncommittal as he studied those around him through heavy-lidded eyes.

The high court nobles, dressed in a wide range of colors, knelt below him on either side while the lower-ranking nobles, mostly in the green of the sixth rank, stood shoulder to shoulder before a painted screen in the background.

The reading of the Imperial lists was a tedious affair to everyone except those being promoted. The nobles' attention wandered; there was a constant low buzz of conversation... until the final announcement... Kiso's appointment as *shogun.*

The appointment came with the shock of an earthquake, a complete surprise to everyone in the Great Hall. The low buzz became a cacophony of questions, exclamations, and loud remarks. The nobles knew that Kiso and Go-Shirakawa were at odds. What had prompted Go-Shirakawa to take this step? Especially when Yoritomo's army was near the city gates and Kiso's army was close to mutiny.

When the uproar subsided, Go-Shirakawa continued the ceremony as though nothing unusual had occurred. Wine cups were distributed to toast the new promotions. Go-Shirakawa watched the guests and saw that several nobles withheld their cups to silently toast Yoritomo. He smiled in self-satisfaction. He had kept his promise to Kiso. Now he was ready to exact his full price.

That night, at Go-Shirakawa's suggestion, the newly appointed *shogun* went to the theater in the northeast quarter to celebrate his promotion.

· · ·

The gatekeeper turned away a hundred nobles before the performance started. Ohana cried at the thought of the lost revenue; Yoshi assured him the crowd would return another night.

During the late afternoon, Yukitaka had come to tell Yoshi that Kiso would attend the performance but that Yoshi must do nothing rash. Go-Shirakawa had not received the reinforcements he requested of Yoritomo. Yukitaka handed Yoshi a folded mulberry paper tied with a crimson strip of silk. Inside was inscribed one word—"Wait."

Yoshi studied the audience while the musicians played Ito's introductory music. His vigil was rewarded. Kiso, surrounded by the *shi-tenno*, entered at the last minute. They sat in the place of honor on a raised balcony at the back of the theater.

The lower gallery was filled with nobles, and Imperial officials jostled one another in unaccustomed familiarity.

Word of *Haya-Susa-no-wo*'s success had spread like brush-fire on Mount Fuji. Overnight it became a mark of distinction to have seen the production.

Yoshi put Kiso out of his mind. Though he was impatient, close to the end of his mission, he would wait until the proper time to act.

When the performance ended, the company earned an even louder ovation than that of opening night. Ohana played his part less effectively, but the mask covered his acting flaws. Aki was brilliant. The part of the maiden daughter had been written to enhance her talent, and she made the most of the role.

The recently promoted nobles came backstage to pay their respects. Yoshi, in makeup and costume, was discussing the play with a group who fancied themselves poets and musicians. He noted it was ever thus; the dilettantes who scratched the surface of an art came backstage to impress the professionals with their knowledge and ability. Just as professional artists always had, so Yoshi held the nobles in mild contempt while acting as if he was impressed with their knowledge and appreciation of his art.

Surrounded by strangers, Yoshi became aware that Kiso and Imai dominated the group around Aki. In the light of the smoking oil lamps, the nobles made a dazzling spectacle with their ornate and colorful robes as they clustered around the white-costumed Aki. Red with golden embroidered dragons, blue with painted scenes of battle, colors in endless profusion swirled in the lamplight like an oil slick on a whirlpool. The dancing shadows made the crowd more human and less human at the same time.

Two figures stood out—Aki at the center, the pale white heart of the multicolored flower, and facing her, Kiso, in black Chinese silk with a tiger's head embroidered on his back.

Yoshi was struck by the aura of power radiating from the hatchet-faced, hot-eyed Kiso. It was the first time Yoshi had seen him in over a year. Kiso had flourished in his position of power.

From the distance of five feet, Yoshi felt a mixture of admiration and loathing. This was the swine who had taken advantage of Nami. Advantage? The crude mountaineer had raped her! But Kiso had changed; he had developed the presence, strength, ease, and physical appearance of royalty. His hair, which had once been ragged and unkempt, was arranged in a neatly combed top-knot under a black silk court hat. No more rope *hachimaki* for the ruler of Kyoto. Yoshi recognized the luxurious quality of Kiso's robe, an import from the court of China. Was there justice in this gossamer world? Kiso the rough mountain man had disappeared; Kiso the newly appointed *shogun* had been polished to a diamond hardness by his year at the court.

Yoshi tried to get closer. It was useless; the people surrounding Yoshi were not about to allow the famous Haya-Susa-no-wo to escape their grasp. Tomorrow they would repeat what he said, and what they thought he said, to their friends at court.

The party ended. The actors felt the pull of fatigue that came inexorably after the euphoria of performance. The less aggressive visitors, those relegated to the fringes, left. Soon even the most persistent bowed and excused themselves.

Kiso and Imai remained . . . with Aki.

Yoshi joined them. He remembered Go-Shirakawa's warning to wait, but Nami's revelation compelled him to face Kiso. Onstage, Yoshi was not recognized, though many nobles in the audience had known him at the court. This, because he was physically so close, was more dangerous. Yoshi's pulse was rapid and a thin film of sweat beaded his makeup. Kiso and Imai wore swords; Yoshi was unarmed. If he was recognized, he would be cut down on the spot. If Kiso suspected the surprising identity of Haya-Susa-no-wo, the vendetta might end now.

Yoshi felt a nerve twitch in his cheek. Kiso stared at him, his thin face registering disinterested curiosity. No flicker of recognition crossed his features. "Congratulations, hero," he said. "I am told that you are more than an actor and I believe it. You used the sword well onstage. Is it true you wrote and produced tonight's program?"

"With Ohana's help. I am just a poor actor working to eke out a living," said Yoshi with a sarcastic bow. He had gained confidence; his disguise was secure. He wished he could reveal himself to Kiso. Patience, a small voice counseled. Yoritomo will exact revenge.

"You speak well, and one does not expect *esemono* to write poetry."

"It is my gift for mimicry, Lord Kiso."

"You know my name?"

"Everyone knows your illustrious name. It has become synonymous with kindness, generosity, and understanding of us, the lower orders." Yoshi grew bolder. His voice was toneless, but the set of his body conveyed a subtle mockery.

Kiso turned to Imai. "I think the actor makes fun of me. Is that possible? If it were so, I'd have to remove his head and lose out on the next night's entertainment."

"He is too outspoken for a player. We should teach him about the kind of manners we expect," snarled Imai.

"Perhaps." Kiso, who had not lowered his voice when he spoke to Imai, turned back to Yoshi. "There is something familiar about you. I can't place it, but it suggests some unpleasantness. Remove yourself from my presence before I am forced to help you along. You played well tonight. You amused me, but now you try my patience." Kiso's eyes became chips of hard black onyx.

"As to that, my lord, I would cut out my tongue if it offended you, but I must point out that my place is here. You are the visitor."

"A little more of this conversation and I might cut out your tongue myself. What a pity that would be."

Before Yoshi could retort in the gradually escalating verbal battle, Aki stepped between them. "Suruga, you embarrass me," she hissed. "And bring trouble to all of us. Please leave."

"As you wish. Perhaps we can finish our conversation another time, Lord Kiso."

"At your service, actor."

• • •

When Aki returned to the inn, it was morning. There was a smug look on her face; strands of hair were loosened from the bow that held them in place.

Yoshi had thought a great deal about his actions while he waited for Aki. He had been wrong to taunt Kiso, wrong and dangerously foolish. He excused himself by saying he had acted to protect Aki from the disaster that would surely befall her if she went with Kiso. After Nami's revelation, Yoshi thought Kiso little more than a beast.

Yoshi had worked long hours to leave a legacy of the theater to Aki and her father. Neither deserved it, but he felt he owed it to them since he could not tell the truth . . . that he was using them to help him arrange Kiso's capture. How could he discourage Aki from going with Kiso and gaining heartbreak instead of reward? Yoshi was in an infuriating position. What could he say to save Aki from her greed? He wanted to shout at her. Instead, he forced his voice to a normal level. "Leaving with Kiso was unwise," he said. "He threatened and insulted me, yet you went with him."

"I do as I please," said Aki with icy calm. "You were childish tonight. You provoked Kiso for no reason. Well, I do not need or want your approval or advice. Kiso loves a woman as a man should. You rejected me . . . twice. You will never be given another chance."

"Listen to me. Don't go to him. He will betray you!"

"Are you jealous of him? How can you know him? You are a commoner, he is the *shogun*."

"I know him and he is evil," said Yoshi, angry at Aki's intransigence. "He lives with the famous woman warrior Tomoe. They have been together since childhood. She will never allow you to share Kiso with her."

"I won't listen. Kiso is more honest than you. He told me of Tomoe and of the others. He is a virile man who has the means to maintain more than one woman. I do not care about the others. I believe Kiso will make me an official consort."

"Kiso is an animal who takes advantage of women. He will discard you as he has the others before you."

"I am not one of them. I find it better to be a nobleman's mistress with a place at the court than an actress who must depend on the theater for her livelihood."

• • •

Haya-Susa-no-wo was the talk of the Kyoto winter season. Every night the theater was full, and every night Kiso and Aki left together after the performance.

"Aki is foolish," Yoshi told Ohana as they sat together after a show. "She should not throw herself at Kiso. You are her father. Advise her to stop before she is destroyed along with him. Kiso is doomed. His enemies are approaching the city . . ."

"Everyone has advice for an old man," said Ohana. "One would think the world was full of wise men except for me. Yet somehow I've survived well for a person of low birth. I am the founder and manager of a successful theater . . ." He looked at Yoshi's face and hastily added, "I take nothing from you. Let us say we helped each other. I guarded your secret when it would have been to my advantage to betray you. Thus far, despite the reward, I have kept my silence." Ohana peered drunkenly at Yoshi to see how the implied threat was received. He read nothing in Yoshi's impassive features.

Ohana cleared his throat nervously. "Why do you try to spoil our success? I know my duty as a father. You are too young to instruct me in that role."

"Where is Aki tonight?"

"She is undoubtedly with Lord Kiso."

"And you don't object?" Yoshi shook his head. Ohana was beyond his comprehension.

"Object? Of course not. I am flattered. Kiso is a great lord. The *shogun!* With his favor, we will be rich."

"Yoritomo comes closer to Kyoto every day. If Kiso lives through the forthcoming battle, he will remain loyal to Tomoe. When he becomes tired of Aki, he will discard her without a thought."

"You are too quick to sell Kiso into defeat. He is not as helpless as you believe. Kiso has discussed the situation with Aki and has convinced her that he will be victorious. With the support of a man as rich as Kiso, we can live a life of ease. What can an acting company offer besides work and uncertainty? We have outgrown it!"

Aki came in later than usual, wearing a robe of apple-green Chinese silk embroidered with golden dragons. The robe was new and obviously expensive. She smiled triumphantly at her father and Yoshi.

seventy-five

The night of the eighteenth day of the first month was bitterly cold. Oil lamps and a scattering of wooden braziers gave little heat to the drafty theater. The audience huddled in winter robes in an effort to stay warm. Those in the open gallery were pale-faced and soft, white powder and blackened teeth accentuating the roundness of their faces. Sprinkled among these scented courtiers were men who sat in ominous silence, with swords hung loosely from their waists, no insignia on their heavy robes. Too dark-skinned to be fashionable, their faces were uniformly thin and hard. If they had been in a group, the faces, swords, and utilitarian clothing would have marked them as hard-bitten warriors of the north. Among the crowd, hidden in shadows, they remained inconspicuous.

Yoshi noted them from his place at the side of the stage. Despite the cold, Yoshi's makeup was scored by rivulets of nervous sweat. He constantly fingered his sword as he studied the crowd.

Where was the man?

At that moment Go-Shirakawa arrived, creating a stir in the audience and excitement backstage. Yoshi had promised the company they would play for the Emperor. No one had really believed him, yet it had come to pass.

Go-Shirakawa was helped to his seat by Yukitaka and Nami. They were surrounded by a party of courtiers. Go-Shirakawa took his seat in a special box prepared in the balcony. He inspected the audience warily, nodding slightly when he saw the dark men in place.

Yoshi caught Nami's eye after she settled into her seat. She immediately recognized him despite the disguise. Yoshi's heart melted at her beauty. He had scarcely seen her face when he had visited the month before . . . only a quick glimpse in the moonlight. Now he studied her from a distance and enjoyed her loveliness.

He tore himself away. If he was to rescue Nami tonight,

his plan would have to work on an exact schedule. He could not afford to be inattentive.

The program was ready to begin. Much of the audience shifted restlessly because of the cold. Where was Kiso's party? Would they come? While Kiso courted Aki, he always arrived early to bring gifts and wish her well before the performance.

He had never been late. Where was he?

Yoshi caught Go-Shirakawa's eye and raised his brows to indicate puzzlement. Go-Shirakawa responded with a shrug. There was nothing more he could do. The rest was in the hands of Yoshi, Yoritomo, and the gods.

There had been much activity in the month since Yoshi's visit to Nami. After Kiso's army had been weakened by Yukiie's defection and losses to Koremori and Shigehira, Yoritomo had launched a two-pronged attack on Kyoto, converging from the south over the bridge at Uji and from the north at Seta, dividing Kiso's weakened forces further.

Go-Shirakawa had used his wiles to bring Kiso, Tomoe, and Nami to the theater tonight. He had offered the celebration of the Bowmen's Wager to Kiso's honor. The celebration was normally confined to a contest between the inner and middle Palace guards, to mark the traditional ending of the New Year period. This year, Go-Shirakawa changed the procedure to allow a contingent of Kiso's soldiers to compete.

Kiso's men won, and the Emperor insisted that Kiso and his group attend the theater as his guests. Kiso could not refuse without directly insulting the Emperor. Go-Shirakawa, seemingly on a whim, requested the presence of Kiso's prisoner, Nami, as his personal guest.

That afternoon, Yukitaka, Go-Shirakawa's ancient retainer, had come to the theater to alert Yoshi about the conclusion of their plan. Yoshi was informed that Kiso had resisted the suggestion of the theater but that Go-Shirakawa had arranged for Kiso's men to win the archery contest, making it impossible for him to refuse. Tonight was their last chance to capture Kiso before he joined his men in the field. Yoritomo had been called upon and, as prearranged, had furnished men who would be located at strategic points throughout the theater. They would respond to Yoshi's command. Go-Shirakawa sent his regards and best wishes. His final message was, "Kiso must not escape from the theater. Our lives depend on his capture or death."

After Yukitaka left, Yoshi had a conversation with Ohana

that angered him. Ohana said, "I should have informed the authorities about you long ago. The reward, my company and its success, would be totally mine today." He drew his rooster body up in a simulation of dignity.

Yoshi realized Ohana was drunk. Yoshi wanted to feel regret about what would happen at the performance that night. He could not. If the plan succeeded, Ohana would have the theater . . . more than he deserved.

Yoshi retained his equilibrium and asked in a level tone, "The company's success? Without me, you and the troupe were doomed to a life of drudgery, playing in fields to rice harvesters. Your thanks are not necessary, but once, admit you owe your prosperity to me."

"Never! You are a common criminal who did no more than I could have done myself."

"Ohana, you play the fool." Yoshi shook his head. How could a man be so blind to his limitations?

"I may play the fool as you've suggested so often, but it is my daughter who will make me rich. My theater has already made me famous. I've had enough of you. I don't need you anymore. Tonight is your last night with us. I have employed another actor to play your roles. Be wise. Go before my generosity fails and I give you to Kiso's samurai for the reward."

Yoshi sighed. Tonight would be his last performance; at last he could speak freely to Ohana. "Ohana," he said. "I am sorry for you and your grasping daughter. I am well rid of you both. Tonight will be my farewell. It will be my greatest performance . . ." That ended the conversation, and Yoshi left, wondering how he had tolerated Ohana so long. Yoshi's course was set; there would be no change of plan. Ohana's dismissal gave Yoshi the excuse to say farewell to his friends and prepare for his departure.

The stage swords he left to Tsure, his costumes to Koetsu, his personal articles to the musician Ito, and a bolt of cloth, intended for Aki, he gave to Ume. He wished them good luck and shared their tears of sorrow. As the sky deepened from light blue to deepest black, he readied himself for the night's activity.

Yoshi took a real sword in place of the dull-edged stage prop and spent an hour polishing the blade to be sure it was at its sharpest. It felt good to work with decent steel. With a bittersweet pang, he recalled his happy days in the *dojo* and the pleasures inherent in doing a hard job well.

During Yoshi's last afternoon with the company, a messenger arrived with a box for Aki. It was decorated with Kiso's crest. Aki opened it before the company and smilingly removed a bolt of rich brocaded cloth. Then she read the enclosed message. Her face broke into a dozen harsh planes and angles. She turned away, sobbing, and ran to her dressing room. Yoshi understood. Kiso had discarded her with a gift of cloth—the wages of greed.

The night brought heavy clouds and the threat of a rare winter electrical storm. The air was charged, smelling of ozone. Strange how Yoshi's gods arranged moments of crisis on the nights when demons roared and threw their thunderbolts across the heavens . . .

Yoshi waited, looking across the crowded theater at the empty seats in the back. Had the threat of the storm changed Kiso's mind? Would he dare offend Go-Shirakawa?

The musicians finished their overture; reluctantly, Yoshi left his vantage point and joined the other actors for their entrance up the ramp onto the stage.

One half of the chorus sang the opening *Kagura*.

> "...As for Haya-Susa-no-wo
> He comes from the heavens
> With the sword of a god
> Haya-Susa-no-wo
> From the heavenly skies
> With the sword of a god."

And the other half answered:

> "Oh, how I wish for the sword of a god."

Yoshi briefly reflected on the irony of this *Kagura*, so apt an introduction to what he would do this night.

By a trick of atmospherics, the voices of the chorus rolled and reverberated from the earthen echo jars beneath the stage to the mass of ice-filled, electric-charged clouds above. The effect was a supernatural sonority. It was as if the old Shinto gods focused their powers on this tiny theater.

Haya-Susa-no-wo made his entrance, right leg raised, sword overhead. He stamped his foot and adopted the powerful *ki-badachi*, riding-horse stance. Tonight there was extra meaning in every move. The audience was transfixed by the power projected from the stage. Heavy clothes and frozen faces were forgotten. This was a transcendent moment of theater art, the infrequent aesthetic shock that must be zealously guarded and savored.

> *"When began the earth and heaven*
> *By the margin of the river . . ."*

Yoshi saw Kiso's seat being filled. Yoshi raised his voice in a paean of triumph. The walls trembled from the strength in his voice.

> *"Of the firmament eternal*
> *Met the gods in high assemble . . ."*

Haya-Susa-no-wo was again in performance . . . for the last time.

The electric storm held itself in abeyance, as though waiting for its cue. The air grew colder and more thickly charged. The audience was spellbound except for the dark men, who periodically inspected the theater and checked their swords.

The eightfold dragon was dispatched, and Haya-Susa-no-wo opened its belly to find the great sword *Kusanagi*. He delivered his final song:

> *"In the Palace at Kyoto*
> *The great seat of power Imperial*
> *God-like ruled the true descendant*
> *August High-Shining-Sun-Prince*
> *Mighty Prince if thou hast deigned*
> *This sublunar world to govern*
> *Thou hast been to all thy people*
> *Dear as are the flowers of spring*
> *As welcome as the rain from heaven*
> *All the nation does await thee . . ."*

The first flakes of snow fell on the upturned faces of the audience in the center pit, breaking the spell of the song.

The actors were confused. This was not the finale as rehearsed!

Yoshi continued, ignoring the snowflakes:

*"But at morn thy voice is heard not.
Days, weeks, months have passed in silence,
Till thy servants, sad and weary ..."*

The dark men rose from the audience.

"Strike a blow for peace and justice."

Yoshi's voice boomed from the stage, giving the password that signaled Yoritomo's men to action. Swords flashed in the lamp light, flicking snowflakes into decorative sprays. Sudden bursts of lightning and a roar of winter thunder came as if on cue from the spirits of the underworld.

A jagged flash of lightning struck the balcony behind Kiso and a tongue of flame licked out from a broken oil lamp. Fire, the most dreaded occurrence in a world of wood and paper. Fire!

Yoshi stood transfixed. The image of Kiso silhouetted against the bolt of lightning burned on his retina. The sign! The sign from the gods!

Courtiers and ladies screeched and scrambled in panic, running from the dreaded fire. The exits were jammed in a stampede of humanity that carried Yoritomo's swordsmen away from their target.

From the stage, Yoshi saw Kiso's dark figure rise and kick the seat cushions aside as he turned toward the exit. Yoshi called above the heads of the crowd, "Kiso, coward. Come back and meet your fate."

Kiso spun around in confusion. He stepped into the circle of growing fire, his narrow, saturnine face ghastly in the dancing light. His black silk robe blended into the moving shadows, making his white face an inhuman mask.

"Who calls to challenge me?" Kiso's voice rang over the cries of the audience.

"I, Tadamori-no-Yoshi of Suruga, who have sworn vengeance for the death of Santaro and the defilement of one dear to me."

"Yoshi? Suruga?" Kiso was dumbstruck. "Where are you? Which are you?"

Yoshi realized that in the unsteady light of the fire and falling snow the players were a solid indistinguishable mass.

The fire grew fiercer, but Kiso made no move to escape.

Rather, he edged forward to see his challenger.

"It is I, Haya-Susa-no-wo," Yoshi shouted, stepping forward to the apron of the stage, brandishing his sword overhead.

The crowd heaved, grunted, and squealed like varicolored pigs. Yoritomo's men struggled against them, trying to get near their target. Kiso did not move. He stood his ground, but between Kiso and Yoritomo's men was a boiling river of humanity.

"Come, then. Face me here," roared Kiso, slashing the air with his blade. "I am the demon warrior of Kiso and fear no man, god, or spirit."

Onstage, the cast was in turmoil. Aki collapsed. Ume was crying hysterically. Ito led old Obaasen away. Tsure and Koetsu struggled to hold Ohana, who was acting like a madman, shouting obscenities and trying to attack Yoshi from the rear. His mask had been torn from his face. His eyes shone red in the firelight; froth flecked his mouth and chin. Despite Ohana's small stature, he flung the two men back and forth as if they were dolls. He saw his dream destroyed, his theater collapsing around him. It was the fault of the vagabond, Suruga or Yoshi, or whatever accursed name he called himself.

As Yoshi prepared to leap from the stage into the crowd, Ohana broke loose. He tore the stage sword from Tsure's side and lunged at Yoshi's back. Koetsu's scream of warning cut through the din of the crowd. Yoshi turned to see Ohana descending on him with a sword. Reflexively, Yoshi struck across the mad eyes.

The sword tip cut Ohana's face from temple to temple. The wound spurted a mixture of blood and optic fluid that stained the snow-flecked stage. Ohana dropped his sword; he staggered forward, blindly clawing at the place where he had last seen Yoshi.

Yoshi stepped backward and fell from the stage into the surging mob. He caught one last glimpse of Kiso and his men, surrounded by flames, leading Go-Shirakawa and Nami out of the rear exit. He thought he saw Tomoe place herself between Nami and Kiso as if to shield her. Then they were gone from sight, and Yoshi was carried toward an exit and out into the street.

The plan had failed. Was this to be the result of his sign from the gods?

seventy-six

Kiso's silk court hat was askew. His robe had caught fire, and smudges of soot marked his smooth hard cheeks. The crooked hat and black smears combined to give his features an inhuman quality. He felt inhuman. Kiso was in a fury; Yoshi had been almost in his grasp! Yoshi had talked with him, mocking him all the while. Kiso's lips drew back, turning his face into a demon mask. He angrily pushed Go-Shirakawa ahead of him, and when Yukitaka protested, he struck the old man aside with his open hand.

Yukitaka fell back in shock. Kiso and his mountaineers had proved themselves barbarians a thousand times . . . but this was unheard of. Kiso had jostled the Emperor and struck his retainer. Truly, the latter days of the law were at hand.

"Bring her with us." Kiso's voice was distorted with rage.

Imai shoved Nami ahead while she struggled against him.

"Both of them into the palanquin," ordered Kiso.

The royal palanquin was waiting outside the theater. Thirty-two bearers, shivering in their scanty robes, nervously watched the threatening fire. They straightened to attention when the Emperor appeared.

"Tomoe, you will ride with the prisoners. Guard them well. Imai will follow you on his horse. Go to the house of the nun of Hahaki. I will ride ahead and tell the sentries to expect you."

When Go-Shirakawa had returned to Kyoto, he had placed the mansion of the nun of Hahaki at Kiso's disposal. It was located at Rokujo and Horikawa streets. The mansion belonged to a wealthy lady-in-waiting to the Empress Hachijo-In; its walls were high and thought to be impregnable. Kiso seldom used it, preferring the opulence of Rokuhara palace, on the far side of the Sanjo Bridge. The Hahaki nun's estate would be ideal as a place of confinement for the Emperor and Nami.

In the palanquin, Go-Shirakawa tightened his robe around himself and slumped against the shutters, moodily staring at the snow covered streets. Nami looked defiant, but a tremor at the corner of her mouth showed her fear. She was in Kiso's hands again.

Tomoe studied her face. "Have no fear, Nami. I will see that no evil befalls you."

Nami smiled weakly and nodded in acknowledgment of Tomoe's words. She said, "Tomoe, you are a kind friend, but you cannot speak for Kiso. He has harmed me in the past, and I do not trust him. He is mad with rage. Even you cannot control him."

"Nami, I said nothing will harm you. I will guard you with my life, upon my word as a samurai."

Go-Shirakawa turned to Tomoe. "You will be generously rewarded if you can save us."

"I seek no rewards. What I do I do in friendship."

"Nevertheless . . ."

Tomoe interrupted brusquely, "We are at the nun's house. Prepare to leave."

As soon as Go-Shirakawa, Nami, and Tomoe entered the palanquin, Kiso ordered the bearers to the nun's house. He viciously kicked his horse and galloped ahead of them. On the way to his destination, Kiso made several decisions. He had once fancied Nami for himself, but in Kyoto he had seldom seen her; Tomoe had interceded and made it impossible for him to approach her. Thinking about Nami rekindled his anger; she was Yoshi's woman, and though Yoshi had escaped again, Kiso could exact his vengeance through Nami. She would have to die. Kiso would have her head mounted on a stake in the public square for Yoshi to see.

As for the Emperor . . . he was too crafty a politician. With Yoritomo near the capital, Go-Shirakawa would have to be confined, under guard. Otherwise he might escape and join Yoritomo . . . giving Yoritomo more legitimacy. Go-Shirakawa claimed he spent his days reciting sutras and meditating. He could now prove it. No retainers, no servants, no visitors. Let him spend his time with his favorite Lotus Sutra. Let him demonstrate the depth of his religious commitment.

Kiso had a sudden realization that tonight had not been coincidence; Go-Shirakawa and Yoshi conspired together. Thinking back, he remembered the shadowy figures rising from the audience . . . Yoritomo's men. The lightning and the fire had saved him from the plot. An auspicious sign. The Emperor had tried to keep him from returning to his troops, but he had been saved by supernatural forces. Now he would lead his men to victory against Yoritomo.

The Uji River formed a natural barrier between the capital and the east. To reach Kyoto, there were only two places where Yoritomo's army could cross: the Seta Bridge at the mouth of Lake Biwa, and the Uji Bridge in the southeast. Yoritomo's troops approached the bridges in a pincer movement. After the military disasters at Mizushima and Muroyama, Kiso had sworn not to divide his army again. Now it seemed he would have no choice.

The plot became clear—Go-Shirakawa's demand that Kiso be honored at the archery contest was part of the plan to keep Kiso from leading his troops.

Another revelation—Go-Shirakawa arranged the archers' victory! How complex was the plot against him? Kiso cursed aloud and kicked his horse to vent his anger.

At Rokujo and Horikawa, Kiso arranged for a suite for the Emperor and a small well-guarded room in an outlying wing for Nami. She wouldn't need it very long. The palanquin arrived soon afterward and the guards led a protesting Go-Shirakawa to his suite.

Kiso ordered two samurai to escort Nami to her room. Tomoe started to follow them.

"Stop," ordered Kiso. "That will not be necessary. You are to go to Rokuhara and prepare for an early departure. We ride for Uji at dawn." He turned to his hard-faced second-in-command. "Imai, you will take charge of the army at Seta."

"Before you order me to Seta," said Imai, "I will speak my mind. Yoshi was in the theater. He is in Kyoto. My task should be to find and kill him."

"That is exactly what Yoritomo and Go-Shirakawa would want . . . for us to waste time chasing Yoshi about the city. No! If we do not personally command our troops, we will lose Kyoto to Yoritomo's forces. We cannot afford that. Our troops must fight and win. Yoritomo must be stopped at the bridges before he crosses the Ujigawa."

"Then will Yoshi escape unpunished?"

"No. My revenge will cost him more than his life. He'll wish he had died."

Tomoe felt a rush of apprehension. "What do you intend?"

"Never mind, woman. You need go to Rokuhara. I command here."

"As a samurai captain, I have a right to know." Tomoe's

dark features were set in a stubborn mold.

Kiso stared at Tomoe stonily. She was close to insubordination. Damn her to Yomi. She was samurai, but she was first a woman; why wouldn't she listen and obey his orders? He would have to reveal his plan or be embarrassed before Imai.

Kiso spoke calmly, patiently. It required effort. "We cannot wait for Yoshi to reappear. We are needed at Uji. Yoshi will come searching for us. When he finds this mansion and Nami, I want him to find her head waiting. She will die tonight, before we leave."

"No! I gave my word that no harm would befall her. Kill her, and you must kill me."

Imai interrupted. "Sister, please. Kiso is right. The woman's death will be our revenge. Her life means nothing. We will kill her and concentrate on defeating Yoritomo. You understand . . ."

"I understand that you and Kiso are like children, thinking only of revenge. Fight Yoritomo, and I'll fight beside you. Make me dishonor my word and, brother or not, you will fight me to the death."

Kiso blew out his lips in exasperation. "There is no time for disagreement. Tomorrow we face a major battle. Tomoe, if you find it necessary to disobey my direct order, you will not fight at Uji. You will stay behind and guard the prisoners. When Imai and I return victorious, we will speak again. I want Yoshi. The woman can live . . . temporarily."

"I deserve to fight at your side. You shame me by leaving me behind."

"Enough! You will come with me only if the woman dies. She is my hold on Yoshi. If you disobey me because of her, you cannot be trusted to fight beside me." Kiso paused, drew in a long breath, and added as an afterthought, "To fight with me and perhaps die gloriously, sacrifice Nami."

Tomoe's mouth set in a rigid line. "I gave my word," she said. "I will remain here. Damn you to the Avichi hell. I've always loved you and fought for you. You push me away when you need me the most. Change your mind. Let Nami live and let me ride with you to glory."

"If she dies, you ride."

"So be it." Tomoe turned away from Kiso and strode, stiff-backed, from the room.

Kiso's lip curled in anger and frustration. Tomoe's defection was an inauspicious sign. He felt the stab of rejection. Kiso

had never fought without Tomoe and Imai flanking him. Tomorrow, Imai would go to Seta and Kiso would ride to Uji
alone.

Kiso cleared his throat and said huskily, "Imai, let's not
wait for morning. Let us put on honest armor and ride tonight."

For hours, Yoshi and the others fought the fire that blazed
through every part of the theater. The freak electrical storm
passed as quickly as it had come. Shortly before dawn, a sporadic snowstorm arrived and the fire died down. Puffs of smoke
and steam rose from the blackened stumps of the stage supports
as thick snowflakes hit the remaining embers.

Koetsu, his face covered with soot, his hands blistered from
the heat, paused and wiped his face with a charred sleeve. He
succeeded in smearing the soot further. "It's no use," he said
to Yoshi, who was working at his side. "There is nothing left
worth saving."

"At least the fire was confined to the theater and no one
was hurt," said Yoshi.

Koetsu gave him a searching look. "Except for Ohana," he
said.

"Amida, yes. I must help him. Where is he?"

"Too late. Aki led him away hours ago. He will be blind
if he lives."

"Buddha forgive me. Much as I disliked him, he was not
my target."

"Ohana was crazed. I saw him. If you had not protected
yourself, he would have killed you."

"Yet..."

"You cannot blame yourself. He was at fault."

"Without Ohana, what will you and the others do?"

"We have little choice. We will stay together and rebuild
the theater. You have shown us the way. We will continue
your work. I will act as manager, and Ume will assume Aki's
role. We have very little money, but with persistence we will
succeed."

"Though I must leave you, I'll help in any way I can," said
Yoshi.

"The man you challenged, where did he go?" asked Koetsu.

"If I knew, I would have followed." Yoshi continued in an
abstracted tone, "I feel our paths are destined to cross in the
near future."

At that moment, one of the acrobats approached and whispered to Koetsu. "An old man waits in the street," said Koetsu. "He asks to talk to you. He says it is important."

Yoshi's brow furrowed. An old man?

"I'll return as quickly as I can," Yoshi said.

Yukitaka stood in the snow next to an oxcart. "You must act at once," he said without preamble. "Imperial guards followed the royal palanquin to the nun of Hahaki's estate. The Emperor and your wife are being held there as prisoners. Kiso and Imai have gone to fight against Yoritomo's army. You must ride at once and rescue the Emperor and the Lady Nami from Kiso's guards."

Yoshi rode one of the acting company's horses toward Sixth Street and the nun of Hahaki's house. He arrived as the first rays of Amaterasu fanned up from the eastern horizon.

Yoshi was too late. The house and grounds were deserted. He cursed under his breath and turned back toward the northeast quarter.

After Kiso and Imai rode to their destinies, Tomoe went directly to Nami's quarters in the north wing. She found Nami kneeling on a floor mat with her eyes closed, her face as still as death; her delicately carved features were waxen in the light of a single tripod oil lamp.

"Dear Nami, forgive us the pain we've caused you," said Tomoe.

Nami's eyes opened slowly. She stared ahead as if in a dream. "Yoshi was so close," she said at last. "I thought..."

"I know," said Tomoe, taking Nami's hand. "Do not despair. You will be with him soon."

"Fate conspires against us. Mystical powers influence Yoshi's passage through this cycle. What could he have done in his previous life to cause this strange Karma?"

"All will be well," said Tomoe, distracted by the sorrow on Nami's face.

"How can it be well? I belong with Yoshi. Yet whenever I am with him, more tragedy occurs."

"And I belong with Kiso. He rode south to join his troops at Uji. My brother rode east to Seta. I was left to guard you . . . but my place is with Kiso, fighting back to back. I must join him, though I fear our cause is lost. Despite his mistakes, I cannot desert him when I know his last days are at hand." Tomoe swallowed and brushed at her eyes with the sleeve of her court robe. She continued, speaking softly, gently, "I will order the guards to the bridges of Seta and Uji. When they leave, I will join Kiso in his last battle. Go to Go-Shirakawa and lead him away from this accursed house."

"I can't allow you to do this, much as I cherish the thought of freedom. Releasing us will be a betrayal of the one you love. Kiso will never forgive you."

"He will never know what I have done. I will tell him you are safely captive and well guarded."

"Tomoe, when he returns and finds us gone . . ."

Tomoe clutched Nami's hand tightly. "Kiso is doomed," she said. "His army is a travesty. They cannot stand against the combined forces of Yoritomo, Yoshitsune, Noriyori, the Miuras, the Dois, and the Ochiais. I am joining him so I may die honorably by his side."

"Tomoe, please stay with me and save yourself."

"I cannot." Tomoe rose to her feet. "As soon as I have changed these court robes and donned proper warrior's armor, I ride to Uji. Perhaps Kiso will think to use the same tactic Yoshi once used—dismantle the bridge and hold off the superior army."

"Yoshi lost that battle of Uji."

"We may win. Our mountaineers are hardy stock, the best samurai in the world."

Nami rose to face Tomoe and held her arms out to her.

They clung to each other for several seconds, then Tomoe released Nami and said briskly, "Within a half hour. I will dismiss the men from guard duty. They will be eager to ride with me to glory."

So it was that shortly before dawn Nami led Go-Shirakawa through the barred gate of the nun's estate and into the street.

They raised their faces to the dark sky and felt snowflakes on their cheeks and tongues, the taste of freedom.

"I am unaccustomed to walking," said the Emperor, "but if you will lead the way, I will follow."

They had started the trek down the wide street to the Imperial enclosure when they heard a drumbeat of hooves approaching behind them. The Emperor and Nami hastily withdrew to the side of the street, seeking shelter from the pursuer. In the dim light, Nami tried to identify the rider. She held out her arm to urge Go-Shirakawa to silence as the rider drew closer.

Her heart lifted when she saw who it was. "Yoshi," she cried. "Yoshi, we are here."

seventy-seven

The scene evoked a vision of the coldest hell of Yomi's underworld. The Uji River, fed by underground springs from the mountains around Lake Biwa, flooded its banks in a rushing, roaring, tumbling torrent. Sixty thousand horsemen milled and stamped on the eastern bank. Retainers scurried from group to group with messages. Supply carts skidded on the icy banks. Shouts, the clang of arms and armor, whinnying horses, and complaining oxen added to the confusion. The scene was lit by the cold three-quarter moon of the twenty-second day of the first lunar month of 1184. Bedlam. Cacophony. Chaos.

General Yoshitsune, younger brother of the clan leader Yoritomo, commanded the army at Uji. Yoshitsune was a brave but relatively inexperienced general. His men reached the river bank in a frenzy of enthusiasm. Yoshitsune's orders to hold firm went unheard in the noise and confusion. He lost control of his army; soldiers and horses plunged into the icy waters by the thousands, to be swept away by the powerful current.

The bridge across the Uji had been dismantled. Kiso's men had removed it plank by plank. They followed the example of Yoshi, who, four years earlier, had used the same tactic to hold off Lord Chikara's superior forces.

Inspired by Yoshi's tactics at Hiuchi-yama, Kiso's men planted underwater stakes and stretched a thick rope along the length of the river. Those of Yoshitsune's men who passed the center of the torrent were blocked by the rope barrier until they, too, were swept away.

The sun rose, lighting the scene more fully. The morning was filled with the cries of men and animals caught by the treacherous waters.

The wild spirit of Yoshitsune's soldiers was not to be denied. The threat of death lay on their shoulders with less weight than a feather. They vied with each other to be the first to cross the Uji, and in their excess of spirits, friends tricked one another to win that honor.

Hatakeyama, an old warrior, was first to succeed. As he reached the far bank, a voice called to him from behind. He turned to see a young man named Oguchi struggling against the current, blood trailing like a long pennant from a shoulder wound. Oguchi's horse had been swept downstream, and Oguchi, weakened from loss of blood, would surely suffer the same fate.

Hatakeyama, having known the young samurai since childhood, went back into the river, reached out, and lifted him ashore. Standing on the bank, Oguchi drew his sword with his good arm, and announced, "I, Oguchi Shigechika, born in the province of Musashi, loyal servant to Minamoto Yoritomo, declare myself first to reach the bank of the Uji on foot."

Hundreds of others joined Hatakeyama and Oguchi . . . and on they came, regardless of their lives. Many tumbled downstream like cherry blossoms tossed on the racing river; many others reached the far shore and challenged Kiso's defenders to individual combat. Hundreds of pairs fought with *naginata*, swords, and even daggers. Men slashed wildly as they slid on a surface of mud, icy slush, and blood.

By ten o'clock, Kiso's army had lost; their morale was not strong enough to sustain them in the face of overwhelming numbers.

Kiso and Tomoe fought bravely. Each killed more than a dozen men. Back to back, they fought against the best of the enemy. Tomoe was clad in blue and silver man's armor. Her hair, so recently combed and scented, was carelessly pulled back by a rope *hachimaki*. It whipped around her face in the cold morning wind as she protected her lover's back against a score of attackers.

One horn of Kiso's golden helmet, knocked askew by a war arrow, gave him a rakish air. His red brocaded *hitatare* was slit in a half-dozen places, and he had suffered a myriad of minor wounds, but his Chinese armor had held up well under the onslaught of his enemies.

As Kiso smashed his blade through the helmet of an attacker, splitting the man's skull from top to chin, he shouted to Tomoe, "I'm glad you came to join me. Without you, I am incomplete."

In the din of challenges, cries of the wounded, and the clash of arms, Tomoe barely heard him. "How could I not come, my lord?" she answered over her shoulder as she completed a butterfly stroke that sank deep into the armpit of an opponent.

"The guards will care for the prisoners." She lied with a clear conscience. Kiso would never know the truth. They were doomed to die.

Before Tomoe's opponent fell to the cold ground, another took up the challenge. As she parried his attack, she heard Kiso call to her. "We were wrong to separate. Imai deserved to fight this last battle with me. We should have fought and died together."

Tomoe responded, "I don't want to die without my brother. The battle is lost, and I grow tired. Let us fight our way out while we have the strength. We can ride north to join Imai. Then let the gods decide our fate."

"Well said, Tomoe." Kiso, instead of merely holding his ground, opened a demonic attack against the man in front of him. His blade flashed in an unpredictable pattern of steel. "Follow me," he ordered.

They gained ground, slowly at first, then more rapidly as they fought out of the center of the melee.

Once in the clear, Kiso looked back to see that, indeed, the battle was lost, as were his dreams. He was *shogun*. His ambition had been realized, and so quickly turned to ashes. Mounds of dead men and horses filled the icy field. More attackers poured across the Uji. The defenders shrank to small pockets of two or three men, fighting against hundreds who swarmed around them. In one quick glance, Kiso saw more of his samurai being overrun by Yoshitsune's men.

"North to join Imai," Kiso cried as he reached the tree where his gray charger and Tomoe's horse were tethered.

As Kiso and Tomoe galloped away, there was a shout behind them.

"Kiso escapes!" The shout turned to a roar. "Follow him. Don't let him get away!"

The sky was thick with roiling clouds. Although it was only midafternoon, the day was dark as night. Kiso and Tomoe drove their mounts through icy rice paddies and frozen fields, through thick forest and dense bamboo groves. They had lost their pursuers an hour earlier, but though the distance to Seta was not great, they constantly backtracked and hid when they sighted groups searching the countryside.

Kiso slumped forward in his gold-embossed saddle. He was fatigued and worn from the bleeding of a dozen small wounds, and he was dispirited by running from battle. The energy that drove him at the Uji had sapped away during the hours of hiding and dodging.

Tomoe's tough mountain horse stepped lightly alongside Kiso's huge gray charger. Though Tomoe's armor had been scored and dented in many places, she had suffered no wounds. Kiso's emblem on a white Minamoto field was tightly furled on a flagstaff attached to her saddle.

"Come, Kiso. Courage," she said. "We cannot lose more time. We must reach Seta before nightfall."

Kiso forced himself erect. He had thrown off the helmet that marked him as leader; his hair was wild, his axelike features drawn and heavy with sorrow. His eyes, which usually burned like coals, were dull and apathetic.

"I was wrong. We should not have separated from Imai," he muttered. "We'll never find him. Perhaps he died at Seta without us. A bad omen. We swore to live and die together . . . and I sent him away."

"We must not give up," Tomoe insisted.

Gusts of wind drove thick snowflakes horizontally along the ground. The riders could see little more than a few *cho* before them as the horses plodded on. They had been driven northwest of Seta and approached the bridge from the shore of Lake Biwa at Otsu.

"Stop!" Tomoe hissed under her breath. She pulled her horse to a halt. Someone was crossing the field at the boundaries of her vision.

Kiso waited apathetically.

"One man," said Tomoe with spirit. "Let him come closer and we'll take his head."

Yoshi reached Uji Bridge soon after Yoshitsune's men succeeded in crossing the river. He was on the western bank and joined the battle in its earliest stages. In the first minutes of battle, his horse was struck by an arrow and collapsed under him. The gods' sign of lightning and fire at the theater had released Yoshi from his vow, and now he leaped from the dying horse and fought on foot in a kind of ecstatic trance. As he wielded his blade, he searched for Kiso among the enemy. In the disorder of the field, he searched in vain.

Yoshi announced his challenge repeatedly. "I, Tadamori-no-Yoshi of Suruga province, challenge the traitor called Kiso to single combat in the name of the Emperor and Lord Minamoto Yoritomo." The noise and confusion at the battlefield

were so great, he was heard only by the few immediately around
him. Many accepted the challenge, but Kiso was not among
them. Yoshi wore no armor, his sleeves were slit, his robe
torn, but he fought with the speed of a divine *kami,* and no
sword or *naginata* touched his flesh. He was covered with
blood . . . the blood of his opponents smeared, spurted, and
sprayed as he left them dead on the icy ground.

"Kiso, Kiso!" he shouted again and again. There was no
response.

Yoshi's blade whistled through the air in deadly patterns,
cutting through his opponents as though flesh were paper. He
moved with godlike grace, impervious to the men around him.
Still, he searched for one special opponent.

The battle swung in favor of Yoshitsune's superior numbers.
Kiso's defenders were isolated in small groups. It was the hour
of the snake, ten in the morning. Yoshi withdrew from the
battle and surveyed the trampled field. There he was! Kiso!
Running toward his horse, with a smaller samurai behind him.
Yoshi gave the alarm. "Kiso escapes! Follow him. Don't let
him get away!"

Yoshi tore across the field after the escaping *shogun.* Kiso
was too far away. There had been only two horses tied to the
tree; Kiso and his companion had taken them and fled.

Yoshi raced headlong back toward the battle. He must find
a horse.

"Imai! It is Imai," said Tomoe with dark intensity. Kiso sat
up as if prodded by a sword. His woebegone expression disappeared. "Imai, Imai," he shouted triumphantly as he rode
into the wind toward his foster-brother, his eyes stinging from
the cold and emotion.

Imai stood high in his stirrups; he threw his head back and
roared with joy, "Kiso! Tomoe!"

"I feared for you alone at Seta," said Kiso. "I could not die
without knowing your fate. Imai, friend, brother, I left my
troops to come to your side."

"How much your care means to me," said Imai. "My men
face General Noriyori alone because I feared you would die
without me."

Tomoe studied one, then the other. She marveled at the
tears coursing down their faces, the hard-planed broad face of
her brother and the narrow hawklike face of her lover. She felt

the moisture at her own eyes. They rode close and clasped each other joyfully.

Tomoe recovered from the grip of emotion. She wiped her cheeks with her sleeve and said, "Now that we are together, let us unfurl our flag and rally those of our followers who live. Let us die gloriously together."

Kiso passed his sleeve across his face and looked to Imai. They were as one—one thought, one heart. Imai nodded agreement, though Kiso had not spoken.

"No, Tomoe. You must ride for your life. Our vow is to each other...not to you."

"You cannot exclude me. I fought as bravely as any man. I proved myself today. Without me, you would not have been reunited in Seta."

"Nevertheless, it is not fitting for me to die in battle with a woman at my side." Kiso motioned to Imai with his head. They spurred their chargers and galloped away, leaving Tomoe in the field.

"You cannot lose me so easily. I've earned my place with you," Tomoe shouted after them. She unfurled the white flag on her saddle and kicked her horse into action, following their path.

At the outskirts of Seta, Kiso surveyed a scene of carnage that surpassed any he had ever seen before. Of the eight thousand men who had been under Imai's command, three hundred remained. Clouds rolled close to the ground and clear patches over the battlefield revealed bodies and parts of bodies trampled into the icy ground by panic-stricken riderless horses.

Imai rose in his saddle and announced in a stentorian roar, "Lord Kiso of Shinano has returned. Brave warriors, join us in our final glory."

From the bloody field, men disengaged themselves from individual combat and joined Kiso and Imai. Among the warriors who remained alive were the brothers Jiro and Taro. They rode to Kiso's side, slashing left and right at Noriyori's men, who clustered around them like flies on carrion.

"Ho, Kiso," shouted Taro. "Now we will show these dogs how the men of Shinano fight."

"How many are we?" demanded Kiso.

"Less than three hundred," was the response.

"And the enemy?"

"More than six thousand."

"Then the battle is fair. Follow me!" Kiso waved his sword overhead, pointed it at the enemy, and galloped directly at the center of the six thousand. His mouth was open in a demonic grimace. Men fell back before the raw power shining from his eyes.

"Kiso Yoshinaka," he cried. "I am lord of Iyo, lord of Shinano, *shogun* of the Empire. Stand and fight if you dare."

Three hundred ravening engines of destruction hit the center of six thousand armored, disciplined fighting men; only fifty reached the other side. They burst out in an orgy of killing, of heads, arms, and legs, sliced and chopped.

As Kiso gathered the wounded remnants of his force, two thousand fresh troops appeared from the fog at the river's edge. "I am Doi-no-Sanehira. Where is the so-called demon warrior? Let him face me," proclaimed Sanehira, their leader.

The challenge was issued and Kiso's fifty survivors spurred forward in a death charge. Heedless of life and limb, the worn, battered, wounded mountaineers flailed their swords in an impenetrable wall of steel. Sanehira's men tried to close on them, only to fall back before their reckless fury.

Kiso led the way through the wall of men a second time. When he reached the other side, he counted five left of the original thousands.

Noriyori's men and Doi Sanehira's men held their mounts in respectful silence, waiting for Kiso's next move.

The afternoon light disappeared. Fog rolled in, mercifully covering the dead and dying. Kiso raised his gray charger on its hind legs. The horse whinnied wildly and turned around three times. Two thousand men of Doi Sanehira on Kiso's right, six thousand of Noriyori on his left. Kiso studied his companions; there was brave Imai, there was Jiro and Taro, and there was Tomoe, with a streak of blood running from her hairline into the neck of her armor jacket.

Kiso calmed his mount and turned to Tomoe. He leaned from his saddle to thrust his face close to hers. "You will leave us now," he ordered in a voice that brooked no discussion. "I will not be shamed before my enemies by dying with a woman. I have always loved you..." his voice choked on the words "...but my honor will not allow this. You must go."

Tomoe's gaze moved from one face to the other. "Imai, my brother..." she said. He turned away. "Jiro, Taro, we are comrades." They refused to meet her eyes.

She snarled, "Be shamed when you see the death I die." Tomoe kicked her horse and charged at a group of thirty samurai who had edged forward in the fog. "I am Tomoe Gozen," she screeched as she bore down on the leader, "braver than a hundred men. Face me if you dare!"

"I am Onda-no Hachiro Moroshige," answered the leader hastily, "captain in the service of Yoritomo. No woman can face me."

He had scarcely finished his declaration when Tomoe crashed into his horse, knocking him to the ground. As he rose, half-dazed, she yelled like a doomed spirit, twisted his head against her saddle and, with a vicious slice of her short killing sword, took his head.

She was immediately overwhelmed by Moroshige's followers. Two held her while the rest raced to battle Kiso. One of her captors pulled her head back by the hair to expose her throat. Tomoe opened her eyes to look at her killer and spit in his face.

seventy-eight

Yoshi arrived at the battleground with a score of General Miura's men. They had searched for Kiso in the foggy lowlands until the sounds of combat drew them to Seta Bridge. They reached the field in time to see Jiro and Taro fall to arrows from the bows of Onda Moroshige's soldiers.

"There!" shouted Yoshi, pointing. "Kiso!"

Kiso and Imai separated, and Kiso spurred his charger into the fog toward the pine forest of Awazu. Imai guided his mount in a tight circle, challenging the surrounding soldiers.

Imai was a brave sight, floating above the mist. His horse reared and snorted wildly, kicking up streamers of white vapor. "Imai Shirō-no-Kanehira am I," shouted Imai. "Foster-brother of the *shogun*, Kiso Yoshinaka. Take my head if you dare."

One of Onda Moroshige's men accepted the challenge. Yoshi was riding toward Imai when he saw the samurai who held his blade to Tomoe's throat. "Stop," he ordered, and leaped from his horse. He caught the samurai's arm in a grip of steel. Yoshi applied pressure to the man's elbow. "I am General Tadamori-no-Yoshi," he said. "I order you to release her."

The samurai rose with bad grace but, recognizing Yoshi's rank, withdrew.

Yoshi lifted Tomoe to her feet.

"Kill me," she demanded.

"No. You saved Nami's life and now I will repay you."

"You can only repay me if you let Kiso and my brother live."

"That is not within my power," said Yoshi firmly.

"Then let me die at my brother's side."

There was a shout of triumph from the battlefield. Tomoe and Yoshi saw Imai, high in the saddle, holding aloft the head of one of Onda Moroshige's samurai.

"Second to Kiso, I am the mightiest warrior alive. Let me show you how I can die." Imai threw the head in the face of an advancing samurai, placed his short sword in his mouth, and jumped face first from his horse. The blade drove through the back of his throat and up into his skull with enough force to penetrate the steel helmet at the back of his head.

Tomoe's mouth quivered as she saw her brother die. "So brave, but so foolish," she cried. "I do not fear death, but to die that way serves no purpose. I choose life . . . and Yoshi . . ."

"Yes, Tomoe?"

"Repay me for Nami's life with another favor."

"Anything within my power."

"Don't take Kiso's head. Let him die with dignity."

"I can promise that."

Tomoe threw off her armor and disappeared into the fog at the edge of the clearing.

Kiso guided his gray charger through the Awazu pine forest. The energy that burned like a sun in his belly and upheld him against his enemies was spent, a dull ember that scarcely left him the strength to control the gray.

Imai's last words to him echoed in his mind as he rode: "Since we both will die today, we have satisfied our vows. Let me fight them alone while you escape to the woods and end your life in peace."

He should not have deserted Imai. He was confused by the rush of events. He should not . . . and he recalled all that he should not have done. The list was endless. He had developed from a half-starved mountaineer to *shogun* of the Empire and had allowed greed, lust, and sloth to undo him.

Night settled. Fog drifted among the pines, making the path treacherous. It was difficult to know if he rode on solid ground or on the frozen surfaces of the small ponds that abounded in the area. Tumbled rocks made dangerous footing. In places, thin ice crackled as the horse passed. Kiso guided the gray by instinct, feeling his way through the medium of the horse's hooves. Fatigued and depressed as he was, his senses were alert. He was aware of a wild monkey screeching miles away, of small animals close by crashing through the underbrush, of an owl hooting from a pine overhead, of snow falling from the branches as he passed . . . but no pursuers.

How could he have left Imai? Again he heard Imai's words. "Let me fight them alone," Imai had begged, "while you escape to the woods and end your life in peace." Imai had pleaded for the chance to prove himself and to save his foster-brother from the indignity of dying at the hands of an ordinary samurai. Kiso smiled thinly as he remembered the bravado in Imai's voice when he said, "I, Imai Shirō-no-Kanehira, can fight a thousand ordinary men. Let me hold them at bay."

Kiso's smile turned sour. Imai had been a rough, unpolished mountaineer, but if loyalty and bravery brought a higher place on the wheel of destiny, he would return in the next cycle as Emperor.

Kiso urged the gray out of the pines and onto a broad field. Thick mist rolled along the ground, covering it as far as the eye could see. Tsukiyomi's quarter face lit the fields with an eerie pale light. The mist absorbed the light to create a milky opaque carpet. In the distance, a farmhouse was brightly etched against the stars. Wind cut through the pines, whipping up tendrils of fog and biting through the back of Kiso's armor. Dogs barked from the farmhouse. Although the dogs were fully ten *cho* away, they sensed Kiso's presence and reacted to the scent of blood.

Kiso would run no more. The enemy was miles behind. The peaceful death Imai had bequeathed him was at hand. He would cross the clearing, find a secluded corner, and end his life with dignity.

The quiet night was disturbed by a shout from the pine woods. Kiso turned in his saddle to see a horseman galloping toward him. Kiso's eyes widened for one split second. The figure that descended on him was a reincarnation of the terrible war god, Fudo. The horseman stood in his stirrups, sword raised, catching the moon's rays on its circling blade.

"Ki-i-i-s-s-s-o-o-o!" The cry would have frozen the blood of a lesser man, but it served to stir Kiso from his lethargy. He recognized the voice and knew at once . . . Yoshi had found him.

And he had found Yoshi!

His energy flared with an otherworldly light. Kiso's domineering face, sharp-planed features set in a mask of death, turned to Yoshi with a snarl. "Yoshi," he grunted in acknowledgment as Yoshi drove his mount full force into the gray charger.

There was a crash of metal on metal, leather on leather, flesh on flesh, as both riders were thrown to the ground. Kiso landed on his shoulder and back. He saw Yoshi spin in midair and roll on the ground with an acrobat's precision. Kiso forced himself to rise. Yoshi, with superhuman speed, was already at him, delivering the windcutter stroke.

Kiso deflected the blade at the last moment. Steel rang on

steel. There was a smell of death and decay in the field; the
ground was invisible under its mantle of fog. Kiso breathed
heavily; a wreath of mist formed from his nostrils.

Kiso retaliated against Yoshi's first attack with a series of
strokes that wove a pattern of steel around him. The blade
moved so quickly, it held the reflected moonlight and seemed
a solid wall.

Yoshi fell back until Kiso's attack was over, then he answered with a vicious water-wheel to Kiso's head, followed
by a torso-splitter, and a reverse figure eight. The strength and
speed of Yoshi's attack was awesome, but by reaching deep
into his soul for strength, Kiso parried every stroke.

The two blades locked and the men glared into each other's
eyes. Vapor from their breath merged into one cloud that surrounded their faces as each pressed for the advantage, searching
for the weakness in the other's defense. Kiso's features were
drawn into an expression of hate and determination. Yoshi's
square-jawed face remained calm and icily cold.

"I should have killed you the first time we met at Hikuma,"
grunted Kiso as they swayed back and forth, locked in their
death struggle.

Yoshi responded by increasing the pressure against Kiso's
sword arm. Suddenly, Kiso fell back, disengaged his blade,
and used it to sweep at Yoshi's ankles.

Yoshi leaped over the silver arc and thrust the point of his
blade, as though it were a *naginata*, at Kiso's breastplate. The
unorthodox tactic caught Kiso by surprise. He barely escaped
as the point was deflected by his armor.

Despite the biting wind, picking and prying at the chinks
in his armor, Kiso began to sweat. He had never known fear
and he did not recognize it, but something set his hands to
trembling; his throat was in the grip of a mighty fist that made
him gasp for breath. Kiso fell back again and again. What was
wrong? Was he losing heart...feeling guilt for what he had
done to Yoshi...and to Nami? Impossible. He was Kiso, *shogun* of the Empire, the demon warrior! His lips curled back,
exposing his teeth in a wolflike snarl, and he launched another
attack.

Yoshi parried and blocked with a minimum of effort; his
face showed no strain, no emotion beyond cold detachment.
Kiso felt Yoshi studying him as if he were a fly waiting to
have its wings torn off. Now...Kiso realized he felt fear.

When they had first clashed, they were equal. Kiso had

been confident his skill would quickly dispatch his enemy. As their battle progressed and Kiso's every move was anticipated, the balance of power shifted to Yoshi. Yoshi's unearthly calm and his supernatural speed made Kiso feel he fought a ghost, a terrible *kami* who demanded revenge for the weaker souls Kiso had wronged.

Sweat popped out on Kiso's brow and froze in the chill wind. His fingers refused to obey his commands. He looked over a rolling sea of mist, empty except for the demon that attacked and counterattacked effortlessly... Kiso trembled. His mouth hung open as he tried to suck in enough air. He told himself he would not succumb to fear... he was Kiso, who had won a thousand duels; if he were to lose this time, he would face death bravely. He screamed his war cry and launched his final attack; a sequence that had never before failed to overcome his opponent. Yoshi easily side-stepped the glittering steel. He seemed to float like an evil dream on the carpet of mist.

Kiso stopped in despair. Was there no way to kill the *kami?* Yoshi came closer, gliding smoothly through the milky carpet of mist, his sword raised overhead. Kiso had one move left... a technique he had practiced for years but had never used. A technique of desperation, unorthodox, unexpected; it could not fail.

Kiso shifted his grip to the blade, pointed his sword at Yoshi's chest, and threw it like a spear with all the strength at his command. The sword flew straight as an arrow. Kiso felt the power in his arm, the trueness of his throw. The sword could not miss.

Kiso extended his entire body, tensing his abdominal muscles with a grunt that was guaranteed to squeeze the last ounce of strength from his tiring body. His triumphant yell became a moan. Yoshi did not even move his feet, only twisted sideways. The sword spear passed harmlessly by his chest to disappear in the mist.

Kiso's eyes widened. Yoshi smiled! A humorless smile, colder than the night.

Kiso sank to his knees; his strength gone. He felt he was in the presence of a supernatural spirit. He was afraid... but he struggled to control his fear. He was Kiso Yoshinaka; he would die as bravely as he had lived.

He raised his eyes and composed himself in the face of the

angel of death. He handed Yoshi his short killing sword. "Kill me," he said. "I am ready."

There was a faint clatter of horses and armor from the pines of Awazu. Soldiers approached from the south.

Yoshi studied Kiso, kneeling in the mist, his throat exposed to the killing blade. Kiso had fought bravely and well. There were times during their battle when Yoshi had doubted his ability to win, but sloth and easy living had taken their toll on Kiso's strength.

Yoshi recalled what Kiso had done to Nami, to Santaro, and to the cause of Yoritomo. Kiso had destroyed the unity of the Minamoto clan. Single-handedly, he had almost lost Yoritomo the Empire. Yoshi lifted the blade, waiting for Kiso to flinch, to quiver, to beg for mercy.

Nothing.

Kiso watched Yoshi calmly. Now Yoshi questioned: his vow? the sign? the stroke of lightning? the fire? Did the gods release him from his vow? He had fought and killed at Uji and felt a divine rapture at steel cutting through flesh. Yes! Yoshi had been freed from his vows, and the moment of retribution was at hand. Kiso was his.

Yoshi thought of Tomoe, saving Nami, loving Kiso, begging for Kiso's right to die with dignity. He studied Kiso and saw the cruelty and arrogance behind the narrow features and calm eyes. And he saw the bravery and loyalty to his comrades...Kiso was the best and the worst of the samurai.

But to kill in battle was not the same as killing a defenseless man. Yoshi would not do it. Someone else would kill Kiso. Yoshi flicked his blade past Kiso's throat.

Kiso did not flinch; he glared defiantly at Yoshi.

Yoshi snapped his blade into its sheath.

Kiso's eyes widened. "What are you doing?" he asked. "Kill me. You've won. I have nothing to live for."

"Take your horse and ride north to Tomoe," said Yoshi. "I grant you your life on her behalf."

"No. No! You cannot do this. You dishonor me. I lost in single combat. You must take my head."

"Go."

"Damn you to Yomi. Take my life. My four kings are dead, my foster-brother, Imai...I have only my honor left. Kill me...please."

Yoshi turned away and walked to Kiso's gray charger. He

led the horse to where Kiso knelt with tears shining on his cheeks. "Go!" Yoshi repeated. He left the reins at Kiso's feet.

"Please," pleaded Kiso. "Take my head."

Yoshi mounted his horse.

"At least leave me a sword so I can take my own life."

Yoshi guided his horse toward the misty Awazu pines. The sounds of horses and men were closer. They would be out of the forest and into the field in minutes.

"Go while you can," Yoshi called over his shoulder for the last time.

With a curse, Kiso mounted his gray and turned north. Yoshi would regret this insult. If he had to accept his life as an unwanted gift, he would use it to make Yoshi rue this day. Kiso started across the field as the soldiers rode out of the pines.

Kiso urged his mount to a slow gallop. Underfoot, ice crackled; he was on one of the myriad of frozen lakes. Behind him, Kiso heard a soldier call a challenge.

"Who rode away?" the soldier asked.

"No one of importance," was Yoshi's reply.

"It's one of Kiso's men," cried the samurai, and kicked his horse around Yoshi, following Kiso's path.

"I am Miura-no-Tamehisa of Sagami," the samurai shouted. "Coward, stand and face me if you dare."

Kiso tried to turn the gray to face his challenger only to feel the frozen lake crack underfoot. With a high-pitched shriek, the horse sank to the withers in black icy water. Kiso kicked it and cursed. This was not how he wanted to die, without a weapon, drowned in a rice field. He wanted to live more than ever to avenge himself against Yoshi.

The gray floundered against the jagged ice, sinking deeper into the frozen ooze of the lake bed. Kiso raised himself out of his saddle and looked back to find his pursuer.

Miura-no-Tamehisa let loose a war arrow from horseback. It struck Kiso's face under his helmet. The arrow sank in at the center of the arrogant nose and drove out through the back of the helmet in a spray of red and gray particles that froze in the frigid air and spread like an otherworldly mist around his upright figure.

Kiso slumped over the horse's neck and slipped off to disappear into the black water. The horse screeched wildly until a merciful arrow silenced its screams and it sank to join its master.

Tamehisa reined in his horse alongside Yoshi as they watched Kiso and his gray charger sink beneath the ice. Tamehisa said, "That man wore Kiso's crest. Do you know who he was?"

"No one important," answered Yoshi. "It is not worth getting wet to collect his head."

seventy-nine

It had been three weeks since the defeat of Kiso Yoshinaka's army by his cousin Yoritomo.

Kyoto was in a state of celebration. There were some in the court whose joy was tempered by the fear that Yoritomo's army of occupation, under the generals Yoshitsune and Noriyori, would be no less ill-mannered and unruly than Kiso's. Their fears were unfounded. Yoritomo's well-disciplined men were firmly controlled by Yoritomo himself.

The eleventh day of the second month of 1184 was the official day of examination at the Great Council. Go-Shirakawa and Yoritomo knelt side by side on the center dais at the Great Council Hall. On this day, officials who were being considered for promotion from the sixth to the fifth rank—a giant step from minor to major councillor—were interrogated by the Great Ministers. If the officials passed the examination, their names would be inscribed on the Roll of Selections and they would be inducted into the ranks of major councillors with a three-times-three wine cup ceremony.

On this occasion, Yoshi was asked to take his place on the councillors' platform. There were many changes since his last appearance. The loyal Taira members had fled south before the advent of Kiso, taking with them Antoku, the child Emperor, his family, and the Imperial regalia. Yet Yoshi recognized many of the councillors as those who had supported Munemori two years ago. Often with men in positions of power, their allegiance changed when self-interest dictated. These men had renounced their former Taira allies and now supported Yoritomo.

Go-Shirakawa's shaved head reflected light from the dozens of torches and lanterns that lit the Great Council Hall. He nodded repeatedly as names were read from a scroll. When the last name was announced, he cleared his throat and looked to Yoritomo.

Yoritomo smiled faintly. It was apparent to the onlookers they shared a pleasant secret.

Go-Shirakawa cleared his throat again. Silence fell on the

assemblage. "We welcome new members to our august ranks and look forward to a long period of mutual prosperity."

The council applauded politely.

When silence was restored, Yoritomo took up the announcement. "Our task is far from ended," he said portentously. "The Imperial regalia is in the hands of the child Antoku, and his grandmother, the Nii-Dono. The regalia must be recovered before a new Emperor can be accepted by the gods. There is an army of Taira loyalists who, though weakened by our efforts, are a threat to our stability. But these are concerns for the future. Today, we welcome the new major councillors and we announce one additional promotion, raising a fifth-rank councillor to the fourth rank."

There was a buzz of curiosity in the council. This was indeed unusual. Promotions from fifth to fourth rank were reserved for the Bestowal of Ranks ceremony on the fifth day of the first month.

Yoritomo waited until the councillors quieted. "General Tadamori-no-Yoshi has rendered unparalleled service to the cloistered Emperor and to me. Today, he will be rewarded." Yoritomo craned his neck in Yoshi's direction. "General Yoshi, come forward," he said.

Yoshi was astonished by the command, but covering his surprise, he walked to the mat before the center dais, knelt, and touched his forehead to the floor three times.

"The lands and estates of Lord Fumio . . . plus the lands and estates of Lord Chikara are transferred by Imperial edict to your name. General Yoshi, from this day on you will serve as governor of Suruga province."

The councillors burst into spontaneous applause. Yoshi bowed again and accepted the cup of wine handed him by a retainer. He raised the cup and toasted, "May I serve the Emperor and Lord Yoritomo as well as they have served me. And may we enjoy the peaceful fruits of our endeavors for ten times ten thousand years."

The cups were filled and emptied, filled and emptied, filled and emptied while Yoshi's heart swelled with joy. He would return to the land of his birth in triumph. Lord Fumio's castle would be rebuilt with income from the land. He and Nami would lead a full and happy life . . .

Despite the cool night, Yoshi had opened the shutters and raised the bamboo blinds on the south wall. A breeze wafted

the scent of early blooming plum blossoms through the opening
The glow from a round wood brazier outlined the *chodai*
sleeping platform, where Yoshi lay entwined in Nami's arms

In the northeast, the thousand temple bells of Mount Hie
pealed the hour of the hare. From the west, a deer cried, an
owl hooted, and the first cuckoo of the season sang his *ho-to-
to-gisu* in the pre-dawn darkness. The world was filled with
the sounds and scents of the coming spring.

In the semi-darkness, Yoshi's and Nami's blood pulsed in
unison. Their bodies created a common heat under the heavy
glossed silk robes of their bedclothes. A faint odor of perfume
and sex joined the scents of the garden to encase them in a
sensuous cocoon. Yoshi was stretched out under the robes
completely relaxed. He felt the sweet pressure of Nami's breast
on his chest as she curled against him, her head pillowed in
the crook of his arm. Yoshi pressed his body closer, luxuriating
in her firm softness. There was no need for words. They had
discussed and shared their triumphs and sorrows through the
night. They had exchanged vows of love, and celebrated the
vows with their bodies.

Yoshi tenderly drew his hand along Nami's side, tracing
the swell of her hips, the swoop of her waist, and the tender
curve of her breast.

Nami murmured sleepily, "Yoshi beloved, I have something
to tell you."

Yoshi's eyes snapped open and for a moment he was
apprehensive. Was anything wrong on this the greatest day of
his life?

Nami continued in a voice soft as velvet:

> "Clouds will fade with dawn.
> Amaterasu's warm smile
> Melts winter's sorrow.
> A new sun quickens the dark
> In my heart's secret caverns."

A feeling of ineffable joy suffused Yoshi's heart. He felt
tears building within him. A child by Nami. A son? A daughter?
No matter. The cycle was complete. The child would be born
in his ancestral home, and the family would continue.

Yoshi brushed his cheek against Nami's and whispered his
response:

*"Transitory world
Where sorrow is forgotten
With the dawn cuckoo
Singing his sweet melodies
In praise of the coming sun."*

As Yoshi finished reciting his poem, a warm wash of golden light from the east illuminated the flower garden. Winter's sorrows were far behind them.

Yoshi kissed a tear of joy from Nami's cheek and whispered, "I love you, Nami."

"And I you," she responded.

about the author

———————◆———————

David Charney's interest in Japan was kindled by his study of the oriental martial arts. For the past twenty years he has been involved with Tae Kwon Do, several styles of Karate, plus Aikido, Judo, Tai-Chi, and Kendo, the art of the sword.

Charney fought at Madison Square Garden and won the All-American senior Karate title in 1970 and 1975. He holds a fifth-degree black belt and teaches Tae Kwon Do.

He has been a competitive gymnast, a ranking table-tennis player, an ice-skater, a magician, a concert flamenco guitarist, and an artist.

Charney is senior vice-president and executive art director of a pharmaceutical advertising agency.

He is author of *Magic: the great illusions revealed and explained,* and various science-fiction stories and magazine articles.

Charney lives in Westchester County, a suburb of New York, with his wife, Louise, and their two dogs and two cats. He has three grown children.